HIDDEN

THE DARK FORGOTTEN

SHARON ASHWOOD

This is a work of fiction. Names, characters, places, and incidents are a product of the author's imagination. Locales and public names are sometimes used for atmospheric purposes. Any resemblance to actual people, living or dead, or to businesses, companies, events, institutions, or locales is completely coincidental.

Cover art by The Illustrated Author

Edited by Jacqui Nelson.

PRAISE FOR SHARON ASHWOOD

Sharon Ashwood is all that is good and right in the paranormal romance genre.

— BITTEN BY BOOKS

Fast paced and captivating… chemistry is immediate and undeniable, and the love scenes are scorching hot.

— PUBLISHERS WEEKLY

Multiply the Wow Factor, the Dark Forgotten saga must continue!

— SINGLE TITLES

This is a splendid way to spend your precious leisure time!

— ROMANTIC TIMES BOOK REVIEWS TOP PICK!

INTRODUCTION

Not even magic can hide forever ...

Elite tracker Rafe Devries is summoned home to hunt the fae. He isn't the first to track the mysterious Magician, but every other wolf who caught the enemy's scent has disappeared. Rafe would sooner refuse the job—he's already left the pack once to escape his Alpha father—but the Magician is luring innocents to their destruction. If Rafe doesn't step up, the wolves have no future.

Lila, maverick daughter of an ancient fae family, meets her brother at a hidden way station in the woods. The secretive setting is a bad sign. Though she loves her kin, they're experts at finding trouble—especially when blood loyalty and courtly ambition collide. The night only gets worse when a wolf shifter and his vampire sidekick break into the station, igniting a chain of lethal events. With her brother wounded and the rest of her family in peril, Lila must fight to save them.

When Lila captures Rafe, a battle of wits—and a dangerous attraction—begins. But surviving each other is just the beginning. The Magician holds sway over the faery court's savage political games, where wolves and fae alike are mere puppets. Lila and Rafe must learn to trust one another enough to uncover their enemy's true identity, or no one—least of all two unlikely lovers—will survive.

CHAPTER 1

*T*here.

Scent danced on the breeze, an elusive wisp that beckoned Rafe Devries forward. He traveled in wolf form, a gray shadow gliding under the trees. He pushed through the ferns and low-hanging branches, but that invisible beacon—elusive even to his sensitive nose—vanished like a dancer beneath her veils. With a frustrated growl, he backtracked, enormous paws silent on the forest floor.

The bowl of the valley surrounded him like cupped palms, holding in the soft whisper of stream and lake. He worked alone, using his beast's senses to tease out what surveillance technology could not. His quarry was somewhere in this wilderness—that much was certain—but no one had caught a glimpse of the fae for weeks.

Rafe tasted the breeze, sifting through the smells. Each had a texture and color in his mind, as unique as faces in a crowd. He would—No, he *must* find his prey. The search hadn't started with one lone wolf. The extended kin of the Devries family—bereft and furious—had been part of the hunt. Not many creatures could evade an entire werewolf pack hungry for vengeance.

But this fae could—and did. With every search, they had tracked the vile bastard to this valley, only to lose him like one more needle in the vast carpet of cedar and fir. In the end, the pack had sent for Rafe, their prodigal son, to come home and collect their debt in blood.

There.

This time, the tantalizing hint was stronger. Rafe turned toward it, breathing deeply. At first, the astringent wash of pine and loam drowned it out, but he caught that lingering note of something else—cinnamon on ice, hot and cold as freshly forged steel quenched in snow. The signature was uniquely fae. He'd found the trail once more.

He picked up his pace, moving as fast as stealth would allow. His quarry was directly ahead where the land rose out of the valley, exchanging dark shadows for fitful moonlight. Dense brush gave way to a sketchy path that wound toward still higher ground. Rafe broke into a loping run, unable to rein himself in.

A figure emerged from between the trees, striding steadily up the path. The broken light traced the silhouette. Graceful. Tall. Slender as a reed. Long, straight hair the shade of palest wheat.

Definitely fae. Definitely female.

He was hunting a male.

Rafe stopped dead, leaves flying as he skidded to a halt. Not even the backpack and loose jacket could hide those curves. A mix of disappointment and interest coursed through him. This creature was not his prey, but she was beautiful, even if she was one of *them.*

As if hearing his thoughts, she turned to search the darkness. Rafe flattened himself to the ground, silently cursing. He'd been too eager, too noisy. A fae's hearing missed nothing.

The moonlight caught her features, confirming his suspicions. She was a light fae, with features almost alien in their fine-boned perfection. Rafe's pulse quickened, the fae's sheer loveliness demanding a response.

But this wasn't his first hunt, and he knew better than to roll over for one of *them*. He remained as still as the twisted roots around him, cool and self-contained. The fae studied the path behind her, head tilted at a haughty angle.

Arrogant, like all the rest.

Eventually, her shoulders relaxed. With a half-shrug, she turned and resumed her climb up the hill, moving a little faster now.

Rafe rose to his feet. She wasn't the one he wanted, yet he wouldn't let her slip away. There were only so many reasons a fae —or anyone—would take a stroll through this remote valley. If he tracked this female, surely she'd lead him to his quarry.

He followed, soundless as mist. Where was she going? There were no buildings, no campgrounds, not even a treehouse in these woods.

Rafe paused long enough to scan the direction she'd come from. There was a secondary road on the other side of the valley, used mostly by outdoor enthusiasts on the way to campgrounds another thirty miles to the east. Had she parked on the roadside and walked in?

He returned his attention to the female's dark-clad form, her long legs and elegantly curved hips. She moved in and out of the scattered moonlight as silently as a dream. Narrowing the gap between them was risky, but it allowed him to catch her scent again—wild, spicy, tantalizing. Now it seemed ludicrous that he ever thought something so attractive might belong to his real quarry.

The foul one. The killer. Memories of grief—his own and the pack's—focused him.

The fae they sought was popular among the supernatural youth of East Bay—those old enough to attend a club and young enough to enjoy the noise and erratic hours. And wherever there was a hot, sweaty crowd with drink, dancing, and not enough clothes, this fae showed up.

That in itself was curious. Usually fae—especially light fae—kept to their own kind. They were an ancient people and, unlike the vampires, had never known what it was to be mortal. This one, though, he befriended the young—those caught just at the first glimmer of independence.

No one had thought anything about this fae's influence until their cubs began to die. The only clue that linked the deaths was the fact that they'd recently spoken to that fae. Then the wolves—and vampires and witches—had howled for blood. For the one they called the Magician and whatever foul magic he used.

And for some reason, his trail led here.

Rafe followed the female, struggling to ignore everything but her usefulness as a guide. He kept that concentration at a cost. Without warning, an owl dove from the sky, snatching a vole from the ground. Rafe startled, caught unawares.

The female spun, a sleek pistol in one hand. Rafe dove for the shadows, but not before he heard her intake of breath.

"Who's there?" she demanded in a voice like chilled velvet.

The night was silent but for the beat of wings. He could almost feel the fae's gaze searching the darkness. The way she held herself—and the gun—said she was trained to use it.

Her fierce confidence made her even more compelling. The itch to confront her—to see who had the superior battle skills—almost made him forget his carefully maintained calm. His pulse thundered in his ears.

She turned away, shattering the moment. With a hop and scramble, she reached the lip of the valley, vanishing for a moment into the gloom beneath a pair of giant cedar trees. When she emerged again, she was outlined against the sky.

Then she raised her hand and spread her fingers wide. Rafe blinked as spears of light arced between them like a fistful of lightning. A spell crackled, raising the fur along his spine.

The brilliance rippled outward, making a corona against the horizon. Forgetting all caution, Rafe stood for a better look.

Afterimages of the woman's silhouette danced in his vision, merging with the trees.

What was she doing?

The sky wavered like the surface of a pond. Stars swirled and ran, reminding him of a Van Gogh painting. Then the darkness around her melted away, replaced by a modern, white-walled mansion sparkling with lights. It stood a hundred yards away, as if plucked from the cover of an architecture magazine.

The female stepped onto the smooth concrete path that led to the door.

Finally, Rafe understood. This was a glamour—a fae spell that confused the senses of their victims. Sight, sound, and scent could be confused. *And a villain could hide in plain sight.*

The fae had hidden an entire mansion behind their spell. The one they sought had been here all along, so close the wolves might have run him to ground like an autumn stag. No wonder the cubs called him the Magician.

The depth of the deception dragged an angry rumble from his chest. The female's head turned slightly, catching the sound. She hurried forward, her boots all but silent on the walk. It was like watching a phantom falling into a dream. A moment later, the mansion—and the female—vanished. The horizon was nothing but stars and trees, empty of fae.

His gaze probed the darkness. Even in that short time, he'd learned the female's form, and he wanted her within his sight. That made no sense. She was not for him.

Fae. The enemy. Anger crackled through him, bright as her magic spell—and now he could act on it. The killer had hidden himself away, but Rafe had found his den.

The hunt was on.

A SILENT RUSH of magic activated the concealment spell, hiding the house and the yard around it once more. Lila shivered slightly, the tingle of power leaving gooseflesh behind. When she glanced back, only a faint blur showed where a film of magic interrupted her view of sky and trees.

Lila exhaled, wishing she could relax. Something had been watching as she crossed the valley and climbed the trail to this place. She had felt the weight of its gaze like a physical pressure, though she couldn't tell whether it had been a two- or four-legged beast. Fae had good night vision, but she hadn't been able to spot it among the forest growth. An expert stalker, then. A predator.

Her shoulders twitched, as if shrugging off that gaze. She should have felt protected here, inside the circle of fae magic, but calm eluded her. Hopefully, that wasn't an omen. Maybe it was just the awkwardness of coming here uninvited.

She started up the smooth path to the front door. Now that she was closer, she could see how far the building rambled, hugging the uneven landscape all the way to the rocky shore of the lake beyond. A quick count of windows said there was enough room to house dozens of people, though she saw no sign of anyone now. No lights shone in the windows or above the doors. The place seemed deserted.

Her brother should be there. It had been her older sister, Sala, who'd insisted someone visit and see what Ademar had got himself into. Now Lila wondered if the address was correct—not that this place technically had one.

Nothing with her family ever went according to plan.

Mounting the porch steps, Lila scanned for defensive wards. This was no ordinary dwelling, but a way station under the command of the Forest King. Such places existed wherever royalty traveled between palaces—or, more likely, luxury condos if they were in the city.

In theory, the laws of hospitality governed the way stations—

all comers got a bed and a meal. Even the lesser fae—the tiny winged beings who frequented gardens and riversides—would find a bed and mug of nectar. As a result, the way stations were usually bustling with guests.

Most way stations were ancient, measured in hundreds if not thousands of human years. This place was brand new, which was interesting. Lila studied the sweep of the roof, the soaring arch over the door. Whoever built this had powers similar to her own. She'd made a career in magic-assisted architecture and knew how to coax living wood to bend and shape as she desired. Without even touching a single beam, she sensed someone had spelled this place from the forest within the last few months. And while one individual may have created the building, more than one would have pooled their energies to ensure the magic endured.

Why build this one, and not use one that already existed? And why was no one here? That was just—odd.

Lila paused before the door, fingering the butt of her pistol for a moment before placing her palm against the white paneled door. A faint surge of power tingled against her hand as the locking spell tested her. Once it recognized her as one of the wood fae, it released with a soft click.

The door swung open. Lila's hand returned to her weapon as she stepped inside. She'd trained in defensive magic, but sometimes—like in an ambush—a bullet was faster and more reliable. With a pounding heart, she listened to the profound silence.

The overhead light blinked on, triggered by her presence. The entry hall was large but as impersonal as a hotel, with white walls framing a checkerboard marble floor. She took a few steps forward, ears straining for sounds. There should have been dozens of servants tending to the needs of guests, but there was only silence.

"Hello?" she called.

Echoes pulsed against the high ceiling, mimicking her heartbeat. She was about to call again when something moved overhead. She froze, her jaw aching with tension.

"Ademar?"

Another footfall, barely there. She turned toward the noise. On the left side of the entry hall, a massive staircase swept to the upper floor. She glided across the hall and began mounting the stairs, weapon drawn.

A faint light shone at the top.

Lila cleared the last step, sweeping her gun from right to left. "Hello?"

"Lila?" Her brother's tall form came into view. He was a head taller than her, but otherwise they might have been twins, with the same dark gray eyes and pale, straight hair. A scar marked one cheek, but the imperfection heightened his otherwise flawless features. Even by the exacting standards of the light fae, Ademar was handsome.

With a sigh of relief, she holstered her gun. "Why are you lurking alone in the dark?"

"What are you doing here?" he replied, a frown pleating his brow.

She hugged him, ignoring his stiff tone. "I'm so glad to see you. It's been ages."

He responded with a one-armed embrace, pulling her off balance with his easy strength. "Did you come alone?"

"I did. Sala was worried. She made me promise to check on you and tell her everything. She seems to think you're in trouble."

He closed his eyes for a long moment, clearly exasperated. "You shouldn't have come, and Sala should mind her own affairs. Let her be content with ruling her children's lives."

"Hmm." As the eldest, Sala could be overbearing, but Lila was beginning to think her sister's suspicions were correct. Something was wrong. "Where is everyone?"

"Those who were here when I arrived have moved on. Others

have yet to reach this destination." Ademar started down the hall, his step quick and light on the bare tiles.

She fell in behind him, just as she had when she'd been a child and he a dozen years older. To her young eyes, he'd been filled with sophistication and mystery. Now he just seemed full of —something.

"Try again," she said dryly. "That wasn't an answer. Why are you here?"

"I am here because Lord Farras asked me to come."

Lila did her best to hide a grimace. Farras was a highborn courtier and cousin to the king. At times, he'd been a generous patron to her family. Nonetheless, his smile made the hair rise along her nape. "Why? What's on his mind?"

Her brother led them to a darkened sitting room with floor-to-ceiling windows overlooking the moonlit forest. The view was the best thing about the space. Usually, when fae built a home, it was harmonious, lush with color and detail. This house was all angles, done in shades of ice and gray, as if the builder had been depressed.

With a flick of his fingers, Ademar lit a candle lamp that sat on a low table in the center of the room. He still hadn't explained the lack of light, but Lila would circle back to that. The fact that Lord Farras was involved trumped every other concern.

"Ademar?" she prompted.

"If Lord Farras requests my presence here, I obey. Given our sagging family fortunes in recent years, I can't very well refuse."

She shrugged one shoulder. Their mother complained long and bitterly about how King Elroth ignored the old alliances with House Fernblade, but Lila had never paid much attention. What could she do about it?

"I am lucky to have a patron who finds me and my interests useful," Ademar added. "He is supporting my research connecting fae communication with modern transmission systems."

"So then, why don't you answer my phone calls? And Sala's, too?"

Ademar's only reply was a faint smile. He sank into a chair and crossed his long legs, resting one elbow on the white upholstered arm.

Annoyed, Lila circled to face her brother so she could argue properly. "Are you going to fill me in or not?"

"You can see with your own eyes that I am perfectly fine."

Except he wasn't. Lila could feel his anxiety from across the room. "I dragged myself out here to see if you're okay. I want answers now."

Ademar said nothing, but his silence was loud. He was just as stubborn as she was.

"Sala said two vampires knocked on her door. They were asking for you, and they weren't happy. What have you got yourself into?"

He looked away, the fall of his long hair obscuring his expression.

"When Sala told me about her visitors, I dropped everything and hunted until I found out where you were," Lila said. "You owe your family some answers. Whatever you're doing is causing ripples."

"Tell Sala I apologize," Ademar replied. "I will ensure no future ripples will reach my sisters. And I don't owe you anything. You're the one who turned your back on us."

That stung. "We've already lost two sisters. Excuse me for asking questions."

He shot her a venomous look. "That had nothing to do with me."

She stepped closer, refusing to let him avoid her glare. "Is it too much to ask for an explanation?"

"You can ask for anything. That does not mean you'll receive it."

His long-fingered hands clenched and unclenched, but his

features remained cold, still marble. He was anxious, maybe angry, but he'd never acknowledge it.

"I had plans for the weekend." She flung herself into one of the white velvet chairs. "Confess, and I'll still have time to make it back to town before breakfast."

Ademar's gray eyes flicked away again. "You're being trivial."

"Since you won't answer when I talk in my serious voice, you're leaving me few alternatives." Lila came to her real point. "I may be living in town and away from court, but I still hear whispers. People are worried about some bogeyman they call the Magician. I hear the king is considering a withdrawal of the fae from human habitations."

Some believed contact with humans was weakening their magic. Lila didn't believe it, but her opinion was irrelevant. The nobles couldn't afford to take chances, especially not the kings and queens, whose birthright of power was far greater than even the most accomplished students of the magic arts.

"King Elroth isn't thinking about leaving. He's doing it. How is that relevant?"

"This way station is new and far better hidden than the old ones—so hidden that I wouldn't have found it without specific directions. One might say it was fit for nobility that didn't want to be found. Should I assume any of these facts are connected?"

He winced. "It's complicated."

"Complicated enough to bring vampires to Sala's door?" Frustration burned in her belly. "Where do they fit in? Did someone commit a crime? Did you?"

"The Undead have no business bothering us." His gaze hardened. "We don't owe them an explanation, either."

Hot annoyance morphed into fear. "By the Abyss, Ademar, what did you do? What does it have to do with Lord Farras?"

"You're making a drama out of nothing," Ademar replied coolly. "Lord Farras invited us to wait for him here. He should have arrived by now, so I expect him at any time."

"What's he up to? And who is *us*? Is there someone else here?"

Ademar opened his mouth to reply, but was interrupted by the sound of breaking glass. She jumped up, reaching for her gun, but Ademar caught her hand and held a finger to his lips.

"I was expecting an annoyance," he murmured. "I was hoping to get rid of you before the annoyance arrived."

"Who is it?" she breathed. Sweat trickled down the small of her back.

He bent, picking up a sword belt and scabbard hidden in the shadows beside his chair. Rising to his feet, he buckled on the belt and drew the sword. Candlelight danced along the blade, as if mocking Lila's choice to carry a human weapon. In the hands of a warrior such as Ademar, trained in battle magic, fae steel had no equal.

A second crash shattered the silence, this time of splintering wood.

Ademar's eyes sparked with anticipation. "It's time to say hello."

CHAPTER 2

Once the female fae had vanished from sight, Rafe spun around and loped back into the valley. There was no time to spare.

Earlier that night, he'd left a knapsack of clothes and supplies at the foot of an ancient tree, right where several deer paths crossed. He reached it in a matter of minutes. It took him slightly longer to change back to human form, dress, and text for backup.

Possible location. Concealment spell. Bring supplies.

He'd barely finished strapping on his weapons when a rush of air stirred the branches. With quicksilver reflexes, Rafe snatched his pistol from its holster, sighting on the fluttering leaves. A moment later, a woman stepped from the trees. Despite legend, vampires didn't turn into bats or crows, but Izetta still moved like the wind.

Rafe relaxed, putting away his weapon. "Sorry. I'm not taking any chances."

"You saw the fae?" she asked, not bothering with small talk.

He'd never quite placed her accent. It was Mediterranean—maybe Spanish—with a generous helping of old South. Her low voice was like the purr of a big cat—relaxed and lazy until the teeth came out.

"I followed another fae up the side of the valley," Rafe replied. "There's a glamour hiding an enormous modern mansion. That has to be the fae headquarters."

"Or not. Their headquarters would be inaccessible by mere mortals. That sounds like a way station."

"A what?"

"It's like a fae hotel. I thought I knew them all, but apparently this one is off the radar. They use them as staging points for a long journey."

Izetta stood with her weight on one hip, arms folded. She was dressed in black jeans and a leather jacket, a cloud of curling dark hair framing her face. Despite her youthful appearance, Rafe knew she had more battle experience than he would ever see.

"Journey to where?" Rafe asked.

Izetta gave a small shrug. "I've heard rumors the Forest King is moving his court. I don't know why and don't really care. This, though, is different."

She pulled out her phone. "A contact sent me this. It's from a security camera at the Widow's Walk." She handed him the device.

A video was cued to play on the screen. Rafe tapped it and watched as the inside of a club came into view. It was good quality for surveillance video, although as usual there was no sound. The camera was aimed at the bar, but he could see part of the dance floor on the right.

"What am I looking for?" he asked.

"The end of the bar. Wait."

A tall figure in a loose tunic and tight pants climbed onto one of the tall stools. He lounged against the bar with his back to the camera, managing never to show his face. All Rafe could see was a thick fall of pale hair held back with a fancy clip.

"Definitely a fae," he said.

"I know, right?" Izetta said. "I think half their body weight is leave-in conditioner."

A second later, two more figures, both female, came into the frame. Rafe zoomed in as the smaller of the two leaned in to kiss the fae with enthusiasm and a good deal of tongue. A long necklace of freshwater pearls swung as she moved. "I know her. She's one of yours."

"Malatest's girl. Her name is Sadie." Malatest was one of the major players among the Undead. "She's a few nails short of a coffin, if you know what I mean."

It was then he caught sight of the second female. A werecat who'd turned up dead a week ago. "That's one of the Magician's victims."

"The last known sighting of her. By all indications, we're looking at footage of the Magician himself."

"Damn." Rafe scrolled back and watched the whole thing again, confirming that the Magician never showed his face. "What does he do to them?"

Izetta shook her head. "I don't know."

"But this is good." Rafe handed her phone back. "This is as close as we've got to him."

"Unless he's inside your invisible mansion."

"Let's find out." Rafe started toward the path.

"Not so fast." Izetta unzipped one of her jacket's many pockets and extracted a blue glass jar. "Faery ointment. It has to touch your eyeballs, even if it stings. Very traditional."

In his haste, Rafe had forgotten that he'd asked her to bring a charm against the glamour spell. "Who made this?"

"Madam Corbeau. I shop at New Broom Metaphysical Supplies in West Harbor."

"That's a bit out of your way."

Her smile showed fang. "It's a specialty item. When it comes to fae, it pays to get the best protection."

He took the jar from her hand. When he unscrewed the lid,

his nose wrinkled at the medicinal scent. The green paste inside was half-gone and crusty around the edges.

"It's still fresh," she said, as if sensing his hesitation. "I keep a ready supply for work."

That made sense. Izetta was a busy freelancer. One vampire king or another hired her to be his blade in the dark when diplomacy became inconvenient.

Rafe cast her a curious look. "Are you hunting fae that often?"

"Dark fae play dirty." She gave an impatient flick of her hand. "Are you going to stare at the ointment or use it?"

Reluctantly, he dipped a finger into the jar. Years ago, he'd worn contact lenses as part of a disguise. He'd hated touching his eyes then, and he didn't like it now. Bracing himself, he smeared the paste above his lower lids before he could change his mind. Instantly, his eyes stung as if he'd rubbed them with acid. Tears blinded him. "Fido's balls!"

Izetta plucked the jar from his hand. "Don't rub. That will only make it worse."

Rafe blinked furiously. His vision was gradually clearing, but the heat had spread into his sinuses. He sneezed, then sneezed again. It felt like his entire skull was on fire.

But the damned stuff worked. Now he could see the mansion's roofline at the top of the rise, black against the stars. The ointment apparently worked on other senses, too. He could smell fae, including the female he'd seen earlier. Anticipation shivered over his skin.

"This way," he said, setting off toward their quarry.

Izetta followed, quiet as a phantom as they ascended the side of the valley, following the same path he'd taken before. This time, though, he could see his destination and choose the best approach. The terraced yard had a pool and hot tub that overlooked a moonlit lake and rolling hills. Everything said elegance and hard cash.

"Who says crime doesn't pay?" he muttered under his breath.

"We'll see about that." Izetta replied, her soft drawl deceptively sweet. "What does your doggy nose tell you?"

"The scents are all new," Rafe replied. "It's as if the construction crew just left."

"Residents?"

"Fae passed through the garden. Hard to tell how many." He sniffed again. "Not much foot traffic in the last day or so."

She gave a slow nod. "Almost as if they're expecting trouble."

Rafe swore under his breath. Whoever had built the mansion had chosen the location well. To the north, the woods were so dense a squirrel would need a machete. The west side faced onto the lake. The east lawn led to a sheer drop. That left the southern approach Rafe and Izetta had taken from the valley. The place was easy to defend.

Rafe glanced over his shoulder. The winding path they had climbed to get near the building was too narrow for most vehicles. "How the hell did they get equipment up here to build?"

"Magic? It's way easier than getting contractors to arrive on time."

Rafe didn't comment. Instead, he crept forward, the cold air seeping in through his open jacket. He approached the south wall of the house, pausing at the edge of the trees. There was a faint light—a candle, maybe—moving in one of the upstairs windows. A place like this was sure to have electricity, so someone was avoiding company.

A second later, Izetta joined him. "What now?"

"We get closer."

Keeping to the deepest shadows, they crossed the lawn. Rafe reached the house first and crouched beneath the low sill of an oversized window. Izetta knelt beside him.

Had they been seen? He counted to ten, listening for footfalls or the whisper of a weapon leaving its holster. When nothing came, he raised himself enough to peer through the gap beneath the lowered window blind. It was dark inside, but shifters had excellent night vision.

The decor was completely white. Clearly, no one here ate pizza without a napkin.

"Fae," he whispered with a sneer. For a moment he regretted not bringing some tech toys—long-distance listening equipment, for a start—but then dismissed the notion. Magic raised merry hell with technology. "There's got to be a way in."

Rafe skirted to the right, the vampire on his heels. As they passed the next window, Rafe glanced inside. The room looked perfectly ordinary, if expensive and maniacally clean. White marble tile added to the Arctic color scheme. Across the room, a stainless-steel sink and backsplash glimmered in the ambient moonlight.

Rafe stopped, pulled out his pocketknife, and wiggled it into the space between the window sill and sash.

"What about a security system?" Izetta asked blandly.

"You have a better idea?"

"I dunno," Izetta countered. "You just set the bar pretty low."

Rafe ignored her. The prey was inside, and his pack needed this villain to die. It was the one thing his father wanted that Rafe could deliver.

After a long minute of cursing, he pried the sash up until the slider lock cleared its hole. He then pushed the window open with barely a sound.

"Fortune favors the bold." Rafe crawled inside, his boots landing softly on the tile floor.

Izetta followed. By the ancient rules of magic, vampires needed an invitation to enter a home—but not here. Clearly, this wasn't a private residence, which made the occupants fair game for the Undead.

They stood together for a long moment, listening for the mansion's unseen inhabitants. The only sound was the whisper of the forest outside, the only motion the flutter of curtains beside the open window.

The breeze carried more than the scent of grass and trees. Rafe spun, instinctively ducking out of sight. Izetta gave a faint, startled hiss.

"Company," he murmured. "Outside."

He rose from his crouched position until he could glimpse two fae warriors in high-collared jackets and tall boots. A uniform, but he didn't recognize it.

Izetta darted to a position beside the window, peering around the frame so that she could see out without being seen. "Light fae. They belong to the Royal Guard."

That didn't mean a lot to Rafe. The fae had more kings and queens than a poker tournament. "What do they want?"

The leader held up a fist, and his companion stopped. Then, with a whisper of steel, they drew heavy broadswords from sheaths at their back.

The vampire made a soft noise that wasn't quite a laugh. "I don't think they're here to borrow the lawnmower."

The leader pointed his blade toward something Rafe couldn't see. Glass shattered. A moment later, he heard a door crash open with a squeal of splintering wood.

The tromp of booted feet echoed below. The intruders—military, by the way they marched—were making no effort to be quiet. Lila's stomach knotted with panic. Ademar glared toward the door and the stairway beyond. White-faced, he visibly gathered his strength.

"He knew this would happen," he murmured under his breath. "He should have been here by now."

"Who? Farras?" Lila grabbed her brother's arm, argument forgotten. "What's happening?"

It wasn't hard to jump to conclusions. The lord had asked Ademar to wait there and then failed to show up. He'd been expecting trouble.

As if reading her thoughts, Ademar's gaze met hers for the barest second before pulling away. "These will be Captain Teegar's men, maybe Teegar himself. According to Lord Farras, he plots against the king."

Her breath caught in a hiccup of surprise. Teegar was an officer in the Royal Guard and had a stellar reputation for loyalty. "That's impossible."

"Are you sure?" he replied with a humorless smile. "Those aren't mice downstairs."

"Why are they here?"

"Lord Farras knows Teegar's plans. I imagine Teegar is here to kill him. Or me, since I'm available."

She blinked. "Is that why you're sitting here in the dark? You're hiding from the Royal Guard?"

"Not any longer. Evidently, hiding didn't work."

"But—"

He waved her words away. "Save your breath until we've greeted our guests. Then ask your questions."

Lila swallowed hard. If the Royal Guard had come with murder in mind, Ademar was in serious trouble. It was no secret he was loyal to Lord Farras—and yet, none of this made sense. Her brother could be difficult, but he wasn't worth killing. He just wasn't that important.

"What do you plan to do?" She adjusted her grip on her gun as they inched toward the door to the hallway.

He bared his teeth in a mocking grin. "Show Captain Teegar that he is not the only warrior worthy of respect."

Lila's stomach flipped. "Fighting isn't a real plan. Not against the guard."

"I'm not about to surrender." Ademar's jaw hardened as he picked up speed.

Still gripping his arm, Lila stumbled, let go, then fell in behind him. As soon as they were through the door, Lila moved to cover her brother's right side.

"This will be dangerous," he said. "You don't need to come with me."

"Don't be ridiculous," she snapped back.

His smile was brief but grateful. They drifted silently down the staircase, Lila half a step behind Ademar. She pulled out her phone, thinking she'd send Sala a text just in case something went wrong. But, as in so many fae-occupied buildings, there wasn't a single bar. Magic and tech didn't mix. She put her phone away.

Ademar stopped halfway down the stairs, pressing his palm against the carved wainscoting to his left. A panel sprang open, revealing a cramped passageway. Ademar stepped through, signaling Lila to follow. The panel slid shut behind her, and the crystal globes set along the ceiling sprang to life with a soft glow.

"Escape route?" she whispered, gazing around her.

"Not exactly," he replied, beckoning her onward.

Lila followed, thoughts swirling. Secret passages were nothing new, but she hadn't expected them in a way station. This was supposed to be a refuge, not a place for spies. And how had Ademar known this was here? Only those closest to the king should know such secrets.

She glimpsed a half-open door that led to a tiny chamber off the passageway. A wooden desk sat before shelves filled with dismantled electronics. A pink quartz crystal, shaped like an obelisk, pulsed faintly on the desktop. Fae used that type of stone for relaying messages through magic. Unfortunately, modern technology interfered with magic as well as the reverse. Ademar was trying to resolve the conflict.

"Is that where you do your research?" she asked.

"Yes," he replied with a distracted wave. "So far, I've managed to piggyback a simple spelled message on the cellular network."

From that point forward, the ceiling sloped low enough that he had to stoop and narrow enough that they had to walk single file. That bothered Lila less than the intense aura of fresh magic that permeated the space. Someone had been casting strong spells nearby.

Lila's urge to bolt for the open air welled up, almost irresistible. She shifted her grip on her gun, the familiar shape of it comforting. "Where does this corridor go?"

He didn't answer. The passageway made a sharp right, then descended in a narrow flight of steps that ended at an ordinary-looking door. Ademar stopped, the cramped space forcing Lila to do the same. She could hear footfalls on the other side of the wall. Her brother had moved toward danger, not away from it.

"*Ademar*," she whispered, a tidal wave of misgivings in that single word.

He glanced over his shoulder, his eyes unreadable in the soft glow of the crystals. "Trust me. There is only one way out of this where no one gets hurt."

That failed to reassure her. Whatever was brewing between Lord Farras and Teegar, escalating the conflict seemed like a very bad idea.

With steady hands, Ademar rummaged in the pocket of his loose shirt, plucking something from inside the silky folds. At first, she didn't see what it was, but once he held it up, she glimpsed a gauzy bundle.

Shock froze her in place. The object was no bigger than a walnut and shrouded with spiderweb and the glittering feathers of a moon moth's wing. Its scent was pleasant, but her senses shuddered like the inside of a ringing bell. If this was the kind of charm someone was making inside this house, no wonder it vibrated with power.

"This is no way to prove your innocence," she murmured, her thoughts clouding from so much magic leaking into the confined space.

"But this way you and I live long enough to make them listen," he said, curling his fingers around the charm. "I won't put my family in danger."

He threw open the door, blocking Lila's view with his tall frame. Someone shouted with surprise. Weapons hissed from scabbards. Despite herself, Lila took a step back into the passage.

"Good evening, gentlemen," Ademar said with cool sarcasm.

"Surrender in the name of the king!" That was Teegar—Lila recognized the captain's stentorian voice. "We found your sister's vehicle on the roadside at the head of this valley. We know she's here somewhere. Come quietly and we'll spare her."

Ademar gave a bark of laughter. "What a generous offer."

He tossed the spell in one short, sharp motion. Lila ducked, covering her face before a bright flash of magic seared the air. Lilac afterimages danced along the back of her eyelids as sweet-smelling smoke all but gagged her. She held her breath, counting the beat of her pulse in a vain effort to guess when the worst of it would pass.

After what seemed like hours, Ademar squeezed her shoulder. "It's safe."

Slowly, she peeled her hands from her face. The smoke had thinned, but she still felt groggy. She gazed up at her brother, studying his expression. "What have you done?"

Wordlessly, he picked up her gun and handed it to her. She must have dropped it—a sure sign the magic had impacted her despite such brief exposure. She snatched the weapon, ashamed of herself, and holstered it.

"Come on," he said.

Lila straightened almost reluctantly. She'd come here to find out what Ademar was up to, and now she wasn't sure she wanted the answer. She said nothing as she followed her brother out of the secret passage.

Two uniformed guards sprawled on the marble floor of the entrance hall, Captain Teegar was the tallest, the golden pommel of his massive sword resting in slack fingers. The other guard had crumpled like a stringless puppet, arms outflung.

Lila shuffled to a halt, suddenly light-headed with shock. "You shouldn't have done this. Self-defense…"

"Is acceptable as long as it isn't *too* successful," he replied, a touch of mockery in his tone. "They aren't injured, you know."

"For now."

Slow, rhythmic breaths echoed through the entrance hall, punctuated by the occasional snore. Fae called this bit of magic the Sleeping Beauty spell. It got the name from a human tale that, as usual, made a fae the villain of the story. While the romantic yarn was simple entertainment, the magic at the center of the plot was real and serious enough to be outlawed. Permanent sleep ended in death, even for an immortal.

"Ademar," she began, wondering how to erase what had just happened.

"I've bought time." Ademar's tone grew defensive. "Help will come."

"Who?"

"They told me this would happen. I prepared for it."

The numbness flooding her began to recede, replaced by fury. "I can't speak for your allies, but no *friend* would encourage this madness. Nor would they tell you to be here and then leave you alone without support." She pushed past him, picking her way around the sleeping guards.

"Where are you going?" Ademar demanded.

"To the kitchen. The spell can't be deep yet. A bucket of cold water should wake them."

"Wait!" Ademar reached for her arm.

Lila broke into a run and prayed the house followed the usual layout of a fae dwelling. If so, the kitchen should be to the right. She ducked down a short hall and through another door.

And came face to face with a wolf-eyed stranger.

CHAPTER 3

The soles of Lila's boots skidded with her sudden stop. The stranger before her was tall and broad-chested, his shaggy walnut hair framing a lean face. He froze in place at her sudden appearance, knees bent and arms slightly spread, as if he were about to leap away rather than attack.

He was not threatening her—at least not yet—but he was in a location no one but a fae should tread.

Her fingers closed around the hilt of her gun, though she kept the weapon out of sight. Raising the tension between them would be foolish, and she might not win a fight. Shifters had power of their own, and energy hummed around this one like crackling static, raising the hair along her arms.

Wolf. And by the yellow cast of his eyes, a wolf about to shift to animal form. Her stomach fluttered, as if she could already feel fangs sliding into her flesh.

"Let me leave," he said, raising one hand, palm out, as if to keep her away.

"Who are you?" Lila demanded, keeping her voice sharp.

The stranger took a slow step back, and Lila caught a flutter of cloth behind him. Someone else was there, behind the wolf, but there was no time to get a better look.

"Did Teegar bring a pet?" Ademar caught up with her and moved to her right, hemming the stranger in.

"No." Her response was instant. The wolf wore stained jeans and mud-caked boots. "A captain's servant would be clean."

Before she'd stopped speaking, the stranger spun and lunged back the way he'd come, vanishing through the kitchen door. After a split second of shock, Lila sprinted after him. Werefolk were agile, but this one was lightning fast.

She burst into the kitchen, but the beast had vanished. Instead, there was a vampire crouched by an open window. The compact figure was half-hidden in the shadows, her presence more a feeling than a distinct physical form. As Lila turned her way, the vampire flowed into motion, one hand on the sill. In half a second, she would be gone.

And news of what had happened today would be loose in the world—Teegar, the sleeping spell, and her brother's hiding place. Lila couldn't allow that—not until she understood what battles Ademar was fighting.

"Stop!" she commanded.

The vampire bared her teeth. Lila raised her weapon and fired. The sound cracked the air, echoing off the bare surfaces of the kitchen. It took a moment to realize that she had missed.

Fangs and darkness hurtled toward Lila with a snarl.

A white streak crackled through the air, engulfing the vampire. Lila recognized Ademar's magic, as unique to him as the sound of his voice. The moment it struck, the Undead dropped to the ground.

Slowly, Lila lowered her weapon, a tremor of delayed fright passing through her. The bullet had missed, but it had bought her brother time to summon a spell.

"Lila?" Ademar called.

"Fine." Lila stumbled back, away from the vampire's crumpled form.

Dark curls spread around the female, stark against her pale skin. Even unconscious, she looked deadly.

"I couldn't let her leave," Ademar said, echoing Lila's earlier thought.

"No argument."

A rumbling growl vibrated through Lila's bones. She'd forgotten the shifter for the briefest moment. All she could see were the yellow eyes of the creature padding around the corner of the kitchen island. The beast had a dark gray coat shading to brown and paws the size of dinner plates. The second their eyes met, the wolf crouched, ready to spring.

In an instant, Ademar was between her and the beast, swinging his blade in a twisting motion surely meant to slash the creature's throat. The wolf sprang backward, losing a tuft of fur. Ademar spun, coming in for a second attack. The fae steel hummed through the air, the sound almost sultry. With a snarl, the wolf feinted, letting Ademar's stroke cleave the space between them. The moment Ademar stepped into the swing, his balance compromised, the wolf attacked.

Long fangs sliced into Ademar's flesh. Bones crunched and her brother screamed, pain mixed with surprise. The wolf shook Ademar like a rat, toppling him from his feet. His sword spun away, useless, as blood splashed to the kitchen tiles, paler than human but still smelling of copper and meat. Flesh tore with a sickening sound, and Ademar screamed again, clearly in too much shock to fight back. Blood sprayed, then gushed, spattering the black and white tile of the kitchen floor.

Lila pulled the trigger of her weapon, but nothing happened. The fresh round hadn't fed properly, leaving the chamber empty. Time slowed as the beast lifted its red muzzle and fixed her with rage-filled eyes. She was next.

Pure instinct took over, drawing power through her as if

she'd touched a live electric wire. Pins and needles swept over her skin, tingling through her breastbone and upward to the bones of her skull. She didn't use battle magic often, and she had to brace herself against the dizzying wave.

The wolf gathered itself, haunches tensing as it prepared to spring. She let the attack fly as the wolf's paws left the floor. Her bolt was fainter than Ademar's, but it worked. The spell twisted around the beast like a wind-blown scarf, binding it in a trail of light. The creature jerked as if electrocuted, jaws snapping on empty air. Then it fell heavily on its side, legs flailing as it blacked out. The wolf lay motionless but for one twitching paw.

Lila staggered back, her gaze fixed on her brother. Ademar was still but for the blood pooling around him in a steady flow.

"No!" cried a voice from behind her.

Lila spun, ready for another attack. A female stood in the doorway, her tall form clad in emerald and silver robes. Two figures—servants?—robed in gray stood beside her, their hands hidden in long sleeves and faces shadowed by deep hoods.

"Mother," Lila said, her voice faint with disbelief. Lady Galeeta of House Fernblade was a creature of the High Court— not the aftermath of a bloody fight. "What are you—?"

Before Lila could finish her question, Galeeta hitched up the hem of her skirts and ran toward Ademar. The moment she reached his side, she sank down, caressing his face even as her costly robes soaked in his blood.

Lila remembered her brother's words: *Lord Farras invited us to wait for him here.* Was this who Ademar had meant by *us*? It had to be. *I won't put my family in danger.*

No, he'd sacrifice himself instead.

"My beautiful boy." Galeeta's voice cracked, though she said the words ever so softly.

Lila's shock finally broke. The hard tile bruised her flesh as she fell to her knees beside her brother. His right leg was torn open, bone obscenely white against raw, glistening flesh. Her mother was already weaving a spell to stop the gushing blood, but the damage would take far more to heal.

Lila gulped, the lump in her throat suffocating. Ademar had fainted, his face chalky and damp with sweat. Grief sawed at her chest. "We need to get help."

"There is none." Her mother's elegant features twisted with grief and anger. "We are alone here. Unprotected."

Lila flinched at the words, or maybe it was the unfamiliar bitterness in her mother's voice. With a visible effort, Galeeta drew herself up and signaled to the robed figures. The two servants straightened, like hounds ready to give chase.

"Take Ademar upstairs," she ordered. "Quickly."

They sprang forward, moving in eerie unison. Lila rose and backed away, reluctant to be near them. There was something unnatural in their movements that made her think of long-legged spiders.

Galeeta gestured toward the unconscious intruders sprawled on the floor. "When you're done, remove those two. You don't need to be gentle."

Lila followed the procession to the upper level of the way station. Once Ademar was in his own room, the servants vanished to deal with the intruders as well as the unconscious guards. Lila took a seat in the room across from her brother's, leaving her mother to work her healing magic on Ademar's wound. That had been minutes ago, and then the minutes had stretched into hours. The night slid by, time oddly elastic. Eventually, Lila rose to watch the heavy moon tangle in the branches of the forest beyond the windowpane.

It was impossible to know how long she stood there, fatigue and distress robbing her strength. She had left her apartment only a few hours ago, hoping to find Ademar buried in his work and forgetful of details like food and drink.

It had happened before. The vampires who'd frightened Sala might well have been collecting an unpaid bill. Her older sister had a tendency to panic whenever she had to deal with anyone but another fae. Lila had fielded a few such mini-dramas without complaint—it kept her in touch with family to a bearable degree. She loved them and missed them—missed the daily sense of belonging to a tribe, even if it drove her crazy—but she had no intention of vanishing down the House Fernblade rabbit hole, never to see her real life again.

So, yes, she'd expected to return home tonight in time for a midnight movie and bed. She hadn't expected two sets of attackers in what should have been a safe space. Certainly not a fight that left her brother severely injured.

Lila yawned, exhausted despite the nervous energy coursing through her body. It had been months since she'd used real magic, and she'd lost her stamina. Ademar would say she was going soft.

She closed her eyes, imagining her brother's frown as he said it. This time, anger rose instead of grief. She'd questioned Ademar's actions when she'd first arrived, but now her loyalty was roused. Her brother had been wounded defending fae territory against a werewolf who couldn't have entered the hidden way station by chance. Someone had sent it—him—and by the Abyss, she'd find out who was responsible.

She turned from the window, needing action. The house was perfectly silent. For a disoriented moment, she wondered if everyone else had left—or simply vanished like ghosts in an old fireside tale. Even her mother's servants were nowhere in sight.

Lila crossed the hall to Ademar's bedroom door and pressed her ear to the wood. There was no sound. A morbid fear seized her, and she pushed the door open, expecting the worst.

Ademar lay unmoving under the silken bedcovers, his hands

limp at his sides. The regular rise and fall of his chest said he was asleep. A knot between Lila's shoulder blades released, and she took another step across the thick wool carpet.

Light from the bedside lamp pooled around Ademar, leaving the rest of the large room in shadow. The black and white furnishings stood like phantoms, a discarded coat and empty mug the only signs of disorder.

Her brother was alone, which meant Galeeta must have slipped away unnoticed. Lila knew healing as well as her mother did, although she lacked the centuries of experience that made Galeeta an acknowledged master. So, Lila hovered by the bed, wanting to inspect his leg but afraid to disturb her mother's healing work. The bleeding had clearly stopped, but a wound like that... Lila pressed her hand to her stomach, suddenly queasy. Her brother was light on his feet, a swordsman of exceptional ability. Was. Had been. She didn't know how much to fear.

"I'm proud of you," said her mother.

Lila spun. Galeeta stood in the doorway, one hand on the frame as if she needed support. Like all the Fernblade fae, her face was elegantly sculpted, with gray eyes and light gold hair. Healing drained the practitioner in a way other magic did not. Dark circles rimmed her eyes, stark against the unusual pallor of her skin.

"What did I do?" Lila asked, almost startled. Galeeta rarely praised anyone, much less her wayward daughter.

"You struck down the wolf. I didn't think you had the courage for that." The words were quiet, suitable for a sickroom, but they still had the sting of a two-edged compliment.

"I trained in combat," Lila replied. "I served my time, like everyone else."

"A few years in the auxiliary guard is one thing. Real combat is another matter." Galeeta swept forward, taking the chair next to Ademar's bed. The lamplight shimmered on her gown's silver trim. "You showed your true colors tonight. You're one of the family, after all."

Lila flinched inside, but the pain quickly flared to anger. "Just because I choose to live in the city instead of the palace doesn't change the fact that I love my family."

Galeeta gave a dismissive shrug. "I never know what to expect from you, daughter."

It was an old, old argument about obedience and duty. She'd moved away to escape the conversation, and she wasn't about to resume it now. "Expect that I'll sit by your side tonight and keep you company."

"Very well." Galeeta studied her sleeping son. "You literally snatched him from the jaws of death. I hope I can save his life."

"How bad is the injury?"

"Time alone will tell, but he heals well. Only one scar from that duel with Lord Patrus. Otherwise, he is perfect."

"Nonsense. He is *entirely* perfect. The best of brothers." Lila had almost forgotten the duel between Ademar and the spiteful lordling. Patrus had learned the hard way that when Lila said no, she meant it. Her only regret was not skewering him herself.

"Immortals bear unhealed wounds forever," Galeeta said softly. "I hope with all my heart this fresh injury mends."

Emotion quickened Lila's breath—a wave of something between protectiveness and rage. The wolf had much to answer for, sneaking in where he didn't belong. What had he and the vampire been doing here? Spying? Thieving?

"Where's Father?" she asked. "He needs to know about this."

"He wasn't able to come," Galeeta replied. "I'll tell you about that later."

That wasn't unusual—as close as they were, her parents pursued very different interests. They had been a love match and remained that way through five children and as many centuries. Gareth and Galeeta. Galeeta and Gareth. Together when it counted, but very much their own independent personalities.

"But you'll contact him?" Lila persisted.

"Absolutely," Galeeta said lightly. "Just as soon as I can."

Lila drew closer to the bed, her fingers trailing along the edge of the silken comforter. Ademar remained still, only his slow, steady breath showing he was anything but an effigy. She reached out, aching to touch her brother, to draw reassurance from the warmth of his skin. Galeeta seized her wrist, but softened the gesture by folding Lila's hand in her own.

"He needs to sleep." Galeeta caught her lip in her teeth, an oddly vulnerable expression.

Lila squeezed her mother's hand. "Perhaps you should, too."

Her mother's thin slice of a smile spoke volumes. "These are complicated times. Sleep is a luxury I haven't enjoyed much lately."

"I have questions. A lot of them." Lila met her mother's clear gaze. "And not just about that wolf. Who or what are those guards of yours? And why was Ademar the one waiting for Lord Teegar?"

Galeeta paused, clearly choosing her words. "Trust me, your brother was doing his duty."

"Is that all you're going to say? He bespelled a captain of the Royal Guard."

Raising her free hand, Galeeta brushed her fingers over Lila's cheek. "I promise to tell you everything I know, but first I need you to do something for me."

Lila hesitated, torn between the desire to help and her instinctive caution. Since she'd arrived, four people had been left unconscious. A sensible person would leave. "What do you need?"

Her mother slipped a hand into the pouch at her waist and drew out a plastic fob that looked incongruous against the silk and gems of her robe. "First, beware of using magic in the underground levels of this building. The area is warded against intruders, and most spells will not work or will work in an unpredictable fashion. Some might trigger a dangerous counterattack."

Lila digested this in silence, unease knotting the muscles in her back. "And that fob?"

"It opens the doors confining our unexpected guests. There is also a key code I will give you. The doors lock automatically, so you do not need either to close them again."

Lila remained still, unsure how to react. She'd been a guard and made her share of arrests, but those had been partygoers with a skinful of wine. This was something far darker. "You have cells here? In a way station?"

Her mother's gaze strayed from Lila to Ademar and back. "Find out what the wolf was doing here. We may as well get answers before we make the beast pay for hurting your brother."

The air in the room seemed to thicken as Lila studied her brother's still figure. The scar on his cheek was livid against his extreme pallor. In her mind's eye, she saw fangs rending flesh all over again. Bright blood spilled on the black and white floor.

Before she formed a conscious thought, Lila grasped the fob.

CHAPTER 4

Rafe woke up in human form, every muscle pulsing with a slow, languid ache. His mouth watered, gagging on the burnt-toast aftertaste of magic and fae blood. It was like licking the inside of a dirty oven sprayed with air freshener.

Reluctantly, Rafe opened his eyes. He was greeted by walls and a dim overhead light—a bare bulb caged and recessed into the ceiling. He sat up slowly, half-expecting restraints. There were none, but one side of the room held a steel door. He was in a cell. Alone.

It didn't surprise him that they'd separated him and Izetta, but a sick worry gelled in his gut. Vampires—who inspired much fear and little compassion—did not fare well as prisoners. More often than not, they starved or became a science experiment.

Rafe rolled to his feet, stumbling as his muscles got over being knocked out cold. Shifters normally healed when they changed, but the spell that brought him down wasn't a normal injury. His back felt like trolls had been line dancing along his spine.

Then he started to shiver. He was naked—he'd shed his clothes before shifting in the kitchen—and the cell was frigid.

Fortunately, someone had dumped his abandoned garments in the corner.

He dressed as fast as he could, hopping as he pulled on his socks. His pockets were empty. Someone had taken everything—from his wallet and phone to the ointment that protected him from fae illusions. They'd even taken his snack pack of beef jerky. That was just petty.

As he dressed, his predicament sank in yet deeper. He was alone and imprisoned in fae territory—just one more wolf who had disappeared in this valley. He looked around at the blank walls, realizing they weren't concrete but some sort of iron-hard wood. Exactly what was this place?

A cold fist gripped his gut, making his heart pound and his breath go shallow. Rafe leaned against the wall, allowing the fear to pass through his flesh like the insubstantial thing it was. He didn't do cages well—not one bit—but right now, he had no choice but to cope. He sucked in air, held it, and let it go slowly, willing his pulse to slow. He had to think. He had to live, escape, and crush the vermin who was preying on his pack.

He'd had rough missions before this. He'd been captured before. He'd get out of trouble, like he always did.

Come home, his father, the Devries Alpha, had said. The words came first in a text message and then by phone when Rafe ignored them. *The pack needs you. I need you. We're losing our people. Soon, there won't be enough strong wolves to hunt.*

It was the first time his father had ever asked him for help. Hell, it was the first time he'd hinted Rafe might be worth something. Until then, it had been plain neither of them saw Rafe as anything but a misfit. He'd been trouble, a fighter, challenging every rule until he'd finally run away to the Silent Wolves, a shifter-run group of special operatives.

But he was still pack, and he'd finally agreed. Maybe, after all, it was possible to come home and make a life within the pack.

Maybe, just maybe—if he could find the Magician and tear out his throat. That was a trophy not even his father could deny.

Rafe began circling the room, examining every inch of the bare, blank walls. There was no furniture, no fixtures, not even a bucket. The only exit beyond the actual door was a floor drain with minuscule holes. A garter snake might get out that way, but not a wolf.

He jumped when a series of beeps broke the silence, then a motor hummed. The top half of the door slid sideways into the wall, revealing a set of heavy vertical bars. On the other side of the bars stood the female fae, a furrow between her pale brows.

He'd pegged the male fae as the ringleader, but the level look in the female's eyes said she was no pushover. So did the confident set of her shoulders. She was arrogant, like all the fae.

Anger rose. She'd knocked him out cold. He could still feel a strange numbness in his limbs.

Beneath his temper, the icy hand of fear fingered the spot between his shoulder blades. A wolf could face bullets, but magic was something else. He couldn't bite a spell.

Rafe drew himself up and folded his arms, pretending a nonchalance he didn't feel. He had a thousand questions—about Izetta, about his own fate—but he knew better than to blurt them out. He would let the fae show her cards first. "Is there something I can do for you?"

"Who are you?" she asked, her voice tight.

"Rafe." He took a slow step closer, studying her features. The delicate, slanting arch of her brows. The gentle point of her ears, all but hidden by her thick white-gold hair. Despite all that had happened, her beauty still drew him, but that meant nothing. She'd proven she was dangerous. "And who are you?"

"I'm the one asking the questions."

"Your companion called you Lila. Is that your name?"

She ignored his query. "Why did you come to this house, Rafe?"

The sound of his name on her lips sounded strange. She was an immortal creature of enchantment, not an earthbound beast like him. He was practical, a warrior, and that meant boundaries, discipline, and sticking with facts.

He didn't have time to answer before she leaned closer, spots of color staining her cheeks. "What makes you think you can harm my brother and live?"

Her brother? Not her mate? Either way, the creature had left a foul taste in his mouth. Rafe met the fae's eyes and glared right back. "He struck first."

The moment in the kitchen had been simple. The brother lashed out. Izetta flailed like a storm-tossed crow, smashing to the floor. Instinct demanded Rafe protect his own, so he'd bitten the fool.

The crunch of bone still lingered like a vibration inside his skull.

"I'm sure he'll get over it," Rafe said with a shrug.

Her eyes widened, as if seeing all the ways she would destroy him. If she hadn't proven so capable, he might have been amused.

"Fae are immortal, not indestructible," she said softly. "You're a monster."

Rafe's pulse jumped. So that bite had put one enemy on the sidelines. Lila—if that was indeed her name—had made a beginner's mistake by letting him know that. A real Alpha would have kept that to themselves. She was dangerous, but she was an amateur in the chess match of power.

"So, are you in charge now?" he asked.

Her chin jutted forward. "I'm the problem in front of you. Concentrate on that."

Now *that* was a good answer, one he might have used. "So you are."

"Just tell me why you're here." She folded her arms, mirroring his stance. "The whole world knows better than to encroach on the fae. Why put yourself at our mercy?"

"I have my reasons."

"Are you a thief?"

"No."

She huffed in disbelief. "What about your friend, the vampire? What's her role here?"

"The ways of the Undead are inscrutable." Worry twisted in his chest. He wanted to ask about Izetta's condition, but then the fae would use her as leverage, putting them both worse off than before. He had to trust his friend's talent for survival.

Lila regarded him as if he were a faintly annoying bug. "Start talking, wolf."

Her chill tone roused his temper. It said he was no better than the slime in the prison floor drain, but then that was how light fae talked to the rest of the world. They kept aloof from other supernatural races, as if mortality were a nasty social disease.

A flash of bitterness seared through him, acid in his blood—but he kept his face neutral. "How many have you killed before me?"

For an instant, she looked taken aback. She hid the emotion quickly, but not fast enough. "What are you talking about?"

"My kin." There was no advantage in hiding this particular truth. "They came into this valley and never returned. The vampire is helping me search for them."

Lila took a step back from the bars, as if his words had physically pushed her. "What makes you think they came to this house?"

"It's the only building around here."

"That's your reason for breaking in?" She waved a hand. "Because we are here?"

He lifted a brow. "I know my people were in these woods. I'm an expert tracker."

The Silent Wolves were specialists, working alone or embedded in a human unit. A trained operative could follow their mark across any terrain—snow or sand, jungle or forest. Over the last decade, he'd been deployed to them all.

But he wasn't about to advertise his combat experience to the fae. He'd already proven himself a threat, and scary wolves ended up as throw rugs.

Silence fell between them for a moment. Her scent tugged at him, reminding him of woodlands where the soft moss cooled his paws. There was something floral in it. Lily of the valley?

He jerked himself back to the confines of the cell, reminding himself that she was the enemy, a mistress of glamour and illusion, not to be trusted. The walls felt heavy again, as if they were crushing his lungs.

She was frowning at him, still angry but clearly curious. "Are you sure other wolves came here? Why would they do that?"

He took another step closer, moving so slowly she didn't seem to notice. "They were hunting a criminal. They were good trackers, but not as good as me."

A shadow passed over her—not just her features, but her entire being, as if some inner light had dimmed. "Who were they hunting? I want a name."

Rafe took that flicker of doubt as an admission. She knew who he was looking for, or she suspected something. He debated how much to tell her. "I don't have a name."

Doubt flickered in her eyes. "You went to a lot of effort to break into our property. That's a big risk for a nameless villain."

"Maybe."

Her eyes narrowed. "Who sent you?"

"Pack."

She curled her fingers around the bars. "Even though all the wolves who came here disappeared? Are you that much better or just that much easier to throw away?"

Something deep inside him flinched. "Maybe both."

Her jaw hardened. "The fae are patient. We have all the time in the world, and you aren't going anywhere. Sooner or later, one of you will give me real answers."

His stomach twisted, the old terror of confinement closing in. She began to pull away, but he caught her hand before she let go of the bars. Her skin was cool beneath his. "You can't cage me. You've got to let us go. All of us wolves, and my vampire friend."

She snatched her hand away. "We don't kidnap random strangers."

"Then what is this prison for?" Rafe gave the walls a casual wave. "This isn't a wine cellar, and I'm not merlot."

Lila shook her head. "You're not the victim here. There's no coming back from what you've done."

Heat rose with his wrath, prickling his skin. When he spoke, his voice dropped to a growl. "You can't cage me, Lila."

She tensed. "I already have."

He'd let the beast slip out, and that breach of discipline was a costly mistake. She reached sideways to something he couldn't see. Then he heard the multi-toned beeping of a keypad. Panic seized him, drowning him like a deadly wave.

"Lila," he cried. "Hear me out!"

He slipped his hand between the bars to touch her sleeve, but she dodged away. "Stay away from me, or you'll lose that paw."

A steel plate slid across the bars from left to right.

"Wait!" He lunged, trying to stop the plate with his hand, but the metal edge dug deep. The mechanism coughed out a grinding noise, and he had to let go. "Lila!"

He barely pulled his hand inside before the panel clanged shut, blocking her from view.

"Lila?" he called, but the only answer was the echo of his voice against bare walls.

He was trapped.

CHAPTER 5

The clang of the heavy lock reverberated in Lila's chest. Rattled, she glared at the steel door, as if it was at fault for her nerves. He'd been cool as ice, but then the mask slipped. What she'd just glimpsed was the stuff of nightmares. One Ademar already knew was real.

Lila spun and strode past the row of doors set into the gray walls. She wanted distance between herself and the werewolf. Questioning the beast had resolved nothing.

He'd broken into the way station and attacked her brother. Rabid dogs had to be put down. And yet that bite was only one of his offenses. He'd made outrageous allegations against her people, and something told her he was just getting started. If she hadn't walked away, he would have kept spewing accusations about kidnappings and evil fae.

But that was the problem, wasn't it? Hadn't she been asking some of the same things? Lila slowed to catch her breath. Why was there a prison here, anyway? A way station was meant to be neutral ground, a place of peace. Not even traditionalist vampires had dungeons anymore—not when there were so many more creative ways to inconvenience the enemy.

Plus, this was a brand-new way station, so the cells weren't relics of a previous era. Someone had *meant* to build a jail for a particular reason—and she doubted it was for the purpose of snatching a parade of werewolves sniffing around the valley. For one thing, what would one do with them? They weren't exactly purse dogs.

For another, she'd lived in the city with its mix of shifters, witches, vampires, and every other supernatural species. Some were quick to pick a fight, but rarely wolves. The wolf's story about looking for someone made more sense than an Alpha stirring up trouble just because.

What had she—and the rabid wolf—stumbled upon?

She continued hurrying past door after door, wishing she'd paid better attention when she'd entered the basement level. It was strange that she was alone—there were no guards keeping watch over the cells—but then what was normal in this place?

That nervous, queasy feeling in her gut rose up again, cresting before Lila ruthlessly slammed it down. By the Abyss, she shouldn't have spoken with the wolf, whether or not her mother had asked it of her. Every time she got involved with her family or the fae in general, she ended up tangled in some complicated problem.

She stopped, suddenly winded. She'd been speed walking for —she wasn't sure how long, but longer than it should have taken to reach the stairs to get out of this basement. Was she going the right way? She surveyed the doors on either side of the hall, wondering who was behind each one. Lord Teegar? The vampire? The wolf's missing kin?

Retracing her steps, Lila nearly made a wrong turn into a side-corridor she hadn't known was there. Or was it? The harder Lila concentrated, the more the angles of the walls seemed to shift, making her sway as if the earth itself was tilting. A throbbing headache crept in.

A confusion spell was at work. Her mother had warned her

this level had magical wards against intruders. Whoever entered this part of the house wasn't supposed to leave. Lila closed her eyes and pressed a hand to the hard, cold wall. Slowly, the ground beneath her feet grew still. She could figure this out.

Without looking, she used her fingertips to guide her down the corridor. Before she'd gone twenty steps, she found the stairway. About three steps up, a spell pushed her back hard enough she felt the pressure against her cheeks.

"*Aberethon*," she whispered, sending a push of power into the barrier. The word was less important than the magic behind it, and her power was born of true Fernblade blood.

She hoped the small spell wouldn't trigger a counterattack, and it didn't. Lila ran up the stairs, her heart thudding. If she hadn't been fae—if she hadn't been powerful—she would have been stuck in the dismal place. Grateful for her escape, she grabbed the handle, fumbling because her palms were damp. The door swung open with a faint squeak. A moment later, she was back in the entry hall where Ademar had put Teegar to sleep.

It had still been dark when she'd entered the dungeon. It was just past dawn now, the sun spilling in through the tall windows. Given everything that had happened, the cheerful daylight didn't seem real. Nothing did. Lila eyed the front door, which someone —presumably her mother's servants—had repaired. There was no trace of Teegar's violent entry, much less Teegar.

Her gaze turned to the view of the trees outside. In a matter of moments, she could be back in the forest, then back in her car, and on her way to her own snug apartment. She'd walked away from the insanity of the fae world before and been far happier for it.

But the first time she'd left, everyone had been fine. Now Ademar was hurt, vampires were knocking on Sala's door, and her mother was exhausted. As strong as the pull to leave might be, Lila couldn't turn her back on them. She had to understand what was happening.

She mounted the stairs and turned her steps toward her brother's room. As soon as the doorway came into view, she stopped. Her mother stood just outside, speaking to one of the two hooded servants. Judging by Galeeta's gestures, she was giving instructions. Lila hung back, a sense of foreboding creeping down her back. It wasn't unusual for lesser fae—pixies, bogles, and the like—to serve their noble masters, but she would recognize their kind. She certainly wouldn't fear them.

This silent, looming servant wasn't any more reassuring in daylight than it had been last night. A moment later, the figure turned and strode away in the opposite direction from where Lila stood, the robes billowing around its feet. Were those talons? The thing moved too fast to be sure.

Her mother looked up, then beckoned Lila to approach.

After a moment's hesitation, Lila complied. "What are those creatures?"

"Gargoyles," Galeeta replied with a dismissive shrug. "A special breed of the species. They've proven themselves invaluable."

"They're terrifying. Why not use your regular staff?"

"These two don't gossip."

"About what?"

Her mother's silence said that was all the answer Lila would get. *For now*, Lila thought to herself. Strategic was better than stubborn where her mother was concerned. Lila had played that game often enough.

She changed the topic. "How is Ademar?"

"He sleeps, which is the best thing for him." Her mother closed the bedroom door, leaving them standing in the hallway. The spark in her eyes had dimmed with fatigue, and tendrils of hair had slipped from their pins. "I want to hear what you learned from the wolf. Follow me. You need to eat."

Lila tried to remember the last time her mother had suggested something as mundane as food. It had been her father who never turned down a good meal and far preferred wine and old books to the political games and derring-do that were his wife's breath and blood. It was no surprise that he wasn't in the thick of the action, but still…

"Did you have a chance to reach Father?"

"I'm glad you asked." Galeeta put her hand on Lila's shoulder, the light touch lasting but a second. "I wish to speak of him, among other things."

Curiosity sparked, but so did apprehension. Something in Galeeta's tone promised nothing good.

They came to the same room where Lila had found Ademar waiting in the dark last night. With the blinds drawn, the room remained plunged in shadows. Lila hesitated on the threshold, seized by a sudden urge to return to brighter light. Galeeta gave Lila a gentle push and then followed her inside.

Someone—presumably the mysterious servants—had laid out food. Tall white candles flickered on the coffee table, framing a tray of cut fruit, soft cheeses, jams, and pastries. A carafe of hot water and a selection of herbal teas stood next to a stack of fine china cups. The rich array of food jarred her senses after the night's bloodshed. And yet, her stomach grumbled a complaint.

"Please, help yourself." Her mother sat in the armchair closest to the window, releasing a sigh of fatigue. "I'll fetch some tea for myself in a moment."

Lila, used to being around humans and their vices, wished for strong, black coffee. Again, an image of her father crossed her mind, leaving an ache behind. He'd love the city's cafés, but had never found time to visit once she'd moved there.

Forcing her shoulders to relax, she crossed the room and picked up a plate, filling it with morsels of everything. "I have a lot of questions."

"Then ask them."

Her first impulse was to ask again about her father, but she stopped herself. Galeeta rarely offered information, and this might be her one chance. She had to pose her questions in a logical order and keep them brief. "I know I'm out of touch with the family, and I'm sorry about that."

"You haven't been back to a fae territory since you left," Galeeta replied. "It's been two years."

"Well, I'm sorry to be so blunt, but I need to catch up now. First question: Is Ademar in some kind of trouble?"

"Whatever gives you that idea?" Galeeta countered.

"Sala sent me to check on him. Apparently, vampires went to her place, looking for Ademar. She was alarmed."

Galeeta couldn't quite hide the slight widening of her eyes—a tell that she was far more upset by that news than she was letting on. "Is that all?"

"There was the captain of the guard who broke in waving a sword." Lila replied, putting a final wisp of pastry on a plate and handing it to her mother, along with a cup of Galeeta's favorite tea. "Here. You need to eat as much as I do."

"Thank you." Her mother took the refreshments gratefully. "But tea doesn't erase the fact that sarcasm is unbecoming in a daughter."

Lila served herself and settled into the chair across from where her mother sat. A ball of anxiety lodged in her stomach. "Forget decorum. It's time we spoke frankly. I can't help if I don't understand what's going on."

"Ademar is not in trouble," Galeeta said in a chilly tone. "He is a warrior, and he was performing his duty. He has done nothing wrong. What is your next question?"

"Who built this way station and why?"

"The other way stations are well known and hardly secure. Lord Farras made this one in secret for King Elroth, to ensure the king could travel without risk."

Farras again. His name was coming up a great deal. "Who else was involved? There had to be others to help him set the spell." Magic did not always survive its creator. No one took chances with something as large as a way station, so it would be anchored to a group for safety's sake.

Galeeta gave a slight shrug. "I don't know the answer to that, but Lord Farras has many powerful friends to call upon for that. Is there anything else you want to know?"

Lila set her plate aside, her breakfast untouched. "Mother, why is there a magic-infested dungeon in the basement?" *Do other children ask this kind of thing?*

Galeeta blinked. "For prisoners, of course. By now, you've figured out this is not an ordinary station." Her mother sipped her tea, her expression carefully blank. "As I said, it was created explicitly for the king's safety. There is a struggle for the throne. Lord Farras is the king's cousin and his supporter."

"Then what was Captain Teegar doing here?"

"The captain hails from a rival clan. Farras believes he is part of a conspiracy against King Elroth's life. If such a plot succeeds, every light fae will be forced to pick a side."

Lila's stomach lurched. "Civil war."

"Exactly. And then the dark fae will move in to take advantage of the chaos."

"As they do," Lila added dryly. "We love blaming them for wrecks of our own making."

Galeeta shot her a sharp look. "This is serious. The fate of all the fae hangs in the balance. You saw Teegar break down the door to the way station, sword drawn. What if the king had been here?"

Lila wasn't sure of the answer. "Well, thanks to Ademar, Teegar is in the dungeon."

Galeeta nodded again, her expression satisfied. "Yes, he is."

"The Sleeping Beauty spell can be fatal."

"It can, but I won't let Captain Teegar die." Galeeta picked a purple grape from her plate and popped it into her mouth. "His ultimate fate is not up to us."

"Then what will you do?"

"We will take the fae prisoners with us once Lord Farras arrives. We'll join King Elroth in Gilden Wood, and once we are there, Teegar will kneel before his sovereign. He will be exposed for the traitor he is, as we shall be on the side of his captors. It never hurts to remind royalty who supports them, and who does not."

That scene was likely to end with an execution. Lila picked up her plate again, needing something to distract herself from that image. She bit into a slice of apple, but was too distracted to taste it. "What are you going to do with the other prisoners?"

"What did you learn from the wolf?"

Lila shivered at the memory of his fingers on her wrist.

"You look frozen, my dear." Galeeta rose, setting her cup and plate on the table. Then she pulled up the blinds of one window. A rectangle of light fell across her, turning her golden hair to pale fire. "The one drawback of my new servants is that they can't abide the light or heat of the sun."

Lila stifled a sigh of relief. Daylight made her feel safer. "I spoke to the prisoner. He said other wolves came into the valley looking for a criminal. They never returned home, so he and the vampire came to investigate. He thought we killed or kidnapped them."

"That's a lie." Galeeta turned to face Lila. "As one would expect. No matter which face they wear, shifters are mere beasts."

Rafe—tall, dark, and wild—rose up in her imagination. "There is nothing *mere* about this one."

"I will question the vampire. Go back and question the wolf again."

"I just left him."

"Get the truth this time. Lord Farras will be here shortly."

"So, the lord will arrive now that Captain Teegar is safely under lock and key?" Sarcasm again, but Lila couldn't help it.

"Lord Farras is our good friend," Galeeta chided. "Ademar is his protégé. He has paid many of our debts. You'd do well to remember what our family owes him."

She remembered all too well. House Fernblade had been fading in wealth and power, until the king's cousin had bestowed his friendship. At one time there had even been talk of betrothing Lila to the lord, but her father had insisted she'd been too young.

A lucky escape. She set down her tea, her stomach too upset to drink it.

"Are all your questions answered now?" Galeeta asked.

Lila met her gaze, refusing to look away. "Some."

Galeeta's eyebrows rose, gently mocking her daughter. "What did I miss?"

Lila pushed to her feet, needing to pace. "Why put yourself and Ademar in the middle of this mess? Why not leave court for a while?"

"I'm afraid there's not much chance of that." For the first time, panic leaked into her mother's voice. "I didn't want to talk about this until the time was right. Your father urgently needs the king's help."

"Father? Why?"

Dread crept over Lila. Something told her this was what Galeeta really wanted to tell her, why she'd plied her with tea and breakfast nibbles. Answering questions had been a means to gain her trust. Even with her own children, Galeeta calculated every move.

Except now, her mother's face had drained of color. Something was genuinely wrong. Lila rose and knelt by her mother's chair, and Galeeta gripped her hand.

"Why does Father need the king's help?" Lila asked. "He's not the type to make enemies, much less ask for royal favors."

Her mother's chin wobbled. "He's still a player at court, or enough of one to make himself a pawn."

Lila watched in horror as her mother blinked back tears. "What does that mean?"

For the first time in the conversation, a flush of anger rose in Galeeta's pale cheeks. "Teegar's faction is holding him hostage. If we walk away from this fight, we forfeit your father's life."

CHAPTER 6

*I*zetta studied the ceiling, imagining pictures in the rough surface. One bit looked like a bear; another smudge might have been trolls in a lewd embrace. It was a trick she'd learned in more than one prison over the years. Better to distract herself than let her imagination run to darker places.

Her captors had chained her to a steel table in the middle of the cell, flat on her back, with the links of her bonds so heavy not even a vampire could break them. Clearly, she and Rafe had made someone nervous. Why not simply kill them? Not that she was complaining—yet.

She hoped Rafe was alive. She didn't like many people, but his was a good soul, even if he didn't understand his own heart. So few mortals had that kind of time.

The heavy lock clanked as it released. Izetta raised her head enough to see the door swing open. A tall, slender female fae stepped in, an impersonal smile on her perfectly-sculpted mouth. Her long, platinum hair was elaborately braided and woven with strands of glittering gems. She was someone important, or at least rich—which was usually the same thing.

"I see you are finally awake," the fae said, approaching the table but still keeping a respectful distance. "How do you feel?"

"You don't care, so tell me what you want." Izetta's voice came out rough, as if she hadn't used it in a long time. Maybe she hadn't. There was no way to tell how long she'd been unconscious beyond the fact that her vampire powers had healed her wounds. Without fresh blood to replenish her strength, that would have taken time.

"I imagine you're thirsty." The female held up a plastic bottle, turning the label so Izetta could see the logo. It was just ordinary water, a common brand. "I assume you find water an acceptable beverage?"

"Yeah."

The female set the bottle next to Izetta's chained hand and stepped back. Izetta could brush the cool surface with her fingertips but couldn't quite grasp it. A frustrated noise escaped her throat.

A flicker of hard amusement crossed the fae's features. "Cooperate, and I'll unchain your wrist so you can drink."

Izetta studied her jailor, saying nothing for a long moment. She sensed the female was older than the two fae in the kitchen, though there was a strong resemblance around the eyes. Mind you, it was hard to tell light fae apart. They all looked like shampoo models.

"Who are you?" Izetta said at last. "What do you want?"

"My name is Galeeta," the female replied. "You met my children, Ademar and Lila."

Izetta tensed. Mothers were mothers, and she and Rafe had injured her young. The thought must have shown on her face, because the fae's smile sharpened.

"As to my reason for keeping you here," Galeeta went on, "I want to know why an ancient Undead is keeping company with a barely-tamed wolf."

"Why does it matter?"

"It's strange how you arrived without an invitation, and then you were able to get inside."

"This isn't a real home," Izetta replied. "Even if it was, it's too new to repel the Undead. That power takes time to build."

"You're right. This place was recently constructed, with extra accommodations." The fae swept her hand around the cell's blank walls.

"I've heard King Elroth is doing a bit of traveling," Izetta said casually. "Word gets around."

Galeeta frowned. She probably thought no one but other fae had noticed the Forest King left the city with his court in tow. Rumor had it that there had been a dip in the effectiveness of certain kinds of spells. Some fae believed it was caused by living away from their natural environment. Others thought it was living near humans, as if mortality was catching.

Was fae power actually tanking? Izetta had no idea, but it meant this court noble—what else could she be?—was left behind while her king bolted for the hills. That had to burn. Maybe it explained the vaguely panicked look in her eyes—or maybe Galeeta wasn't the badass she liked to believe.

The fae stepped closer and lightly ran a finger over Izetta's belly, as if slashing it from side to side. A hot prickle of energy followed her touch, making Izetta flinch. "People don't break into other people's places for legitimate reasons. I think you're a thief. What did you come here to take?"

Izetta said nothing, letting the silence stretch. She'd been a captive many times before—in her line of work, it happened. She'd learned to bide her time and wait for opportunity.

Galeeta took a step back, her large gray eyes narrowing. There was a nervous tic in her jaw. "Being Undead does not make you impervious to persuasion. I have servants who are expert in such arts."

Izetta grinned, letting fang show. "I've been persuaded by the best."

"Don't be a fool. I don't *want* to hurt you."

"I'm a realist," Izetta replied. "You might be looking for information, but that's a small part of the story."

"Oh?"

"You're really looking to assign blame, because that makes you a victim instead of the villain."

The fae gave an annoyed frown. "Why would I want that?"

"Your boss—and everyone has a boss—will ask how someone got inside your secret playhouse. More specifically, how you let that happen." Izetta licked her lips, which were starting to crack with thirst. "Having someone to blame comes in handy, except blame leads to killing innocent people."

Galeeta made a faint sound of derision. "What does a vampire care about collateral damage?"

"Besides getting damaged? Age actually makes some of us thoughtful. Sadly, I think it makes you cling to whatever self-justification keeps you going."

The fae's eyes glittered with temper. "Popular psychology won't keep you whole."

Izetta curled her lip. "You fae have something to hide, and you're afraid I've found out what that is. You want to know who sent me snooping around. Otherwise, I would be dead."

From the female's expression, Izetta had hit the mark. Now she knew what the woman wanted. Maybe Rafe had been right about the Magician hiding within these walls.

"You are not the first vampire that's fallen captive to House Fernblade," Galeeta said in frozen tones. "We know the Undead can heal one injury, then another, and then yet another, but eventually you will need fresh blood."

A cold fist of fear seized Izetta's gut. So few understood how to truly torture her kind.

Galeeta folded her slender arms. "Eventually, you will break. Then you will tell me everything I want to know."

~

LILA CROSSED the black and white tiles of the entry hall, her heart pounding. She'd learned enough on her last visit to the dungeon to be wary, both of the occupants and the magic guarding them. She could disarm or circumvent many spells—she had been trained well from the time she was a child—but some of what she'd sensed was beyond her skill.

Ademar had excelled at higher level magic, such as the Sleeping Beauty spell. He had probably learned it from Lord Farras, who was no doubt responsible for much of the magic around this place. Apparently, there was a perimeter spell in the surrounding forest that prevented visitors from reaching the road. No one got away once the fae took a prisoner.

Her father was a prisoner. The very idea made her want to retch. The king's dungeon was no joke, and King Elroth had a particular hatred for traitors. Once inside that tower, few ever got out. If pleasing Farras convinced him to advocate for her father, she'd play along. And if getting information out of the wolf got her useful answers, she'd do that, too. She hated fae politics with a passion, but she'd suck it up for the sake of her father's life.

The door that hid the basement stairs stood just to the right of the grand staircase leading to the upper floors. The knob was enameled to match the stark white walls. The door was almost as well-concealed as the secret passage Ademar had used during Teegar's attack, which begged the question of how many hidden entrances she hadn't found yet.

Lila opened the door and stared down the barely lit steps. Last time she'd come this way, she'd been riding a wave of fury over Ademar's wounds. This time she was attuned to the wave of subtle magic that invited visitors in while never intending to let them go. There was a kickstand on the inside of the door, so she propped it open to safeguard her retreat. Dry-mouthed, she thrust her hand into her pocket, fingered the key fob, and made herself descend the stairs.

As before, the corridors below were empty of guards. Lila went the same way as she had the first time, studying whatever landmarks she could find—a scuffed bit of wall, the number of light fixtures until she came to the right-hand turn. Rafe's door was the first, halfway along the hallway. There were other cells—Teegar and the vampire had to be there, too—but Lila kept her focus on the wolf.

One problem at a time. She turned her attention to Rafe's cell.

As before, a steady red light shone from the security panel to the right of the door. Older fae were often slow to adapt to human technology, but if Lord Farras had added modern gadgets to the way station, he was clearly comfortable with modern tech. That made sense. He was acting as a patron to Ademar, whose passion was marrying magic and machines. Maybe it was her brother's expertise that ensured these locks worked in the presence of so many spells.

Lila swiped the key fob over the security panel and waited for the light to go from red to green. Then she pushed the button that slid open the top panel of the door. With a metallic click and scraping noise, the steel plate slid open to reveal the barred top section of the door. Lila watched as Rafe looked up from where he sat on the bed, elbows on his knees. At the sight of her, his lips curled into a snarl before the cold human mask slammed into place. Lila stifled the urge to step back from the bars.

At least she knew where she stood with him. That kept things simple.

Rafe rose and approached the door, his body language wary. Unlike the first time she'd come, full of fury, she gave herself time to study the shifter. From the first, she'd noticed his long limbs and broad shoulders. Now she saw smaller details. That weathered tan said he spent much of his time outdoors. The dark hair was a lush, heavy texture only a shifter could claim. Her fingers itched to see if it was as soft as she imagined. By the time he reached the door, Lila had to concentrate on the reason she was there.

He folded his arms and regarded her with steady hazel eyes. The color held the possibility of wolf gold, a glimpse of the predator within. It was hard to stand still and meet that gaze. She wanted to shuffle away. He was so—cold.

"Have you been given food and water?" she asked in a flat tone, wondering if her mother's mysterious servants had been there.

"Yes," he replied, "although I gotta say, if this is a fae hotel, your concept of fine cuisine needs work."

"So give us two stars." She shrugged. "I doubt the manager will care."

He lounged against the heavy stone that formed the doorframe. There was an insolence to the posture that almost hid his wariness. "What do you want from me?"

"I want you to pay for the injury you dealt my brother, but we've been over that."

"I understand." His expression didn't change. "You and your brother are pack."

"You could put it that way."

"I just did."

She shifted a little to the left, trying to see his entire face between the bars. "You're not sorry for biting him, are you?"

"There is a difference between remorse and regret. I regret that it was necessary."

His calm, cool tone infuriated Lila. "Just like it was necessary to hunt us in our own way station?"

"I told you why we came here. We were hunting someone who is a threat to the pack."

Lila's breath hitched. They'd just arrived at the first topic she wanted to explore. "I want to know more about this criminal the wolves are hunting."

~

RAFE STRAIGHTENED, something in the fae's voice putting him on guard. The last time Lila had come here, he'd pushed her too hard, withheld too much. He let emotion outrun reason, which was against every scrap of Silent Wolf training. *Be careful.* He'd get nowhere if she stormed away a second time.

"I don't know his real name," Rafe admitted.

She tilted her head, her gray eyes narrowing. "What do you know?"

Rafe sucked in a breath. He was treading on very dangerous ground. "Whoever he is, he's popular with the youth of the city's supernatural quarter. They call him the Magician."

Lila folded her arms, hugging her ribs tight. "The Magician? Are you serious?"

"He meets them in bars and dance clubs. Within hours, at least some of them have gone mad. Others are dead. No one knows why."

"And you say he is a fae?" She spat the words out as if they tasted foul.

Rafe stalked closer to the bars. "I've seen a surveillance recording. He was light fae, all right, and I recognized one of the victims. What is he doing to them?"

Her brows gathered into a frown. "I don't know. I've heard something about a spate of recent deaths, but never dreamed a fae was responsible."

As they'd been talking, she'd pulled out her phone and swiped the screen. After typing a moment, she held it up so that Rafe could see a news article. Another headline, another dead kid. Rafe skimmed the first few lines. This time, the victim had been a newly-made vampire. His gaze flicked back to the top of the screen. The by-line read *Errata Jones.* He vaguely recognized the reporter's name from other articles, or maybe it had been a blog.

"So you believe me?" he asked.

"The deceased lived in my apartment block," she said. "I know these deaths are real. I get why you want to stop the carnage, but I don't know how to help. Your Magician isn't here."

Rafe was confused. "Did you say the last victim was your neighbor?"

"Yes."

"Light fae don't live side-by-side with vamps."

Her mouth twisted in a half-smile. "Except for me. I'm the only light fae in town with an address in a mixed-species building."

She began to put the phone away, but had to pull a key fob from her pocket before the phone would fit. Rafe tried not to watch as she tucked it in her breast pocket.

"Why live there?"

She hesitated so long he thought she wouldn't answer. Then she spoke quickly and quietly, as if she were afraid of being overheard. "I wanted something different."

For a fleeting instant, he understood her. "You wanted to know who you might be outside your pack."

The look she shot him said he'd got it in one. "Maybe."

"Good for you."

"What do you know about it?"

"A shifter community can be pretty smothering, too."

That was how he'd ended up half a world away, tracking bad guys for fun and profit. The hard part was coming home and finding out he still didn't fit in, even if he was the Alpha's son.

She straightened, as if remembering this wasn't a casual conversation. Her eyes lost their momentary warmth as she grasped the bars, leaning close. "Let's get back to the Magician. Tell me again why you came here to find him?"

Rafe gave up being friendly. It hadn't exactly been a pretense, but he'd known it was doomed. "Like I said, we tracked him to this valley by his scent."

"Right to this door?" She bit off each syllable. "Are you sure?"

"Yes."

"I believe your bogeyman is real, but you're sniffing in the wrong place." She began to pull away, but he caught her wrist. Her skin was cool, the bones fragile beneath his grip.

"Our young are dying," he said in a voice like ice. "I can't ignore evidence."

Her scent tickled his nostrils, driving straight into the most primal centers of his brain. She was like a drug, though he could not tell if that signaled poison or pleasure. His fingers grazed the crisp fabric of her shirt, as her breath warmed his face. If he leaned in another inch, he could have pressed his lips to hers.

"No." She snatched her hand away, jumping back and rubbing her wrist as if he'd left a bruise. "We're not criminals. We don't lure party-goers to their deaths. And we didn't kidnap your missing pack mates."

Rafe deftly palmed the fob he'd plucked from her shirt pocket and slipped it out of sight. "You can't blame us for searching."

"You had no right to attack us."

They were right back to where they had ended last time, snarling and snapping. She had spirit, even if she stuck to her opinions like a barnacle. He'd be wild with frustration except now the fob felt warm in his hand, heavy with promise.

"You can't keep me locked up forever." It was all Rafe could do to keep mockery from his tone. He *would* find a way out. "Or my pack mates."

"Do you have fur in your ears? We don't kidnap people."

"Then explain where they went."

"Not my problem. It has nothing to do with us." Despite her denial, the conversation had clearly struck a nerve.

"So you're saying I wasn't kidnapped?"

With a darting movement, she pushed the button that closed the panel over the door. "I'm done arguing with you."

The panel began to grind shut.

"Let me go, Lila."

"Oh, but you'll stay," she said, eyes snapping. "Even if you made it out of your cell, no living thing can leave this way station without permission. That's old magic, woven straight from the soul of the forest. Cross that line, and no one will find so much as a finger bone."

Rafe took a breath to object, but he was staring at the closed door. Her words had just ripped his careful plan to shreds.

He sank to the floor, his back pressed against the wall. A low, frustrated growl escaped him, echoing against the hard walls. His fist closed around the fob.

What good was it now, when nothing alive could escape?

CHAPTER 7

Time passed, but how much was a mystery. The walls didn't move, but they seemed to gather weight. Rafe felt their heaviness in every breath he took, as if the in and out of air got harder each time. He had to get out. If he didn't, he'd suffocate on nothing.

He got up, spurred by the need to pace … move … something. A therapist—the Silent Wolves insisted on monitoring the mental health of their operatives—had blamed his claustrophobia on the excessive self-discipline he'd wrapped around his rebellious psyche. Or something. He'd blame the bars and cold floors for his discomfort because those were hard facts.

Still, his thoughts yammered without mercy. It was his own fault he was there. He should have known better than to answer his father's text—but the unexpected request had been impossible to ignore. And, there was so much past to erase. He had started challenging his father young, picking a fight whenever and wherever he saw a need for justice. It had come to a head when he'd mounted a raiding party on a rival pack against his father's explicit orders. When Rafe had left the pack, there had been anger on both sides. It was only later he figured out that a wolf without a pack was a wolf with no home.

But they needed his skills now, and playing the hero might be his way back. Yes, he should have known the job would be more complicated than what he'd learned over the phone. Dad wasn't a detail kinda guy, sometimes by nature and sometimes on purpose.

To be fair, a fae dungeon beneath a trendy ultramodern mansion was a definite curve ball. No one would have seen this one coming. And now? Now Rafe would vanish like all the wolves who searched the valley before him. Or not. He rarely failed—and wasn't planning to take up the habit.

His pacing had taken him around the cell three times. He turned back to the door, examining its structure one more time. The bottom half was solid, the top inset with a barred window sealed by a sliding metal panel on the side closest to the hallway. The lock appeared to be magnetic, probably operated through the control pad.

He examined the spot where he'd dropped his shirt button into the track right as Lila had closed the panel. As intended, it had stopped the panel from closing completely, leaving the thinnest gap along the frame. A good system would have detected an object, but the electronic security in this place was designed by amateurs. Fae copied tech with an artist's eye, but rarely understood the principles behind it, probably because it conflicted with their own magic. Maybe the more sensitive the system, the more problems it would have around the fae.

Rafe peered closer. It was hard to tell, but it looked as if the pressure had cracked the button into several pieces. Experimentally, Rafe probed the gap, but it was too small for human fingers to slide into the opening. He needed to rethink his next step.

And the one after that. His original plan had withered with Lila's last words. According to her, a spell trapped him inside the way station. Fae were tricksters, but they rarely—if ever—told a barefaced lie. Still, there were always loopholes.

A snarling scream ripped through his musing. Rafe froze.

Izetta. He knew her hunting cry, but this was fraught with as much pain as anger. He snapped to alert. Shifting his nails into strong, deadly claws, he slipped them into the gap between the panel and its frame and began pulling it open to reveal the bars.

The metal groaned as the system fought to close the panel tight. The force dragged against Rafe's claws, bending them at a painful angle, but soon he could slip his fingers around the edge. As he tried to slide the panel to an open position, the bars blocked his progress. They were too tightly spaced for his human arm to pass through, but he was a shifter with exceptional control. He could shift a part of himself at a time. A paw could go where a hand could not, and it was every bit as strong. Still, he strained against the force driving the panel shut. Muscle and tendon bunched to resist it. More than once, he had visions of the mechanism snapping closed and breaking his bones. He was bathed in sweat before he'd worked the panel along its tracks far enough to reach the keypad and shift back to a fully human form.

The scream came again, fainter than before. A prickle chased down the back of his neck. As a rule, vampires didn't feel much pain. This had to be bad.

He fumbled the fob out of his pocket and juggled it to the hand he'd worked through the bars, all the while keeping the door from chopping off his arm. The keypad was to the left of the door, completely out of his line of sight. After a few blind swipes, he heard the beep that said the keypad had come to life.

Now to enter the code he'd heard Lila enter. He played the sequence of tones over in his mind, remembering the slight variations and the silences between each beep. *Beep. Beep. Beebee-ba-beep.*

Experimentally, he pushed two buttons, one after the other,

then another two. The button at the top of the keypad was a slightly higher pitch than the button below. The left key was a lower pitch than the one on the right. The differences were slight —so slight that a human would never have noticed.

Another bead of sweat snaked down the back of his neck. He slowly tapped out the code, got it wrong, then tried again. With sudden force, the sliding panel stopped fighting back and locked into the open position with a sturdy *clank*. Rafe stumbled, off balance now that he didn't need to push for all he was worth. His palm tingled as blood rushed back to his half-crushed flesh.

In the distance, he heard a door close, then footfalls. Perfectly still, he held his breath until he was sure they were moving away from his cell. Another door, this one farther away, opened and shut. At the very edge of his sensitive hearing, Izetta cursed.

There was no time to waste. He searched around the keypad with his fingertips and found a large button beneath the keypad. It was an awkward reach through the bars, forcing him to rise up on his toes before he could press the button all the way down.

The door released with a heavy click. Rafe pulled his arm back through the bars, rubbing the chafed skin, and pushed the door. It swung open without a sound. Rafe cautiously stepped into the hall, scanning from right to left. There was no one in sight, but the scent of blood hung heavy in the air. Beneath it was the leathery musk of vampire.

There had to be a way out of this dungeon, a door to the daylight world and freedom. Rafe pushed the idea aside and followed Izetta's scent down the hall to his right. He passed three cells before he found the one where the tang of blood was thickest. Listening carefully, he waited a full minute before he decided she was alone.

He waved the fob over the keypad outside her door and entered the code, praying that all the cells used the same one. He drew a deep breath when the light beside the pad turned from red to green and the panel at the top of the door slid open, revealing the cell inside. His first view was of a small table on casters that held a tray of sharp implements. The sight of it made him flinch.

Izetta was bound to a table in the middle of the room, her eyes shut and skin slicked with blood. She didn't stir at the sound of the sliding panel. With silent rage, Rafe pushed the button that released the door lock and stepped inside the cell.

Now her gaze flicked his way, her dark eyes widening a fraction when she saw it was him. Yet she didn't waste time with questions.

"Get these off me," she said, voice cracking as she strained against the straps that bound her.

Rafe picked up a long, thin knife, then discarded it for a pair of shears that sliced the thick straps like tissue paper. As soon as she was free, Izetta lunged for the bottled drink that sat nearby. While Rafe freed her ankles, the vampire drank the entire bottle without pausing for breath.

"Here," he said, passing her the fob. "The door code is 7-2-3-3-5-7. Go get help."

Izetta's brows drew into a sharp V. "You're not coming?"

"Nothing living can leave without permission. At least that's what the female fae said."

"And I'm not alive." The vampire gave a small nod. "I'll do what I can."

With anyone else, that wouldn't be much of a promise, but Izetta always meant what she said. She would do whatever was in her power.

"Good enough," Rafe said. "Let's get you out of here."

She got to her feet, but it was obviously a struggle. Rafe steadied her until she shrugged off his hand with a disgusted wave. They got as far as the hallway.

A bullet skimmed over Rafe's shoulder, leaving a hot kiss of pain in its wake. He grabbed Izetta, pulling her flat against the wall, shielding her body with his own. Lila stood a dozen yards away, gun held in a perfect shooting stance.

"Did you think no one would notice the cell doors were open?" she demanded. "They have silent alarms."

Two enormous robed and hooded figures were coming down the hall. Lila glanced their way, going a little pale at the sight of them, then focused her aim on Rafe.

"Run," Rafe said to Izetta, whispering it in her ear. If anyone could pull a disappearing act, it was a vampire.

There was no time to shift. Rafe leaped forward, somersaulting over Lila's next bullet to launch himself at the robed minions. He grabbed the closest one, heaving the tall figure backward with enough force that its feet left the floor. Snarling, the hooded minion pulled free and wheeled around, breaking Rafe's grip with a sweep of its arm.

Rafe caught a glimpse of the second minion's fist just as it swooped toward his temple. He ducked, driving his shoulder into Hood One's middle. Pain needled through his joints—hitting the creature was like hitting concrete—but at least the thing was vulnerable. Rafe heard a whoosh of breath, then the thump of flesh as his opponent's back hit the wall. He let out a wolfish snarl, his beast applauding the violence.

The celebration didn't last. Pain sliced through him as a fist pounded into his right kidney. Eyes watering, Rafe sidestepped and spun, using the momentum to deliver a cross to Hood Two's jaw. Rafe felt the skin of his knuckles split as they connected with rock-hard flesh and bone.

Hood One launched toward Rafe once more, talons sprouting through its fine leather gloves. Rafe roared in fury as they raked his cheek, barely missing his eye. As he shoved Hood One away, hot blood trickled down his face like tears. The pain called to his wolf, urging it to join in bloody, senseless abandon.

The next time Hood One lunged, Rafe grappled his enemy

close, limiting its ability to strike. Whatever the Hoods were, they were powerfully strong, with ropey, bunching muscles beneath the robes. Rafe smashed Hood One's head into the wall. It slumped to the ground, the hood falling away to reveal a flash of leathery flesh.

From the corner of his eye, Rafe saw Izetta fly from the shadows, swooping for Lila's gun. Lila wheeled on the vampire, but the second minion got to Izetta first. Izetta and Hood Two tumbled to the floor. Rafe lunged toward them, but Lila flung herself in the way. Rafe grabbed her arm, twisting it until she was forced to her knees. A noise escaped her, half cry, half snarl of rage. Rafe snatched the gun from her grasp and grabbed a fistful of her thick, pale hair, so she couldn't stir an inch.

He pressed the muzzle of the gun to her temple, but his gaze went to Izetta. Though clearly wounded, Izetta had pinned the creature facedown, her knee between its shoulder blades and both arms trapped behind its back. Rafe sucked in a full breath for the first time since breaking into the way station.

He bent over Lila. "Let her leave."

She twisted her head as far as his grip allowed, murder in her eyes. "And then what? She brings all your friends over for a party?"

A frustrated growl rumbled through Rafe's chest as he tightened his grip on her. She hissed in pain, until he loosened his fist, aware of the soft silk of her hair tangled through his fingers. Up close, her skin was almost translucent, the veins beneath a faint tracery of blue.

Somewhere distant, a door slammed. Rafe didn't understand magic, but he could feel the air changing, as if spells were starting and stopping all around them.

"What's going on?" he demanded, his pulse thundering in his ears.

He caught a whiff of something burning, then grunted in surprise at a sudden, searing pain in his fingers. He dropped the gun to the floor. It sizzled, blackening the tile while a brutal thump on Rafe's back made him stumble. When he glanced over his shoulder, nothing was there.

But the distraction had done its work. Lila melted from Rafe's hands. Before he could react, she was on the other side of the room, her hands clenched into fists. Electricity rippled through the room, leaving the faint smell of ozone behind. A moment later, the two Hoods began to rise to their feet, the motion fluid and graceful despite their bulk.

The moment they stood, a blazing light filled the room, like a thousand cameras flashing at once. Rafe hurtled backward and landed awkwardly, wrenching his shoulder as he rolled upright. His ribs ached like he'd taken a roundhouse kick.

Rafe swayed a moment, senses reeling from the impact. Then shock speared through him. The robes of the minions had fallen open during the fight, revealing the figures beneath. They were taller than Rafe and equipped with beaks, wings, and claws the length of lawnmower blades. Their skin was a dark mud color, leathery and pebbled with sharp spines sticking from each joint. Gargoyles?

He didn't have time to think about it—they weren't alone. A female fae he hadn't seen before stood between them, appearing as suddenly as if she'd stepped through a rift in space and time.

"Mother," Lila said. The word held uncertainty, as if she expected a reprimand.

Mother? Rafe held his breath as the newcomer scanned the scene, a frown tugging at the corners of her full mouth.

"Where is the vampire?" the older fae demanded.

He heard Lila's wordless exclamation. His own heart raced with a mix of triumph and tension, because Izetta was no longer there.

"I don't know," Lila replied. "I'm sorry."

Lila's mother turned to Rafe. "And what is he doing out of his cell?" She took a step forward and grabbed his chin, forcing him to look her in the eye.

Rafe stopped breathing until she let him go and wiped her fingers on her robe.

"Deal with him," she said to her pet monsters. "He's more trouble than he's worth."

CHAPTER 8

"No," Lila said. "Stop."

She didn't raise her voice, but the effect was as swift as if she'd screamed the words. The two hooded figures froze in place, their tattered robes eddying around their feet. Lila swallowed, her mouth suddenly dry.

Galeeta's brows raised in question. "Daughter?"

Lila faltered, wondering why she'd spoken—and why she'd used a voice of compulsion. Maybe she didn't want to witness what her mother would do next.

It wasn't sympathy for the wolf. He was their adversary, and they both knew it—in fact, now he was giving her a puzzled look.

"Let him live," Lila said, her cheeks heating beneath his curious stare. "Please."

"Why do you care?" Galeeta asked, raising her brows. "Did he win your heart with his sad tale?"

"No. His teeth are too sharp for that." Lila groped for excuses. "He's got more information. There's something he's not telling me. I'm not done questioning him."

Rafe's lips curled back, showing teeth that were a little too pointed for his human form. Without a word or sound, he made it clear he would tell her nothing. That kind of bravery only came from someone with little to lose.

After a pointed pause, Galeeta waved a hand at her retainers. "Put the beast in a cell. One he hasn't broken yet."

Lila ducked her chin, avoiding Rafe's eyes. He'd just gambled away his freedom—and probably his life—to protect his friend. This beast was heroic—or stupid—to a fault.

With cool efficiency, her mother's servants frisked Rafe and found the key fob, silently dropping it into Lila's palm. Then they dragged their prisoner away. Rafe cast one last glance over his shoulder, which Lila pretended not to see.

Galeeta studied her with a frown. "How did this happen?"

Lila's hand traveled to her breast pocket. He'd brushed against her for the barest second, but now her cheeks burned at the half-remembered touch. "He's a thief."

A distant door clanged, deep as a mourning bell. The wolf was caged again. Both Lila and her mother turned toward the sound to see the servants were on their way back, clawed hands hidden in their sleeves.

"Go search for the vampire," Galeeta said to them. "It should be an easy task, since she was bleeding just minutes ago. Bring me proof you found her and dispose of the rest."

The two bowed and moved silently toward the stairs. Although they didn't run, they moved faster than Lila's gaze could follow.

Galeeta took Lila's arm and drew her down the hall at a brisk pace. A frown puckered her brow. "This should not have happened. No one escapes the fae."

"I'm sorry," Lila answered.

They stopped before Rafe's previous cell. The sliding panel at the top of the door was buckled, wrenched open by brute force. The bars were warped, as if they'd been made of putty.

"This wasn't your fault," her mother said, running the tips of her long, slim fingers over the damage. "Such a creature is hard to deny."

A frisson passed through Lila's frame. *Deny how?* Her gaze locked on the crumpled metal, mesmerized by such raw strength. Fear rose like bubbles in her blood, but so did fascination. Physical power alone hadn't opened Rafe's door. He had brains and courage, too. *He's fighting for the young of his pack, trying to save them from someone he thinks might be us.*

"Still," Galeeta continued, "that can't happen again. We can't afford to look weak right now."

Lila turned away from the ruined door. It was too distracting. "What do you mean?"

"Remember that I'm fighting to save your father." Galeeta's lips thinned. "Let's not lose any more family members."

Lila looked down, unable to meet her mother's eyes. She'd had four siblings once, not just Sala and Ademar. "No."

"You spoke with the wolf again. Did you learn anything new?"

"He says the Magician is a light fae."

Galeeta made a dismissive noise. "Nonsense. He's holding out on you. How do we make him give us information?"

As they began walking again, Lila replayed her conversations with the wolf. He was a highly skilled fighter. Self-contained. She could tell from the way he held himself, the confident lift of his head, that he trusted his own abilities. He was a loyal friend, based on the fact he'd saved his vampire.

And behind all that bravado, he had the saddest eyes she'd ever seen. Maybe that's why she'd spared him. She wanted to know why.

"He's proud," Lila said as they reached the staircase and mounted the steps. "He knows who he is."

"Males like that are easy to break," Galeeta replied with a shrug. "They assume everyone fights fairly."

Not like a fae, Lila thought darkly.

"In the meantime," her mother went on, "go assist the others to capture the Undead. If she reaches her Master, word of this place will spread like fire."

Then all Galeeta's plans—whatever those were—would be lost. Lila cared only about saving her father, but that was more than enough. "On my way."

~

RAFE LANDED BADLY, knocking his elbow on the cell floor. Pins and needles swarmed up his arm, but he had no time to think about it. Hoods One and Two flipped him onto his stomach, pinning him down. He writhed, using all his strength, but he was no match for two of them.

Rafe turned his head so he could breathe and caught a glimpse of the closest creature's face looming over him. The mouth and chin formed a serrated beak that could easily slice through a limb. These had to be gargoyles. That was the only species that made sense, but they weren't like any he'd seen before. Where in all the Hells had the fae found them?

When the closest monster saw him looking, it opened its mouth to hiss, showing off a wormlike black tongue.

Cold metal slid around his wrists, snapping tight. Immediately, he felt a prickling burn against his skin. *Silver.* It affected shifters almost as badly as cold iron poisoned fae.

Hoods One and Two abruptly let him go. He rolled over, expecting a rattle of chains, but found his arms free but for a cuff on each wrist. By the time he jumped to his feet, his guards had retreated to the cell door and were leaving. The last one out turned, an unreadable look on its alien face, and studied Rafe before slamming the door shut. The metallic locks clicked into place.

The sound sent a stab of panic through his gut, but he forced it down, putting a paw on its throat. He needed facts. Logic. Discipline. That was how he'd survive.

His first step was to take stock. The whole process, from dragging him here to locking him in, had taken less than a minute. His captors had been brutal, efficient, and impersonal. He had cuts and bruises, but nothing too bad. He flexed his arm. His elbow complained, but it wasn't broken.

Rafe paced to the wall, then to the door. This cell was identical to his old one, taking exactly the same number of steps to get from end to end. The last few hours had only changed three things. One, it would be far harder to break out of this cell now that they knew what he could do. Two, he had freed Izetta. Three, they had put him in cuffs.

He stopped moving long enough to examine them. They were about three inches wide and perfectly plain. The only blemish on their smooth surface was a tiny keyhole on the edge of each band. Hair prickled at the base of his neck as he thought about who might hold that key. Lila's mother? The fool he'd bitten? The only reason the fae would create these cuffs was to keep him under control.

His beast rose, begging to be let out, and Rafe discovered the first thing his new bonds did. The power that let him change form slipped out of his reach as soon as it stirred. He was trapped in man form, half of him cut away.

A wave of breathless nausea made him sit down on the floor.

Discipline. Boundaries. Draw a line of ice around your emotions, a perfect box. Your feelings can flow up to that line, but they can't spill over. What's outside the line can't get inside to touch you. Keep yourself separate, and you can weather any storm. The thicker the ice, the harder it is to crack.

Slowly, slowly, he formed the picture in his mind. As he did so, his pulse and heart rate fell to a normal level. He'd learned the technique in the Silent Wolves. They'd given him the combination of freedom and self-mastery he'd needed. Now he was trained, steady, followed orders, and delivered results. For all the harsh words and disappointment heaped on Rafe when he'd left home, he knew he'd taken the right path. The old Rafe wouldn't have survived a day in these cells.

The therapist—going had never been his idea, but the order had come down after that thing with the rusalka—said he should be careful not to take the ice wall too far. That he had isolated himself. Well, as long as he was around the fae, those walls had better be a mile thick. They pushed every one of his buttons.

And it wasn't the first time. Rafe had been too young to remember details, but a hunting party of dark fae had killed his cousin, Trevor, while he was running as a wolf. They had speared him for sport, then sent a purse of gold coin to Trevor's dad. The Alpha—his grandfather back then—had called the money *weregild* and according to ancient law, the wolves had been obligated to accept the price.

If Rafe had been Alpha, no amount of coin would have bought those fae peace. Laws be damned. That was a big part of why he'd agreed to hunt the Magician. He was sick of his people being murdered by the fae.

Where were the missing wolves of Pack Devries? Old Jasper, too stubborn to let time and rheumatism keep him by the fire? Hot-headed Rand? Alexi and Lars? Those last two were brothers who ran an auto shop during the day and street races when no humans were looking. And there were more. Twelve had gone missing—he was number thirteen. Had the others found the Magician? Was that why they'd vanished?

Rafe got to his feet just long enough to flop onto the hard bed. He stared at the ceiling, repeating the boundary exercise to quiet his thoughts. It mostly worked, but one worry still niggled.

Had Izetta escaped to find help? If not, he was in this cell for good.

～

Between the drama of the escape and her mother's worries, Lila had lost track of time. She was a little surprised to find the afternoon light was already dimming when she got outside, the ragged skyline of fir and pine melting into a dark silhouette. A rising wind brought the scent of the woods like a sharp perfume. Lila drank it in, grateful to be free of the way station.

She turned in place, wondering where to begin her search. An escaped prisoner would try to put distance between themselves and their jail, but even a sliver of daylight robbed the Undead of their strength. Galeeta had been right—the vampire couldn't have gone far.

Lila paused, using her fae senses to scan the forest around her. The servants were straight ahead, their presence prickling at the edge of her awareness. Lila turned in the opposite direction, heading into the deep woods behind the house. She had no desire to meet those two on a dark, deserted path.

The terrain was almost impassable for anyone but a fae—clearly not a well-used route. Insects buzzed a lazy drone as she picked her way forward. The brush was thick, hiding steep boulders and equally unexpected drops. In places, the thickets looked almost woven together. Insects buzzed a lazy drone. There was a faint path hidden beneath the drifts of leaves, but it took a sharp eye and imagination to find it.

Lila used her magic to clear the clinging branches. They lifted with a crackle of twigs, but just long enough to let her slip past. The one time she was slow, she nearly got a face full of brambles. Soon the brush and trees towered above her, blocking out the sky.

The deeper she went, the darker it got, and she was forced to summon a ball of light into her palm. She held it high to see the ground in front of her, but the shadows gobbled up the light's rays. Instinctively, she stopped, wary. Dead ahead, an extra-thick tangle blocked her way, steeped in a spell she'd not encountered before.

A familiar resonance in the spell said it was fae work, not something their escaped vampire might have conjured. Under normal circumstances, she'd leave another fae's work alone. Still, the last days—was it even that long?—had burned through any hesitation. Whatever was hidden here might be an answer. At the very least, it was blocking her path.

Unweave. Pull back. Stand aside. Lila infused the words with her will, forming the syllables first in the common language and then in her own native tongue. The magic caught and twisted, pulling on her store of power the way a spinner teases out their wool. The branches shifted as before, but not without resistance. Every inch took force. Pain shot along her nerves, finding each ending from her fingertips all the way to the root of her spine. It seared like lightning, molten and radiant. Lila let out a cry and fell forward, jarring her knees.

She bent over, head to the ground, as a wave of sickness engulfed her. She hadn't used that much power in years, and she was out of practice. She pressed her palms to the earth, grounding herself with the feel of cool, damp moss.

When she raised her head, a narrow gap had appeared in the underbrush. She got to her feet, awkward with fatigue, and took a tentative step forward to make out what lay beyond the barrier. The scent of freshly turned dirt filled the air.

Lila paused, letting the woods speak to her. *Secret. Quiet. Sleeping the long rest below.*

She fell back a step, but not before she'd counted six graves. She took two more steps back, then slid to the ground with her back to a tree.

The white moon sails, but our voices are silent. An ice-cold fist gripped her gut. Rafe hadn't lied. The wolf *had* come here looking for his pack.

She'd found them.

CHAPTER 9

*L*ila mounted the stairs to the way station's upper floors, the scent of the woods still clinging to her clothes and hair. Where there should have been nothing but the tang of moss and cedar, now she caught the faint whiff of acrid decay. Was it real or her imagination? She couldn't tell. Her nerves were twisted tight, afraid of what those graves meant.

For the last hundred years, the fae had lived in uneasy peace with the other supernatural communities. Humans, for all their weakness, were a challenge that united the others. But that newfound harmony was far from guaranteed. Those graves could ignite a wildfire of enmity and bloodshed between shifters and fae.

Lila could pretend she hadn't found them, but there was too much at stake to take the easy road. Truth was the only way.

She reached the top of the stairs and started down the corridor, her feet silent on the thick carpet. The house was quiet, no other footfalls disturbing the deep hush. Lila's gaze searched the shadows, as if her unanswered questions lurked in the doorways. Had her mother's servants caught the vampire yet? Would there be more wolves coming? What would happen to Rafe?

The image of the wolf—his generous mouth and sad, intelligent eyes, rose in her mind. An uneasy flutter of guilt quickened her pace. Surely this new information would influence his fate. At the very least, he deserved to know what had happened to his kin.

When she finally heard voices, they came from Ademar's room. Had a physician come? Had he taken a turn for the worse? With a surge of alarm, she broke into a run, the graves momentarily forgotten. The door stood open.

"Ademar!" She sprang through the door, then barely skittered to a stop before she crashed into the foot of the bed. She finally grabbed the bedpost and stood gaping.

Her brother was propped up on pillows, his pale face even paler against the white linens. But he was awake and talking softly with Galeeta, who sat beside his bed, cradling his hand in hers. He wore a clean nightshirt, and his hair was combed. Clearly Galeeta, in a motherly mood, had tidied her son.

Ademar barely turned his head at Lila's approach, as if too weak to move much, but a smile lit his eyes. With a sharp stab of relief, Lila bent over the bed, gently embracing her brother. His skin felt hot. A thread of worry tightened in her chest.

"How do you feel?" she asked as she stepped back, holding his gaze with her own. The question was woefully clumsy, barely hiding her anxiety. "Tell the truth."

Ademar hesitated, his gaze dropping to where his hands rested on the bedcovers. Candlelight glistened on his fever-damp skin, highlighting the sharp elegance of his features. "My leg hurts," he snapped, voice rasping. "Is that truth enough?"

Lila drew back, a little stung by his impatient tone. "I'm sorry."

Shaking his head, Ademar sank back onto the pillows. "My apologies. I'm not at my finest."

Galeeta adjusted the bedcovers. "But you are mending, and that is what counts."

"Is there anything I can do?" Lila asked.

"You're a good sister." Galeeta stroked Lila's hair, smoothing it into place.

Such affectionate gestures were rare, and Lila barely stopped herself from leaning into it like a cat. For the briefest moment, she felt safe. It didn't last.

Lila sensed the servant's presence before the robed figure appeared in the doorway. It loomed, head bowed and hands hidden by the gray habit. The stance reminded Lila of a medieval monk, except she had glimpsed the horror beneath the cowl. A medieval demon, perhaps, like the kind from a nightmarish painting of Hell.

Without another word, her mother glided from the room to join the creature, closing the door behind her. Lila drew closer to the bed and clasped her brother's hand. He returned the squeeze, but without much force. Lila opened her mouth to speak, but her thoughts collided. She should have been filled with simple pleasure that Ademar was awake, but the servant's arrival filled her with foreboding.

Ademar closed his eyes, the pale blue veins in his lids visible in the pool of lamplight. Lines of pain bracketed his mouth.

Lila took a deep breath to ease the heaviness over her heart. "Mother was frantic trying to heal you," she said, filling the silence. "She barely left your side."

"I know."

"I don't think she can admit how badly scared she was for you."

"Maybe," Ademar murmured. "As bad as this is, I am the fortunate one. Unlike Father, I have my freedom."

Lila knew she should leave and let her brother sleep, but she had to ask just one question. "Did you know about Father?"

Ademar gave a silent nod.

"Do you know why or how he was captured?"

"I was not there when it happened." He opened his eyes to the merest slits. "From what Mother said, the Royal Guard came one night and took him without warning."

"What of our servants? Didn't they defend him?"

"The soldiers came armed to the teeth, and they brought a spellcaster with them. The staff had no chance. Neither did our father."

Lila's head swam. "But why? What did Father do? And why did nobody tell me?"

"That was Mother's choice. She wanted to keep you and Sala safe. She loves you, you know."

The door opened again before Ademar could say more. Galeeta swept in, tension surrounding her like a cloak.

"The vampire is still loose in the woods." Their mother's chill tone couldn't hide the swirl of fear and anger beneath it. "But she won't escape. She can't. Not until we are through with this place."

"What do you propose?" Ademar asked.

"It's time we reduce our liabilities."

Lila's breath caught as her mother stepped aside and the second servant dragged Rafe into the room. He was gagged with a strip of leather, and a heavy chain hobbled his feet and wrists and wound around his waist. But the real bonds were the plain, almost elegant cuffs around his wrists. Silver was painful to shifters and sapped away strength and magic. The color had drained from Rafe's skin, leaving him pasty beneath his tan. His gaze crossed Lila's for a moment. The frozen hatred in it almost made her fall back.

Prisoner and guard stopped at the foot of Ademar's bed. With a brutal shove, the servant forced Rafe to his knees. The wolf tried to twist away, but the servant grabbed his shaggy hair, wrenching his head up to face his captors.

Ademar pushed himself up to sit forward. "Why is this creature here?"

"The beast escaped his cell, and then helped the vampire escape," Galeeta said, her voice cold. "He has squandered whatever dim chance for clemency he had. He is here to beg your forgiveness before I decide his end."

"Forgiveness?" Ademar's features twisted. "This thief trespassed against the fae and maimed me when I forbade him."

The heat of her brother's words jolted Lila, clearing her head. "Wait a minute."

Silence fell over the room, brutal in its absolute quality. Lila's pulse thundered in her ears.

"What?" her brother finally demanded.

Lila widened her stance, as if bracing for a blow. "Whatever else happened, Rafe isn't a thief. He was telling the truth about looking for his kin."

"Why would you possibly believe that?" Galeeta asked, sounding weary.

"I found the graves in the woods a few minutes ago."

Rafe jerked, making a strangled sound around the gag. The servant wrenched his bonds, silencing him. Even so, Lila heard his soft moan.

"Graves?" Galeeta said softly. "Graves of other wolves?"

"Yes." Lila steadied her thundering heart and pressed on. "He told me he came looking for other wolves, and apparently that was true. Someone killed them and wove a thicket around their graves. I found them when I was looking for the vampire. Whoever buried them invested a lot of magic to keep the place secret."

"Are you saying a fae is responsible?" her mother asked. Where she'd been haughty before, now there was apprehension.

Lila looked from Galeeta to Ademar, considering the shock on their faces. In a deep corner of her soul, she felt relief. Not that she'd suspected them of the crime—not really, but ever since arriving at the way station, it was hard to know what to believe.

"A fae spell hid the graves," she answered, sticking to the facts. "Their families deserve to know they've been found."

She glanced Rafe's way, but his head was bowed, features

hidden. She looked away. It seemed wrong not to allow even a beast his private grief.

"Not so fast," her mother said. "A crime like this deserves justice, but our own authorities must be informed first. There is protocol for a crime between our communities."

"Very well," Lila said. She distrusted delays but wasn't going to spoil the fact that her mother was actually listening. "But let's not lose sight of the fact that the wolf told the truth about his missing pack."

Her brother frowned. "Then as little as I like it, we owe him some leniency." The words were grudging, anger still thick in his tone.

"His life for that of the victims." Galeeta replied slowly. "But only that. He attacked us. And, if he came here in search of his missing packmates, it is unlikely he knows anything of value to us. By the same token, he knows too much to be set free."

Lila winced. "Then what will we do with him?"

Galeeta flicked a hand. "Since you pleaded his innocence, he can serve you."

Lila balked. "I don't need a servant, especially not a wolf. It's plain that fae and wolves don't mix well."

"Don't be hasty," Galeeta said, circling Rafe and the servant as if inspecting them for purchase. Her eyes were still troubled, as if pondering problems Lila could barely see. "Lord Farras will be here soon, and he must be received as befits a noble of royal blood. He is leaving his estates and joining the king in Gilden Wood. He will be stopping at this way station and has commanded that there be a feast here to initiate the journey. You will see to the arrangements."

Lila gaped. "Me?"

"Of course you," her mother said in a way that left no doubt. "I raised you properly. You know what to do, and you will need a servant's help."

As the daughter of a noble house, Lila knew what wine to

serve and who to seat next to whom and in what order they ought to be greeted. That didn't mean she enjoyed any of it.

Her mother watched her, reading her silence for the resistance it was. "I'll repeat what I said before. Lord Farras is our greatest supporter. If he chooses, he will intercede with the king to get your father released. We need the lord's favor."

Lila cursed silently. "Very well. I'll make a comfortable bed and cook a good meal if that will help Father, but that's all. I don't like Lord Farras. You know that."

Her mother's smile was brief. "Of course. Thank you for doing your part."

Lila looked from her mother to Ademar, whose eyes were closed again. A wave of uneasiness swept over her. Too much was happening at once. "We should let him rest."

"For now, yes," Galeeta replied. "You're a good sister."

Lila wavered a moment. "The graves in the forest—who do you think killed the wolves? Could it have been the Magician?"

Her mother shook her head. "I don't know, but I will find out. There is a risk to our own security when such a crime is committed on our doorstep."

Lila turned to go, but the servant and Rafe blocked her path. With a heave, the hooded figure dragged Rafe to his feet and shoved him toward the door. Her stomach a cold ball of dread, Lila followed the two into the corridor.

Galeeta shut the bedroom door behind them, leaving Lila to face her future servant and his guard. The hooded figure still held Rafe's chains in its grip, keeping the wolf all but motionless. For a moment, the only sign of life was the rise and fall of Rafe's chest. He'd closed his eyes, as if willing himself anywhere else.

Lila had a decision to make. She could feel the gargoyle's hidden gaze fall upon her like a physical weight.

"Give me the key to his cuffs," she said, putting a touch of iron into her words.

The creature produced a key that look ridiculously small in its claws. After it dropped the key into her palm, she hung it on her neck chain and tucked it beneath her shirt. She'd long ago developed the habit of keeping keys and amulets with her at all times —first as a girl with four older siblings and a diary full of childhood secrets. Nothing in adulthood had convinced her to change the practice—not where the fae were concerned.

She tried to look the hideous creature in the eye and failed. "Now take off his chains and that gag. If he attacks, you have my permission to put him down."

After a moment's pause, the servant complied with swift, economical movements. The gag came off first, then the chains slithered away with a rattle. The hooded guard gathered them up and stepped aside, clearly waiting to see what would happen next.

Rafe barely moved except to wipe away the feel of the gag. He regarded her with narrowed eyes. "You spoke up for me."

"I just told the truth."

"Even for a beast?"

He might have been gagged and bound, but he'd been listening. Lila frowned, thinking of the graves and that strangled cry he'd made. Grief was still there like a radiant heat, challenging the icy reserve of his expression. She didn't blame him for keeping it private.

"Everyone deserves honesty," she replied. "Even hungry wolves."

"And now I am your servant." He swept a bow as graceful as that of any fae courtier. As he straightened, he seemed to grow taller, as if even partial freedom had unleashed a dangerous power. "What is your command, my lady?"

The oh-so-polite words were sharp with barely leashed mockery. Lila pressed her lips together, locking his gaze with her own.

"Walk with me," she said. There was a lot to do if she was going to play hostess.

He raised a brow. "Shall I stay five paces behind you? Isn't that what a servant does?"

"I said walk, not stalk. I'm not a fool."

They went a few steps in silence. Rage vibrated behind the wolf's nonchalance. Rage and sorrow and a touch of fear, burning with unbearable intensity. Lila could feel that fury like the first rumble of a quake, ready to rip through his civil mask.

"You don't want me," he said, the words edged in frost. "Like you said, fae and wolves don't mix well."

The chill in his tone was more explosive than a shout. He was challenging her, proving he still had a will of his own.

She knew better than to take that bait. "I intend to get out of here alive and unbitten."

"Yet you're forced to take me on." He gave her a steady, cool look that couldn't quite hide what he was feeling. "Understand this—I want answers, and this way station is where I will find them."

She stopped walking and turned to face him. "Is that meant to be reassuring?"

"There is a spell in the forest that won't let me leave," he said. "Your brother will try to kill me as soon as he can walk. You, of all the fae here, are willing to listen to reason, making you my best chance of survival."

"Meaning?"

He gave the slightest of shrugs. "I'm motivated to keep you alive."

"Even if I am your enemy?" she asked.

A ghost of a smile flickered over his face and was gone. "That keeps things interesting, don't you think?"

CHAPTER 10

Izetta limped across the downtown intersection, hiding her face from the well-dressed humans lining up outside restaurants and movie theaters. What the fae hadn't broken, the fight with the gargoyles had. With her limbs bruised and her clothes in tatters, she was a pitiable sight. A few bystanders threw her scornful looks. More pretended she wasn't there.

Rage and shame thrummed through her, but she thrust it down for later. The path from the forest had been brutal, and she'd had no blood to give her strength to heal. Pain stabbed with each step, a molten blade first in her leg, then her ribs, sometimes the small of her back. The fae had understood how to draw out the act of injury, and even a vampire had limits.

If Rafe hadn't helped her, she'd still be in the fae's dungeon. She owed him, and she'd return with reinforcements, whatever it cost her. But her first task was survival.

One stumbling lurch at a time, she turned from the bright, well-swept main street into a side alley and, from there, to a seedy part of town. This was a no-man's-land between the human neighborhoods and the streets run by the supernatural set. Neither wanted the blame for this block, but both made use of its so-called services.

She paused, sluggish and shivering, as she leaned against the grime-streaked bricks of the closest building. The amber lights of the Beacon Pub puddled on the wet sidewalk, bringing to mind the many other spilled liquids associated with the dive. Like most of the businesses along Skinner Street, it was a front for something else—in this case, the business HQ of the local vampire nest. They'd pay well for what she'd learned in the forest. With an act of will, Izetta pushed herself away from the wall and down the street.

The Beacon's narrow door had lost most of its paint. The remainder was mottled by Christmas lights strung around the entrance and front window. If the decorations were out of season, no one cared. It was as close to fancy signage as the dive was going to get.

Izetta pushed the door open and was met by a wall of rock music from decades past. The tables were full, with more customers leaning against the poster-covered wall, pints in hand. The fragrance of warm flesh and warmer blood was a caress and a gut-punch. Hunger unhinged her already wobbling knees. Her jaw throbbing with the need to bite, she elbowed her way directly to the bar and grabbed the only free stool.

Henry, the werebear owner, was pouring drinks. He took one look at Izetta and pulled a carton from the fridge beneath the counter. When he poured it into a glass, it looked like ruby cream, only a few bubbles glittering along the rim.

"Heat the second glass," she said, her voice a dusty croak. "Give me the first one now."

Henry didn't argue, thrusting the drink at her before pouring another and putting it in the microwave. Izetta gulped the slimy liquid, not needing to pause for breath. The plasma-infused beverage clung to her tongue, cloyingly sweet, but she immediately felt warmer. It would tide her over until she could hunt.

"What happened to you?" Henry rumbled as he put the warmed second glass in front of her, his dark eyes searching her face. He was six and a half feet tall and built like a concrete block wrapped in plaid flannel and suspenders. The patrons knew better than to mock his fashion choices.

"Long story, and not a good one," Izetta replied, resting her forearms on the sticky wood of the bar. Already, the pain was backing off, so the disgusting drink was doing its job. "I was out Dunbury way. Had to walk back."

Henry grunted, leaning closer to hear her over the din. "Too hurt to fly?"

Izetta shrugged. Vampires didn't fly so much as levitate short distances. She'd been able to get away from the hellhole in the woods, but then her abilities had stuttered like bad Wi-Fi—not that she'd admit that out loud.

She sipped the warmed liquid and made a face at the chemical aftertaste. She pushed the glass back toward Henry. "Put something in this."

He splashed in vodka, a trace of amusement crinkling his eyes. The rest of his face was too buried in his reddish beard to reveal much expression. "Glad you made it home."

"I'm not home yet. I stopped here to talk to Malatest. He'll want to hear about what I found."

Henry frowned. "He's got the lieutenants with him tonight."

"Lieutenants," she huffed. They were mere boys, mean-spirited toddlers grasping at the scraps of power Malatest dangled before them. She could take any of the brats one-on-one, but as a gang they made her wary.

She held out her glass again. It took a lot to get a vampire drunk, and she needed something to ease the knot between her shoulders.

The werebear obeyed, being generous. "I wouldn't talk to Malatest tonight if I were you."

"Because?" She swigged the drink, the alcohol fumes burning her nose.

He arched a brow. "Sadie has put him in an unforgiving mood, and you smell like wounded prey."

"Running up his gold card?"

"He wouldn't mind that nearly half as much. Let's just say she prefers the dance clubs to this joint."

That fit. Sadie and the Magician had been together on the surveillance video—which raised questions Izetta intended to answer before her second drink was done. "How did Malatest find out where she goes?"

Henry gave her a droll look. "He *is* an Undead crime boss. I suppose he knows a few tricks."

"Including pumping you for gossip."

Henry shrugged. "Drunks can't keep a secret worth troll dung."

Which is why Henry heard everything first. Acting as confessor and shrink was all part of a bartender's role, and the werebear was excellent at his job.

"Let me guess," she said. "The club crowd comes here to wind down after their fancy night out."

He gave a rumbling laugh. "Slumming, you mean?"

Izetta opened her mouth to retort, but an inhuman shriek rent the air. Every head at the bar turned toward the back corner. Someone—some*thing*—had jumped onto a table. Chairs clattered to the wooden floor as customers scrambled away. The creature swung around, scanning the crowd. When the light hit its face, Izetta saw it—he—was a half-shifted wolf. The hairless snout didn't quite contain all his fangs.

Izetta slid off her bar stool, flexing her claws. She still hurt all over, but she felt better on her feet. The air stank of fear and a subtler hint of anticipation.

"A-rooo," the half-wolf yodeled from a throat neither beast nor man.

The crowd—mostly shifters themselves—snarled a response. One picked up a chair, ready to brawl.

Henry heaved an exasperated sigh and grabbed a wooden club from under the bar. It was an Irish *shillelagh*, thick enough to crush skulls. He set it on the counter with a thud. "In case anyone gets ideas."

Izetta understood. Fights were bad for business and getting furry only made things harder if the law got involved. Monsters didn't get a pass.

"Second one this week," Henry muttered. "Half-in, half-out."

"What's that about?"

"The Magician's been passing out party favors again."

Quick as a snake, she caught Henry's wrist. "Tell me."

He flinched at what he saw in her eyes. He had to deal with the half-shifted wolf, but she was the threat just inches away. "Tell you what?"

"Do you know anything about the spell he uses?"

"Everyone thinks it's magic. It's not." He stared at Izetta's hand until she let him go.

"Then what is it?"

"Bacchante." He rubbed his wrist. "I heard the name last night."

"Bacchante?" she repeated. "Are you saying this is—what?"

"A party drug. And they bring the stuff here after their big night out. Bad news for me."

Pins and needles ran down her arms as her mouth dropped open with incredulous shock. She fought a sudden urge to laugh. "A drug?"

She was parroting Henry like an imbecile, but she couldn't believe what she'd heard. "No. People like you and me, we don't react to drugs. I can barely get drunk if I try."

"This one works. Leaves a pile of bodies, too."

Izetta swore again. It made sense. The Magician preyed on the young, the fast and fabulous who thought a crowded dance floor and high-priced bloodtinis made them somebody. The fae had been luring innocents forever. But she'd expected enchantment from a fae. Hypnotism. Glamour. The gorgeous and deadly. Not something so mundane.

By then, Henry had turned to the other bartender, who was built like a rugby player, but was still just a human. "Get as many customers as you can out of here."

"What? Why?" the young man asked, eyes wide.

"Do the math," Henry growled.

When one shifter lost control, others struggled. Add enough beer and good times, and inhibitions were already low.

Izetta flexed her shoulders, testing how well she'd healed. She winced, but Henry was a friend. She'd help if she could.

While the werebear locked up the till, she pulled herself to her full five foot four and strode into the crowd, her steps in time to the loud, thudding music. Bodies formed a wall close to the table-dancing shifter, but Izetta had sharp elbows. Soon, she'd forced her way to the front. There, she had a full view of the wolf.

He'd changed a little more, growing into his teeth but losing the ability to balance on two legs. Now he seemed confused as what to do with his forelegs and alternated between grabbing at bystanders and scrabbling to stay on the table.

"Chuck!" a round man cried at the creature. "Chuck, knock it off!"

The speaker looked more like a pug than a wolf, and Izetta couldn't pinpoint his species. There were too many scents in the room.

"Chuck, get a grip! You're gonna be sorry in the morning."

But Chuck's human brain had left the building. He howled as his palms elongated, sliding into a sickening, bone-crunching stretch that made Izetta swallow hard. Claws sprouted with a meaty squelch. Images flashed through Izetta's mind—carnage, remorse, execution. Scenes like this never ended well for the wolf.

"Chuck!" called his friend.

The half-wolf wheeled on the man, who was standing far too close. One paw lashed out, claws spread for maximum damage. Pug-face ducked in time, but his pint of beer went flying in a spray of lager.

A drum solo thundered through the sound system.

"Woohoo!" someone yelled, tossing his own beer at the wolf. At the touch of the liquid, the creature snarled and spun.

"Stop it!" Izetta yelled, but the words were lost in the chaos.

The music shifted to a fast, heavy beat. Izetta sensed the pulses around her quicken to keep time. If potential violence had a scent, the air thickened with it.

"Whoa," another laughed as more drinks sprayed in the air.

The half-wolf snarled, drawing yips and growls from the raucous crowd. A crow shifter cawed a laugh. Izetta tensed, second-guessing her chances in a fight with so many stupid drunks. She was still healing, and her reflexes weren't sharp enough to take on a crowd.

And not this bunch. Eyes glinted yellow in the gloomy bar. Customers shed jackets and sweaters as their temperature spiked right before a shift. Izetta glanced around to see other patrons hurrying outside, the staff holding the door and all but pushing them through. At least some folks had sense.

"What's the matter?" a female shouted at the creature on the table. "Can't get your wolf all the way up?"

Izetta grabbed her and pushed her toward the door. The woman stumbled, her balance drowned in house red. Others hooted and laughed.

Henry shouldered his way to Izetta's side, the shillelagh braced against one massive shoulder. Someone pelted beer nuts at the half-shifted wolf.

"Give the lad some space," the werebear boomed.

A few shuffled resentfully away, but most weren't listening.

The creature spun in place, gnashing fangs at the taunts and jeers. Even Izetta could feel the crackle of energy passing from shifter to shifter. One customer sprouted fur and dashed for the exit, pausing to lift a leg against the bar. Two others began tussling in the spilled beer. The yips turned into howls, winding up the crowd. One—out of beer now—went to throw his mug.

Henry grabbed his wrist. "Enough!"

The suicidal idiot took a swing at Henry. The blow connected with the werebear's jaw, splitting skin. With a roar, Henry hurled his attacker into the crowd, landing on two werecats scrapping on the beer-soaked floor. The sharp scent of blood ignited the mob. More shifted, baring claws and fangs. A bundle of black feathers—the crow shifter—exploded from the crowd and flew toward the safety of the bar.

The half-were leaped from the table into the crowd, limbs spreading as he plunged into the fray. Shorter than most, Izetta lost sight of him in the crush of bodies. *Blood of Ancients!* That was like losing a knife in dark water—nothing was safe until the blade was found. She hopped onto the table for a better view, her injured ankle throbbing a sharp protest.

She didn't see the half-wolf leap from behind, sweeping her from the table and into the milling throng. Izetta twisted mid-flight, taking the brunt of the landing on her hip instead of her face. The beast pounced, fangs snapping a millimeter from her nose. She slammed the heel of her hand into his throat, forcing him off her aching ribs. She scrambled away on hands and knees just in time for Henry to bring his club down on the creature's shoulder. The beast scrambled away, one arm dangling, to cower against the wall.

"Anyone else?" Henry roared, raising his weapon.

Noise and motion stopped as if a switch was thrown. Actual damage had been done, and now Izetta sensed each participant sizing up the stakes. Only the music played on, the aggressive beat echoing in her throbbing head.

Then the pug-faced man stumbled toward his friend, a

worried frown wrinkling his face. The beast was nosing his useless arm and licking it.

"Chuck, are you okay?" the man asked, reaching out.

Izetta's breath caught. "No!"

The wounded wolf's reaction was too quick even for a vampire's eye. With one paw, Chuck slashed, the long claws scooping out his friend's insides with a slurp of wet flesh. Izetta sprang to her feet, but the pug-faced man was already done screaming.

Before Chuck recovered his balance, she grabbed his snout and twisted hard. Vertebrae snapped. Once the light left his eyes, she let the werewolf's body drop into the sticky puddle that had been his friend.

Someone killed the music, leaving a deafening quiet in its wake. Chuck didn't shift back to human, remaining a grotesque mix of species. Another effect of bacchante? Izetta sucked in a breath, steadying herself against a wave of sudden grief.

A drug—a chemical formula—had triggered this carnage. With morbid dread, Izetta tried to picture it. Was it a powder? A pill? Did it have a taste? What would happen if became easy to get?

With a whine of old hinges, the door to the back office opened. Heads snapped to attention, as if the crowd had forgotten what lay beyond beer and blood. Izetta smoothed her torn jacket, wondering if she still smelled like prey.

Roman Malatest, leader of the local vampires, strolled into the room, a shark sizing up the chum.

CHAPTER 11

Malatest turned and scanned the room, a frown of annoyance pleating his brow. The patrons stood among the upended tables like embarrassed schoolchildren, only their wide, dilated eyes hinting at barely-banked bloodlust. Someone began clattering dishes at the distant bar, as if tidiness had become a sudden priority.

His eyebrows arched when his survey reached Chuck's crumpled body on the floor. "That's going to leave a stain."

No one dared to reply as the awkward silence congealed. Izetta shifted, easing wounds that had reopened during the scuffle. The movement caught Malatest's attention. His gaze landed on her lightly, like the brush of an ink-black moth, but it stirred every nerve. Malatest was dark-eyed, dark-haired, and as chiseled as an old-fashioned matinee idol. He might have played a ruthless millionaire or swashbuckling pirate with equal ease, and his reputation was all that and a dash of crime lord, too.

Malatest planted his feet wide and folded his arms. With a scrape of feet against the wooden floor, the patrons bowed or bent a knee. Izetta followed suit. No one disrespected Roman Malatest and survived.

Izetta looked up through her lashes, studying him. She'd only met Malatest a few times before, but his type wasn't hard to read. His stance—the way he moved, the set of his head—belonged to an apex predator. Or should have done. Malatest had been sitting in the back room while the bar had spun out of control. It wasn't a good look for the bloodsucker in charge, and someone was going to pay for that.

With a jerk of his chin, he beckoned Izetta forward. She rose slowly, the tension in the air almost solid. The scent of blood—even shifter blood—made it hard to think. She came to a stop before him, keeping a respectful distance.

He was more than a head taller, making it easy to look down his perfectly straight nose. This close, she could see he'd died young, before life had etched character into his features. It gave him the look of a vulnerable, if wicked, angel.

Not her type, though her blood still heated at the glint of interest in his eyes. She couldn't be blamed for a flicker of response. Immortality got lonely, but nothing about Malatest said he was worth the sacrifice. For an independent agent like her, reputation was all.

"What are you doing here?" he asked. "I hired you to do a job. And you're hurt."

That was almost an insult among vampires. Injury was weakness, and the weak were prey—and she'd heard tales of this one's ruthless appetites.

"I'm fine. I came to tell you what I found out," she replied, smoothing the line of her battered leather jacket. "The floor show was just an extra."

His lips thinned at the tasteless joke, but it seemed to strike the right note of cool nonchalance. He nodded. "Did you find your mark?"

Izetta looked behind her, ensuring there was no one else within earshot. The music had started up again, but soft enough to allow for conversation. "That's what I came here to discuss."

He gave a satisfied grunt. "Give me a moment."

Malatest motioned to two of his henchmen. They stepped forward instantly, their motions eerily in synch. Izetta wondered if they rehearsed.

He pointed to Chuck. "Clean that up."

"Yes, sir," one of them answered with a smart bow. Then the two strode to the body in a way that said this wasn't their first time.

Malatest beckoned to Izetta. "This way."

She followed him through the door at the back of the bar's seating area and into Malatest's office. The room was pretty much what she'd expected. An antique safe, probably dating from the venue's speakeasy days, squatted in the corner. An old desk sat beside it, facing the door and a worn leather sofa.

Sadie reclined on the sofa, wearing a plum-colored slip dress and her signature string of freshwater pearls. Her long legs were bare but for silver high-heeled sandals that clearly cost more than Izetta's entire wardrobe.

"Hey, pumpkin," she said as Malatest entered the room.

"Hey, yourself. Where did you come from?" he asked, bending down to kiss her lips.

"I stopped by on my way out." She flicked her strawberry-blonde mane. "It looks like you're too busy for me tonight."

"For now," he replied. "I should be free in a couple of hours. Why don't you stay here and wait?"

"Nah." She gave a tiny shudder as she stood, picking up a miniscule handbag on a chain. "I don't like your place tonight. I'll come back later."

"Where are you going?" Malatest asked, his voice hard.

"Out."

"Where?"

"Where the mood takes me." She blew him a kiss as she sashayed past Izetta and through the door.

"Be careful."

"Be good and I'll be back before dawn."

Izetta watched her go and tried to ignore the faint growl coming from the vampire who'd hired her. Sadie wasn't playing the obedient female, and Izetta could hardly blame her. Still, she had questions about anyone who went dancing with a murderous fae.

"You hired me to find the Magician," Izetta said, opening with the most basic fact.

Malatest circled the desk and sat. He leaned back, the glow from the green banker's lamp highlighting the clean lines of his face. He did not invite her to sit.

"Did you find him?" he asked.

"I found much that will interest you, but I have a question first. Are you aware that the Magician's been seen in the same clubs that Sadie visits? That they've been seen together?"

Izetta wished she still had her phone with the video, but that was lost somewhere in the fae way station. She'd meant to show it now, as proof of her investigation.

"I wondered." Malatest glared down at his hands resting on the desk. Then he looked up again, erasing every hint of vulnerability from his face. "I didn't know when we last spoke. Now I'm certain."

Finding that answer was probably the motivation for hiring Izetta—or at least part of it. "And you know about the drug because you've been talking to Henry."

"Yes."

"Sadie is in danger."

He made a strangled sound. "I've tried reason, and I've tried locks. She will not be tamed."

There was no question an Undead with his power could make Sadie obey. The fact that he hadn't made Izetta like him better. "Your only course of action is to get rid of the Magician."

"Yes, so tell me what I don't already know," he said, making it an order and not a request. His eyes darkened, taking on a dangerous glow.

"Of course," Izetta agreed pleasantly. "I will, according to our arrangement."

He accepted the hint with a lift of one brow and turned to the safe. The ornate gold scrollwork had worn away, but it still had presence. He extracted a key ring from his vest pocket and unlocked the heavy door. When he turned back to Izetta, he held a stack of hundred-dollar bills. "Start talking."

"I coordinated with one of the Devries wolf shifters," she began. "We tracked the Magician to a dwelling in the wilderness off the highway east of town."

As she continued, he counted out a bill for every tidbit of useful information. She had just got to the part where they'd broken in when a figure appeared in the doorway and lingered there, clearly intrigued by Izetta's story.

"Did you see where the drug was made?" the newcomer interrupted, pulling a spiral-bound notebook from her large shoulder bag.

"This is Errata Jones," Malatest supplied with a touch of exasperation. "A reporter."

"A reporter?" Izetta echoed in confusion. Vampires—especially those with vaguely criminal pedigrees—usually avoided the media. Or drained the blood from its representatives.

"Freelancer," the female said, taking a seat on the sofa. "I'm here because I share an interest in locating the cause of so many deaths. The drug connection is one explosive headline."

Errata's smile was confident, as if she had every right to be in the room. She had dark, shoulder-length hair, high cheekbones, and olive skin that contrasted with bright green eyes. She wore a tight blue jacket with figure-hugging jeans and high-heeled boots. Her only jewelry was a diamond-shaped metal pendant on a leather thong. Izetta guessed she was some sort of cat shifter. A werecougar, maybe?

"To answer your question," Izetta said, "I didn't see anything like a lab."

"Too bad," the cat said. "I want to know how it's made."

"Any useful theories?" Izetta asked.

Errata shook her head. "We've just started hearing about the deaths in Fairview. Some think the root cause comes from the Castle, but the earliest reports seem to be from your neck of the woods, not ours."

"Could be."

The Castle was a supernatural prison in Fairview, a university town to the north. The prison had a complicated history and even more complex inhabitants, and it wasn't unreasonable to assume that a strange and powerful drug had come from there. But Errata was right—the first deaths had been local.

Izetta picked up the stack of money Malatest pushed her way and flipped through the bills, double checking the total.

"Who lives in the forest house?" Errata Jones asked, jotting on her notepad.

"Nobody lives in a fae way station," Izetta replied. "Not on a permanent basis. It's like an upscale hotel, except this one had a dungeon."

Errata's pen froze, and she looked up. "Seriously?"

"They still have my friend in a cell." Satisfied, Izetta folded the money, stuffing it into her pocket. "They want their secrets to stay secret."

Malatest frowned, locking the safe again. "You got away. They won't let that slide."

"Neither should we," Izetta replied. "We tracked the Magician there, but I think he's just the cherry on top of a big bowl of crazy. Whatever is going on in that way station is likely to spill over into everyone's business."

"Like what?" he demanded.

"They were expecting someone else to show up. For all that

they were breaking out the thumbscrews, my hosts were nervous."

"Who frightens the immortal fae?" Malatest sat back in his desk chair, the old springs creaking. "Their magic terrifies the rest of us, not the other way around."

Errata had stopped writing and was watching Malatest with a frown. "What are you thinking?"

"I'm considering motive. The supernatural community is an untapped market for narcotics." He stared at the ceiling, his hands behind his head, for a long moment. Then he leaned forward again, bracing his arms on the desk. "All the victims are new to this life. Our young—the newly made—are still struggling to learn how to survive as one of the Undead. The Magician tempts them with oblivion before they make peace with their new existence. He preys on their grief and doubt."

"How will you stop him?" Izetta prompted.

He laughed, and it was bitter. His already pale face had lost what color he had. "I thought your investigation would find a single fae, a murderous misfit his own kind would despise. We could survive exterminating one such madman."

Errata closed her book, a grave look settling over her features. It was as if she sensed an end to the story and needed no more notes. "But now?"

"Way stations belong to the fae kings and queens." Malatest rose, pacing from his desk to the wall and back, shoulders stiff. "Whatever happens there is royal business. And this place is not the norm, not with a dungeon and gargoyle servants. It's a death trap."

Izetta's shoulders ached with tension. "I heard you were careful, but not bloodless. I accepted your job because I thought you'd get rid of the Magician."

Malatest swung back to her, anger in his dark eyes. "You took the job for money, and I gave it to you. There is no debt between us."

"But we know where he is. Rafe tracked him to the door," Izetta protested.

"I have a strong nest, but it's small." Done pacing, Malatest dropped into the chair again. "I'm not starting a war with an entire kingdom of fae. We have weapons, but not enough warriors and zero magic."

Izetta's skin went cold, fatigue catching up with her. The urge to shout at Malatest bubbled up like lava, but she forced it down with a brutal act of will. "You saw what happened in the bar tonight. Are you going to let them get away with this?"

"I'm a realist," he said. "Losing a war would finish my nest. I need a less costly solution."

Izetta clenched her fists to hide the rage-filled tremor in her hands. "They still have my friend."

Rafe had risked his life so she could escape. She had made him a promise.

"I'm sorry," Malatest replied.

"You're going to abandon him?"

Malatest spread his hands in an empty gesture. "He's your friend, not mine."

Izetta sucked in air, taking a breath she didn't need to ease the pressure in her chest. Disgust and disappointment crowded in. She'd seen her brethren fed to the lions of Rome. This felt the same.

Izetta leaned over the desk, locking eyes with Malatest. He was powerful, but she was older, far older, and that made them equals. His smooth, pretty features seemed a shallow mask she longed to crush. Dark thoughts flitted through her mind, mostly involving knives and teeth. But ending Malatest's existence wouldn't defeat the fae. The fallout would just complicate her future plans.

She picked up the stapler and crushed it in one hand. When she dropped it back to the desk, it was twisted scrap. The skin around the vampire king's eyes tightened, but his only response was a soundless chuckle.

"You've got nothing else to say?" she demanded in a soft snarl.

"No." His tone was ice. "I've made my decision. I'm sorry it doesn't meet with your approval."

She cursed under her breath.

Malatest drew a laptop toward him and opened it, logging in with a quick flurry of keystrokes. It was as good as a dismissal. "Go get cleaned up. You look a mess."

Izetta heard Errata's stifled gasp but didn't turn her way. Instead, she spun and walked out without closing the door in her wake. Pushing the few remaining patrons out of her path, she stalked by the janitor sweeping blood-soaked sawdust from the floor. With a quick wave to Henry, she stiff-armed the door and burst onto the street.

She got half a block before she came to a stop and wondered where to go next. This wasn't her town. At least the bastard had paid her so she could get a hotel room and grab someone to drink. Then she'd plan her next move.

Izetta picked a direction at random and began scanning for hotel signs. A few places still had neon letters glowing over their facades, as if the street had been caught in a time warp. She started walking again just as she heard someone call her name.

"Izetta." It was Errata, sprinting after her despite the high-heeled boots. "Wait."

She turned. "What do you want?"

"He's not the only game in town."

Monumental weariness swept over her. "He's the local boss. He has the clout." *And he's afraid.*

"Malatest is the boss of his nest," Errata replied. "But don't forget the shifters. There's a large pack in town."

Rafe's pack. She'd have to explain how one more wolf got swallowed up by the forest. That made her stomach hurt. "What's your point?"

"I want answers." Errata smiled, and this time it showed sharp, feline teeth. "And shifters don't quit."

CHAPTER 12

*L*ila ran her hand down the tendril of ivy, finding the joint where a cut would do the least damage to the plant. The woods were fragrant with new growth, and the early afternoon sun was a warm blanket across her shoulders.

She'd changed from her city clothes to a pale green dress that fell to the ground and swished around her ankles. Like all fae garments, it was softly tailored to fit without restricting natural movement. With warm earth beneath her bare feet, such creature comforts should have added up to a perfect outing. She ached with tension nonetheless.

Rafe stood a few feet away, a wide basket of the greenery she had gathered at his feet. He was dressed in fae garments—a loose tunic and slim fitting pants—since his own clothes were beyond repair after the last fight. The simple garments only emphasized his stature. The sun was behind him, turning his broad-shouldered form into a looming silhouette.

She didn't need to see his features to gauge his mood. The bracelets kept him obedient, but they couldn't change his nature. Her mother had said shifters were, by definition, mere beasts.

Rafe was anything but *mere*. He radiated wild energy as if the primal force of his wolf had been distilled into flesh.

Angry flesh. The angular lines of his form broadcast outrage louder than any words. He had a right to his fury, but it made Lila acutely uncomfortable. Fae rarely allowed themselves so much emotion. Not before a stranger, and not when magic was in the mix. That path led to chaos.

Lila drew her knife. It had a silver handle and curved blade so sharp that the woodiest stems cut like silk. She looped the ivy into a bundle and dropped it into the basket, the variegated leaves pale against the blooms and branches already there. She might be overdoing the greenery, but the stark house needed a lot of help before it would feel welcoming.

It was probably a lost cause. There were too many uncomfortable undercurrents in the place. Lila had gone back to the dungeon to look for Captain Teegar—she had questions for the man who'd arrested her father—but found the cells empty. There had been one filled with packing crates, another that still had traces of vampire blood, but none with prisoners. Wherever her mother had put the captain, she didn't want him easily found. Lila had thought about questioning her, but then decided she'd find out more on her own. She'd try again later when her mother was busy with the influx of guests.

"Don't you have servants to gather greenery?" Rafe asked as she wandered the few feet back to the trees. "Gardeners?"

His deep voice startled Lila. They'd barely spoken since they left the house. "I understand Lord Farras is bringing his retinue. There will be plenty of staff then."

"So why not wait until your lord arrives?"

She examined a holly bush, wondering if its shining leaves were worth the prickles. When she looked up, Rafe's expression was hard to read. "He is an honored guest. He shouldn't have to prepare his own welcome."

A faint smile tugged at the corners of his mouth, then vanished. "You don't like him much, do you?"

Lila shrugged, reminding herself to be more guarded. "My opinion does not matter."

She cut a branch of holly and turned to drop it in the basket. The motion brought her within an arm's reach of Rafe. Only the basket stood between them. There had been yards before, so the wolf had moved closer, staying right on her heels. Just as he had for the better part of the last hour.

He was acting as her servant, but he was also stalking her. Lila felt a sudden, terrified impulse to bolt, but knew better. That would make her prey.

"Your opinion *should* matter," he said. "You are part of your pack."

"Not for long. I'm not staying," she replied. "I have a job and a home in the city that say I don't need to care. Or impress anyone."

She hadn't meant to be so blunt—or even talk to the wolf at all—but voicing her defiance felt good. It also left her feeling lonely. Going her own way was a two-edged blade.

"I'm sure you impress them. They would not ask for your help otherwise." That faint smile was back, more knowing than happy. He understood her position every bit as well as she did.

Her gaze lingered on his expression, narrowing to his smile, and then his mouth. Not for the first time, she wondered if wolves were good kissers.

Lila pulled her thoughts up short. The wolf wasn't there to satisfy her curiosity. He wasn't even a friend, and was certainly not her confidante. He was here for information, for payback, and to protect his pack.

"I didn't ask for sympathy," she said, finally letting the holly drop into the basket. It fell with a rustle.

"We've both been pulled into a situation we didn't bargain for," he said. "That's not sympathy, just observation."

"You're trying to find common ground so you can build trust between us. That trick is as old as Stonehenge." She stepped back to return to her work, but he caught her arm. A bold move, for a captive. She met his frown with a glare.

"Neither of us understand what's going on." He slowly released her. "That's plain enough from the questions you ask your kin."

Lila wondered exactly how much he'd seen and heard. "What's that to you?"

"We both want the truth. Together we stand a better chance of finding it."

He'd leaned so close she could see the touch of panic in his eyes. Rafe was gambling she wouldn't end him then and there. It was rare to find a male—even a fae male—who acknowledged her power and still trusted her enough to lay himself bare. This mortal wolf was doing just that.

Surprise flooded Lila. "What do you propose?"

It wasn't agreement, but it was enough that he looked away, finally ending his intense scrutiny of her every move. "First, I want to see the graves of my kin."

He ducked his head then, hiding from her gaze an instant before he straightened, his features blank once more. The show of vulnerability was brief but real, rousing the tumult of emotions that had drowned Lila over the last few days. His pain found an answering chord inside her—one she'd barely acknowledged for fear she'd crack in two.

Without warning, their lips met. It took Lila a moment to realize she had been the one to lean in, but he'd responded with instant intensity. The pressure of his kiss made her ache in forgotten places. She jumped back in shock, her fingers pressing to her lips as if to rub away the sensation of his warm mouth against hers. A scalding heat spread over her skin, turning her cheeks to flame. "I'm sorry."

His dark eyebrows quirked. "Are you? Shall I demand a stronger apology?"

His banter rang hollow, embarrassing her more. The air between them was thick with feeling—fear, desire, anger—and there was no room to be lighthearted. She turned away, desperate to end the moment.

What had she been thinking? And yet, her heart couldn't witness that much hurt without trying to heal it. *Fool, what comfort could a fae give to a wolf?*

"If you want to see the graves, come this way," she said briskly, striking out along a narrow path.

Rafe picked up the basket and followed. Lila led them on a half-hour walk that circled the house and angled up the slope behind it. As before, the forest thickened before they reached the hidden cluster of mounds. When they passed through the final barrier of branches, she stepped aside to allow Rafe a complete view of the small clearing.

Rafe froze, as if seeing the graves made the death of his pack-mates real. He set down the basket of greenery, all but dropping it before it touched the ground. Then he hesitantly stepped around it, slowly moving to stand among his buried kin. Every line of his body held grief, but he did not speak a word.

Lila swallowed hard, fighting a piercing ache inside her. Rafe bent, placing a palm upon the freshly turned earth, as if speaking to his dead.

He had been right. Neither of them had bargained for this—either the losses or the possibilities. Her lips still felt the pressure of his. He had firmly responded, but the episode unsettled her. Somewhere between her arrival at the way station and this burial site, the landscape of her world had become something she didn't recognize.

Lila bent over the basket, carefully moving the holly aside before sorting through the cuttings. She picked out an armful of the wild peas and shooting stars that bloomed wild along the lakeside and began laying them on the graves. She came to a stop beside Rafe, who remained still and silent as if in shock. Lila put a hand on his arm.

He drew in a long breath and let it out in an angry gust. "Why did this happen?"

"Someone has a secret," she replied. "Whatever it is, it's not worth this many lives."

A twig cracked. They both turned toward the path leading to the small clearing. Lila tensed, readying a spell, while Rafe stepped to one side. They'd both want room to move if it came to a battle—and by unspoken agreement, they were facing that fight together.

For a long moment, there was only the hush of wind in the leaves broken by an occasional footfall. Then Lila's breath caught as Ademar emerged from the trees, leaning on a tall walking stick. Fae usually moved without a sound, but his injury explained why they'd heard his approach. He looked haggard, the sheer weight of the healing spells and amulets upon him turning his complexion a waxy hue. His gray eyes took in the two of them and the flowers on the graves in one disapproving sweep.

"What are you doing up and walking this far from the house?" Lila asked in surprise.

"I came to the woods to heal," her brother replied, his tone curt. "Or have you forgotten how to be a fae of the forest?"

Lila didn't respond as Ademar looked again at the mounded earth. "By the Abyss, these are the dead shifters."

"They are," she said quietly, grateful that Rafe kept silent. Maybe it was enough that Ademar sounded subdued.

"I don't understand what happened here," her brother mused.

"I don't know either," she replied. So far, all she'd uncovered was a tangled mass of fae politics. Had it been Lord Farras? Captain Teegar? "Why would anyone kill these wolves?"

Ademar raised his chin. "I wasn't speaking of the dead. I was wondering aloud why you brought your prisoner to this place."

Lila opened her mouth to protest, but then bit back the words. She could feel Ademar's loathing for Rafe as if it were a touchable thing. She understood it, but it was every bit as dangerous as the wolf's fangs.

"My prisoner is wearing spelled bracelets," she said evenly. "You know that."

Her brother frowned. "Even so, I question bringing him to an outdoor location where escape is easy—and he does seem to specialize in picking locks."

Annoyed, Lila busied herself tidying her basket. "It's my call."

"Are you certain about that?" Ademar moved toward her, leaning heavily on his staff. The white wood was carved in a pattern of leaves and vines set with glittering quartz. "Are you certain of your decision to bring a dangerous captive to the one place guaranteed to rouse his resentment of us?"

His words struck deep, mostly because Lila shared that doubt. The difference between them was her willingness to believe an outsider's word. She straightened, doing her best to keep her temper. "I'll take that risk."

"But the rest of us disagree. Your duty to family comes first, and that includes keeping your prisoner secure."

"Has it occurred to you that a killer is loose in the area, and I may require protection?"

"He's wearing cuffs," Ademar replied, his tone flat.

"The cuffs won't stop him from defending whoever holds the key." She put her hand to her throat, where the key hung on its chain. "Where is this coming from? As little as I like it, I'm decorating your halls and preparing a chamber for his lordship. There's no reason to dog my steps with your accusations."

Ademar's smile was sharp. "No one doubts your ability to fluff a pillow."

"If I can't be trusted, then don't give me the responsibility," she shot back. "I did not ask for it and would sooner be on my way back home. In fact, that is exactly where I'm going the moment this is over."

Ademar gripped her arm, just as Rafe had minutes ago. The wolf had been gentler, and Lila gave an involuntary yelp.

"You've had your own way far too long," her brother snapped.

Rafe had been a statue until that moment. Now, as fast as any fae, he grabbed Ademar and flung him back from Lila. Ademar flew, arms spread, before the bushes at the edge of the clearing broke his fall. Lila cried out, cradling her bruised arm even as she sprang forward to help her brother.

Ademar's glare froze her where she stood. "I didn't ask you to coddle me."

Digging his staff into the soft earth, he heaved himself upright again, stumbling to regain his balance despite his bad leg. Lila flinched but couldn't tell whether it was from her brother's words or the growl ripping from Rafe's chest. She held up her hands, palms out, as Ademar pointed his staff at the wolf.

"Stop it," she commanded. "Both of you *stop*."

She didn't raise her voice, but she did push a thread of compulsion into her words. Instantly, the clearing fell silent, even the wind holding its breath. Rafe's growl faded, and Ademar grudgingly lowered his weapon. Lila held her position, the sun hot on her back as her attention shifted from one male to the other.

Rafe's anger was like a physical weight over the scene, ready to crush them given the chance, but he remained silent and still. Ademar was another matter.

"You have no right to show that beast mercy," her brother said into the silence. "Not after what he did to me."

Guilt twisted inside her. "Go back to the house. Go back to bed. We can talk this out when I'm done."

Ademar's look hit her like ice water. "Yes, we'll speak later. As a family."

Which meant Galeeta would be involved. She watched with foreboding as Ademar retreated the way he'd come, using his glittering staff to support his weight. As the branches waved and bowed with his passage, gooseflesh crept down her arms.

"Will that be a problem?" Rafe asked.

"Nothing I'm not used to," Lila said easily, but didn't believe it.

CHAPTER 13

Once Lila's brother left, the circle of mounded earth fell silent but for the bees in the wildflowers. The spirit of the pack surrounded Rafe, elusive and yet as tangible as the sun on his skin. The lost wolves were there, but not there; connected, but the threads that bound them ended in the realm of the dead. Ewan. Connor. His uncle. Many others, youngsters and seasoned hunters both. Rafe could not follow them any more than he could reel them back from the grave.

He let fury burn through his grief, cauterizing the raw wound in his soul. Like them, he'd come to this cursed valley to find the Magician. Prisoner or not, he'd finish the job and leave a bloody trail of vengeance. It would just take longer than he'd thought.

Assuming he lived. Fresh graves had a way of sowing doubt, even for a survivor like him.

His gaze slid from the circle of the dead to Lila, who stood lean and graceful beside him. Her head was bowed as if in prayer. He didn't doubt her dismay over the slain wolves was real, but he reminded himself that meant next to nothing. Her loyalties lay with her own kin.

She looked up as if hearing his thoughts. "I've kept my

promise to show you this place. Now it's time to return to the house."

Reluctant to leave, Rafe was slow to pick up the basket of greenery and fall into step behind her. As he hesitated, his limbs grew clumsy, alien. Even the sensation of the wicker basket in his hands seemed to belong to someone else. Suffocating panic rose, swamping him before he pushed it down and hastened to obey Lila's command. The strange sensation faded the instant he did what he was told. As long as he wore the bracelets, there was no breaking a promise to one of her kind.

The trees closed around them, blocking out the sun and cooling the air. Lila walked ahead, her pale hair loose around her shoulders like a cape. Every step she took was in rhythm with the swaying branches, as if she were dancing with the wind in the trees.

Her unexpected kiss still burned deep inside him, branding him with her taste. He didn't want the lingering memory. The bracelets tugged at him like a tether, but so did desire. It was hard to know where magic ended and unwanted longing began.

His sole spark of hope came from the precious few hours each day that Lila required his help and he got out of his cell. Somehow—between fetching, carrying, and outwitting the bracelets—he'd find the Magician and avenge the murdered wolves. Maybe even escape.

Lila knew he would try. She had to, and yet she let him walk behind her, certain he wouldn't overcome the magic of his bonds and attack. She was a madwoman, or a terminal optimist who thought taking a werewolf for daily walkies was a bright idea. He'd never understand the fae mind.

Or maybe he underestimated the warrior she was. That idea intrigued him the most.

Before long, the white walls of the way station rose from the landscape. Lila rounded the corner, choosing a modest door at the back of the house. When he followed her through, the gloom inside made him blink. They'd entered a storage room lined with shelves. Half were empty, but the rest were stacked with enough glassware and expensive-looking dishes for an epic banquet.

Lila led the way past the shelves and into another room. This space was huge, almost too large given the dimensions of the house. Maybe magic made it possible to cheat the laws of square footage, because the glossy wooden pillars of the ballroom seemed to march to a vanishing horizon like the trees in an orchard. Lila stopped at the head of the room, dwarfed by the vaulted ceiling supported by ribs of polished oak. Rafe stopped beside her and set the basket of vines and branches at their feet.

"You said you were going to decorate for a reception," he ventured. "You're going to need more than what we gathered."

Her mouth quirked. "You don't know much about fae."

"As little as possible. Even less about party planning."

She cast him a sidelong glance. "Your invite got lost in the mail?"

"I'm a bratwurst and beer kinda guy."

She gave a small huff of amusement and tucked a strand of hair behind one gently-pointed ear. "Truly, I'm shocked."

She plucked a vine from the basket and twined it about the nearest pillar, making a loose knot as she murmured in a tongue he didn't know. Then she took the branches and berries, the garlands of flowers and swatches of moss they had gathered and bound them to the pillar with the length of vine. All the while, she kept speaking in a lilting, sing-song voice.

Rafe felt the spell gather before he saw its effects. As Lila raised her hands, palms out, the air seemed to thicken, the scent of something sweet and slightly burnt clogging the back of his throat. Sounds grew muffled for a long, disorienting moment before the earth bucked beneath his feet. Rafe stumbled, barely catching himself as the building air pressure seemed to release with a pop.

Green ran along the pillars like ink flowing from a brush. One after another, vines spiraled up the polished wood and then crawled along the ceiling until reaching the next pillar, then the next. Wherever they passed, flowering branches of every hue sprang from the wood, weaving above the now-mossy floor. White blooms opened along the ceiling like a carpet of stars, each glowing with a gentle, otherworldly radiance.

Finally, long, ornately carved tables and benches grew in even rows, each one of rare wood polished to a mirror shine. As Rafe watched, open-mouthed, the chamber shifted and shrank until it comfortably fit dozens of tables. When the buzzing presence of the spell faded, he was aware of the gentle perfume of new vegetation. The room was alive, called into being from the woods around them.

Lila lowered her arms. She'd gone pale but for a bright flush of pink along her cheekbones. With a shaky breath, she spun in a circle, admiring her handiwork. Her hair swung as she moved, fanning out in a wheat-pale wave. For a fleeting instant, he saw the young girl she must have been, innocent and astonished by her first glimmers of power. Dazzling.

Her spin brought her close enough to brush against his side. Unthinking, he caught her, fingers closing around the bare skin of her arm. There was lean muscle beneath the soft warmth. Instinctively, he pulled her close, drinking in the electric scent he'd first detected in the midnight woods. She'd been his prey that night, something to be tracked.

The enemy. Someone to outwit, outsmart, outfight. But now none of that seemed wise or right.

A heady wave of confusion made him pull back, though he still held her arm. Her silvery gaze locked with his, watchful but unafraid. Whatever vulnerability he'd seen a moment ago had vanished.

He released her arm and fell back a step. Fear he could have coped with. Even anger. Not the penetrating assessment written across her face—or her frank refusal to judge.

He didn't know how to weave his way through her contradictions. Her mouth parted, as if to speak, but hesitation filled her eyes. Was she just as perplexed?

A prickle against his consciousness made him turn. The other fae—the mother—lurked at the opposite end of the hall, her brow creased in a frown. The two hooded monsters she called her servants flanked the door.

"There you are," Galeeta said, starting toward Lila. "You took your time."

Lila tensed, drawing inward like a turtle ducking into its shell. Rafe barely stopped himself from stepping between them. He contented himself with glaring at the servants, who didn't stir from their posts.

"Do you like the result?" Lila asked her mother.

The older fae glanced around the room, then gave a judicious nod. "You remembered your lessons."

Lila folded her arms, guarding herself even as she braced her feet a little wider. "I should hope so."

He'd seen that reaction among wolves—seeking approval and safety but getting neither so choosing defiance instead. This was a pack without a good Alpha.

As if sensing his judgement, Galeeta scowled. "Time to kennel your pet. We need to talk."

Lila glanced Rafe's way, her expression saying she'd rather he stayed. He was a buffer she didn't want to give up. His protective instinct, foolish puppy that it was, rolled over and showed its belly.

Every instinct screamed not to abandon Lila. Fido's balls, what was he thinking? The fae were the enemy who'd put him in chains. They'd killed his kin. He was there to seek and destroy at least one of their kind.

Now the servants approached, their steps silent on the moss-strewn floor. Rafe gave a silent bow to the two females and surrendered to the monsters without a fight. He had priorities, and survival was at the top of the list.

❦

LILA WATCHED Rafe go with an unexpected sense of loss. The first time non-fae witnessed a display of her green magic, it inspired awe in some and fear in others. The power eclipsed Lila herself in their minds. Ever after, she was just a vessel for her spells.

Rafe wasn't exactly on her side, but since they'd met, she felt Rafe had seen *her*. Warmth kindled inside her like a tiny glowing star. She wished it meant more—could mean more—than it did.

Galeeta waited until the doors closed behind the wolf and his two guards. Then she made a sweeping gesture that captured the leafy room. "A fine job with the vines. Not all fae manage so well after living in the city. Their magic grows weak. Some say it's the bad air, or the amount of technology spewing out harmful vibrations."

"I'm not sure that's a thing," Lila said.

Galeeta gave a delicate shrug. "It doesn't matter. What's important is that the power in House Fernblade runs strong. That will matter to Lord Farras."

"Why? He's known our family forever."

"Our houses were meant to be joined, if you recall."

Lila kept her features still, but her dislike must have shown anyhow.

Her mother gave a sympathetic smile. "I know you're not fond of him, but he is an important ally."

"So you said."

"We're an old house, and the power proves it. The king has no heirs. With houses like ours supporting Farras, he has a legitimate claim to succession."

Lila froze where she stood, wary of the direction this was taking. "We are more than the magic in our veins."

Galeeta didn't reply for a moment, but strolled between the tables, her hands clasped before her. "I think you may need a few more tables. I understand Lord Farras is bringing two hundred with him, although half of those will be servants and guards. I suppose we'll have to make one of the glades into a parking lot, although I can't be sure how they're traveling."

Lila heaved a heavy sigh. "Please don't change the subject."

Galeeta frowned, the expression there and gone like a thunderclap. "We want Lord Farras to owe us favors. Think of your father."

"Of course." Lila felt a conversational trap opening wide. "And I am quite willing to put on a meal and air his bedchamber, but that is all. I have no interest in getting to know him. Remember that."

Galeeta raised her hands in a gesture of exasperation. "Must you be so difficult?"

"Whatever you think of the city, I have a life there. One I like."

"Fae need their people around them."

"I can live well enough on my own. But I'm not alone. I'm surrounded by co-workers, neighbors, people of all kinds."

"Humans," Galeeta said darkly.

"And others. I've made friends. Think about it, even Sala lives in the city, and she was the ultimate fae princess."

Her mother put a gentle hand on Lila's shoulder. "Sala never forgets who she is. She asked you to come here at my request."

Lila drew back, confused. "She said Ademar was in trouble and needed me to find him."

Galeeta smiled.

"Are you saying that was a trick? What about the vampires who knocked on her door?"

Her mother's smile faded. "I did not invent the vampires. But I need you here for this visit, and so we found a way to nudge you. And it turned out Ademar did need you here, so we weren't wrong."

"We? Who is we?"

Her mother reached out to touch Lila's shoulder again but drew back at Lila's flinch. Galeeta clasped her hands together instead. "I rarely ask you for anything. I really need you to cooperate now."

Lila studied her mother, seeing strain in the line of her shoulders and the set of her jaw. With a kind of amazement, she realized her mother was afraid.

Galeeta had never balked at anything, ever. She was as cool as glacial snow. What had changed that?

What would happen if Lila refused?

ell, that leaves us with a whole new and squirmy bag of questions. Whether we're talking humans, non-humans, or the undecided, is it wrong to slip the leash of sobriety from time to time? And if we choose to nope out of reality for a while, what if we can't come back?

This has long been a human-only issue—until recent developments, the supernatural set hasn't had access to drugs or intoxicants that stayed in the system long enough to matter. Bacchante has changed all that, and even in the short time since its existence has come to light, speculation has run wild about its origins. Some claim it emerged from deep in the Castle, one more mystery from the prison dimension we can't readily explain. Is this unfounded rumor, or a chance to finally understand the possible dangers of a drug whose use is bound to spread? Or are the mysterious deaths that stretch beyond East Bay's border evidence that widespread distribution of bacchante has already occurred?

That's the focus of our next installment of this special podcast series. Good night for now, darklings.

Izetta stabbed the screen of her freshly-purchased phone, silencing Errata's husky voice. The hotel room fell quiet except for the rush of traffic on the street below. Seated on the edge of the bed—the room was too small to hold much furniture—Izetta scrolled through the list of episodes on her phone only to find she'd listened to the last in the series. Another one was scheduled to drop in a week.

There was a comment button on the podcast's web page, and for an instant, she was tempted to leave a response. *C'mon folks, if this really came from the Castle, the true mystery is why we'd put something from a demon dimension in our mouths. Isn't that kind of stupidity how we ended up dead and fangy in the first place?*

She closed the comment box instead. Snarking wouldn't help the situation, and the forty-eight previous respondents already had that covered, including a spirited diatribe about werelemmings.

Izetta hit the page's home button shaped like a tiny cat. The werecougar's website showed a decade's worth of solid reporting for online news sources as well as a longer career as a radio personality at CSUP in Fairview. In other words, Errata Jones seemed legit. Enough for Izetta to believe the werecougar was, in fact, researching a news story.

Izetta flopped back onto the shabby hotel bedspread, staring up at the cracked ceiling and the psychedelic wallpaper half a century out of date. She thumbed the phone again, checking the SolAlert app that told her it was another half hour until full dark. She was old enough to function during the day, but no member of the supernatural set entertained visitors before sundown.

She tossed the phone aside. She'd bought it—along with fresh clothes—at an all-night store catering to nocturnal clients. Her last cell was still in the fae hellhole along with Rafe. And her favorite knives. Her list of grievances against the fae was getting longer by the minute.

Izetta scowled at the damp spot on the ceiling above. Speaking of hellholes, Errata's mention of the Castle gave her pause. She'd heard about the place twice in twenty-four hours.

Malatest had mentioned it, too. She'd never been there herself, but she'd heard stories. The Castle prison dimension was home to old and scary supernaturals with far too much time on their hands. Millenia, in fact. Was it possible they'd concocted the drug there from who-knew-what ingredients? Did anyone actually care, as long as distribution was stopped in a graphic and memorable manner?

She fumbled for the phone again. The kitsune clerk in the store had somehow managed to deactivate her lost phone and download the contents to her new one—including the surveillance video of the Magician. That had been the first thing she'd checked. The second had been her contacts list.

She found Errata's number and hit the text icon.

Pick me up. I'm at the Ambassador.

A beat passed, then three dots danced on the screen before a text bubble appeared with the reply.

On my way. Meet me out front in ten.

Efficient and to the point. Izetta liked that. She rolled off the bed and ran a comb through the mop of messy black curls that fell to the small of her back, then gave up when the comb got stuck. Unlike fae hair, hers had attitude. Bad attitude. She tossed the comb back on the dresser, shrugged into her black leather jacket, and left the dingy room.

The elevator was deader than she was, so she took the stairs and emerged into the cool darkness just as Errata pulled up to the curb in an older model Jaguar coupe. The car purred in a way that said it had been lovingly maintained.

Izetta pulled open the passenger door. "Classic ride."

"We've been together a while." Errata patted the dashboard.

Izetta slid inside, appreciating the soft leather seats. "Nice."

"Have you had breakfast?" The question was casual, but the reporter's tone was firm.

Izetta flashed fang. "You don't want to hang out with a hangry bloodsucker?"

Errata's smile was cool. "No, and not when we're about to stroll into a den of wolves. You'll push each other's buttons enough as it is."

Izetta slumped in her seat. This clearly wasn't Errata's first rodeo—not with so many interviews and stories on her CV. She knew her subjects well.

"I stopped for takeout," Izetta replied, looking out the window to hide her expression. "A youthful vintage, but full-bodied enough to satisfy."

It had been hard to let him go. She'd found the man in the back of the all-night store—or he'd found her. Young, but not too young. Healthy, but probably not for long. Those addicted to vampire venom always knew where to find the Undead. Maybe it was a universal impulse to put the unspeakable in one's mouth— or have the unspeakable put their mouth where it didn't belong.

She'd been starving by then, almost clumsy in her need, but he'd survive once the haze of euphoria wore off. She'd left him sleeping in the housewares section, nestled among the scatter rugs. He'd provided excellent customer service all around.

"Good to be fed and ready, because I think we'll need all our persuasive talents." Errata pulled away from the curb, immediately accelerating to a heart-pounding speed. "The Devries Alpha is known for being a difficult customer."

From what Rafe had said about his dad, that was putting things mildly.

"Did the Alpha say he would help us?"

"He only agreed to meet," Errata replied. "Although once he knows the truth, surely he'll help his own son. I'm good at getting Alphas to see reason. It's all about making them think it's their idea to do the right thing."

"We'll see." Izetta's breath caught as the car swung around a corner at top speed. "Whoa!"

"Sorry." Errata grinned. "Sometimes I get the zoomies."

"Uh-huh." Izetta felt her still heart make one startled beat as they roared across the bridge spanning East Bay's inlet. The lights from the bridge streaked the black water below, shimmering as wind ruffled the surface.

"What do you get out of this?" Izetta asked.

"A story," the werecougar replied. "And, frankly, there are enough terrifying things out there without a drug trade aimed at our people. If I can do something to stop it, I'm in."

"We're dealing with fae," Izetta said. "Their magic makes this next-level dangerous. You know that, right?"

Errata tapped the pendant she wore. "I got this amulet from a witch friend of mine. The core is ancient iron. It cuts through fae spells."

"Keep it close," Izetta replied. "But don't count on anything they can take away."

Conversation faded as traffic thickened and the car was forced to slow. This side of town was different, with fewer businesses and more homes. They passed schools and shopping centers, and eventually the houses grew sparser with parkland between. That made sense. Wolves needed room to run.

The road narrowed until there was little to see but gate posts with house numbers stenciled in reflective paint. After about three miles of twists and turns, Errata turned up a drive shrouded in cedars. The view soon opened to a starlit clearing. In the midst was a sprawling rancher with a wrap-around porch. Automatic lights came on as Errata pulled onto the parking pad to the right of the main entrance, beside a brown station wagon and an RV. If this was a den of wolves, it was a domestic one.

Errata had barely killed the engine when two wolves in animal form and another in blue jeans approached the car. Izetta got out and was immediately blocked by the gray wolf closest to her. Its back was as high as her hip.

"We're here to speak to your Alpha," Izetta said, looking the beast in its amber eyes. She'd never met Rafe's father, Roy

Devries, but this wouldn't be him. The pack leader wouldn't be on parking patrol. "It's about his son."

"I called ahead," Errata added, pocketing the Jaguar's key fob. "He's expecting us."

"A kitty cat and a vampire?" scoffed the one in human form. "This should be fun."

He turned and sauntered toward the house, entering through a side door into a daylight basement.

Izetta followed, Errata and the wolves bringing up the rear. Once they were in the room, Izetta heard the door close and lock behind them. At the sound, their guide stopped abruptly, standing to one side.

The space had the messy comfort she expected in a wolf den. A pool table stood at one end. At the other were couches and a bar piled with bags of junk food. It smelled of wet dog and young male. Around a dozen werewolves crowded the space, some bearing a slight resemblance to Rafe. Very few struck her as mature warriors, and she remembered Rafe's story about his disappearing kinsmen. Maybe the experienced hunters had already gone missing.

The wolves formed a ring around them, trapping them in the middle of the room. Only two of those present were female. From what Izetta knew, that didn't bode well for a pack's smooth operation and usually indicated a group in decline. Females went where their young would be looked after.

Without seeming obvious, Izetta shifted her stance, ready to fight. Beside her, Errata's heartbeat sped up, the light *thud-thud* audible despite the jostling males. Izetta kept her expression calm, though her hand drifted toward her jacket pocket where she'd hidden a blade. It was a sign of supreme confidence—or sloppiness—that they hadn't searched her at the door.

A figure rose from the couch, pushing through the circle of wolves. In his late fifties, he had the same square jaw, the same sure way of carrying himself as Rafe. Unfortunately, he had none of his son's manners. He fixed his two guests with an unreadable look.

"Roy Devries?" Errata asked.

"The same." He smoothed the front of his shirt. "Are you the reporter who asked to speak with me?"

His tone said he liked the idea, as if a newshound's interest made him important.

"I am," Errata replied. "Thank you for seeing us."

He glanced at Izetta. "And you're the vampire who knows my son?"

"I know Rafe," she answered, keeping her tone friendly. "I went with him on his mission to find the fae they call the Magician."

The Alpha's expression grew stony. "And where is my fool of a son? On a plane, running away again? It's like him to do as he's asked just long enough to satisfy his conscience."

No wonder Rafe rarely came home.

Izetta sucked in air to cool her temper. "The fae captured him. He's their prisoner."

"Prisoner?" This time there was worry in his tone.

Errata saw the opening and jumped on it. "Help us get him back. They took him because he found the Magician."

Izetta froze, barely concealing her reaction. It was a lie—they'd found a pile of nasty business, but no one they could point to with certainty. Not that she was going to point that out.

"He tracked them right to their door," Izetta added. "He—and I—made it inside their way station. It's right in the valley, hidden by a glamour."

The Alpha folded his arms. "Of course he did. He's the best tracker going. That doesn't tell me what you were doing there."

"I went on behalf of the local vampires. Their leader also wanted information about the Magician."

"Is Malatest making a move against the fae?"

"Malatest is considering his options," Errata said quickly,

meeting Izetta's gaze. "He wants to know if the wolves have enough courage to join him."

A murmur went around the room, those in wolf form sending up soft yips of agreement.

The Alpha held up his hand to silence them. "We have more than enough courage. That has never been in question."

The room fell silent. Errata opened her mouth to speak, but his look silenced her.

"I've heard your message, now hear mine," he continued. "We hunted the Magician to save our young. I sent one scout, then another to investigate the valley where we suspected the fae hid from sight. Neither of my kin returned. Then I sent more warriors who never came home. When I forbid others to go, they went anyhow, my brother included."

Here he stopped, swallowing hard. "It became clear that my pack, with or without permission, would not let the fae's crimes go unanswered. I had to stop the endless drain of our best people."

"So you sent for Rafe," Izetta said. "He came."

"For all his failings, my son has training and expertise that the rest of the pack does not. He was always our best tracker. This was his chance to erase the anger between us. But now he's lost as well."

"He's not lost yet," Izetta said. "That's why we're here."

The Alpha's grief curdled to fury. "Is the Magician dead?"

Izetta bristled. "No."

"Then my son failed," he spat. "Yes, we have the courage to fight, but can I risk the wolves I have left while Malatest considers his options?"

His rage pulsed through the room, raising the hair on Izetta's arms. The other wolves felt it, too. They rose as one, their circle closing around them. Errata was wide-eyed, looking around as if readying to bolt.

Izetta itched to grab her knife. "Malatest doesn't have a son to rescue."

"No," Devries agreed. "He sent you, and somehow you came back, but my boy didn't."

At some invisible signal, the circle of wolves drew closer, and closer still. The ones in animal form pushed in, lips curled in silent snarls.

Devries leaned in, eyes gone wolfish yellow. "Care to explain why you're here and he isn't?"

CHAPTER 15

Izetta's hand inched toward the folding knife she'd picked up during her shopping spree. She could feel the weight of it inside the pocket of her jacket, beckoning her to put an end to Devries's posturing. It wasn't as good as her custom blades, but it would get the job done.

"Hmm?" the Alpha prompted. His breath smelled like ham and mustard. "Why'd you leave my boy behind? Was it just so you could lead the rest of my pack into a trap and hand over my territory to your Undead boss?"

Izetta's fingers brushed the outside of her pocket and felt the outline of her knife. As if reading her intent, the wolves tightened the circle, every breath pulling them closer. It was a motley group. Those not wearing fur dressed in graphic tees and ragged jeans. But there was nothing casual about the way their eyes followed her every motion. They were primed for violence.

She recognized this game of threaten-the-stranger. The reasonable part of her knew there were too many wolves to fight, but a slice of her soul itched to gamble. There was a reason she'd courted death in the arena in front of a roaring crowd—but she wasn't deciding for herself alone. Errata hadn't signed up for recreational carnage.

Izetta drew her hand back, putting an end to temptation. "Rafe ran interference so I could get free and find help. I was in a bad way."

The Alpha's brow furrowed. "He couldn't run himself?"

He wasn't bothering to disguise the worry beneath his words now. However difficult Rafe's relationship was with his father, there was no question the elder Devries cared about his son. Beside her, Errata shifted nervously. If the werecougar had been wearing her tail, it would have been thrashing.

"No," Izetta replied. "He risked his own safety to ensure I survived."

Puzzlement flickered in the Alpha's eyes. "What was he thinking?"

"Rafe is a good friend, and I don't have many." Begging this Alpha almost physically hurt, but she steeled herself. "That's why I'm here, asking for your help. Please."

Devries made a noise of derision, but he stepped back, taking his ham breath with him. "His job was to save the pack, not a vampire."

"I could get past the fae. He couldn't. It was a practical choice."

"How is sacrificing my son practical?"

Izetta shrugged, refusing to be rattled. "I could ask you the same thing. Are you really going to leave your son to rot in a fae prison, or are you going to help me get him out?"

Devries's shoulders hunched with tension. "As a father, I say yes. He's my boy. As an Alpha, I see a fool who can't remember his pack comes first. And then there's the wolf, who sees a blood-sucker standing where his flesh and blood should be."

Errata made a noise low in her throat. The werecougar had been so silent, Izetta had almost forgotten her. She held up a hand to keep the cat from interfering. The Alpha was close to crossing the line, but she'd give him another inch before teaching him a lesson.

"Decide what you want to do," she told him, voice cool. "I will keep asking anyone I think worthy of the fight."

He leaned in again, eyes going a wolfish gold. "And you think I'm worthy, do you?"

Izetta could feel the eyes of the wolves following her every movement. She stepped forward, showing them all she wasn't afraid. "Not everyone can stand up to the fae. That's why I came to you."

The werewolf laughed, but it wasn't pleasant. Neither was his huge hand squeezing her shoulder so hard she felt the bones shift. "Flattery won't get you far, darling."

Fast as thought, the knife was in Izetta's hand. The shiny blade flicked open with a glint of silver. "Don't ever call me darling," she said, her voice dropping to a snarl. "You're not my Alpha dog."

The air in the room all but crackled. Devries's gaze fixed on the knife, twin spots of color flaring on his cheekbones. Izetta's jaw ached with the urge to bite. One of the wolves whimpered.

A car honked outside, startling them all. Errata spun toward the door with a hiss.

"Who's on watch?" Devries waved toward the door, sending the flunky who had ushered them into the room scurrying to obey. The circle of wolves broke, fading back so he could pass.

The Alpha folded his arms and glared at his guests. If she had to guess, he was both annoyed and relieved at the interruption. Truth be told, so was she.

A moment later, the wolf returned. "Someone's here to see you, boss."

Devries answered with a snarl. "Who?"

"It's vampires. Mr. Malatest."

"Really?" Errata muttered under her breath. "What's he doing here?"

A speculative murmur rippled through the room, but Izetta had expected this. She'd rattled Malatest's cage, and any crime boss worth his salt would keep tabs on her movements. He'd know she'd gone to his chief rival and would get here quick to do some damage control.

She snapped the knife shut with a flick of her wrist. "Now the real conversation begins."

"What does that mean?" Devries muttered.

Izetta flashed fang. "Either we learn to play together, or the fae get away with literal murder. My guess is that you're too good an Alpha to let Malatest take all the glory."

Errata's eyebrows shot up, but Izetta had said what she needed to say. She'd met a thousand Devries in her time. They were bullies, sometimes cruel ones, and yet they could make excellent partners in a fight. The trick was to set the ground rules before they did.

His chin jerked up defiantly. "Don't push me."

"What you do is up to you," Izetta said, pocketing the knife. "Me, I don't leave friends behind, so I'm in the fight whether you like it or not."

She felt the Alpha's anger like a wash of heat, but Malatest chose that moment to swan through the door, a train of flunkies on his heels. Devries swung to face the newcomers, a low growl rumbling through his barrel-chested frame. His wolves sprang to attention, intercepting the vampires until he waved his pack aside.

"What do you want, Malatest?" he growled.

"I need soldiers. We have a score to settle with the fae."

The words came out clipped, more an order than a request. It was exactly the wrong tone. The werewolves stirred anew, slouching and resentful.

"I thought you wanted no part of the hunt for the Magician," Izetta put in, more to needle him than anything else. "What changed?"

Malatest cast her a resentful look, then reached into the pocket of his long coat. He drew out a long chain studded with freshwater pearls. He held it up, the ornate chain softly glinting as it swung from his hand. The last time Izetta had seen the necklace, it had been around Sadie's neck. Her stomach sank as she remembered the girl lingering in Malatest's office. Malatest kissing her. The insouciant swing of her hips as she slipped out his door.

"She proved more curious than smart," the vampire king said, his face like stone.

Errata's breath caught. "What happened?"

He held the chain higher, twisting it so that the light from the bare bulb in the ceiling caught the links. "I've heard two different stories in the last hour. I'll hear a dozen more by morning."

"Malatest?" Izetta asked softly.

"After Sadie left my office, she went out with friends. I had her followed. There was still a chance we could catch the Magician alone, remove him quietly from this world, but he was nowhere in sight." He cleared his throat. "She went to a dance club frequented by a mixed supernatural crowd. That much everyone agrees on."

"What don't they agree on?" Izetta asked.

Malatest's mouth twisted, as if what he was about to say tasted bad. "Some say she met the Magician and fell under his spell. She went mad for love and walked into the rising sun."

Devries made a sound of disbelief. "That's a storybook tale."

The vampire king raised a brow. "Every story involving the fae is a thinly disguised horror tale."

"What really happened?" Izetta asked.

"Sadie got bored and found someone selling bacchante. She was too fragile for the drug." There was real grief in his voice.

Izetta's chest twisted with compassion she didn't want to feel. Malatest was easier to despise than to pity—but even Devries was nodding slowly.

"I'm sorry to hear of another loss," the werewolf said, his tone formal. "Both our communities have paid a price. But what is bacchante?"

Malatest stuffed the necklace back in his pocket, his expression grim. "He's killing our people with a substance masquerading as a drug. It might be magic or chemical or both, but he is the source."

A mutter ran through the crowd of wolves. Izetta couldn't help wondering which of the young ones already knew exactly what the rogue fae offered and yet hadn't breathed a word of it to their sworn Alpha. Rebellion and recklessness were often twins.

"I need your soldiers," Malatest repeated. Half the iron haughtiness in his voice was grief, but it still sounded like an ill-considered command.

"And what do the wolves need, leech?" The Alpha bristled, his sympathy forgotten. "What gives you the right to march into my den and make demands?"

An angry clamor rose. Izetta heard car doors slamming outside. If she guessed right, more vampires were arriving to back up their boss.

"Wait." Errata stepped forward, slicing the air with her hand. Her dark hair swung as she looked from Devries to Malatest, quelling them with a fierce green glare. "Stop talking and listen. We all want the same thing."

Izetta reached out to grab the cat's sleeve, certain she'd lost her kitty mind. Provoking two of the most powerful supernaturals in town wasn't a good survival plan. Devries opened his mouth to speak, but Errata held up her palm, stopping him midgape. Long claws sprouted from her fingertips as they watched. A gentle reminder she wasn't just a helpless fluff they could bully.

At the sight of the claws, Izetta felt the situation slip out of her control. She stepped back, making herself wait and see how it would play out.

"Think this through." Errata paced from one leader to the

other and then back, her movements smooth and eerily quick. "We all want to stop the Magician and anyone helping him, and Rafe is being held captive. He deserves to be rescued. Those are easy goals if we don't start off by fighting."

"And you think lecturing us will help?" Devries demanded, finally finding his voice.

Errata stopped in front of him, poking his chest with a claw. "I'm trying to make you understand you have a common interest."

"Why?"

"I'm neither vampire nor wolf," she said, finally stopping to claim the center of the room. "I favor neither side, and I know the laws and pacts that rule among all our kinds."

"Good for you," Malatest retorted. "How does that matter?"

"You're both waiting for the other to commit to an invasion of the way station."

The two leaders exchanged wary looks.

"Neither one of you wishes to proceed without guarantees."

"We're not stupid," the vampire king agreed.

Errata gave a satisfied nod. "Then, if you allow it, I will help you negotiate an agreement that shares the risk and the glory between you both."

"That's a bold proposition," Malatest said. "And a difficult one."

"Easy wouldn't be worth my effort."

"What do you get out of this?" Devries demanded.

"People do like to ask me that." A hint of impatience crept into Errata's voice. "I get the satisfaction of stopping the Magician. I don't want this problem reaching my home town. I want our cubs to live."

"How very noble," Malatest said with a sneer. "I think the truth is you're here to make your name. You're an entertainer, a radio personality with dreams of scooping a hard news story."

Errata tensed, a fine tremble of anger passing over her. But the cat woman had self-control. She smoothed her hair from her eyes and gave him a pointed smile. "You want hard? I've negotiated intellectual property rights with telepaths. You two are well within my wheelhouse."

The werecougar had the confidence to give her words weight. Malatest looked away, pretending to brush a wrinkle from his sleeve.

"I do far more than talk shows," Errata added. "I make people pay attention to what matters."

Izetta leaned on one hip, hands loose at her sides, ready to fight. This would either be a slam dunk or a bloodbath, and Izetta wasn't an optimist. The uncomfortable pause lasted until Devries rolled his eyes to the ceiling, visibly giving in.

"Why is it that cats always think they're in charge?"

CHAPTER 16

Sleep was a blessed oblivion—until it wasn't.

The ability to nap anywhere, anytime, was a survival skill Rafe had learned early in his career with the Silent Wolves. Rest was never guaranteed during an assignment, so he grabbed sleep when he could to stay in top physical and mental shape.

That was until he'd been taken captive during the extraction of a valued asset in Eastern Europe. His captors had been rusalki —beautiful water spirits who had gone to the other side of the war. Then the nightmares had begun, night after night, dreams of drowning in a net made from the maidens' sea-green hair. There was no wrestling with the creatures who dissolved at his touch. He might as well have tried to grapple a wave. Cold, dark water pressed in, robbing sound and sight, and choking every breath until his lungs burned for air. He'd wake up gasping, the pain too great to move. As a means to break his spirit, it had been an effective technique.

He'd killed three and escaped. It was only later that he learned he'd been captive for only two weeks. It had felt like months, and he hadn't been able to sleep in a locked room since. The way station, with its graveyard and its cells, brought the dreams back with the force of a speeding truck.

Rafe lay awake, fully clothed and staring at the ceiling. The Silent Wolf shrink had claimed the dreams wouldn't bother him unless they resonated with his psyche. The boundaries he'd put on himself. His isolation from the pack. His reluctance to share emotions. That self-repression was a means to cover up his guilt for disappointing his father, and his subconscious turned that guilt into strangling locks of hair.

Maybe some of that was true, maybe it wasn't. Self-actualization took a back seat when job number one was staying alive, and survival was all about discipline and training. He knew how to be invisible, gather information, and cover his tracks. If he dropped a body on the way to the exit, he was quick and quiet. A Silent Wolf had no room for feelings. Maybe that's why he took the riskiest assignments. They kept him too busy to think. Or hope. Or sleep, for that matter.

A faint scent teased him, one he'd noticed in the clearing where his kin lay buried. It was the animal stink of fear, as if the wolves had been helpless and aware right up until the killing blow. The stench of despair had followed him to this cell like a ghost. Or a warning?

Where was Izetta? If she was still among the Undead, she would have reached town. If she hadn't …

He sprang to his feet, pulse thrumming, at the now-familiar beep and clatter of the door release. Lila stood at the entrance. The memory of their kiss rose like an exotic butterfly, lovely and utterly out of place.

A sudden warmth in his chest betrayed every hard lesson he'd endured. Discipline demanded that he shouldn't be glad to see her. Wolf and fae didn't mix. He knew that, and yet his body and soul disagreed.

"Come," she said, her voice flat with weariness. "There is much to do before Lord Farras arrives tonight."

Even without the benefit of windows, Rafe's internal clock said it was dawn. For a fae, it was the middle of the night. "You should be sleeping."

"Like I said, there is much to do." She stood back, indicating the hallway beyond.

Rafe paused only to pull on his boots. Wordlessly, Lila turned and led the way to the stairs, her usually straight posture ever so slightly wilted. Her light-blonde hair was carelessly braided, as if she'd left her chambers in a hurry. Fae were pathologically careful of their appearance—worse than any cat.

"Is something wrong?" he asked. He couldn't decide if he was genuinely concerned or looking for an opportunity he could exploit. Maybe because he was confused, the question came out with a hint of sarcasm.

She slowed just enough to glance over her shoulder but didn't meet his eyes. The outer curve of her gently pointed ears flushed pink.

"I require practical help, not questions," she replied, then turned and quickened her pace. "Right now, my job is to prepare sleeping chambers for the lord and his men. This will take some time. He has exacting tastes."

They climbed several sets of stairs and emerged in a hallway Rafe hadn't yet seen. The walls were white and the floors a light oak. Judging by the view from the window of the stairway landing, they were several floors up. She entered the first doorway on the right, which appeared to be lined with cupboard doors. She opened and closed several before she found the one she wanted. It was stocked floor to ceiling with bed linens.

"Here, take these." She held out a pile of sheets with one arm and rummaged in the cupboard for more.

As he reached to accept the stack, she grabbed his hand and pushed back his sleeve. There was a red welt where the silver bracelet touched his skin.

"What's this?" she asked, setting the linens aside so she could take a better look.

He swallowed back a sliver of resentment that she didn't already know the answer. "Silver irritates a shifter's skin, especially something this tight."

"Oh." A flush crept up her ears. "That's easily fixed."

She cupped the right-hand bracelet between her palms. It immediately heated, at first a gentle warmth and then to an almost painful temperature. Rafe drew in his breath to protest, but then the metal shifted away from his flesh. A cool tingling ran all the way to his elbow. When she drew back her hands, the silver band hung ever-so-slightly loose and the skin beneath was whole.

"You should be able to slide your shirtsleeve beneath the bracelet," she said, then went to work on his other wrist.

"Thank you." Rafe couldn't quite feel grateful—he was still bound by magic—but the absence of itching pain was a profound relief.

She stepped back, finished with his other bracelet. "I'm extremely sorry that happened."

For an instant, Lila seemed plunged into embarrassed confusion. She closed her eyes, sucking in a breath before opening them again with a look of shaky resolve that didn't convince him one bit. This was not where she wanted to be.

She picked up the sheets again, thrusting them into his arms. "No time to waste."

"Don't your servants take care of this?" he asked.

Her face lost all expression. "It is customary for the eldest unmarried daughter of the house to make the beds of the honored guests. I decorate the hall and plan the meal. That is the tradition of our noble houses. To do less is considered an insult."

"You can't magic the rooms ready?"

"No. That lacks the required personal touch."

Rafe considered that. Werewolves were good at hospitality,

but no female would tolerate someone around the cubs without sniffing them first. If nothing else, Galeeta seemed just as protective of her family. Something wasn't adding up.

"What hold does this lord have on your kin?"

At that, Lila dropped a pillowcase and quickly bent to scoop it from the floor. "Nothing."

"A two-year-old cub could lie better than that."

"Fae don't lie," she retorted.

"Fae detect untruths. Not the same thing."

With a frown, she placed the pillowcase on top of his load. "Lord Farras is an important ally with the ear of the king and a claim to the throne if the king dies without issue. It would not be wise to offend him."

Rafe had figured that much out already. "And the soldiers who arrived here at the same time as me?"

The crease between her brows deepened. "Lord Teegar is a captain of the Royal Guard and a political rival of Lord Farras. Before you ask, I do not know his side of the story."

Fear swirled beneath the studied neutrality of her tone. No wonder she was doing whatever domestic task was asked of her.

"So, that's why you agreed to play hostess?" He followed her out of the room and down a long hallway to the guest bedrooms.

"It was not my preference, but yes," she said quietly, raising a hand to indicate which room to enter.

It was a corner suite with views of the lake and trees. The stark white walls and plain black furniture were softened by gauzy curtains the shade of new leaves. She'd selected bed clothes and towels to match.

"What do you do when you're not here?" he asked, setting the pile of linens on the bed.

"Architectural design," she replied. "I have a job in the city."

"I thought fae didn't thrive there." Whether he liked it or not, his curiosity was piqued.

"Most don't." She shook out the bottom sheet, letting it settle over the mattress. "It's noisy and far from the forest. There's talk about damage to ancient tradition from too many new ideas, and how human inventions make fae magic less relevant in the modern world."

"So why leave?" He grabbed the other end of the sheet, helping her pull it tight.

For the first time, she smiled. "I like the new. Humans, especially. They're tiny explosions of emotion and energy. Everything is so urgent to them."

"Mortality does that," he said wryly. So did unexpected kisses.

"It's honest, even if it's messy." She began stuffing the feather pillows into embroidered cases. "Shifters have their own dynamic. So do the Undead. That's why I love living in a multi-species building—there are so many different ways of being in the world."

"Not everyone would enjoy that."

"Their loss. It's creative, and an opportunity to learn, especially about yourself. It's hard to see your own blind spots until you get away from the familiar." She tossed him the first pillow.

Rafe settled it among its fellows. Then he cast her a sidelong look. "I heard a rumor that the Forest Fae are leaving the city."

Lila frowned. "They are. The court is leaving first."

"A good Alpha would be the last to leave, but that's just us," he said under his breath. He caught the second pillow and patted it in place, wishing the future occupant nightmares.

In the few minutes they'd been talking, the bed had transformed into a cushioned oasis. Lila moved on to the rest of the room, setting out soaps and towels, toiletries and flowers. Though she added little to what was already there, every surface became a perfectly balanced arrangement. The clean scents of candles and fresh linens melded in perfect harmony, adding to a restful atmosphere. Thinking of his bare cell and sleepless nights, Rafe envied the future occupant with fresh savagery.

Lila completed her circuit of the room, rejoining him at the foot of the bed. Her furtive glance at the carefully piled cushions put a thousand inappropriate thoughts in his head. The bed looked so soft. So did she. Lila stood close enough that her scent overlaid everything else.

"If you love the city so much, why not go back?" he asked, talking so the moment wouldn't end. His head filled with images of what he could do with her on that feather-soft mattress.

She glanced up at him, the gray of her eyes stormy. At first, he thought she wouldn't answer, but then the corners of her mouth turned down. "I will when this is over. Right now, there will be consequences if I don't stay."

Clearly, he'd struck a nerve. And it was just as plain that she needed to talk, even if it was to her captive servant. He wavered a moment, his first instinct to retreat. She was fae, and this was enemy territory. He didn't owe her a shoulder to cry on.

Except she'd shown him compassion. Believed him. Healed him. Probably saved his life. The very least he could do was listen.

"What consequences?" he asked.

"The king holds my father prisoner."

"Ah." That was an obligation he understood. No wonder she'd agreed to play a role she hated.

Lila scrubbed at her face, the gesture angry. "I shouldn't have said that. It's not your affair."

"Who can help?"

"Lord Farras has the power to secure my father's freedom."

Rafe put a gentle hand on her shoulder and was startled to see her eyes glittered with tears. She ducked her chin, hiding her emotion until he pulled her close. To his surprise, she leaned in, letting him take her weight. The top of her head fit beneath his chin, the warmth of her hair like silk against his skin. A painful sensation rose in his chest, urging him to wrap her tightly in his arms.

"Lord Farras holds a lot of cards in this game," he said softly.

She nodded, her body stiff as she fought back her distress.

"What do you want to do about that?" he asked.

NO ONE HAD EVER ASKED her before. As wonderful as it might be to have a say, the prospect terrified her. Action led to reaction, and Farras didn't pull his punches.

She drew away from Rafe, missing the solid feel of him the instant she straightened. But she'd be a fool to listen to him, however sweet his words might be. He was her prisoner, not her friend, and as likely as not to betray her.

"I'm sorry," she said. "This is not your problem."

"No, it's not."

The frank answer caught her off guard. "Well—"

"I understand, though," he said, interrupting her. "The games of power. The obligation to family, even when that bond can hurt."

She nodded, her throat too tight to speak.

"My father is a difficult Alpha," he went on. "When we went hunting, he'd set traps. Not for our prey, but for me and my friends. They were no joke—a wolf could lose a paw or break bones. If we fell into them, he'd call us stupid and weak. If we escaped them, he'd accuse us of cheating."

Rafe was trying to build a bridge between them, to show they had something in common. It was an old tactic to breed trust, but it made Lila feel a little less alone.

"What did you do?"

"When I got old enough, I left home just to put an end to the growling." Rafe gave a short, bitter laugh.

"What are you saying?" His tale sounded awful, and she wasn't sure of the point.

"The Alpha, my father, wanted to scare off the next genera-tion. If their confidence was broken, they would never challenge him." Rafe shrugged. "All too often, power is fear in disguise. The more you have, the more you fear it will be taken. The only way to keep it is to make the other guy fear you more."

"What do you do?"

"Refuse to play the game."

Lila shook her head. He might talk about walking away, but he was an Alpha, too. Maybe not by title, but that dominant spark couldn't be lost or won. She would put down money that—given the chance—he'd attract a pack of his own.

"What about duty?" she asked with a tinge of sarcasm. "What about protecting the people you love? Isn't that why you're here? You came to save the day?"

Rafe pulled a face. "I didn't say running was the final answer. It was all I could think of at the time. I'm not perfect."

But he was, in too many ways. Lila felt easy beside him, utterly safe. That wasn't wise. Nor was the sweet churn she felt in her belly when she studied his form. Unlike a fae, the werewolf had a raw beauty that drew her in a way no perfection could.

Maybe that was why she didn't resist when his lips brushed her hair, then her cheek, and finally her mouth. She froze, her core suddenly weightless with surprise and desire. It left her giddy enough that she bunched her fists in his shirtfront, holding on before she fell.

He was warm—hotter than human or fae. His presence engulfed her, filling her senses as she leaned into the kiss, instinct taking over. His tongue slid against hers, demanding and definitely *other*. It was a taste she'd longed for without knowing it existed, wild and unapologetically male. Yearning thrilled through her like a kindling fire.

They broke the kiss just long enough to change angles, just long enough that she slid her arms around his neck. The move brought them closer, body to body, crushing her breasts against the wall of his chest. She gasped, aroused and sensitized as he stroked the curve of her back, then lower. He seemed to be trying different techniques, keeping what made her squirm with pleasure and discarding the rest.

Lila was acutely aware of the bed. It would be easy to discard every inhibition, to let emotion run away. Whether sincere or not, Rafe made her feel worthy of affection. That was a drug more addictive than any potion or pill.

A door slammed in the corridor. Lila jumped back, stumbling and catching herself on the footboard of the bed. Rafe moved to steady her, but she waved him away, glancing nervously at the bedroom door. Her hand went to her mouth, conscious her lips had to be swollen from such a bruising kiss.

Yes, she'd startled like a guilty teenager, but consorting with a prisoner was a deadly offence. She wished she hadn't seen the look of hurt in Rafe's eyes, but that was swept away by a rush of alarm as the door flew open.

CHAPTER 17

*A*s she turned, Lila caught sight of herself in the mirror above the chest of drawers. The carved and gilded frame was serenely elegant; she was not. The mussed hair and reddened lips screamed guilt. Reflexively, she pressed her palms to her cheeks to cool them. That made her look like a panicked maiden in a silent movie. She jerked her hands away in disgust.

Beside her, Rafe tugged his shirt into place and picked up the remaining linens, barely stifling an amused smirk. Lila refused to return his sidelong glance.

Ademar entered, this time leaning on a cane of polished black wood wrapped in silver filigree. It had the ivy and acorn pattern from their family coat of arms and looked new.

"There you are," her brother said, glancing from her to Rafe and back. "I find you together again."

"You and Mother agreed he would be my servant," she replied. "Where did you get that cane?"

"A gift," he replied. "Lord Farras sent something for you as well. He's most generous."

She barely stopped herself from saying she didn't want it. Provoking Ademar would do no good—not when he'd nearly caught her kissing the shifter who'd torn him open. A flutter of guilt rose, but then it faded under her brother's hard stare.

She redirected the conversation instead. "So, you've been in communication with Lord Farras?"

He gave her a dry look. "You do recall the project I'm working on? Melding cellular communications with crystal magic?"

"So it's working?"

He shrugged.

Ademar continued to look between her and Rafe, visibly pondering the tension between his sister and her servant. Clearly, he didn't like what he saw even though Rafe had retreated several paces so that he stood a respectful distance away. She knew her brother well enough to feel his accusation like a tangible thing, even if he didn't say a word.

Wolf and fae didn't mix. Or at least shouldn't, according to fae standards. If it ever reached Lord Farras that Galeeta's daughter consorted with beasts—well, as the humans put it, he'd lose their number. Any chance of saving her father would be gone.

That was unthinkable. Despite all, she loved her family. In the end, they would always put each other first. That was as true as the green of forest leaves. Or it had been. Now she wasn't certain.

Ademar advanced into the room, shutting the door behind him. He shouldered Lila aside as he pushed forward, leaning heavily on his fancy walking stick.

"So, what have you actually done in here?" he asked, flicking the edge of the coverlet with the tip of his cane. "It looks the same as before."

That was not true. It could not be true for anyone with fae senses, for her presence was imprinted on everything she had touched. The most sensitive could detect the quality of her mood as she'd done each task—which was not a comforting thought.

Lila gave an airy wave. "I have provided clean linens and fresh flowers. What more does Lord Farras need? He can't be staying for long."

Ademar's jaw stiffened. "He deserves whatever courtesy we can provide."

"I chose the nicest room."

It was true. Morning sun flooded the forest outside, falling in gilded shafts through the leaves. The room itself seemed an oasis of tranquility. One might never guess there was a dungeon beneath their feet.

Her brother scanned the room, as if verifying her statement. "It is pleasant enough, but I don't see why you required the dog to help you fluff a few pillows."

Her temper stirred. "He is my servant to do with as I please."

His frown deepened. "You didn't keep him alive just because he can fold a fitted sheet."

"Don't be ridiculous. Only demons can do that."

His reply was a wordless noise of disgust. Lila could feel his foul mood like a dank mist. The cause went beyond Rafe's presence. It was woven with something else—frustration, jealousy, or something she couldn't even put a name to.

"Why do you want me to feel guilty?" she asked. "What good does that do?"

"Maybe you should," he replied softly. "You know the answer to that better than I do."

The words were almost neutral, but his tone was not. Rafe set down the stack of linens and stepped between them, making a protective wall. Ademar took an awkward step back, cursing as he stumbled on his injured leg. He was afraid, and she didn't blame him. Rafe might wear a human face, but a predator liked to finish his kill.

Lila gently pushed Rafe aside. He moved but didn't shift his gaze away from Ademar. The two kept each other in a clear line of sight, even as they put distance between them.

"Stop glowering, both of you," she said.

Ademar twisted the handle of his walking stick to reveal a

thin rapier hid inside the silver and ebony case. "It's time your beast went back to his kennel."

Rafe picked up a stool in one hand, clearly ready to use it like a shield—or a club. He was taller and heavier than her brother, and his temper filled the room like a crackling wave. Lila's pulse quickened. It was impossible not to respond—he was defending her, after all—but someone had to take control.

"I just finished this room," she said, putting a snap in her voice. "Stand down before there's property damage. I don't have time for this nonsense."

Neither male looked happy, but Ademar put away his blade with a swish of metal. Rafe set down the stool and edged closer to Lila with a protective loom. Her brother watched them both with clear dislike.

"I don't like this side of you, Ademar," she said, voice husky with tension. "It's all I've seen since I came here."

Ademar's lip curled. "And all I've seen is someone who isn't sure where she belongs."

Lila drew breath to reply, but then swallowed down her retort. It would just start the fight all over again.

"Control your pet before I do it for you," Ademar said coldly.

"Don't," she said. *Don't threaten. Don't bully. Just don't.*

Her brother shifted his weight onto his good foot. "Say that again."

She swallowed hard and forced herself to say the words Ademar wanted. "Please spare him."

Rafe stirred beside her, his anger almost crackling against her skin. Yet, he wisely said nothing. For all his supposed beastliness, he had better self-control than the fae in the room.

Ademar's gaze slid to Rafe, his loathing plain. The wolf had wounded his pride as well as his flesh and bone, but the damage went even deeper than that. It had left him afraid, and not just of wolves. Lila could taste it like ash in the air.

"I hope you realize that my sister is all that's between you and my blade," Ademar said in silky tones. "A single misstep would end badly for both of you, but especially her. The fae hold their own to high standards."

Rafe's expression burned with fury, but he bowed his head in wordless acknowledgment. Her brother opened the door, allowing the sound of bustling movement to seep into the room. Lila ignored the commotion, too choked with anger to allow for distraction.

"How dare you speak that way?" she breathed.

"I dare, and I do," Ademar replied, leaning into the corridor as he snapped his fingers.

Two fae wearing plain gray livery appeared in the doorway at once and stood stiffly, awaiting Ademar's orders. They were light fae, but Lila did not recognize them.

"Who are they?" she asked, thinking they looked like a pair of puppets.

"Members of Lord Farras's advance guard," Ademar replied. "They got here an hour ago to ensure everything was ready for his arrival."

"Oh." For an instant, she was acutely aware of Rafe's warmth beside her and longed to burrow into it.

Ademar turned to the two servants. "Return the shifter to his cell. One of my mother's creatures will show you the way."

Lila looked up at Rafe, unwilling to let Ademar give the order. Rafe's handsome features were carefully schooled, but his warm hand squeezed hers before he followed his escort from the room. She watched him go with a bitter taste at the back of her throat. As soon as they'd left, Ademar swung the door shut again.

"You're sulking," he said.

She swung around. "And you're acting like a petty despot."

"My apologies, sister." He didn't sound as if he meant it in the least. "And now it's time to end your housekeeping duties and prepare yourself for Lord Farras's arrival. He will get here tonight in time for the banquet. It's important that we make a good impression."

"And I am to provide a decorative function?" she asked with deceptive mildness.

"Mother has organized a selection of gowns for you to choose from," Ademar went on with a smile. "He hasn't seen you for years and will be pleased by what a beauty you've become."

Several thoughts collided, none of them pleasant and all of them making her feel trapped. The way station had no wardrobes of clothes as it did cupboards of sheets and towels, so where had the dresses come from? And why did Ademar look so full of himself? Once upon a time, her family had dangled her in front of Farras to win his favor, but that was long ago and it had come to nothing. She intended it to stay that way.

"No," she replied.

"No?" He raised a brow. "To what, specifically?"

"No to all of it. I decorated the hall and chose a menu. I made up his lordship's room. If you want, I'll leave a mint on his pillow. But that is where custom ends, and I'm not obligated to do more. I'm done now, and I'm going home."

Ademar caught her elbow, his grip gentle but firm. "Most would be delighted to sit beside a powerful lord and ensure that he enjoys himself. Could you not be a normal lady of the court just this once?"

"I think not," Lila said, her voice cracking with emotions she'd held back for too long. "Since I've arrived here, I've seen Captain Teegar of the King's Guard—a lord himself—bespelled and imprisoned. I've seen strangers attacked and tortured for trying to find their kin. There are graves in the woods no one cares to explain, and despite the fact Rafe is innocent of any crime, he is still a prisoner."

Ademar studied her face but said nothing. His hand dropped from her elbow with an air of defeat.

"This is fae politics," Lila continued. "I hate it, and I moved away so that I didn't have to deal with it. That decision stands. I refuse to play the game."

"What about Father?" Ademar asked.

Guilt tugged at her like a strong current, threatening to pull her from her feet. "I want to help. I would shed blood to free him, but I have no confidence anything I do would make a difference."

"I don't understand."

"Neither do I, and that's the problem. I've been patient. I've held my tongue about whatever you and Mother are up to, hoping you'd tell me everything in good time, but that time has run out." She took a deep, shaking breath. "No one is giving me the complete truth. With so many unanswered questions, how am I supposed to make a real choice? There is asking for my help, and then there is entrapment. I won't be coerced."

"Listen." With sudden ferocity, Ademar pushed her.

"Ademar!" She stumbled backward, too surprised to react.

"*Listen.*" He shoved her again.

Lila fell into a sitting position on the bed. He towered over her, the walking stick clutched in both hands. His mouth pinched into a hard line, betraying his anxiety.

"What are you doing?" she demanded, her voice husky with outrage.

"You need to wake up before it's too late." His knuckles whitened where he gripped the cane, as if clutching it was all that kept his temper in check. "You want the truth. Here it is. Lord Farras has all the cards. We're in no position to deny him anything. If you have to sit and simper at him tonight, you will do so."

Lila gulped back bile. She felt as if the floor had suddenly opened and she was falling down, down into an inky pit. "I don't belong to him. Or you. Or Mother."

"Father ended your betrothal because you were too young. Now you're grown and Father is not here."

Her heart pounded, making it difficult to hear. "That doesn't change anything."

She sprang from the bed, dodging around her brother to lunge for the door. As she swept past the bureau, a porcelain vase went smashing to the floor. The explosion of shards stopped her in her tracks, leaving her to stare at the jagged pieces scattered over the floor.

"Calm down, Lila," Ademar said softly. "We're putting on a good show for Lord Farras, that's all."

"You're asking me to tempt him until he gives you what you want," she said, her mind racing so hard her thoughts were almost blank. There was too much to re-evaluate all at once. "If Farras takes your bait, you can't take it back. You can't take me back."

Ademar was silent. Her throat ached with tears, but she refused to let them fall.

"I thought you loved me enough to protect me," she said. "I thought Mother did, and Sala. We were different people, but we were family. I could trust you."

Her brother still said nothing.

Nausea rolled through her like a foul tide. "But Sala was part of this, wasn't she? She asked me to come here to make sure you were all right. And I came, Ademar. I came for her and for you."

Ademar looked at the door, as if expecting someone to enter. Or maybe he couldn't meet her eyes. "She didn't have a choice."

Lila bent and began picking up the tiny shards. It was habit. If she left them, someone might be hurt. "Do you have a choice?"

Leaning on his walking stick, he turned to watch her. "Don't cut yourself."

She caught and held his gaze. "Do you have a choice? Would you save me if you could?"

His mouth worked for a moment. "What do you think?"

He flung himself toward the door, stumbling in his haste. He grabbed at the handle, rattling the knob as he got the door open.

For a long moment, he stood suspended on the threshold, as if he had more to say. But with a sigh, he staggered forward and slammed the door behind him.

Lila jumped at the sound, slicing open her palm so that blood ran into the fine creases of her hand. The crimson transfixed her as it spread like liquid fire. *Noble blood. Blood kin. Magical bloodline. Is that all that matters? What about who I am?*

With a fit of sudden disgust, she tossed the shards to the floor. One of his lordship's servants could sweep up the mess, blood and all. She wasn't going to be Farras's arm candy or his chambermaid. More to the point, she wasn't about to hand her future to someone selfish enough to take it.

If she didn't have a choice, she'd make one.

CHAPTER 18

*L*ila left the guest chambers and slipped through the halls of the way station, not entirely sure where she wanted to go. The temptation to simply leave the way station was strong, but that would leave too much unresolved. Plus, she suspected she'd end up like Sala, with unwelcome visitors on her doorstep. Breaking free of this drama required more than a hasty exit.

She didn't have much time. Sunlight pooled on the polished wood floors, indicating the morning was well advanced. A few more servants in gray livery passed by, no doubt preparing for the lord's entourage. She hoped they'd brought plenty of supplies. Way stations were capable of adding rooms and even entire wings as needed without changing the boundaries of its footprint. Even so, if her mother's estimate of 200 guests was correct, their store cupboards would be stretched to the limit.

She passed another group of servants, these carrying travel bags. It would take time to get everyone settled, and she was certain Lord Farras would not arrive until the initial chaos was over.

That still didn't give her a clear idea of timelines. The

most sophisticated travel magic could bend time and space to cut distances, creating roads that existed beyond the normal realm. Likewise, the king's private domain—Gilden Wood—was in a fold of reality only fae could enter. The gateway and the path that led to it were carefully hidden from mortal eyes.

Lord Farras was capable of treading at least some of those secret byways, which meant he could arrive at any point. Lila might only have a few hours to decide how to deal with his presence and her family's expectations.

She'd barely finished that thought when she heard Ademar's angry voice coming from the second-floor sitting room where she'd played question and answer with their mother. Curious, Lila turned in that direction.

"I don't care," Ademar was saying. "The rewards of this game are high, but the stakes are too great. There is only so much damage this family can endure."

"There is greater risk in sitting idle," her mother replied. "You know that as well as I do."

The door to the sitting room banged shut, cutting off sound. With a glance over her shoulder to ensure there were no onlookers, Lila drew closer to the room. She loathed the idea of eavesdropping, and yet something told her this was a conversation she couldn't afford to ignore. She pressed her ear to the smooth wood of the door.

"Sala's been threatened. I've been injured. Where does this end?" Ademar asked, his voice hard. "I just had a conversation with Lila that gives me no comfort. I revile myself for taking part in it."

Lila inhaled sharply. Was that what had brought him here? A troubled conscience? Her stomach twisted, regret mixing with bitter anger. If only he'd shared his thoughts instead of bullying her, but he'd never been one to make his own decisions.

A long pause followed before her mother spoke. "You only did what I asked. We can't afford to lose courage now. There is something afoot in this place."

Ademar gave a short laugh. "You keep saying that, and still I've seen nothing."

"You arrived here too late for that. So did I." Galeeta's voice faded, as if she were pacing farther away. "We did not witness any crime, though I know one occurred, and more are coming."

"Based on what?"

"We are not like humans. They need evidence typed on a form. We can read the signs."

"Like what?" Ademar demanded, impatience sharp in his tone.

"Unexplained graves," Galeeta replied, "trespassing Undead, and rumors that the Magician has passed this way. What more is required to rouse your curiosity?"

"What more indeed, before we find ourselves in an unmarked grave? I can't afford to indulge in speculation. I'm less concerned with imaginary crimes than offending a powerful lord who will be here by sunset."

"And why would he be offended?" her mother's voice sharpened. "We are doing what he asks."

"You're planning to lure him into a trap."

"It's necessary." Her mother heaved an explosive sigh. "I will surrender my own life before I give up my family's safety."

Ademar's voice rose. "But that's exactly what you risk. We are already half our number."

"I don't have a choice. We've lost too much to walk away. With the right throw of the dice, we could be whole again."

"Lila and I are not your game pieces. We did not consent to be used as bait."

The uneven sound of Ademar's footsteps and cane approached the door. Lila shrank away, her cheeks heating with embarrassment. She didn't want to be caught listening at the keyhole, but she refused to run like a guilty schoolgirl.

The heavy door flung open, crashing into the wall. Lila

jumped at the noise, falling back another step as Ademar swept past as fast as his injury would allow. Anything she might have said shriveled at his stormy expression.

He vanished in the direction of his chambers, giving no sign that he'd even noticed she was there. Lila shifted uncertainly from foot to foot, the wake of his anger like a scent in the air.

The brass door handle had left a dent where it smashed into the wall. Lila fingered the damage, wondering at the force of Ademar's rage. He'd called them both game pieces. What exactly had he meant?

Her mother's steps sounded from inside the room. She was pacing like a frustrated cat, back and forth across the polished floor.

Lila pressed her palm to the wood, covering the damage the handle had left. Magic surged beneath her hand, warm and smooth. It only took a whisper of power to heal every flaw. When she pulled her hand away, the panel showed no trace of what had happened.

Her mother had appeared at Lila's elbow, startling her. Lila stifled a curse.

"Very good," Galeeta said. "Thank you."

"It's nothing," Lila replied. "I do this at work all the time."

It was true. She designed and built places—homes, galleries, commercial spaces—much the way Farras had created the way station from living wood. Except, of course, hers didn't include prison cells, and she understood the use of colors beyond black and white.

She looked away from her handiwork and met her mother's eyes. "Shall we talk?"

Apprehension flickered over Galeeta's face—she was no doubt tired of arguing with her children—but she gestured for Lila to enter the room. "Please."

Lila fell into step beside her, stopping only when she reached the windows at the far side of the chamber. The view was a river of emerald forest under a clear blue sky.

Lila put her back to it to face her mother. "What's going on? I know there's more than a simple banquet afoot. Give me respect enough to tell the truth."

Her mother glanced aside as if unwilling to meet Lila's eyes. "Lord Farras sent you a gift. His courier brought it earlier today."

Crossing to a side table, she picked up a cube-shaped box about eight inches across. It was fashioned from pale oak wood deeply carved with leaves and vines.

Lila accepted it reluctantly. "I heard you arguing with Ademar. He accused you of using us as bait."

Her mother cast her a sharp look. "Open your gift before you decide anything. You might change your mind about Lord Farras."

Frowning, Lila balanced the box in one hand and released the brass clasp with the other. The lid sprang open to reveal a lining of padded azure silk. On a velvet cushion of the same hue sat a pair of hair combs glittering with gems. Lila's stomach knotted with anxiety.

The box alone was worth more than Lila's bank balance. The combs must have cost a king's ransom. This was no casual reward for putting on a nice party. The lord definitely wanted something from her.

She snapped the lid shut and carefully placed the box back on the table. "I won't accept anything from Farras."

Galeeta made an exasperated sound. "What has he done to you, one fae to another, to earn such animosity?"

A small spark of surprise made Lila straighten. Despite her clear dislike of the lord, it was the first time her mother had asked the question. "What does it matter to you?"

Galeeta's expression softened. "You're my daughter. I wouldn't ask if I didn't want to know."

Lila hesitated, wanting to push back but knowing it would get them nowhere. With some misgivings, she opted for a plain answer. "Do you remember the time we visited the castle in Gilden Wood? The first time, when King Elroth was in residence?"

"You were about ten," her mother replied, folding her arms over her stomach. "I remember the jester scared you. What was his name?"

"Bronkin." He'd been a twisted, half-mad creature, less a clown than a vengeful imp lurking behind Elroth's throne. Spiteful and cruel to anything weaker than himself, it was as if the jester had been distilled from every dark impulse of the faery court.

"That's right," her mother said. "He liked to leap out from behind the tapestries and startle the servants."

"He bit them."

"So he did. He tried biting one of the king's mastiffs once, but only once."

Lila grimaced. Years later, she'd heard one of the courtiers had finally run Bronkin through with their sword. No one had objected.

"My story actually starts with the jester," Lila said. "He chased me down the castle hall and threatened to feed me to the pigs. I ran out through the kitchen and into the stables to hide. Bronkin didn't like the big warhorses because they'd kick him if he got near."

Her mother grew still, her expression intent. "And then?"

"I barely reached the stalls when I heard one of the horses whinny—not in greeting but with a sound of pain." Lila closed her eyes, remembering the sweet scent of hay and dusty earth. It had been the height of summer. "I ran closer, and I saw Lord Farras with a stick. Not a crop or a riding whip, but a heavy piece of wood. He was screaming at this beautiful chestnut mare. She'd thrown him off when she refused to jump a fence."

"He pushed his horses hard," her mother said softly. "Quite a few were injured when he raced them across the countryside."

Lila's throat tightened at the memory. "He beat this animal until it was lamed. It wasn't about the horse's courage or its skill. This was about making it obey his will."

"You shouldn't have seen that. You were just a child."

"It shouldn't have happened. I was old enough to recognize an evil soul, and it terrified me. I huddled in the straw and cried until Rosemund and Arabelle came to take me back to the castle."

The names felt odd on Lila's tongue. The family rarely spoke of her lost sisters now.

"I healed that horse, you know," Galeeta said with a half-smile. "Arabelle told me what had happened."

"I didn't know that," Lila replied, a strange pressure in her chest. She couldn't name what she felt. Gratitude? Astonishment? "Thank you."

"Arabelle also told King Elroth. That's why he gave you a pony to practice your riding that summer. He didn't want your first experience of Gilden Wood to be spoiled."

It had been a small horse rather than a true pony—a dainty white mare with a braided mane. Lila remembered the king's kind smile, and how he'd gently shown her—in company with her older sisters—how to guide the animal over the forest trails. She hadn't fully understood the rarity of such attention from a king until she was an adult. He'd gone far out of his way to calm the feelings of one small girl.

Her thoughts lingered in the past, remembering her sisters. They'd left to serve the May Queen as her ladies-in-waiting years before Lila struck out for the city. But not long after she started her design job, there had been word they'd disappeared without a trace. She'd joined in the long search for her sisters, along with the rest of House Fernblade. Even King Elroth had stepped in, sending aid, but the two girls had never been found.

Lila dragged her mind back to the present, glad to leave the past where it was. "That's why I hate Farras. He's unfit to dwell among other living creatures. I will thank Father to the end of my days for stopping any suggestion of marriage between us, and I do not understand why you're encouraging him now."

Her mother blinked. "There was a time when children accepted the plans of their betters without question."

"Those days are over." Lila took a deep breath to quiet her pounding pulse. She was hot and cold at once, her muscles rigid with tension. "I want to know why you're involved in his affairs."

Her mother's shoulders sagged. Lila tried to read her expression, but Galeeta seemed to be seeing something in the distance. Her mother crossed to the chairs and sat down slowly, as if every joint hurt.

"Ademar told me that you would be stubborn," Galeeta said. "That I would do far better to simply ask for your help."

"He was right. And it would save time."

"I've been trying to protect you. Protect us." Her mother bent forward, putting her head in her hands. "The less you know, the safer you will be."

Lila yearned to embrace her, but instinct told her to stand her ground. "I need to know everything, or I walk."

Her mother looked up, her eyes bright with tears. "Then please don't hate me for what I've done."

CHAPTER 19

"Our fortunes were—are—declining." Galeeta drew a shaky breath as she began her story. "When I was a child, in the time of King Elroth's grandfather, House Fernblade was the first in wealth and prestige. Even the high lords bowed before us. But the wheel of the universe turns, and other houses took our place."

"Why?" Lila asked. "What happened?"

Her mother shrugged. "There was no one event, except for our complacency. Other houses won more battles, crafted better magic. They had more gold to tempt the learned and talented to their houses. We fell to the second ranks of the Forest Fae, then the third. Once power goes, so does wealth and opportunity."

"We never lacked for anything." Lila pulled a chair close to Galeeta and sat, their knees almost touching.

"No, but adequate is not the same as enough. Not when one has allowed supremacy to slip between one's fingers." Her mother's smile was wry. "Your father didn't mind, as long as there were books and good company to hold his interest. I wanted our legacy back."

Lila barely dared breathe. These were facts she knew, but her mother had never been so direct. "And Farras?"

"He was charming, and he addressed me as if those glorious days had never passed." Her mother leaned back in her chair, her long neck bowed in thought. She was flawlessly lovely, and with an immortal's ageless health.

Lila would never watch her decline the way humans did. And yet, the light within her was dimmed.

"I confess he made a useful tool of my pride," her mother said. "It worked, at first."

It was the most honest thing Lila had ever heard her say. "And then?"

"His friendship was like a charm. Invitations and advancement sprang up like flowers after rain." Galeeta wavered. "But time passed, and I began to hear from others how their dealings with Farras had gone wrong. It was always the same story—at first, he was all smiles. Then debts were suddenly called in. Marriage plans called off. Fortunes collapsed. People grew afraid to cross him."

"Why? Why did he do that?"

"You said it yourself. He desires mastery, whether it's over a horse or another fae."

"Do you know why? What do we even know about him, other than that he is cousin to the king?"

"He came to court many, many years ago. Some said he was a second son, the only survivor of a family murdered by the dark fae. That is all I know. By the time I met him, he was second only to the king and he did not welcome questions." Galeeta's smile was grim. "He has never confessed anything to me, but I believe he hungers for as much power as any fae can possess."

"Royal power?" Lila shivered at the thought. The power of a king or queen was, by virtue of their role, exponentially greater than their most gifted subject. But it came with the crown, either by birth or by conquest. There was no other way to possess it. "That's treason."

"So it is." Galeeta's tone was weary. "I began to pull away, hoping our acquaintance would naturally cool. But he wasn't about to let me go. He made it impossible to deny him anything."

Lila shifted nervously, dreading what came next. "What did he do?"

"By then, your father had been taken by Lord Teegar. I was alone, and I had you children to think of."

"What did Lord Farras do?" Lila said again, the words a mere whisper.

"His lordship had already taken Ademar under his wing. He was sponsoring Ademar's advancement at court and in his studies. Lord Farras has the power to make or break his fortune."

And to set Ademar up when Lord Teegar came calling, but Lila didn't say that.

"He held my son's interests over me, ensuring my loyalty." Her mother's eyes grew flinty with temper. "And then he threatened Sala."

"What?" Lila exclaimed. "How?"

"You said vampires arrived at her door. That was not the first incident."

"But those were Undead."

"Farras rarely dirties his hands directly. They were his hirelings."

"Is that why she tricked me into coming here?" Lila asked, the cold knot in her chest warming to anger.

"Sala has children." Her mother said it as if that answered everything. "She understood what was at stake."

And if Farras could hurt an innocent animal, would he stop at a child? Her nieces and nephews?

"We need your cooperation," her mother continued. "We meant to get it without involving you more deeply than needs be."

"You mean that you intended to leave me ignorant," Lila asked, her voice sharp. "Am I the sacrifice? The child you can afford to lose?"

"No!" Galeeta's voice was a whip-crack. "You're the one who had the strength to leave for the human world. To change and grow. You can hold your own."

Confused, Lila fell silent.

"I need you to convince him of our desire for an alliance." Her mother's voice was calm even as her hands twisted in her lap. "Our survival depends on making him believe we're his loyal followers at the very same time we're plotting his downfall. He is no fool, so it will take all your cunning. As political games go, this is at a master's level."

"I'm not good at games," Lila answered in a small voice.

"You're like your father. More interested in beauty than battles." Her mother's expression was grim. "That is one good reason why it would have been easier if you knew none of this. Now we have no choice but to play the cards we have, and to play them flawlessly."

"Why not simply run? Or tell the king?"

Galeeta sat forward, her face pale. "Farras has threatened my family, and a challenge will force his hand. I will not tolerate a threat to those I love. That is the one unalterable truth."

Lila groped for something that made sense to her. "I still don't understand. If I'm key to this plan—even if I'm a bad actress— why not tell me everything from the first moment I got here?"

"You've been gone for years." Her mother's eyes grew dark with emotion. "I needed to be sure he hadn't turned you against me first. He's compromised at least a third of the great houses of Forest Fae. Maybe even half."

All at once, puzzle pieces began to fit together. It wasn't the words her mother spoke, but the emotion beneath them that triggered understanding. Lila blinked, seeing her mother as if for the first time. Whatever the family's rank and position, Galeeta had never lacked confidence in her own abilities. She would have been certain of her path right up until the moment she was caught in Lord Farras's power.

That moment of realization would have been poison, especially when the price of failure was her own household.

Lila had gone to the city with the same confident pride. She'd believed herself modern and authentic, a maverick breaking with hidebound tradition. She'd closed her ears to anything the fae had to say about it.

She was more like her mother than she cared to admit. Neither of them willingly questioned their course of action.

"You're setting a trap for him," Lila mused.

"I hope so," her mother answered, her voice barely above a whisper. "I'm improvising."

"That's not like you. You're meticulous."

"These are uncharted waters." Her mother gave a nervous laugh. "You mentioned the Magician and how he steals the lives of the young."

"Yes." The sudden change of topic left Lila even more uneasy.

"And you've heard of how the city fae are losing their powers."

"I've heard the stories."

Galeeta rose suddenly, pacing to the window. "Some believe there is a relationship between the two. That the Magician is behind both calamities, and that Lord Farras is involved."

Lila made a wordless exclamation.

Galeeta turned from the window to face Lila, her gaze fierce. "A fae may lose friends and fortune, but if they lose their magic, they lose themselves. If Farras is responsible, we've found his vulnerability—the one thing even his most devoted followers will never forgive."

Her mother was right. With a spark of both hope and terror, Lila began to see Galeeta's plan. "We need evidence."

Her mother reached out, grasping Lila's hands. "Which is why I volunteered to host this banquet. As I said, it gives us an opportunity both to reassure his lordship of our loyalty and to find proof of his guilt."

Lila pondered that for a moment. "Where does that leave Father? Aren't we relying on Lord Farras to plead his case to the king?"

Galeeta's jaw hardened. "If we hand over the Magician, the king will refuse us nothing. I will save Gareth one way or the other, if I have to tear down the royal dungeon stone after stone with my bare hands."

Lila swayed slightly, as if her mother's words were carried by a storm. She searched for a reply, and finally settled on the only one possible.

"What exactly do you need me to do?"

LILA LEFT her mother close to an hour later. Her mind spun from the conversation, and from the amount of things that could go wrong. The sinking sensation in Lila's gut left her sick and giddy. She finally understood Ademar's anger, because his response to fear was to strike out. Hers had always been to run, but that would solve nothing.

Galeeta had finally spoken the truth, or at least most of it. Her mother was a consummate courtier, used to the cut and thrust of the chambers of power, but even Lila could see she was in over her head. Even if she survived and justice was done, Galeeta was guilty by association with Farras.

Worse, her mother's sudden honesty highlighted everything she'd withheld before. Fae were good at half-truths. Lila still wasn't sure how much of the story was missing.

An ache pierced her chest, along with an unspeakable loneliness. She had no family she could rely on. Sala had to protect her children. Ademar was wounded and in an unpredictable mood. It would be up to her to act, to make decisions that would save or doom her family—maybe all the Forest Fae. It was her against Farras with the fate of their people as the banquet's main course.

She needed someone with real-world experience at her back.

She found Rafe in one of the storerooms, where the advance party of Lord Farras's entourage had unloaded a mountain of dry goods. Rafe had been put to work with a broom.

"One of the porters broke a bag of rice," he said, dark head bent as he swept the scattered mess into a dustpan. "In the old legends fae couldn't pass a spill like this without counting every grain, but they walked away just fine."

Lila shook her head. "It's usually the dark fae who get quirky like that."

"Quirky," Rafe muttered, dumping the pan's contents into a garbage can. The silver bracelets rattled against the metal bin. "I'll remember that description next time a phouka tries to make me its dinner."

More porters passed by in the hall, this time carrying deep baskets heaped with fresh greens, carrots, and edible flowers. Preparation for the feast was already underway. Anticipation pulsed in the air, as if the way station itself was aware of new and busy people.

The tension put Lila even more on edge. Rafe looked up, a question in his eyes, as she shut the door to the hallway.

"I have a question," she began, choosing speed over a subtle approach. They didn't have much time.

Rafe leaned the broom against the wall and gave her his full attention. "Okay."

"When you came here, how did you intend to identify the Magician?"

"Smell. He's been here enough to leave his scent behind." Rafe's brow creased. "And he's the type to injure another without a pang of conscience. Whatever their species, stone-cold killers eventually reveal themselves."

Lila didn't bother asking how. "What about his appearance?"

Rafe froze, as if suddenly making a connection. "I suppose I can say I've seen him."

Lila felt her jaw drop, then snapped it closed. "Where?"

"In a video. Security tape from a club. Izetta had it on her phone."

"What did he look like?"

Rafe shifted uncomfortably, as if embarrassed. "Like a fae. Long fair hair."

"And we all look alike." Lila sounded testy even to herself. "I've heard that one before."

"The camera showed him from the back." Rafe shrugged. "If Izetta returns, maybe she will do better."

"If she returns?" Lila asked.

Rafe's expression fell. "Every prisoner dreams of rescue."

"If she comes with an army big enough to stop Lord Farras, I'll throw confetti."

He released a long breath. "If she was going to come, she'd have done it by now."

Worry tightened his features. His friend had been badly hurt. Even if she'd reached the highway, she might not have survived. But if she'd made it and could bring back reinforcements?

Lila liked that idea. Escape. Coordinate an attack. Make a plan. If House Fernblade had trustworthy allies, Lila would be doing the same thing.

"This banquet may end badly," she said softly. "Watch your back."

"Will there be a fight?" he asked, sounding hopeful.

She almost laughed, but she'd seen what a shifter could do—and she might need him to do it. At first, she'd hated Rafe for wounding Ademar, but the wolf was caught in the web of a wider conflict. Just like her.

"I'm almost certain there will be a battle," she replied. "But fae don't always fight with the usual weapons."

He brushed her hair aside with the back of his fingers, lightly touching her cheek. "Then you be careful, too."

"As strange thing for a wolf to say to a fae," she mused.

"You're the best jailor I've had." The corner of his mouth lifted. "And I thought we agreed to be allies."

"We did."

"Good, because despite your family and magic and all the rest, I rather like you."

The words were lightly mocking, but they held genuine warmth. His touch lingered, comforting her when she had nothing else to cling to. She balanced on her toes to touch his lips with hers. His palm, large and rough with calluses, cupped the back of her head. Body heat radiated through the taut fabric of his shirt. So tempting. So inviting. Lila leaned into him, exploring the hard terrain of his chest with her palms.

She opened her mouth to his, exploring his unfamiliar taste. He was fundamentally different from her—entirely alien, according to most fae—and yet they shared common ground. Both of them were rebels.

Both wanted to survive. His kiss all but promised it, pushing the darkness from her mood. A light, sweet sensation threaded through her as he pulled her close.

Allies. Maybe friends. Certainly forbidden fruit.

The moment of peace couldn't last. Breaking the kiss, Lila stepped back. She was short of breath, her mouth tingling as if he'd bruised it. Heat lurked in Rafe's gaze, as if he knew they'd pick this up at a later time.

"I must get ready for tonight," she said, dread already seeping back into her soul. "I need to think."

He caught her hand. "Why did you ask about the Magician?"

Lila opened her mouth to answer, but then stopped herself. All she had were suspicions, and Rafe was bent on vengeance. She had to be careful. "There are a lot of fae coming to the banquet. He might be there. I don't know anything for certain."

"Will you be in danger?" A faint growl rumbled beneath the words.

She winced. "I don't want to think about that answer."

He took her chin in his hand, tilting her head until their gazes locked. "Remember you're not alone. If you're hunting the Magician, you've got friends you haven't met."

CHAPTER 20

Dusk stole into the way station ballroom. It began in the blue shadows among the fronds and vines of Lila's decorations and slowly crept across the room. Candles bloomed and flickered along the tabletops and tiny stars scattered the ceiling and nestled like brilliant blossoms among the greenery.

Rafe watched the fading daylight from one side of the room, where he stood shoulder to shoulder with a long line of fae servants. He had been issued the same gray uniform and stood in the same alert posture, his chin high and his eyes straight ahead. The one difference between him and his fellow servants was the silver bracelets. Though their magic held, with his shirtsleeves acting as a buffer, they no longer burned his skin. The lack of pain had made the head server's endless instructions much easier to follow.

"Do you know what you're supposed to do?" the fae next to him asked without looking around.

The male was shorter than Rafe, his hair a few shades darker than Lila's. He had a pointed nose and a curved lip that made him appear to be always smiling. The servants were less uniformly perfect than the fae nobles—which made them easier to pick out of the crowd. This one had been part of the pair who had escorted him from the guest room to his cell earlier that day. Rafe had given him no trouble. In return, the fae had been reasonably polite.

"I understand the assignment—more or less," Rafe replied. "Play waiter. Don't spill on the guest of honor." He wasn't worried—he'd watch the others and copy what they did. Years in the Silent Wolves had exposed him to many environments, including those where salad forks mattered.

They stopped talking as the cross-looking head server stalked by, checking every uniform. He paused before Rafe, giving him a long look, but could find nothing wrong with Rafe's dress or posture. He moved on with a sniff, his short indigo cape swirling.

"Why am I here?" Rafe muttered.

"Tradition," the fae replied. "Make the prisoners of note serve guests. It's an old school power play to show off the host's standing."

"In other words, I'm an exhibit."

"Exactly," the fae replied, keeping his voice low so that the official in charge of the servants did not hear. "If the lady of the house is putting on that much of a show, tread carefully. When the courtiers start posturing, they lose common sense. It's like dancing around a roomful of rabid squirrels."

Rafe shot him a glance. "That's descriptive."

"That is life in the service of the great and good. I am Asus."

"Rafe."

"I know. I've been instructed to see that you put on an adequate show. Grovel slightly, but not too much. They like their enemies humbled but still worthy of conquest."

"We aim to please?" Rafe replied.

The fae's mouth quirked at one corner, but he didn't say more. At that moment, the last ray of sunlight faded, leaving the room in spangled night. The muted light played over the long tables loaded with silver and gold dishes, touching the rims of goblets studded with rainbow gems. Then, like embers flaring to life, the candle flames brightened until the space was suffused in a warm glow.

As if someone had opened an oven door, the scent of savory spices flooded into the room, making Rafe's mouth water. Others must have smelled it too, as a shuffle went down the ranks, but no one dared to speak. An expectant silence hung in the air, broken only by the creak of the main doors swinging open.

Music started, first a ripple of notes from a wooden flute, then the heartbeat of a drum. The sound drifted from the far end of the room, but Rafe couldn't see the players. The song settled into a stately march. Twin rows of fae, these wearing indigo braided with silver, came down the central aisle of the room at a solemn pace, each bearing a candelabra to light the way. Two by two, they stopped before the long tables and held up their burdens, bathing the aisle in light.

Then Galeeta appeared, one hand resting on Ademar's arm. She was dressed in a flowing emerald gown that shimmered as she moved. Ademar's garments were darkly sober. Behind those two walked Lila, her long hair piled atop her head and pinned with sparkling combs.

Rafe's breath caught. He'd only seen her in ordinary clothes before, but now she dressed the part of a fae lady. A tight-fitting sheath of pale green silk fell to the floor, hugging her slender form. Over it was a sleeveless gown made from gauzy, glittering layers that made her seem to float. It was as if a star had fallen to glide among them on soundless feet. His heartbeat quickened, his senses suddenly, acutely aware of every breath she took.

A few dozen finely dressed fae followed, but nothing about them captured his interest. They stopped before the servants with the candelabra, forming two lines that faced one another on either side of the center aisle. Then the music changed, adding instruments and kicking up the tempo a notch. It was time for the guest of honor to grace them with his presence. It said something about this Lord Farras that he traveled with his own band just in case he needed to enter a room.

The next servants had fancier uniforms and carried a tall pole topped with a golden bird of prey, Lord Farras's banner hanging from its talons. The fae who came next had to be the lord himself. After so much fanfare, Rafe's curiosity was piqued, and he strained to catch a better look. Farras was dressed in cream and gold, his white-blond hair falling straight to his waist. Even from a distance, his presence was a palpable force. The bones of his face were sharply defined, as if all softness had been pared away to leave nothing but steel and will. The others here might be high-born, but Farras was in command.

There weren't many with such obvious charisma. Rafe's imagination replayed the video of the Magician, comparing the two. There were obvious similarities—the coloring, the hair, the lithe fae grace. But too many fae looked alike, and without being able to use scent as an identifier, Rafe couldn't be sure.

As Farras reached the double line of nobles, they bowed low. So did the servants. Asus tugged on Rafe's sleeve until he did the same. Wolves didn't bow, but this was a matter of fitting in. By the time the servants rose again, the company was taking their places at the long tables. Every seat in the vast hall was taken.

Rafe was closest to the high table, which sat at the front of the room on a dais and faced the other tables. Lila sat to Lord Farras's left while Galeeta and Ademar sat to his right. The lord's expression was carefully neutral, but Galeeta could not hide the flash of triumph in her eyes.

Rafe's concentration broke when Asus thrust a golden ewer into his hands. The metal was warm from the steaming water inside it. Asus draped a thick linen towel over his arm and picked up a matching basin.

"Time to earn our bread," the fae said.

A ripple of nerves flashed through Rafe as he followed his guide to the high table. The ewer was heavier than expected, and he had to walk carefully to keep water from splashing over the rim. Lord Farras sat in a high-backed chair more ornate than the rest. Standing to one side of Farras, Asus held out his basin toward Rafe, signaling for him to fill it with the warm water.

"Is this the wolf shifter you spoke of, my lady?" Farras asked Galeeta. His voice was sure and resonant, as if he were used to being heard on a battlefield.

"Indeed, my lord," she replied. "This is the beast that injured my son. As you can see, he is now tamed by our magic."

Rafe's gaze flicked to Lila to find her studying the embroidery on the tablecloth. She was ethereal, her slender arms pale in the candlelight. He'd almost looked away when she lifted her lashes just enough to meet his eyes. Her expression was shuttered, protecting her secrets. He longed to hold her again. The feeling burned like a hot coal in his guts.

Farras washed his hands in the basin, then dried them on the towel Asus offered. From what little Rafe knew of fae customs, this was a ceremonial cleansing. A good guest shed bad energy before sharing a communal meal. It was also practical, since most of the dishes were finger food. Farras finished by handing Asus the damp towel.

With another low bow, the servant rose and muttered a spell. With a mild flash of light, the basin was empty and the towel clean and dry. Rafe's ewer was just as full as before. They moved behind the chairs to stand next to Galeeta, the next in rank at the table. With a bow, they began the hand-washing ritual again.

Lord Farras turned to Lila. "You should be pleased. From what I see so far, your family has arranged a most acceptable welcome."

Lila nodded. "Thank you, my lord. I'm pleased that we were able to accommodate your retinue."

He laughed. "I designed the way station to always have as many rooms as needed, regardless of numbers. It is a complex piece of magic, but well worth the trouble."

"I can see that."

"I trust that you have looked forward to this event with antic-ipation?"

An unreadable expression passed over her features, there and gone in an instant. "I wish I could say so, my lord, but this event came as a surprise."

Ademar coughed. Galeeta signaled another servant to fetch wine.

Lord Farras turned to Galeeta with a feline smile. "Have you been keeping this meeting a secret?"

Lady Galeeta returned his smile. "I was prudent, in the inter-ests of security."

"Of course."

He lifted Lila's hand and kissed it, letting his lips linger a shade too long. Rafe could not blame him. She was all but edible in that damnable confection of a dress. He barely stifled the low growl aching to escape his chest.

Asus and Rafe finished with Ademar and offered the bowl of hot water to Lila. She quickly disengaged Farras's hold and lowered her hands into the basin for a vigorous scrub. Farras's brow furrowed with displeasure, but there was nothing he could say.

Rafe stood to one side of her chair, close enough that the filmy fabric of her dress grazed his wrist. When she finished drying her hands, Lila dropped the towel at Rafe's feet. They both bent to pick it up.

"Outside. Later," she whispered in his ear.

Rafe straightened, eager to read a signal in her gray eyes, but they were cool and placid. She wasn't taking any chances—at least not until after the banquet.

With a polite bow, he followed Asus to the next table, excite-ment tingling in his chest. *Outside. Later.* Whatever was happening at the way station, it was coming to a head.

Rafe welcomed it.

CHAPTER 21

A server placed a platter of aromatic savories before them —spiced dates, wild mushrooms stuffed with herbs, and dabs of rare cheeses on tiny rounds of flatbread. A scatter of roasted hazelnuts nestled with a garnish of wild berries. The dish was as much artwork as food, an opening prelude for the feast to come, but Lila's appetite was long gone. It had perished the moment Ademar spilled the truth that afternoon.

They were watching her—her mother, Ademar, and her mother's ghastly servants. Ever since that moment in the guest chambers, one of them had kept her in their sight. There would be no way to avoid dinner conversation with Lord Farras. She could endure that much, but no more. The moment the dancing started, she'd be gone. From an early age, she'd learned how to use a crowd to escape.

She scanned the room, finding Rafe in the throng. He was easy to spot, his dark hair and powerful build so different from the rest. He was still with the fae servant, carrying hot water from table to table so that each guest was attended to before their dinner was served. Her group would be done eating by the time the two reached the back of the room. Only when the last table was served would the servants have a chance to sample the feast, providing there was any left.

She had a sudden, irrational vision of him beside her, tasting everything from her plate. She wouldn't mind, as long as she could touch him again. She would feed him morsels of cheese and bread, letting her fingertips linger on his soft lips. Heat prickled under her skin, rising up her throat and into her cheeks.

"Are you well, my dear?"

Farras's voice jerked her from her daydream. He looked down at her with mild curiosity in his dark gray eyes. Their color was unusually deep for a fae, more storm cloud than silver.

"A little overwhelmed, to be truthful." That at least was no lie.

"Does the food not tempt you?"

"I am saving myself," she said, hoping it sounded demure. "There are a great many courses."

"Excess is expected on such occasions."

"Is expectation the same as desire?"

He leaned closer, and she could smell his scent. It was rich but sharp, like spicy resin. She longed to pull away, but he had an arm over the back of her chair, effectively closing her in. She felt surrounded by the force of his presence, as if he radiated an electric charge. Some fae bled power like that, but most had the courtesy to keep their magic to themselves.

"Faery feasts are notorious for a reason," he said with the hint of an indulgent smile. "In the old days, they could last for weeks. Legend had it that if a mortal ate at our table, they would be our slave for a hundred years. But I think that was just an excuse to stay for dessert."

She laughed, as was her role as witless female. "Do you have a favorite dessert, my lord?"

"I do not care for sweets," he replied. "At least not the type served on a plate."

"I enjoy tiramisu."

He lifted a brow. "Is that a human food?"

"It is. A delightful one."

"And where did you learn of this marvel?"

"There is an enormous variety of human restaurants available in the city."

He sat back in his seat, releasing her from the shadow of his magic. She rubbed her arms, as if it had left a residue, then stopped when she realized he was watching. Behind his shoulder, her mother was also studying her every move—no doubt wishing Lila was a better actress.

"Have you tried many of these human cuisines?" he asked.

"Quite a few."

His manner softened, as if he let his public persona slip. "I admire your inquisitive spirit. You have chosen to experience the human world, to learn rather than run from it. That is courageous."

Lila raised a brow. "Not many would say that."

He met her gaze. "They do not look beyond their own horizon. You and I see possibilities."

In that moment, she might have liked him if it hadn't been for the pure, cold calculation in his eyes. He was stroking her vanity to see where it got him. *Into a pit of venomous serpents, if I can arrange it.*

"Then explain your vision to me, my lord," Lila said as a cupbearer filled her goblet with wine. "I am eager to learn it from your own lips."

From the corner of her eye, Lila caught Galeeta's sudden alertness. She was listening to every word.

Farras lifted his goblet and waited for Lila to do the same. They touched the jeweled rims and sipped the straw-colored wine. Lila's senses filled with the taste, tangy and mellow with dew-kissed dawns and the scent of rich earth. She set the heavy cup down, already half-drunk on visions of the harvest.

The lord gave the wine an appreciative nod before he set his goblet aside as well. "My concern is always with the safety and security of our people. There have been threats to the tradition and sanctity of the Crown, and my vision, as you say, is to ensure the sacred power of the Forest King is in the right hands. To this end, I travel to join Elroth. As you know, he is retreating to the royal lands in Gilden Wood. In due course, your family will join me."

"And we are delighted to do so," Galeeta broke in. "Our family interests have long been bound by love and war."

"Indeed," Farras replied, a barb beneath his civil tone. He turned to regard Galeeta without quite taking his eyes off Lila. "No doubt that is why you seated your lovely daughter at my side."

Galeeta smiled, though it did not reach her eyes. "She was once your betrothed."

He put his hand over Lila's, casually possessive. "So I recall. I also recall that betrothal was called off by your husband."

Lila's skin grew suddenly clammy. She wanted to run, hard and desperately, into the night air. She tried to slip her hand from beneath Farras's. Without a flicker of emotion, he tightened his grip.

Servants came, removing the first platters and replacing them with towers of bite sized pastries filled with a spiced mix of wild greens. Gold leaf decorated the shells.

"My lord requires your influence with the king," Galeeta replied. "No doubt he would prove more willing once he is free."

Lila jerked her hand away, unable to stand his touch a moment longer. Farras graced her with a sidelong look of amusement.

"Rest easy," he murmured. "You shall have your chance to speak."

"Indeed, I shall," she said stiffly.

"Your father was working against the king," Farras said, now serious. "He was arrested for a reason. He is, or was, in Lord Teegar's employ."

"No!" Lila protested, unable to stop herself. "He isn't like that."

The father she knew was allergic to anything so labor-intensive as treason. But with sudden clarity, she understood Farras had no intention of freeing him. He wasn't useful enough to make the cost worthwhile. Farras seemed to read her thoughts, for he gave a slow nod.

"Lord Teegar is in our dungeons," her mother said, breaking through the heavy silence. "My son captured him and one of his men."

Farras looked from Galeeta to Ademar with the first real sign of interest. Lila exhaled. At last, her family had something Farras wanted—that wasn't her.

"So I understand. I will take custody of Teegar," Farras said, throwing Galeeta a look that said he wasn't going to bargain. "Then I will take him to the king. The royal questioners will uncover the truth, and our loyalty will be proven beyond question."

"That sounds deceptively simple," Lila murmured to herself. Had Teegar actually committed any crimes, or was he just another game piece?

Despite her soft tone, Farras still heard her. One corner of his mouth turned up. "Why dwell on the unpleasant details?"

"Soundly reasoned, my lord," she replied. "Deniability is useful."

He chuckled. "You are more your mother's daughter than you know."

Lila forced a smile, even though cold prickles skittered down her spine.

"No, my lord," she said quietly. "I am not my mother. I will not underestimate you."

For the first time, genuine interest flickered in his eyes. "You are a surprising young lady."

That smile did nothing to ease the cold lump in her stomach.

Farras was as much a predator as any wolf. She bowed her head, pretending to be overawed by his approval.

"There is one thing I do not understand," she said meekly.

"What is that?"

"What did Lord Teegar do to earn your wrath?"

He sat back, eyes narrowing. "Do you not know?"

"No."

Farras tilted his head back, clearly considering how to answer as he studied the softly glowing lights dotting the darkened room. "It is one thing to be ambitious. There are plenty who would take the throne if they could through legitimate means."

"And Lord Teegar? He seems anxious to uphold authority. He is a captain of the King's Guard, after all."

"So he is. If only he were content with that."

"Meaning what?" Lila laughed softly. "Your statement only communicates innuendo, my lord."

"And so it must remain," he replied, leaning forward to clasp her hand and raise it to his lips. "This is hardly dinner conversation."

Farras's lips were soft but strangely cool, as if his blood ran with ice. On his other side, Galeeta watched them with calculating eyes. Clearly, it looked to the world as if she and Farras were happily flirting.

Lila cast about for a civil reply. Farras's arguments were nothing but cobwebs and poison. No doubt Teegar had stood in Farras's way once too often. Now he paid the price and somehow her family had become tangled in that rivalry—among other things. How many webs was Farras weaving, and how many had her mother stumbled into?

She realized she had been holding his gaze far longer than she'd meant to. He rose from his seat, still holding her hand. With a light tug, he bade her to rise.

"Come," he said, loud enough for his voice to carry. "I have eaten enough for the moment. Let there be dancing before more food arrives."

It was customary to break between courses during a long feast. The guests were free to gossip or go outside for fresh air. Usually, the host offered entertainment, games, or—as now—dance. Used to their master's whims, the musicians immediately struck up a stately tune. It began on a reed flute, high and breathy, and was joined by the bell-like sound of a brass-strung harp. The heartbeat of drums followed.

As the noble of highest rank, Farras began to dance first, leading Lila to the broad expanse between the rows of tables. Other couples followed, weaving an intricate pattern of steps as they moved. In one count of beats, the dancers swayed in a circle, capes and gowns glittering in the errant light. In the next, they were in squares, changing partners and back again. Lila spun with Farras, their palms pressed together and bodies almost touching. Then they pushed apart, circling on feet so light they barely made a sound.

Lila loved to dance, and Farras was an accomplished partner. She flowed into the music, feeling the sound of the fae instruments like the current of a stream against her limbs. She spun in place, the marvelous, gauzy silk of her gown floating in a glittering cloud. The whole room was watching her, watching Farras admire her. And he did—with parted lips and a rising flush to his lean cheeks.

She'd forgotten, living and working in the crowded city, what such intense regard was like among her kind. Pride glowed in her blood like strong wine, urging her to forget the danger that lurked just beyond the dance's last bow.

But she quickly sobered as the final measures came on a trill of the flute. Farras drew near, breathing hard and his pupils dark with an expression she could not name. In another male, she'd call it desire. In him, there was something else. Anger? Did he resent that she'd stirred his emotions, even for the few minutes of the dance?

He took her arm, fingers circling like a vice just above her elbow. But before he could speak, one of his men approached, a sealed message in one hand. Farras's grip dropped as he turned away, everything but the message forgotten as he broke the wax seal.

Grateful though she was, his swift change of focus startled Lila. Whatever the letter held, she doubted it would help her. Swift and silent, she faded into the crowd of dancers still milling about the floor, aiming for the side of the hall farthest from her table. From there, she slid through a servant's entrance behind one of the garlanded columns.

Cool night air bathed her face the moment she stepped outside. She closed the door behind her, leaning against it as if she could contain the insanity inside. A sudden, frustrated weariness gripped her, but she forced herself to straighten her spine as she saw movement at the edge of the woods.

She only had one chance to change fate, and this was it.

CHAPTER 22

By the time the pastries reached the last and least of the dinner guests, the nobles were already dancing, and the servers were returning to the kitchen two at a time. Rafe and Asus reached the large room, staffed by a literal army of Farras's cooks, just as the next dish was being plated. An array of spicy curries—red, green, and yellow—steamed in brightly decorated ceramic dishes. The complex scent wafted toward Rafe on a gust of the kitchen's stifling heat. He sneezed, the peppery fragrance teasing and tormenting at once. It smelled good, but not exactly satisfying.

"Vegetarian again?" he muttered. "When do the meat courses start?"

"The light fae do not eat flesh," Asus said primly.

"Dark fae do," Rafe replied.

"They have more in common with beasts."

"Hurray, Team Gravy."

Asus gave him a narrow look, and they both let the matter drop. There was too much commotion to talk, anyway. The kitchen was a hive of frantic activity, forcing the servers into a disordered crowd near the double swing doors that led to the banquet area. Rafe inched his way to the edge of the group, hoping for a wash of cooler air from inside the hall. The uniform he'd been given was beautifully made but clearly designed for less heat.

The door swung open, and he glanced into the hall, turning his face toward the fresher air. The diners were drifting between tables and sharing a few last words before returning to their seats for the next course. Lila was across the room by one of the ivy-covered pillars. She was unmistakable in that sparkling cloud of gauze that passed for a dress. As Rafe watched, she cast a cautious glance over her shoulder and slipped outside.

Rafe stiffened. Why was she leaving now, in the middle of the event? Had something gone wrong?

He rejoined the huddle of servers who were waiting to pick up the next round of platters. In one smooth movement, he slid backward and picked up a clear glass decanter of ruby wine from the table to the left of the double doors. Stealing into the banquet hall, he made his way through the hall as if he meant to deliver the drink to one of the far tables. No one gave him a second glance.

Still, he had to be careful. He thought about taking a knife, but without joints of meat to cut, there weren't any in sight that would serve as a weapon. He was taking a risk as it was.

Instead of following Lila out the same door she had used, he delivered the wine to a table in the far back corner of the hall. His return route took him past another exit that led almost directly into the woods. It was a mark of the fae's confidence in their superior strength that there were no sentries posted at the exits. Magic would keep a prisoner like him from making an escape from the surrounding trees.

He circled through the woods until he could see the long porch where Lila stood, her hands on the rail and her face lifted to the night breeze. Rafe froze, transfixed by the graceful lines of her posture. He had seen her dancing with Farras, and she had been breathtaking then, but alone and unguarded she was even more lovely. There was no display, no artfulness, only her. It took all his willpower to shake off the spell and keep moving.

When she saw him, Lila ducked under the handrail and jumped to the grass, heedless of the three-foot drop. With a sudden burst of speed, she ran to where he stood in the trees. She grabbed his arm to break her momentum and stood close, panting hard.

"How did you know I was here?" she asked.

He shrugged. The alternative was to say something stalkerish —that he couldn't stop looking for her, that he was always aware of where she was. There was no way to say that without sounding, well, like the big bad wolf of human tales.

"Why did you leave?" he asked instead.

She looked back toward the house, as if expecting trouble. "I am to dazzle Lord Farras into treating my family as favorites of his court."

"That should be easy. The dazzling part, at least." He was dazzled just standing beside her, breathing in the intoxicating perfume of her skin. It acted on him like a happy-making drug. He shouldn't feel that way about a fae, but he couldn't help it.

She turned back to him, her gray eyes the shade of smoldering ash. "He might have magic and power enough to seduce half the light fae this side of the Summerlands, but I would rather he forgot my existence."

Lila started down a path that led deeper into the trees, her arms swinging with determined energy. Rafe followed, not sure what was coming next.

"I take it you disagree with your mother and brother about the value of his favor?" he asked tentatively.

She shrugged. "I question whether someone like Farras would truly value an ally who bought their place in his court by hurling their daughter at his feet."

"That's not an uncommon way of striking a bargain, from what I hear," Rafe replied. "Not just among the fae."

She stopped, turning to face him. "It's ridiculous. Regardless of my feelings, there's no guarantee he would keep a promise, dance and smile as I may. I don't want to know him, much less accept his gifts."

Lila pulled out the gem-studded combs that held her hair and tossed them to the ground with a gesture of disgust. The long, pale mass of braids and curls tumbled free. Rafe's fingers twitched, aching to touch it, to bury his nose in the silk and drink in her essence.

"That's why I asked you to meet me," she went on. "Mother wants me to court him and spy on him at the same time."

"What?" Rafe's chin jerked up, as if she'd hit him. "What parent does that?"

"She has her reasons," Lila said quickly. "He's made threats. But I can't stay. I tried to play the game like she asked, but it's not in me. I need to leave. Find help. Somewhere. Somehow."

Leave. The word hit Rafe like a punch to his chest. She'd believed his story and shielded him from the other fae. She'd even become a partner in his quest for the truth of what happened to his pack. But now he realized there was so much more—she'd become the reason he'd endured this captivity. A bottomless void opened up inside him, even as he admitted she was wise to run.

"I will find help for you and your wolves," Lila said softly. "Fae of good conscience won't stand for what's going on here."

She drew a long chain from around her neck—so long that most of it hid beneath the neckline of her gown. It was fine, the angles of the links designed to catch the light. Now Rafe saw it held a tiny key. She unlocked the silver cuffs from his wrists, letting them fall to the ground beside the combs Farras had given her.

The surge of his natural power warmed Rafe like a shot of

strong liquor. Light-headed, he planted his feet wider on the forest loam. Even rubbing his wrists to chase away the ghost of the chains challenged his balance.

Lila grasped his hands in hers. "I know you can't leave the forest, but maybe you can hide until I bring help."

Now he could hide, he could shift, and he could fight. He'd survived missions with less on his side. "Thank you."

He studied her for a long moment, seeing only Lila, only the woman trying to be true to herself. She'd freed him because she couldn't ignore what was right. Like him, she wasn't an easy pack member, always challenging the rules, however much she loved her kin. She deserved his understanding, and whatever help he could give.

"You need to go." He squeezed her hands. "If what you say is true, Farras won't appreciate being abandoned in the middle of dinner."

"I couldn't sit there and watch him preen. Your vampire friend gave me the inspiration to try a different path." Her jaw took on a stubborn angle. "And I haven't forgotten what you said about rescue."

"Let me give you some contacts," Rafe said. "Use my name and they'll send whatever help you need. You don't have to do this alone."

"I'M NOT ALONE," she said. "You've been with me all along."

Lila's stomach tightened with apprehension as Rafe listed names and places where she could look for help. He was opening the door to his world, giving her permission to call in allies and favors. It was an enormous act of trust.

Had she earned it? Rafe's kin had been murdered. He'd been chained. If anyone had the right to bite back, it was her wolf. And yet he had her back. Even by meeting her here, he was taking a monumental risk.

They had stopped in a small clearing where the ancient cedars soared overhead, watchful and whispering. Moonlight filtered through the trees, just bright enough for fae sight to make out Rafe's features. She stepped closer, feeling his warmth like a beacon against the cool night air.

Why was he taking this risk for her? Yes, he'd given his reasons when they'd bargained as mistress and slave, but that conversation had crumbled away like so much dry leather. A new pact had formed in its place, one based on their shared need for answers. But this moment held something else, too. Something earthy, honest, and simple. He wanted her—not for her family or position or magic, but because she was Lila.

The knowledge slid through her veins like sun-warmed honey. She'd done nothing to earn his regard beyond following her own conscience, and that made it all the sweeter. All that lay between them was truth and raw attraction.

She cupped his cheek with her palm, meeting his eyes. A giddy sensation swooped low in her belly, making her catch her breath.

"What?" he asked, sliding one hand to the small of her back.

"Every female should know what it is to be desired by a wolf."

A crooked smile twisted his mouth. "Maybe, maybe not. We're an acquired taste."

She should be running, not standing and talking. Certainly not kissing.

And yet she was, wholeheartedly. He tasted wild, as if the night wind sang in his blood. His rough cheeks burned against her skin, an arousing counterpoint to the softness of his lips. The giddy feeling in her belly settled into a molten heat.

Barely breaking the kiss, Lila found the buttons of his uniform jacket and unfastened them, then set to work on the shirt beneath. She'd sensed his body heat before, but now her fingers brushed the warm skin of his chest. It made her suddenly aware of how flimsy her gown was, how unsuited to the cold woods—and how welcoming his warmth would be along every inch of her flesh.

Lila ran her hands beneath his shirt, stroking the hard muscle. His heart beneath her fingers, a drumbeat of desire that caught her own pulse in its thrall. Her gown was no barrier to the hard thrust of his arousal against her. She sank into the thrumming heat of his caress, leaving no air between them. No space. No distance to bridge.

She pressed her lips to the hollow of his throat, leaving a trail of kisses and tasting salty flesh. Rafe made a noise low in his throat. She felt the vibration beneath her tongue and understood, for an instant, the Undead's erotic need to bite. All at once she wanted—no *needed*—to be one with him, his flesh and hers united.

He slid the frothy outer gown from her shoulders, letting the fine fabric drift to the forest floor like an exotic bird coming to roost. Rafe murmured something too low and soft to be words. An exclamation or a curse—it was all the same. Lila didn't need words to understand his meaning. Beneath the gown was nothing more than a sleeveless shift of moonlight silk, a whisper of modesty. Beneath that was all her.

Rafe swept her from her feet with careless strength, carrying her deep into the trees. A gust of wind sent the branches rustling, as if the night itself inhaled with anticipation. When Rafe set her down, Lila realized her shoes were gone. She'd lost them but couldn't recall where or when and didn't much care. Her toes dug into the soft loam, sensing the dance of roots beneath. Branches dipped around them, so huge they swept the forest floor. It was private here, thick moss and needles drifted inches deep.

Rafe pulled her close, his hands finding the hem of her shift and inching it upward. Lila rose on her tiptoes pressing her body tight to his.

"Are you sure you want this?" he asked, voice as hushed as the forest around them.

"Yes." She said it without thinking, without hesitation. There would be no hiding this from other fae—not without the subtlest of magics—but she didn't care. She wanted the world to know the choices she'd made. Choices were all she had, and this one came from deep inside her.

With the practiced efficiency of shifters, Rafe had shed his clothes. She slid the straps of her shift from her shoulders and let it drop. Her nipples immediately hardened against the cold. He took her left breast in his mouth, gently laving the tip with his tongue. The shock of heat jolted her, drawing a breathy cry from her throat. The sound turned to a moan as he sucked harder, turning the warmth to exquisite pressure. When he finally released her, she barely noticed the cold again. The beat of her enflamed pulse threatened to ignite her core.

He tasted the other breast, the sensation spearing through her until her legs were weak and trembling. Nothing he did was by halves. His scent, musky and wild, grew stronger as they touched. He nipped her neck, the sharp pain mixing so close to pleasure it nearly pushed her over the brink.

He's marked me. She should have been affronted, but just then it seemed sexy as hell.

Lila pulled him down to the soft, mossy ground. Both of them were growing impatient. But then Rafe paused, pushing the hair from her face and studying her, amber wolf-light sparking in his eyes.

"You're impossibly beautiful," he whispered. "Your hair is the color of the moonlight. Your skin shines like you've bathed in the stars."

And when you think I'm not looking, you let down your shield. Right then, your eyes were the saddest I've ever known. But she didn't say it. Her kind were responsible for much of that sorrow, and yet he had let her past his defenses. If only half her tribe had that much spirit.

He bent to kiss the mark he'd made on her neck, running his tongue over the wound. She moaned, her neck arching to expose her throat. A low rumble sounded in his chest, responding to the primal gesture of surrender.

With new urgency, he worked his way over her body. She responded in kind, rising to meet the hard swell of his chest, raking her nails over the breadth of his shoulders and down the narrowing flare to his hips. Every angle of his form was hard and hot and thickly muscled. If she was a creature of the forest, he was the untamed life that dwelled inside it.

Her thighs parted in invitation. Rafe explored the soft inner flesh, nipping, tasting, coaxing a cry from her.

"Please," she gasped.

He entered, her body straining to accept his size. She was ready, but this was—unexpected. She'd heard rumors of the generously made beast-men, whispered tales among women both human and fae. They were true. She gasped, her eyes wide and staring into his. His frank satisfaction at her astonishment was clear.

Then he began to slowly move. She gripped his shoulders, riding the earthquake with a wonderment that quickly melted to elation. Suddenly she was an elemental force, part of a vortex winding tighter and tighter. The movements increased in speed and force, and then she was responding with equal strength, a dancer adding her own steps. She cried out, losing control, every nerve dazzled. Suddenly the glade seemed filled with light, but whether it was magic or simply madness, she could not tell. It went on and on, driving her up and over again before Rafe made a final, long thrust and gave himself to her utterly.

She rolled on top of him, not willing to let him go just yet. His arms folded around her as if she had always belonged just there, her head tucked under his chin, her hair spilling over them like a cloak. She kissed him, tasting the sweat on his skin. He was still breathing heavily, the rise and fall of his strong chest making her burn for him all over again.

This—this unconditional acceptance, this equality, this partnership—was the emotional ballast she'd never had. It took nothing and gave everything, unlike games of power. And even if this moment never came again, it would not fade. Lila closed her eyes. She wasn't ready for this to be just a memory. If only time would stop.

But she couldn't pretend forever.

CHAPTER 23

"*I* need to go." Lila swallowed down the ache in her throat. The words severed the moment, ending the comfort of his embrace. Just like that, the blissful *now* turned to *then*.

"I know," Rafe replied.

She hated herself for breaking the sweet silence, where only the sound of their breath disturbed the forest's hush. They should have lain there, murmuring endearments and wallowing in the newness of their pairing. They should have been looking for the next bridge to cross. Instead, the journey was done.

There was no telling if there would be another encounter. She might return at the head of an army. She might never make it out of the forest. Even if she made it back, what would she find?

Lila slipped from his arms and rose, finding her dress and shoes. She ignored the sparkly overgown, leaving it where it had fallen.

Rafe rolled to his feet and swiftly dressed, every motion tight with apprehension. "Take my jacket. You'll freeze."

"There will be too many questions if you return to the banquet without it."

"I'm free." He held up his wrists, now without the silver cuffs. "I'm not going back inside."

"Good point." She took the jacket. It was too large, but she was immediately warmer.

Rafe lightly held her shoulders as he leaned in and touched his lips to hers. She drank in his heat and wild energy, running her hands along his hard forearms until she grasped his hands. She pulled him close, twining her fingers through his.

"Remember the names I gave you," he murmured. "Go as swift and silent as moonlight falls."

"Is that a blessing?"

He kissed her forehead. "It's a wish we make for our hunters."

Lila wanted to ask more, but if she waited too long, she'd lose the nerve to go at all. With an act of will, she stepped away, keeping his hand in hers until only their fingertips touched.

"Be safe," she said softly.

Then she darted into the trees, turning only once to see Rafe watching her, his white shirt bright against the mottled darkness. The urge to run back to him almost buckled her knees, yet giving in would help nothing. Lila pushed on.

She'd freed him as far as she could, but he was still a prisoner. She had to find help before that could change. Even so, regret at leaving him behind struck like a knife thrust.

She broke into a run, willing branches from her path as she fled. Feet all but silent on the soft forest floor, she aimed for the road. She'd left her car there nights ago—a sleek but sensible Toyota hybrid—and hopefully no one had towed it. There was a spare key fob beneath the rear bumper, protected with a spell. All she had to do was retrieve it, and she'd be on her way.

Lila slowed as her path climbed to the edge of the property. The trees grew sparser, the pale ribbon of the road easier to glimpse beneath the moon. An uncertain prickle ran down her spine as she neared. She was so close. Soon she should see the outline of her silver-gray vehicle. It was no more than thirty yards away.

She paused, panting as she took one last look around before the final sprint to freedom. There were no headlights on the road, no sentries, no one but an owl shifting its grip on a branch above. With a bound, she launched forward, gathering speed. The quicker she moved, the less chance she'd be seen.

The perimeter spell caught her two steps from the road. Lila tripped, her balance swept from beneath her by a tingling wave. The sharp pins and needles ripped a gasp from her throat, but it didn't stop there. Like an electric bolt, the spell threw her into the air, suspending her for an agonizing heartbeat before hurling her back into the trees.

RAFE WATCHED LILA LEAVE, all too aware of every step she put between them. His conscious mind—the one honed for the logic of daredevil missions—knew she had to get to the city. It was the only way to summon help for their families and themselves. And from what he'd seen, it would take professionals to stop a player like Farras. For one thing, his retinue was large enough to count as a small army of fae.

But she hadn't been the first to leave. Izetta—battle-hardened and wise to the city's underground players—had gone for help and not come back. He'd done what he could by giving Lila the names of his friends and allies, but would she be any safer? She certainly wasn't helpless. She was skilled with magic and cool-headed in a fight—Rafe had learned that the hard way.

He followed her path to the road, anyway. She drew him as if the silver cuffs had been replaced by something forged as they lay together. It was stronger than logic or mere protective instinct. They had come together first as allies, then confidantes, and now because they had called to each other, flesh and soul. There had been no conditions, no expectations but their need for each other.

He'd endured enough battles to know the future held no guarantees. And yet, just this once, he wasn't willing to let the slim chance of holding her again slip away.

Rafe moved silently, ghosting between the trees. Loam and cedar scented the air, along with the bitter, exhaust-flavored tang of the road ahead. Above all that was the intoxicating scent of Lila herself. Maybe he followed her just to breathe it in as long as he could.

Soon he would have to concentrate on his own safety. Hiding from the fae, even for a few days, would test his skills to their limits. He hoped Lila would find help quickly.

She picked up speed, moving too fast for him to follow in human form. He quickened his pace as she vanished from sight, grateful for the path that led through the tangle of trees.

The land began to rise, ascending from the natural valley that separated the south side of the way station from the road. A few places were steep enough he grabbed craggy roots and saplings to keep his footing on the slippery ground. He caught sight of Lila once she neared the edge of the property. He smiled at the confident energy in her stride. She was almost free.

When the flash came, he dropped to his belly, covering his head from hard-won instinct. *Detonation.* But not a kind he recognized.

When he looked up, Lila tumbled down the incline like a discarded toy. Rafe sprinted toward her, clambering up the hillside in a shower of stones and leaves. Lila had landed facedown and unmoving beside a stump hidden by ferns. Rafe dropped to his knees beside her, panic an acid taste on his tongue.

His mind raced. What had she said, back in the dungeon? *No living thing can leave this way station without permission.* But wasn't such magic meant to pen intruders? Prisoners? Surely not other fae?

And hadn't she said it was fatal? Gingerly, Rafe brushed the tangle of hair from her face. Her features were slack and smeared with dirt, but she was breathing. He ran his hands beneath her and down her limbs, checking for blood and broken bones, but found nothing. Then he grasped her shoulder, shaking her gently. "Lila?"

The breeze was carrying the burnt-toast stink of magic from the top of the rise. With only the slightest variations, that scent was always the same. It didn't matter who or what cast the spell, it had the same choking stench.

"Lila, wake up!"

He cursed under his breath from sheer relief when her eyes fluttered open. She moaned weakly, her fingers twitching as she gathered herself to sit up.

"Careful." He kept his tone kind but matter-of-fact, the way he'd been trained by the Silent Wolves. "Think before you move. Where does it hurt?"

"Everywhere." With a groan, Lila pushed herself up until she knelt beside the ferns. She squeezed her eyes shut, rubbing her temples. By her sickly pallor, Rafe guessed it was a lucky thing she'd eaten lightly at the banquet.

"What happened?" Rafe asked once she finally opened her eyes again.

Dawning realization crossed her features, collapsing into what looked to him like dread. It took two swallows before she found her voice. "I can't leave. They fixed it so I can't go home."

Rafe inhaled sharply. A wave of rage froze his brain—fury that someone had put her in danger—but he slowly pushed the anger down. He couldn't help her if he couldn't think straight. "Are you physically hurt?"

"No. I'm no good to them dead." She wrapped her arms around herself, as if suddenly chilled to the bone. "But every fae attuned to the security of the way station will have felt the spell activate. We can't stay here. We have to move."

Rafe rose and helped her to her feet. She swayed, letting him take her weight against his side. Slowly, he guided her a step at a time to level ground.

"I don't understand," she ground out. "Mother. Ademar. Why would they do this to me?"

Rafe couldn't guess fae motives, but he understood pack. "There's something they believe only you can give them."

"Lord Farras." She bit out the name. "Or perhaps Farras himself set the trap. I escaped him once, thanks to Father. Maybe there will be no second time."

"What did your father do?" Rafe asked.

"He ended our betrothal." She stopped moving and pulled away as if she'd finally found her balance. "And now he's in prison on ridiculous charges."

The anguish in her voice seared Rafe's heart. "I'm sorry."

"I want to help him." Her chin trembled, and she bit her lower lip to stop it. "I want to save my family. I can't do it by submitting to a monster. Even if I do, he'll never stop."

That sounded unbearably complicated. Rafe put an arm around her shoulders, drawing her close again. She tilted her face up to his. Tears reflected the moonlight and turned her eyes to silver pools. Rafe's chest filled with a swirling sensation, as if he'd been drinking for days.

"No child, willing or not, should be used as a sacrifice," he said. "That goes against pack and nature."

"What about duty?" Tears slid down her cheeks like liquid jewels.

He kissed them away, tasting salt. "You can't save your village from a dragon if you let the dragon eat you first."

She looked down, her long lashes hiding her eyes as the words sank in. Rafe guessed no one had ever given her permission to save herself before now. Except maybe her father? That would explain her grief.

"Then what do I do?" she asked, her voice thick with emotion.

"I can't leave, and I won't pretend they haven't put a leash around my neck. My only option is to fight back."

He held her at arm's length, studying her face. "How would you do that?"

She wiped away her tears with the back of her hand. "If I can't go for help in person, I can get a message out by magic. Or I think I can. It will be risky."

"We need fighters on our side." Rafe's mind raced. If they couldn't find allies from outside the way station, they needed ones from within. Damn Izetta, why wasn't she here with an army of bloodsuckers at her back?

"Everyone here is part of Lord Farras's entourage."

"What other prisoners do you have?" he asked. "Are there other shifters? Undead?"

"Not that I know of. Just other fae."

"Fighters?"

"Traitors."

"According to whom?"

"Good point." A look of pure inspiration crossed her face.

Rafe's heart lifted at the sight.

Lila started back toward the house, fresh purpose in her stride. "How about Captain Teegar of the Royal Guard?"

CHAPTER 24

*L*ila led the way around the side of the way station, where there were few windows and fewer doors. Guests had begun to wander outside for air between the interminable courses, so Rafe and Lila kept their distance from the building, using the trees for cover.

Once they'd reached the southwest corner of the way station, Lila crouched low and pulled Rafe down beside her. She was aware of his physical presence in a way she hadn't been before—the earthy solidity that made her want to curl around him like a tender vine. When his side brushed hers, his body heat sent a wash of desire straight to her core. She mentally shook herself. Her mind needed to be on the task ahead.

Bushes screened them from sight, leaving only enough of a sightline for her to study the house. In what little time she'd had over the last few days, Lila had retraced her steps through the secret passages of the way station. She'd found more than what Ademar had shown her—a labyrinth that had expanded as Farras had magically added rooms for his horde of hangers-on. She wondered if she remembered all the twists and turns.

"What are you searching for?" Rafe whispered.

"See where the wall jogs inward," she said, pointing. "Notice the ground where the lawn meets the trees."

Rafe did as he was told, forehead pleating in concentration. "The grass is trampled, but faintly."

She nodded. It was hard to make out the tracks, but a werewolf's night vision was as good as a fae's.

"What am I looking for?" Rafe asked. "It appears to be a path leading to a blank wall."

"That's exactly what it is. There's a hidden door, and we're going to use it."

Crouching low, they sprinted across the lawn and sank low into the shadow beside the wall. Ears pricked for approaching footfalls, Lila ran her palms across the smooth surface, searching for the entrance and for any magical tripwires. She found one and, with some effort, disarmed it. Then she searched for the door mechanism. To the naked eye, there was nothing. To her inner sight, it was a coin-sized blur of sparking energy waiting for a small pulse of magic to activate the lock.

Once she pressed it, a piece of the wall slid aside, revealing an entrance. Rafe inhaled sharply but followed her inside. Without prompting, the door slid closed behind them while Lila summoned a ball of light.

"Where are we going?" Rafe asked softly.

Lila beckoned. "I had another idea."

She hadn't been in this exact passage before, but she had a good sense of where she needed to go. She started up a flight of narrow stairs, then along two corridors that turned right and right again. Rafe followed, his steps all but silent. Before long, Lila found herself at the entrance to Ademar's secret hidey-hole. The door was ajar, as if he'd left in a hurry. He had a tendency to forget the time when he was deep in his experiments.

She cautiously pushed the door open. The room was much as she'd seen it before, with the crystal shard on his desk and the shelf of dismantled electronics.

"Captain Teegar is somewhere in the cells, and we will find him. But I can also try to get a message out from here," Lila said with more confidence than she felt. What had seemed like an easy win a moment ago was less certain now that she was looking at the equipment. It might work. It might not. She hadn't used a crystal in years.

As if he sensed her apprehension, Rafe held her gaze for a long moment, then nodded. "All you can do is try."

Lila's mouth was dry. "Of course."

"What's all this?" Rafe asked, peering at the shelves. He picked up a ring of heavy keys she didn't recognize. "Are these useful?"

"I don't know," she replied. "They don't look like they fit ordinary locks. They're too big."

Rafe kept them anyway, then moved on to the next shelf. A handful of phones were charging in a power bar. More phones sat to the side in pieces.

"Magic and telecommunications don't mix well," she said. "It's impossible to get bars in here, so Ademar is trying to combine fae power and conventional tools."

Rafe moved in for a closer look, his hand finding hers and giving it a quick, reassuring squeeze. Then he flipped a phone case over to see the silver and black design. Most of the insides were missing. "This was Izetta's."

Lila moved behind the desk. "I'm sorry for that."

With a soft cry of triumph, Rafe unplugged one of the others, which was still in one piece. "This is mine. But you're right. No bars." He stuffed it into his pants pocket.

Lila was barely listening. She could feel the crystal's hum like a vibration in the bones of her skull. It made her teeth ache. "This will take a few minutes, and I need to concentrate. Will you keep watch?"

"Standing guard is what I do best." With a grim smile, he stepped into the passage, pulling the door closed behind him.

Wasting no time, she sat down and examined the crystal. She

had to do this old school since he had no idea how to use Ademar's experimental enhancements. The obelisk-shaped stone sat in the middle of the blotter, the only object besides a stray paperclip. The stone was pink quartz, about a foot tall and the width of her palm at the base. Big enough for long-distance calls, then. This wasn't mind-to-mind communication, but it would leave a message with every crystal keyed to the person the caller wished to reach.

Lila flicked the paperclip to the floor. She was out of practice and couldn't afford the slightest interference. Taking a deep breath, she touched the peak of the stone with one finger and formed a picture of the recipient in her mind. She'd thought long and hard about whom to call. They had to be fae, as only fae used the crystal network. It had to be someone who wasn't likely to be under Lord Farras's control—and from what her mother had said, that narrowed her choices considerably.

Lila hesitated, a deep wash of foreboding sapping her will. Asking for help meant implicating Galeeta and probably Ademar, too. There was a good chance she would damage her family's fortunes beyond repair, but what was the alternative? If Farras won the day, they would be under his thumb forever.

If his plans failed, he would drag her family down with him. Still, this was bigger than House Fernblade. Murder, unjust imprisonment, plots against the Throne—and the Magician, whose name wove through everything. The only way to save her family—and maybe all the Forest Fae—was to put an end to this madness before they dug themselves in deeper. Perhaps the fact that Lila raised the alarm would count for something when it came to judging the guilty.

And there was only one person she knew with enough clout to take down Lord Farras—King Elroth himself. Maybe he had her father, but she was willing to gamble he didn't have the full story. She pictured him as he'd been the day he'd taken her for a ride on his beautiful white horse. He'd been a prince then, laughing, kind-eyed, and patient with her childish prattle. He was as far above her in rank as the stars overhead, but she had to believe in someone. She had to believe in the justice of that man who knew how to be gentle with a child.

A diffuse glow sprang to life at the heart of the crystal, bathing the room in a soft pink glow. Lila sent her consciousness into the heart of the light, steadying herself against the stream of energy. This part reminded her of sledding down a bumpy hill, at least until she got control of the flow. That wasn't easy. Ademar's obsession with crystals showed in the speed and power of the stone.

Only when the energy was smooth and even did she start her message. It came in words and images like a montage—Teegar, Rafe and his Undead friend, the wolf graves, her father, the prison, Farras, and the barrier that trapped her. She held back nothing. She might not get a second chance to tell this story.

Once she was done pouring out her tale, the stone pulsed with light. Lila sat back, releasing a long breath. The stone would take a moment to gather the information into a concise package ready for transmission. Given all she'd had to say, that would take a moment. All she could do was wait.

Impatient, she jumped up and began an inspection of Ademar's clutter, rummaging through the shelves for keys, weapons, or anything she could use. She found some old shirts and pants that looked human-made—possibly something her brother wore if he went into town. They were too big, but infinitely warmer and more practical than the remains of her ballgown. She changed, then found an elastic to confine her hair. A little more searching revealed a pocketknife she tucked into the fleece jacket she grabbed from the back of the door.

By that time, the crystal had stopped pulsing and settled into a steady, muted glow. It was ready to transmit. She sat down again, focusing once more on the message's destination. The glow narrowed to a pinpoint, bright as a miniature sun in the middle of the stone. She cupped her hands around the base, feeling a faint, warm buzz of power. She licked her lips, remembering the rhyme she'd learned as a child.

"Through fire and rain these words do wend, by stone and air the message send."

In truth, she didn't technically need the incantation, but she was rusty. The rhyme helped summon the exact twist of will that triggered her magic. There was a brief pink flare, and the crystal went dark. And then it shattered.

Lila gave a wordless cry and pulled her hands away from where they cupped the stone. With a noise between a crunch and a tinkle, chips of pink quartz collapsed into a heap. *By the Abyss, I broke it!*

Her first reaction was a childhood echo—Ademar's fury that his baby sister had broken his toy. Lila began to shake. Had there been a flaw in the crystal? Or had her clumsy skills ruined sensitive equipment—and her only chance to set things right?

Then again, it might have fractured because of her brother's experiments. Whatever the reason, her message was lost. There was no chance a communication could have gone—and no chance of sending one in the future.

The door opened and Rafe stepped in. "I heard something. What happened?"

The sick feeling in her stomach threatened to worm its way upward. Lila gulped it down. "No luck."

Rafe scanned the pile of shards on the desk, eyebrows rising. "Onto Plan B?"

She silently blessed him for asking no questions. "Plan B."

There was no way to hide what had become of the crystal, so they simply shut the door to Ademar's room and returned to the hidden passageways. The next destination was the basement cells, where they could search for Lord Teegar and any other captives they might be able to free and send for help. There were no guarantees that the perimeter spell would let anyone pass, fae or not. But the fact that Lila had been caught was most likely personal—which was infuriating, but offered a smidgen of hope.

She followed the same path Ademar had taken the night she'd arrived—which seemed months ago, given how much had happened. She opened the door to the entrance hall a mere crack to peer out. It would only take a few seconds to get from the passageway to the door leading to the cells, but this was the moment when they would be the most exposed.

No one was in the entry, although a dull murmur of voices indicated crowds of guests were near. They slid silently into the entry, closing the passageway door behind them. The only obstacle was the staircase landing that jutted a few yards across the checkerboard tile. All they had to do was circle that to reach the door to the downstairs.

Rafe went first, moving with a sinuous grace. Lila followed, the pocketknife she'd found in one hand. It wasn't much of a weapon, but it made her feel better. They darted around the staircase. The scent of mulled wine hung in the entry. No doubt the smaller, main floor kitchen had been pressed into service to prepare the refreshments served outside the banquet hall. That meant servants would be nearby.

Rafe reached the door and pulled it open. Lila was a few seconds behind, so she pushed her ball of light forward to illuminate the steep stairs. He took the first downward step when a bolt of light skimmed over Lila's shoulder with a crack of shifting air. She ducked, whirling to see where it came from just as the spell caught Rafe between the shoulder blades, pitching him forward into the dark. The door slammed shut behind him.

Lila straightened, numb with shock. Lord Farras took a step forward, moving so close their toes brushed.

"Hello, Lila," he said. "We need to talk."

CHAPTER 25

$\mathcal{A}$ chill smile curved Lord Farras's lips, though his eyes showed nothing. Not for the first time, he reminded Lila of a sleek but deadly serpent. She shifted the tiny pocketknife in her hand, hiding it from sight.

"What did you do to Rafe?" she demanded. It was the wrong tone to take with a lord, but she was done being polite. Rafe might be hurt.

"The wolf? Nothing more than a push and a tumble back to the kennel where he belongs."

Anger heated her cheeks. "You had no right."

"Of course, I did. You failed to keep your pet properly leashed," he replied, making every word precise. "And I don't approve of animals in the house."

"I neither need nor desire your approval."

Cool amusement flickered across his face. "As I said, we need to talk."

He reached for her, but she deflected his grasp with a whisper of magic. If the rebuff surprised him, he didn't let it show.

"What if I have no appetite for conversation?" she asked. "I decked the banquet halls and plumped your pillows. I put on a dress and danced with you. What more welcome do you think you deserve?"

"Are you offended because a messenger interrupted our dance?" He laughed. "That was the king's formal invitation for me to join his retinue on the road to Gilden Wood."

"Judging by your expression, I'd say it was a summons."

Now she saw a gratifying spark of anger in his eyes. She straightened her spine an extra inch, refusing to cower. She'd been waiting for this moment since her girlhood.

With a sound of annoyance, Farras seized her wrist so hard she lost feeling in her fingers. She struggled to keep hold of the knife, but her efforts were useless. He plucked it from her fingers and snapped the blade shut with his free hand before dropping it in his pocket. All the while, he held her gaze with a look of barely-banked rage.

"If you must express your outrage," he snarled, "do me the courtesy of using a proper dagger."

With that, he jerked her arm hard enough to make her stumble forward. A pair of fae walked by, but they wore his gray livery and quickly turned their faces away. No one was going to stop Farras, even for a daughter of House Fernblade.

"Where are we going?" She tried to stop, but the marble floor was too slippery to dig in her heels.

"The closest room where private conversation is possible."

She pushed back with her power again, but this time, he was prepared. She might have been attacking a concrete wall with a birthday cake sparkler. His only response was a disgusted grunt.

He shoved her into the kitchen where she'd first encountered Rafe. The location was already in use by a half-dozen servers preparing refreshments. Several were ladling hot spiced wine into goblets. One startled as they barreled in, narrowly missing his feet with the steaming liquid.

"Out!" Farras ordered, pointing toward the door. "I need the room *now.*"

The servants immediately downed their tools and left, not even pausing to mop up the puddle of spilled wine. Farras pushed Lila forward until she bumped against the steel doors of the refrigerator, then finally let her go. She spun to face him, her hands on her hips.

The bright lights of the kitchen bleached all subtlety from the embroidered hues of his silk tunic, washing the cream color to a dirty white. It did nothing to soften his angry pallor.

"I know you tried to leave," he said, taking in her ill-fitting clothes in one sneering glance. "I adjusted the perimeter wards on this property, but anyone who was paying attention felt them activate."

"Why keep me here?" she demanded. "What good does that do?"

The intense smell of the hot wine made her eyes water. She wondered if it was possible to get drunk by inhalation.

"They say a little knowledge is a dangerous thing." His finely-carved features shifted back to his usual expression of mild amusement. "It's a human saying, but true nonetheless. You have an agile mind—better than either of your parents'. I have no idea what information you've managed to piece together about my activities, but I'm disinclined to let you leave right now. Not until your loyalties are assured."

She heard the threat but refused to show her mounting panic. "Ironic, since I can't get anyone to tell me what's going on."

"What *do* you think is going on? And why are you so quick to make an ally of the wolf?" To her surprise, he seemed genuinely curious.

"The wolf—Rafe—came here on the trail of the Magician. He wasn't the first. We found the graves of his pack members in the woods, and no one here knows a thing about how they died." She flung the last words down as a challenge. "Does that mean anything to you?"

His eyes narrowed. "The Magician. I have heard something about him."

"Who is he?" she demanded. "They say he's a light fae."

A brief silence followed. A clutch of partygoers passed outside the window, their raucous laughter bearing witness to the free-flowing drink. Lila wished herself out there with them. Farras cleared his throat, drawing her attention back into the room.

"I don't have an answer for you," Farras replied. "There are a great many theories, but little proof."

That wasn't the same as not knowing. "The shifters and the Undead have tried to stop him. Have the fae?"

He straightened, pacing the few strides to the cooktop and back again. The floor sounded sticky beneath his feet. "Not officially. There have been informal investigations. In most cases, those revealed who the Magician is not."

"He's killing people."

Farras stood, hands on hips, mirroring her pose. "The dead are not fae and, therefore, not our affair."

"You can't be serious."

He paused to push aside the empty wine bottles resting on the counter. "I am. Our concerns are greater. What the Magician has in his arsenal is access to a kind of power the fae have never considered before now. It is not widely known, but what he offers his victims is a drug popularly known as bacchante. It was named after the murderous fangirls of the Greek god Bacchus."

Lila's mouth drifted open. "A drug? We use occasional potions, yes, but what do fae—or any supernatural, for that matter—have to do with drugs? That's a human vice."

"This one is different from the others. As you've no doubt heard, fae power dims when we're surrounded by concrete."

"People say that, but I don't believe it."

Farras gave a slight shake of the head. "Believe it of those with less magic in their blood. They're fading like cheap paint. The drug sharpens magical powers, brings back what's been lost.

Unfortunately, users develop a craving for the rush of magic, especially when they've feared it lost forever."

"It makes them addicts," Lila replied. "The cost doesn't sound appealing."

"Some users claim to see the angels," Lord Farras said with a hint of laughter. "But who believes in such things?"

She shifted her weight to one hip. "I'm being serious."

"So am I." He was instantly sober again. "The important facts are that the drug exists, the Magician sells it, and any who use it are quite prepared to dance to his tune. It gives him influence and the most democratic power of all—wealth."

"And they pay him even if it might be fatal?"

"No one believes the worst will happen to them." Farras shrugged. "The dead are not fae. Humans can't tolerate bacchante at all, but other species experience a euphoric state once or twice before the drug drives them mad."

"That's appalling."

"The Undead are particularly susceptible. After a thousand years, any new experience has great appeal."

Lila swallowed hard, feeling something inside her erode beneath his words. Maybe it was innocence.

"How do you know all this?" She studied Farras. "Are you the Magician?"

There was a beat of silence. "No. No, I am not."

There was no hint of falsehood in the words. Lila wasn't sure if she was reassured or disappointed. "Then how do you know his business?"

"It *is* my business to know everything," he replied. "Especially when there aren't many strings in the fae world that the Magician can't pull. And before you ask me if I intend to stop him, the answer is yes, if the opportunity presents itself, and if I believe it is to my advantage."

"And not because it would spare so many deaths?" Lila's tone grew sharp.

A snatch of song drifted through the window. Someone outside had a flute.

He gave a low laugh. "Is the foolishness of strangers my responsibility?"

"Those who have much, owe much to their fellows."

"Ah, schoolroom morality." He began to pace again, but this time he moved closer, giving her no room to step out of his way. "Are you truly so unaware of your position? I believe I heard Galeeta mention your father's situation."

Lila stiffened until her calf muscles hurt. "She said you would appeal to the king on his behalf."

"And your cooperation is the price of my aid." He smiled, though it held no warmth.

"Cooperation?" she asked, glancing past him toward the door as footsteps sounded outside. No one came in.

"You will support both our houses."

She swallowed down bile. The smell of wine was starting to turn her stomach. "What support can I possibly offer you?"

The clean lines of Farras's face grew sharp. "The only reason I would assist your father is because he belongs to House Fernblade. What your family lacks in fortune is more than balanced by a long magical lineage."

She gave a hollow laugh that sounded more like a moan. "And having us as allies would somehow boost your power base? Don't you have power enough?"

"I think that question has already been asked and answered today. Power is an infinite good. All species understand it, whether it's gold or land or the right to deflower every bride in the village." He lightly brushed her cheek with his fingertips, laughing under his breath when she flinched away. "Ultimately, it guarantees survival. Your enemy's throat is in your jaws instead of the other way around."

Lila jumped as the door opened suddenly, allowing a wash of conversation to enter. Beneath it, she heard the gong announcing the next course. With a frown, Farras turned to see who had disturbed them. Lila sidestepped enough to see it was Ademar, leaning on his cane. High color flushed his cheeks and the top few buttons of his tunic were undone. It was plain he'd been enjoying the wine Farras had brought from his estates in straw-packed crates.

"Ademar!" she said, putting an urgent plea in her voice.

"Lila?" He frowned at the clothes she'd pilfered from his private room. "What is going on?"

She surged toward her brother, eager for any excuse to get away from Farras. The fae lord gripped her elbow before she could get more than a handful of steps.

"We're enjoying a private conversation," Farras replied. "I heard the summons to return to the feast. You should go. We'll join you when we're done here."

Lila widened her eyes, silently pleading for Ademar's aid. That look had always worked when they'd been children—her big brother had never failed to come to her rescue. Even now, when he acknowledged her with the slightest nod, she had hope.

"Did you have a reason to interrupt us?" Farras asked Ademar in a pointed tone.

Ademar bowed, leaning heavily on his cane. "My apologies, milord, there was supposed to be hot wine to serve guests seated in the garden. I promised my mother I would personally find out why it failed to appear."

Farras waved a dismissive hand. "Galeeta is free to place the blame at my feet."

Ademar bowed again, catching Lila's gaze one last time. "Again, I am sorry for the interruption."

Then he made his exit, leaving her alone with Farras. Lila's stomach hollowed out with dismay. All she could do was stare mutely at the door.

"He is a talented pupil," Farras remarked. "He learns quickly."

"Evidently." The word came out as a mere whisper.

"I trained him as a boy," he said. "Riding. Swordsmanship. The beginnings of a proper magical education."

"I remember that."

"I'm sure you do." Farras's tone had lost its edge, as if he meant to make himself agreeable now. "Those summers at the king's palace. You learned how to ride on that little white horse Elroth gave you."

She said nothing, remembering the stables and Farras's lamed steed.

"Your brother resumed his studies with me a few years ago, shortly after you left for the city. His rapid progress shows how your magical bloodline runs true, from the Grand Duchess, through your mother, and onto her children."

"Congratulations on finding an apt pupil."

"I want more than a student," he said, stepping in front of Lila so that she was trapped against the refrigerator once more. "Don't be deliberately obtuse. Not if you want your father back."

"I would rather be dead than have that conversation."

"A bold statement."

"Why was my father arrested?"

"Your father is a good man, but not a wise one. He was arrested for possessing the proceeds of illegal trade."

"My father would never do anything so dishonorable," Lila replied, somehow staying calm. "That's not who he is."

"You may be right. I personally believe he was ignorant of where the gold came from, but the king's justice will never take that fact into account. Your mother knows that, which is why she sought me out as an advocate to clear his name."

Lila's breath caught. For an instant she felt Galeeta's distress as a physical ache. For all their differences, her parents loved one another fiercely. "That explains a great deal."

He shrugged. "Such devotion would be charming if all she wanted was to clear his name. But Galeeta wants a place at the king's table, even if that entails kidnapping a captain of his guard."

Lila said nothing.

His mouth curled into a predatory grin. "If you recall your pretty horse from that long-ago summer, you should also remember that you were promised to me as my bride. Fernblade blood carries strong magic and my lineage is royal. Our children will have every claim to the Crown."

Not without treason. "That marriage promise was annulled."

He held up his hands, weighing two invisible loads. "Join our houses, and I will free your father. Your family will be safe and happy all their days. Refuse me, and I will send them to join the vermin buried in the woods."

Lila's mind skated over the ultimatum, unable to take it in, until her attention snagged on the last few words. "What do you know about the wolves?"

He gave a short, hard laugh. "I built this house. I keep it secure."

"*You killed them.*" She took a stride forward, forcing him to bump into the steel table behind him.

"I put them to sleep, quite literally. It was a tidy and painless end, if that matters to you."

"Why?"

"They were prying where they had no right to go."

"I heard you don't like getting your hands dirty, but why not kill them right away?"

"Because I could do something more interesting. Because I could test variations of the Sleeping Beauty spell on living subjects." His lip curled in distaste. "And because I thought the prisoners might be leverage with the rest of the pack, should I need their services. Sadly, their spies didn't survive long enough to prove useful."

"Spies? They were looking for the Magician," she shot back, glaring up into his face.

Farras blew out an exasperated breath. "Well, he's not here, is he?"

Everything he'd said solidified at once. He wanted the throne. He'd use her to get it. He'd destroy her family if she refused. And he'd killed Rafe's pack.

What wouldn't he do to get his way?

In one smooth motion, Lila reached behind Farras, grabbed one of the bottles still full of wine, and swung. Surprise was on her side. The glass smashed against the lord's skull, sending a shower of blood and merlot across the black and white tiles. He went down, bouncing against the refrigerator as he fell.

Lila jumped back as he slumped at her feet. She dropped the broken bottle and raced for the door.

She may well have doomed them all.

Rafe came to, his skull throbbing as if an ax had split it open. Pain was the first sensation. The second was the taste of blood and dust, as if he'd breathed in the fine grit from the tiled floor.

Recollection seeped back. He'd fallen—been pushed—through the door to the dungeon. After a moment of confusion, he realized he was facedown with his feet still on the bottom step. His forehead felt bruised and the spot between his shoulder blades burned as if it had been struck with a brand. He slowly tucked in his legs and rolled onto his right side. Happily, nothing seemed broken, although the room swam as he stood. He swallowed his rising nausea and pulled his phone from his pocket. Luckily, it was intact, but despite the time display, he wasn't sure how long he'd been unconscious. Maybe a few minutes? Not more than a half hour, but a lot could happen in that time.

Lila. Rafe hadn't seen what happened in the seconds he'd been plunging down the stairs, but the result was clear. Someone had her.

A series of images flashed through his mind—Lila dancing, Lila at the graves in the woods, Lila soft and welcoming beneath him. She didn't belong in a cage, any more than the wind or rain. Any more than a wolf. A low snarl ripped from Rafe's throat as he considered his next move.

The only light came from dim sconces sunk into the walls at distant intervals. It was enough to see the door at the top of the steps was closed. It was probably locked, but he had to try it anyhow.

As he reached for the stair rail to climb back up, his knuckles hit something hard. He stepped back, confused, then reached again more slowly. It was like bumping into an invisible brick wall a quarter of the way up the stairs. Feeling a little like a French mime, he felt his way from one side of the stairwell to the other, from the steps to as high as he could reach. While his eyes saw nothing, his fingers told him the story of a wall—rough, cold, and tingling with wild energy that raised the hair along his forearms. Whoever had pushed Rafe down meant him to stay down.

Cursing, Rafe backed away from the stairs. Lila was on the other side of that barrier, and instinct begged him to hurl himself at it until it gave way. How strong could an obstacle be if he couldn't even see it? But this was magic, and brute force wouldn't work. He'd have to reason his way past.

He sucked in a breath, forcing himself to think. There were other exits. He'd used some of them in company with his jailors. If he could get out of the basement, he could search for Lila. And he'd take advantage of the search. They'd been on their way here to hunt for Teegar and finding the captain still mattered. Rafe would check the cells while he looked for a way out.

He set off at a brisk pace. He remembered Lila telling him about a confusion spell that kept intruders from finding their way through the dungeon. Since he'd usually been escorted in and out, he hadn't personally suffered its effects. Still, he didn't want to waste time going in circles. When he got to the first corner, he took out the ring of keys he'd found in Ademar's office and scored a mark on the wall. Then he kept going, memory telling him to veer right.

The cells were widely spaced, only one or two doors a side down each hallway. Rafe stopped at the first few, listening for signs of life behind the steel doors. He didn't have one of the fobs that activated the keypads, but he checked the doors for old-fashioned key locks, just in case one of the keys on the ring might prove useful. By the time he checked a half-dozen cells, a sense of futility crept over him. There were no keyholes and no sounds. More to the point, he wasn't finding any exits.

At the next turn, he left two short marks. At the next, he left three. Not a sophisticated system, but it would do. He checked a dozen more cells and was on his way to his fourth corner—how big was this place?—when the sound of footfalls froze him in place. *Step-step-click. Step-step-click.* A man with a cane. Lila's brother.

Sound bounced off the hard surfaces of the corridor, making it hard to tell which direction Ademar was coming from. Rafe pressed himself against the wall, making himself as small as possible as he peered around the corner. It was only then he noticed the faint scratch in the paint. Rafe's stomach dropped. It was the single mark telling him he'd gone in a circle and was no closer to getting out. *Fido's balls!*

He slid around the corner, but it was a miscalculation. Ademar entered the passage from the other direction. Rafe fell back a step while the fae stopped cold, his expression thunderous.

"Face to face at last and without my sister to save you," Ademar drawled. "Unlucky dog."

The possibility of violence hung like a fog in the air. Rafe was unchained and free to shift, but Ademar was too close. The fae would be on him before he fully changed. Rafe had no gun, no knife, nothing but his phone, and he'd never heard of texting a fae to death. Then his hand slid into his pocket and found the bundle of keys. They were almost as good as brass knuckles.

Ademar limped closer, his eyes dark with hatred. "You have no idea how much pleasure I'd find in reducing you to a carpet stain."

Rafe pulled the bundle of keys from his pocket, then closed his fist so the points stuck out from between his fingers. "You won't find me such easy prey."

"Good luck with that." Ademar flicked his hand.

A circle of blue flame ignited around Rafe's feet, penning him where he stood. The fire was blazing hot but left no mark on the floor or walls. Rafe shuffled his feet, inching his boots away from the heat. Smirking, Ademar shrank the circle another inch, clearly prepared to make a game of toast-the-wolf. Then he caught sight of the keys in Rafe's grip, and his brows dipped in fury.

"Give me those," the fae snapped.

The metal ripped from Rafe's fingers, taking skin and leaving deep scratches behind. The bundle flew to Ademar's palm, where he inspected the ring, clearly checking the keys were all there. "You were in my study. I assume Lila took you there."

Rafe said nothing, just closed his fist around his smarting fingers.

"Well?" Ademar shifted forward, leaning on the cane. The jewels dotting the embroidery of his tunic winked coldly in the cheerless light.

"I follow where Lila leads."

Ademar shot him a look of pure loathing as he stuffed the keys in his pocket. "So you do, and she has little protection in this place. Your loyalty to my sister is the only reason you're still breathing."

"Not everyone shares your sentiment," Rafe replied. "Someone pushed me down the stairs."

"Lord Farras," Ademar replied. "I saw them together in the

kitchen. She detests him even more than I hate you, and that's saying something."

"Then why leave her in his company?"

Rafe studied Ademar, comparing him to the video of the Magician. He was tall and fair. He could imagine him moving with the grace and energy of the enemy. And Lila's brother would do what it took to survive. Was selling poison to wolf cubs beyond him? There was no telling with the fae.

"Lila is my sister, and I don't answer to you, wolf." The flames inched closer to Rafe's flesh. "And you don't understand the complexities of the game I play."

"No, I really don't." The heat intensified. Sweat rolled down the small of Rafe's back.

Ademar's mouth twisted. "Well, here is the simple version. Lord Farras is a dangerous enemy, and he already suspects that I don't share his every opinion."

"How do you know?"

"I'm sure Lila mentioned that he left me on my own to capture Captain Teegar of the Royal Guard. It was a test I couldn't afford to fail. As a result, I'm implicated in his schemes. I'm not a free actor."

"What does he want?"

"Farras plans to crown himself king before he's done. He'll crush anyone to do it." Ademar shrugged. "Correction, he'll get his hangers-on to do the crushing. Milord does not dirty his hands."

"Is this a confession or a preamble to incinerating me?" Rafe asked. "I always worry when I get information for free."

"Oh, don't worry." Ademar's smile chilled Rafe to the pit of his stomach. "You'll pay for this. What were you and Lila doing in my study?"

Rafe thought of a dozen lies, but opted for the truth. He couldn't yet see where this was going. "We were looking for help.

She wanted to send a message. Find someone to slow Farras's roll. I don't think it worked."

"Of course not. She's no idea how my system works." Ademar muttered something under his breath about delicate equipment and amateurs. "And when it failed?"

"We planned to get a message out a different way."

Ademar grimaced. "Release a fae prisoner to make it past the perimeter spells?"

Lila's brother was quick. Rafe had to give him that. He nodded, doing his best to ignore the smell of his boots' soles starting to melt.

"Lord Teegar?" Ademar asked sharply. "He is a traitor."

"According to Lord Farras. Do you trust his opinion?"

Ademar jammed a hand through his fair hair. "I don't know."

Rafe thought carefully before he spoke again. "Can Teegar be trusted to leave here and find backup? Will that backup be someone who will help your family so you don't have to tie your-self in knots for a lord you don't respect?"

Ademar's eyes narrowed. "Be careful how you speak of your betters."

The flames shot high for a heartbeat, dazzling Rafe's eyes. He clamped his jaw shut, willing down his roar of fury. Then the fire faded to its previous size. Ademar leaned against the wall, a predatory smirk on his face.

"Fine." Rafe's throat ached with thirst. "I know you and I have very little in common, but we share one thing. We both want safety for our packs."

"So?"

"You say you're not a free actor, but you're not powerless. If you want change, then make it happen."

Ademar straightened from his slouch and gripped the handle of his sword cane, as if he meant to draw the weapon. But then the fae went still and silent for so long that Rafe began to wonder if he'd ever speak.

Finally, Ademar released his grip on the sword. "You're too useful to kill. Not yet. If I let you go, swear you will protect Lila. You took that capability from me, wolf."

"Fair enough." Rafe could have argued the last point, but it was clear Ademar cared for his sister. That would have to do. "You have my word."

The fire at Rafe's feet blinked out as suddenly as it had flared. He almost cried out in relief.

"Follow me," Ademar ordered.

Rafe did, but kept more than an arm's length from the fae. They were having a moment of tolerance, but that was hardly trust. Ademar turned, and turned again, leading him to a part of the dungeon Rafe did not remember. Finally, they stopped before a door a little larger than the rest.

Ademar drew a fob from his pocket, identical to the one Rafe had used to free Izetta. The fae waved it over the keypad and entered a code—a different one than Rafe remembered from the other cells. Clearly, this cell held a special prisoner, because the locks were more complex. When the light beside the pad turned from red to green, a small panel the size of a large postage stamp slid open beside the door, revealing a keyhole.

Ademar flipped through the key ring he'd taken from Rafe and selected a large iron key. He turned it in the lock, selected another, and repeated the process. Only then did the panel at the top of the door swoosh open, revealing the cell inside. Ademar pushed the button that released the lock and stepped aside as the heavy steel door swung open.

He gestured for Rafe to step inside. "He's yours now. I have no intention of being present when he makes his escape. I suggest he use the exit at the end of this corridor. It leads directly to the woods."

Rafe glanced down the hall. There was indeed a door there. Then he looked from the fae to the cell, where a figure lay sleeping on a narrow bunk like the one Rafe used. Something wasn't adding up.

Rafe started with the obvious. "Why isn't he awake?"

"A spell." A flash of what might have been regret crossed Ademar's face. "The soldier we captured the same night did not survive it. He caught it right in the face and stopped breathing."

Rafe's stomach tightened. "How do I get the captain out of here?"

"No need to wake him with a kiss, if that's what you're worried about." Ademar held up the ring by the largest key. "This is iron coated in wax. Scrape the wax off and press the raw iron to his skin. Fae are allergic. Plus, iron counters our magic, including the sleeping spell I used. Teegar will wake up screaming, but he'll wake."

"Are you sure?"

"Mostly, but he's your problem now." Ademar held out the keys. "I was never here."

Rafe reluctantly accepted the ring. "I know nothing about magic. Shouldn't you be here in case of an emergency?"

A bitter smile curled the fae's lips. "You wanted Teegar; you have Teegar. If Farras comes for his prisoner, I will be nowhere nearby."

"Blame the wolf."

"Why not?" He made another gesture toward the open doorway.

Rafe stayed glued to the ground. The only encouraging sign was that Teegar's chest rose and fell. At least he was alive.

Ademar's smile broadened into something fierce. "Don't you trust me?"

Rafe looked inside the cell, imagining what would happen the moment he crossed the threshold with Ademar outside. The fae had already killed one of his own kind with his spell—no telling what he'd do to a creature he loathed, especially when Lila was nowhere in sight.

"If you want change, then make it happen," Ademar quipped, turning Rafe's words back on him. "You and I have cooperated as far as we're going to. Now it's time to put our plans into action. And our promises."

Rafe met his eyes and found nothing there but anger. "I keep my promises," Rafe said.

"Good for you."

"Good for Lila, you mean."

Finally, Ademar nodded. It was all the reassurance Rafe was going to get.

Heart pounding, he stepped inside the cell.

CHAPTER 27

Good evening, gentlecreatures of the night. This is Errata Jones, and I'm recording this podcast live on scene as forces gather at the roadside just outside the border of the valley where a fae way station hides behind a spell of invisibility. The object of this mission is to free prisoners held by the fae and to capture the criminal known as the Magician and any associates we can find. An eyewitness account detailed in episode seven of this podcast series confirms the danger posed by the fae residents within the compound, including violent assault, confinement, and torture. What we have on our side is a significant force of vampires and wolf shifters who are highly motivated to see tonight's action through. What we don't have is enough hours until daylight because carpooling two rival species and their weaponry took longer than loading incontinent toddlers onto a bus for their first day at playschool.

Izetta ducked under a low-hanging tree limb. It was past midnight and the moon had faded, but she could see plenty from her position halfway between the road and the way station. The Undead had volunteered for scout duty since they were able to cross the perimeter spell without harm. Izetta was perched on a rise that offered a clear view of the house.

The place stirred up a mix of dread and rage that left her hollow and hungry. She'd come too close to her final end on these grounds, and she'd be just as happy never to set foot here again. But Rafe was inside, and she wasn't leaving without the wolf. She'd given her word.

There had been just enough time for her supplier to courier fresh ointment so that every member of the strike team could see past the glamour concealing the way station. Unfortunately, what it revealed was far more than anyone anticipated. It looked as if the enemy was throwing a party, and a few hundred of their besties had shown up. An entire field was parked up with an eclectic mix of vehicles, from e-bikes to horses to an old Volkswagen bus. It was a far cry from Malatest's matchy-matchy fleet of shiny black SUVs, and yet somehow more disturbing. For all their elegance, the fae had a chaotic streak that magnified their danger.

As she watched, several sets of doors opened and the party-goers spilled outside, wine goblets in hand. The smell of spices floated out, hinting at a meal inside. It seemed like a typical celebration, with laughter, music, and plenty of drink. A few lit up the long, skinny clay pipes the fae seemed to prefer. All of them were dressed in rich, brilliant colors glittering with jewels.

But why were they there? Up to this point, the activities at the way station had been secretive. What in the name of the Old Gods was going on? And where would she find Rafe?

Errata joined her, her approach as silent as any of the Undead. The only difference in her perfect stillness was the aura of heat that marked her as a living creature. She wore the magic-busting amulet in plain view, as if she wanted to make certain it worked.

"Who are all those people?" Errata asked, her voice barely above a whisper.

"Someone with a title has come to visit," Izetta replied, fingering the set of iron handcuffs tucked into her belt. "Look, you can see there are servants in livery."

"I don't see any patrols."

"That's because they think they're invisible."

Errata sniffed. "Arrogant."

"Yup."

The werecougar's attention shifted suddenly to the left. Izetta heard the rustling noise, too. Anywhere else, she would have assumed it was an animal. Here, though, a wild beast didn't fit. It was coming from too close to the building, and no creature—present company excepted—approached a gathering of fae uninvited. Not even a raccoon.

The wild card creeping away from the way station had to be investigated. They both rose, moving from a crouch to a silent drift toward the noise. It sounded like—she couldn't exactly say, but it started and stopped at random intervals. And it wasn't traveling in a straight line, although the general direction was taking them toward the road.

"I'm going for a better look," Izetta murmured, and launched herself toward the treetops.

Vampire flight was excellent for floating from one rooftop to the next, cloak a-flutter. It had limited use in a crowded forest, where branches snagged hair and clothes. Even so, Izetta threaded her way through the hazards until she came to rest in an oak just ahead of the wild card's path.

She had both feet on a gnarled limb and one hand on the trunk, ready to leap when the bush below swayed. Izetta tensed, then watched with amazement as a tall fae staggered out of the undergrowth, wearing nothing but loose-fitting pants and a baggy shirt. If the figure had been human, she'd say he was seriously drunk, but it took dedicated drinking for a fae to get so much as tipsy. Bacchante? She didn't think so—it had given poor old Chuck a rush of wild energy, and this dude looked anything but energetic as he tripped and fell to his knees in the mud.

Errata was ghosting through the brush below, barely disturbing a leaf as she passed. Izetta signaled, indicating their quarry was found and that the werecougar should cut off his retreat. Not that he was going anywhere quickly. Izetta watched as he struggled to his feet and slapped at the bits of bark and dirt clinging to his pant legs. Then he cast a nervous glance over his shoulder and doggedly lurched forward again.

Izetta stepped off the branch, landing lightly in his path. He fell back, arms wide to keep his balance. From this angle, she could see he was athletic, more heavily muscled than most fae, but badly disheveled. His hair was pulling out of its ponytail, leaving limp strands to fall in his face.

"Get out of my way," he snarled. His speech was slurred, as if his tongue was as uncoordinated as the rest of him.

"No," Izetta replied. "Where do you think you're going?"

"None of your concern." Eyes blazing, he pushed the straggles of blond hair out of his face. There were marks on his wrists as if he'd been bound. An escaped prisoner, then?

"I don't blame you for leaving," Izetta said. "The room service here sucks."

He gave a muffled snort of laughter. "Stand aside."

Errata emerged behind him, eyes glowing yellow in the fugitive light. When she cleared her throat, the fae spun and fumbled for a sword hilt that wasn't there. He caught his balance and dropped into a fighting stance. The cat danced out of reach as he lunged to grab her but caught the amulet instead. Errata lashed out with claws.

Izetta pounced, using the fae's forward motion to knock him facedown. She was a foot shorter and much lighter, but leverage was everything. Errata held him in place while they bound his hands with iron cuffs and hauled him to his feet.

"You're coming with us," Errata said, shoving him forward.

The fae stumbled, nearly taking the werecougar with him. "Stop. I've been asleep. They put me to sleep. When I woke up, nothing worked right."

"A spell hangover?" Izetta asked.

He nodded, then blinked as a curtain of hair fell in his face. He'd lost his hair clip and with his hands bound, he couldn't push the long mop out of his eyes.

"Move." Errata pushed again, but more gently this time. "We'll get you out of here."

That seemed to be enough to convince him to cooperate. They started toward the road, the fae walking at a smooth pace now that he had someone helping him. Izetta fell in behind them, but paused when a dull sheen of silver caught her eye. The fae's hair clip. She picked it up, shoving it in her pocket, and hurried to catch up.

She took over steering the fae when they reached the road, where the vamps and wolves waited for the vampire scouts to report back. It was only then she noticed Errata's amulet was gone.

"Where's your amulet?" Izetta asked.

The werecougar put a hand to her throat and cursed. She was trapped inside the perimeter.

"He must have broken the clasp when he grabbed it." The cat gave the fae a shove.

"Retrace your steps," Izetta suggested. "I can manage our prisoner from here."

With a sharp nod, Errata turned back and Izetta guided the bound fae to the road. She felt a faint tingle as she stepped from the forest, as if she'd passed through a magnetic field. Even if the perimeter spell didn't zap the Undead to a crisp, it sent a shiver of dread down her spine.

"Who is this?" Malatest asked as they approached.

He leaned against the front of his car, checking the edge of a sleek-looking boot knife. Izetta had to hand it to Malatest—when the going got nasty, he wasn't afraid to pitch in. More vampires drifted aimlessly around the double row of vehicles—vamps on one side, wolves on the other—waiting for orders.

"We found him scampering toward freedom and decided to help him along." Izetta finally let the fae go.

The fae glanced from Malatest to Izetta, blinking through his hair. Though he was still cuffed, he seemed to catch his balance more quickly now, as if the sleep spell was finally letting go.

"Who are you?" Malatest asked, straightening from his slouch with the grace of a serpent. He still held the knife.

The fae didn't answer immediately, seeming to frame his reply before he spoke. "I am Captain Teegar."

"And why should we let you live?"

"I'm not your enemy. I was taken captive and held illegally."

"By your pointy-eared king?" Malatest poked him with the knife tip. "How many fae kings are there again? Four for the light and four for the dark? I can never keep track."

Teegar flinched at the flagrant lack of respect, but wisely held his temper in check. "I was taken by the agents of Lord Farras. He is a traitor with designs on the life of His Royal Majesty."

"Is that who is having the party?" Malatest continued. "This Farras guy? Who is he, besides a traitor?"

Teegar shrugged. "Humans would call him a confidence man, except with more killing."

A brief silence followed the statement. Malatest looked impressed.

"How did you get out of the way station?" Izetta asked. "I've been in that dungeon. It's no joke."

"A wolf shifter woke me from the spell. He was not working alone."

"Rafe?"

"Devries," Malatest called. "You need to hear this."

Rafe's father emerged from behind one of the pickup trucks. "What?"

"News of your boy." Malatest pointed the tip of his knife at Teegar.

The fae licked his lips, clearly nervous. "He called himself Rafe. He woke me and led me to freedom."

Devries huffed out a relieved breath. Izetta felt a knot inside her loosen, but not by much. She still had too many questions to relax. The first was why this captain of the Royal Guard hadn't even asked what an army of supernatural predators was doing on the way station's doorstep.

"Now that you know who I am," Teegar said, "please let me go. I must be freed to warn His Majesty there is treachery afoot. That was why your wolf let me go. To summon aid as fast as possible."

"Do you need to borrow my phone?" Malatest asked dryly.

Panic rounded the fae's eyes—or maybe it was a hangover from the spell that had held him prisoner. Either way, he looked jittery and confused. "A phone would not reach His Majesty, or anyone in his party."

Both Izetta and Malatest crowded closer to Teegar. Devries joined them, making a perfect circle of intimidation.

"Where is this king of yours?" Devries asked.

The fae was visibly sweating now. "His Majesty is on the road to his private domain."

"If he's already out of cell range, how are you going to get there?" Izetta asked.

He tried to toss the hair from his eyes again. "I will run on bare feet if I need to."

She didn't doubt it. He wanted to get away just as quickly as he could. But he was a captain, and generally officers had better planning skills. He could, say, ask for a ride in one of the many vehicles parked right there. Or, he could keep his mouth shut about his boss's movements like every other security detail on the planet. "How far do you need to go?"

Defiance entered the fae's eyes. "Our roads can't be measured in miles."

In other words, he wasn't about to give a straight answer.

"I have a better idea." Malatest finally sheathed his knife. "You'll stay with us."

Teegar's face fell. "Why?"

"You know the layout of the building, and we need to get inside. You're going to lead the way."

CHAPTER 28

*L*ila tore down the stairs to the dungeon, stumbling in her haste. After the blast Farras delivered, she half-expected Rafe to be sprawled at the bottom, but there was no one in sight. Was he unhurt, or had someone dragged him away? Jumping down the last few steps, she knelt and examined the tile. There was a smear of blood, but not much. That was something, at least.

Anxiety clawed her. She'd knocked Farras out, but he wouldn't remain unconscious for long. And when he woke, he'd show no mercy. She didn't have long to act.

She rose to her feet, wondering again where Rafe had gone. The house's magic would have made it next to impossible for him to return upstairs. Captive or free, he was most likely still on this level.

Lila followed her usual route through the dungeon, watching the shadows and moving as quickly as she dared. The place was as bleak as ever. The widely spaced lights showed nothing but tile floor and featureless paint, without even a cobweb to give the place personality.

Still, her fae senses caught a shift in energies. It was as hard to describe as the shape of a thought or the movement of song through air, but it was perceptible. The way station felt restless, folding and reforming in subtle ways. When she stopped at Rafe's old cell, ambient magic was all but absent. The room was empty, and the building knew it. Lila moved on.

The next cell she stopped at was the one where she'd seen packing crates stacked against the wall. At the time, she hadn't had a reason to or time to investigate them. But now, after what Farras had told her about the drugs, she was curious enough to have a second look. She opened the door, using her fob and key code, and the overhead light came on as usual. The cell was empty and scrupulously clean, as if an army of pixies had gone over it with toothbrushes.

Frustrated, Lila left and pulled the door shut. The absence of evidence proved nothing, but it stoked her suspicions. Even if Ademar, Farras, and her mother claimed to know nothing about the Magician's presence at the way station, the wolves *had* tracked him there. It seemed too convenient that the crates disappeared the moment she'd asked questions. Then again, they might have held food for the banquet or rolls of duct tape for all she knew. She'd been too slow to investigate, and now she'd lost her chance.

Cursing, Lila pressed on. The confusion spell in this part of the dungeon had weakened, at least for her. She'd been down those corridors too often now for misdirection to work. She continued to check the cells as she went, looking for Rafe and also for Teegar. She found no one and nothing.

She stopped at the last door, frustrated. There might still be a chance to find outside help, but the window of opportunity was closing. Where were the prisoners? Where was Rafe? They had to be hidden behind the shifting veil of the way station's power.

Half-wild with frustration, Lila reached out, touching the living consciousness of the structure. Farras had summoned the place out of the surrounding forest, exactly the same way she shaped wood in her construction designs. The lord was far older than she was, his magic stronger and more sophisticated, but their power was similar enough that she understood every twist in the spell's weave. She hoped that was enough to get the building's cooperation. *You're made of magic. My kind of magic. Help me out.*

Her awareness bumped against a fold of energy, thicker and twice as opaque as the rest. It was keeping her—and anyone else—from freely wandering past the door where she stood. Even so, she sensed her brother had been there recently. Maybe only minutes ago.

Lila deepened her contact with the flow of power. The sensation of pins and needles swept over her skin, then beneath it, reaching deep into her bones. With as much delicacy as her impatience allowed, she pushed against the magic's flow, making herself a path.

A hallway appeared before her—one that hadn't been there a moment ago. It looked the same as the others, with bad lighting and steel doors. This time, though, she could feel life. She'd found prisoners. *I don't have much time.*

An image rose in her mind, but it was of the graves in the woods. Confused, Lila touched one door, then the next in hopes of something more. Something that would make the vision make sense. The third door stopped her in her tracks. The specifics of the image faded, replaced by the sensation of fur under her hands and cold wind in her face. Then it was *her* paws padding on the forest floor, *her* voice lifted in chorus with the pack.

Lila staggered back, shaking her head to clear it. Her perception swirled, jumbling realities for a giddy moment until she was sure what was here and now and what was *other*. By Titania's wingtips, she'd found more of Rafe's pack.

She pulled her necklace from beneath her shirt. The electronic fob for the cells still dangled from the long chain. She swiped the fob and punched the code into the keypad, praying this door used the same number sequence she knew.

When the metal panel slid open and she peered inside, she saw the room was full—not of men, but of beasts huddled together on the floor. She'd heard shifters changed to their animal forms to heal, and it made sense their bodies would try to throw off the spell. Unfortunately, this wasn't an injury that their natural magic could cure.

There were too many furry backs to be sure of the number. Five? Eight? Gray and brown, black and white, they were all huge, even lying down. Every wolf was deeply asleep with a stillness that suggested they were under the same type of sleeping spell Ademar had used.

Lila pushed the button that unlocked the cell door, wincing at the mechanism's loud clank. The sleeping wolves didn't stir as she stepped inside. The floor was full of paws and tails and she was forced to tiptoe around the edge of the pile. Werewolves were larger than their animal cousins, though they shared the same lean, long-legged grace. Closer examination revealed six individuals, all breathing. Rafe would be overjoyed to know at least some of his missing kin still lived.

If only he were here. With some effort, she could break the spell, but she was fae. She was one of the enemy who had trapped them, not to mention selling poison to their young. They could tear her to shreds in an instant if she didn't handle this just right. Memories of Ademar's injury flooded back in vivid shades of red.

It was possible to wake sleepers by administering a sudden shock, usually pain combined with a sundering of the magic that bound them, but that was as likely to kill as cure. For one thing, the spell's victims were usually weak from thirst and hunger. Even against a ticking clock, she wouldn't put them through more distress. Not even if her method held a degree of personal risk.

She found the wolf who was the oldest, judging by his gray

muzzle, and sat cross-legged on the floor beside him. Hopefully, age meant he was a leader who could help with the rest. She pulled his head into her lap and began stroking his fur, all the while searching for the spark of his consciousness. As expected, it was sunk deep in the spell's void—just a pinprick slowly drifting toward oblivion. Lila's throat ached with grief, making her swallow hard. There was a wanton cruelty to simply switching off another being and letting it waste away like a forgotten toy. The dead wolves most likely died of starvation, and that was nothing short of evil.

She murmured soothing nonsense, running her fingers through the wolf's thick fur. Touch belonged to the here and now, where she wanted him to be. At the same time, she sent a thin thread of healing toward the spark in the void. It was important not to overwhelm that ember, but to coax it back to the surface one sip of energy at a time.

Her vision softened as she worked, her gaze fixed on the contrast of thick brindled fur against the hard, featureless floor. The repetitive movement of her hands, petting and soothing, relaxed her as much as her patient. The spark caught and flared, drawing in her healing power. She gave the wolf enough to survive, enough so that he could hunt for himself. The yellow eyes opened and with a thrash, he struggled free of her embrace and got to his feet.

Lila stared up at the creature. A wolf shifter was as much wolf as human, and vice versa. She could see both forms of intelligence in his gaze. She could also see very large teeth as he lifted his lips in a growl. She strained to keep her panic in check.

"Hello," she began. "My name is Lila. I'm a friend of Rafe's."

The wolf kept growling, though the sound grew fainter. He was giving her a chance, but not a big one. She thought of all the things she wanted to say—explanations, instructions, apologies on behalf of fae kind—but discarded them all. Whatever she had to say, the wolf deserved more.

"If you promise not to bite me, I'll wake your friends."

∼

RAFE SWORE UNDER HIS BREATH, a sense of dread sinking like a rock inside his chest.

The last thing Ademar did before vanishing into the guts of the dungeon was unlock a door to the outside so that Teegar could escape. It was up a short flight of stairs and opened almost directly into the forest. Given that this place had a hidden prison and secret passages, it made perfect sense that it would also have an emergency escape route. The way station's creator had a seriously paranoid turn of mind.

Still, escape route or not, Rafe experienced a truckload of reservations as he'd ushered Teegar through the door. Not only was the fae disoriented by the spell, he seemed more intent on running than carrying a message for Rafe. It would be just his luck if the last hope for rescue bolted like a scared bunny.

Rafe yearned to go, too, and lose himself in the sweet-scented forest. But Lila was here, in need of protection. Once outside, he wouldn't find an easy way to get back in. He didn't have her talent with fae locks and hidden passages.

Instead, he retraced his steps through the dungeon. He steeled himself, pushing down a tsunami of thoughts and feelings. It was time to refocus. He'd carried out the mission he and Lila had started. Now he would find her and keep her safe until help arrived. If Teegar failed, there was still a chance Izetta had survived to summon aid.

He'd been walking only a minute when he caught the scent of wolf. *Imagination. False hope that I will see the pack again.* But then … then he saw them rounding the corner in a river of loping fur. He heard the pant of their breath, the click of their nails on the hard floor. His uncle, Jasper. Rand. Alexi. Lars. He knew them all:

cousins, friends, and allies gone missing in the hunt for the Magician. *But they are here. Not all of them were lost.*

They swarmed him, Uncle Jasper first, and then the others—jumping and nipping but silent as hunters had to be. They looked thin and ragged, but they were alive. Rafe buried his fists in their ruffs, felt their hot tongues washing away his grief. The urge to be with them in wolf form nearly buckled his knees, but none of them were safe. Not yet.

"This way." He ran ahead, as swift as the beasts.

Jasper and Alexi flanked him and the rest streamed behind, as if they moved with one mind. In a way, they did. They were pack.

Rafe ran up the steps and opened the door to the forest again, waiting as his wolves hurtled past. They brushed against him with shoulder and tail, reminding him by touch and scent where he belonged. When the last went by, he moved one foot to follow, but something made him look back. Lila stood in the corridor, gazing up to where he stood at the top of the short flight of steps.

"I found the wolves and woke them," she said. "I warned them about the perimeter. They know they should hide in the woods until we break the spell keeping them here."

She woke them. His mouth went dry at the enormity of what she'd done. She'd saved lives. Probably saved the pack.

He had to say something, thank her, acknowledge it somehow, but the words wouldn't come. "I found Teegar and freed him," he blurted instead. "Your brother helped, believe it or not."

"He did?" Her brow furrowed.

She didn't sound certain. He didn't blame her, given what he'd seen of Ademar. Then he remembered he had promised the fae to keep her safe. Rafe glanced back toward the wolves. Jasper stood at the edge of the trees, yellow eyes turned his way.

"You should go with them," Lila said softly. "You're free now."

"I know. You set me free as well."

But he let the door fall closed, cutting off his view of the woods. He looked down at Lila again. She stood tall but somehow dimmed, as if she'd spent all her magic waking his kin. The thought shook him all over again. This was no time to leave herself vulnerable. Surely she knew that?

"You belong with your pack," she said. "You don't have to stay."

"You didn't have to free them, but you did."

"They were my responsibility." She made a weary gesture. "I had to make it right. It was the least I could do."

Generosity. Fair play. Accountability. He never expected any of those from a fae. Her gesture caught him between joy and the profoundest grief. She had an inner beauty invisible to her own people.

"Come with us," he said. "You'd have a grateful pack to protect you."

"I can't."

"What are you staying for?" His words sounded impatient. He hadn't meant them that way.

"I'm not free until my own pack is healed." She looked away. "That won't happen until Farras is stopped. And the Magician."

With an effort of will, Rafe set aside the yearning to be with the wolves. He'd come here to hunt the fae hurting his pack. Lila might have freed him, but he wasn't free of his mission.

Rafe descended the steps, acutely aware of the shrinking space between them. The scent of the wolves was on her, mixing her natural sweetness with their wild musk. "Then I'm not free until you are. You saved my kin. Wolves don't leave a debt unpaid."

"There is no debt," she said.

She would have said more, but he took her by the shoulders and drew her close, his lips finding hers. He didn't want logic. He wanted her taste. He wanted to know her in ways that didn't need words. Lila moaned into his mouth as he ran his hand down the curve of her spine.

The vibration of her voice ran through him, sending a thousand shocks to intimate places. He pushed her against the wall—another steel door, cold beneath his palms. The kiss went on, the heat between them mounting to an excruciating pressure. Something dark inside him chuckled. This fae was as feral at heart as any beast.

Then she froze, suddenly breaking the kiss. Rafe reined himself in with difficulty, expecting a lecture about timing and danger and how he should know better when there were madmen on the loose.

But when she looked up with wide gray eyes, that wasn't what she said. "There's someone in this cell. A fae."

Rafe stepped back, giving her room. "Friend or foe?"

"I can't tell. Not yet." Lila examined the door and made a noise of frustration. "It's got a different locking mechanism than the others."

Rafe fished in his pocket and held up the key ring, holding the bundle by the large iron key he'd used to free Teegar. "Try this."

The door looked the same as Teegar's cell, and it was in the same corridor of the dungeon. It stood to reason this was where the special prisoners were kept. He hoped it also meant the security systems were the same, because he'd listened closely when Ademar had opened the captain's cell.

Rafe took several tries to recreate the code. But, between that and a variety of keys, they eventually opened the door. The cell was pitch dark, but Rafe could hear the rub of fabric as someone shifted positions. This prisoner was not asleep.

"Wait," he said, catching Lila's arm.

Light bloomed above her palm, and she sent it floating along the cell's ceiling. The illumination was weaker than the lights she'd made before, a sign of how much energy she'd used up. Even so, the figure hunched on the bed shielded his eyes with a strangled cry.

To Rafe's eyes, the male fae looked like a jumble of bones and rags. Lila grabbed Rafe's arm for support.

"Father?" she gasped.

CHAPTER 29

*L*ila launched herself forward, dropping to her knees in front of her father. Grief welled up as she took him in her arms. Grief and molten outrage.

Lord Gareth of House Fernblade had never had the stern elegance of some fae nobles, but he had shared the light fae's natural good looks. Now his cheekbones stood out, shadowing a wan complexion. His dark-blond hair lay in thickly matted hanks.

"Father?" Lila murmured, cupping his face.

Her hands trembled, both from the fatigue and fierce emotion. He'd always been her protector, the one who took her side in any family dispute. He'd encouraged her to follow her curiosity and move to the city. No one else had believed she could survive on her own. But now? Now he was barely recognizable.

She'd never seen him with a beard. They were not the custom among the fae, and his was a tangled mess. He wore a loose, casual tunic with a richly embroidered robe thrown over it. Clothing he wore reading a book by the evening fire, and most likely what he was dressed in the night he'd been dragged away by Teegar's troops. The fine fabrics were now threadbare rags.

He squinted down at her, showing red-rimmed, watering eyes. She dimmed the light she'd left floating above them until he could hold her gaze without blinking.

"Lila?" His voice cracked, as if he hadn't used it in a long time. "How did you get here?"

"Never mind that. We're taking you to safety."

"We?" He looked around, seeming bewildered.

Rafe had pulled the door closed without engaging the lock. He stood beside it, hands clasped behind his back.

"Who is he?" her father asked.

"A better friend than we deserve. Come on."

Lila tried to help him stand, but he was too unsteady to keep his feet. Though he had not been spelled into sleep, it was plain that he'd been left in the dark with little food or drink. She sat him down again.

He slumped forward with a deep sigh, shaking his head. "Leave me. I thank you to the depths of the Abyss and beyond for finding me, but I would not risk your lives for mine."

The last words were so faint, Lila could barely make them out. She took her father's hands and held them lightly, all too aware of the bones of his long, almost fleshless fingers. A memory rose of those hands holding a brush. Her father had been known for his fine, flowing calligraphy. He'd always loved beauty more than the sword.

Tears filled her eyes. She blinked them away, refusing to let him see. "Be at peace. As they say in the city, I've got this."

Or she hoped she did. She was shaky herself after healing six wolves already and digging deep into her reserves. But this was her father, who had always done his quiet best to ensure she was happy and—above all—free. Lila could not hold back now.

This time, no finesse was required. There was no spell to break. All she needed to give was her strength. A soft glow gloved their hands as she sent her healing to him. As always, it was like flowing into a maze more than it was filling a cup. There was no central reservoir to supply, but dozens of small places where damage was done.

"Lila," her father said, a note of protest in his voice. "You need your strength."

She squeezed his hands. "I said I've got this."

The injuries she found were weeks old, maybe months. She realized she was not entirely sure when he'd been kidnapped from his own home. One more thing her mother had not shared.

Lila felt the ground list under her feet and realized she was swaying where she stood. Rafe's hand settled on her shoulder, steadying her. She sensed his worry and was thankful he trusted her to work anyway. When she finally released her father's hands, Rafe stood behind her, letting her lean against his solid form.

Her father rose, unsteady at first. Lila reached out, but he caught his balance.

Taking a deep breath, he raised his hands, palms out. "No, daughter, you've done your work well. I will walk out of this place with dignity."

He smiled then, the wry, crooked humor she remembered dimmed but present. Lila's heart squeezed with relief and love, and the tears she'd been holding back spilled down her cheeks. She flung her arms around her father's neck and squeezed him tight.

"How long have you been here?" she asked on a sob. "I thought you were in the king's custody."

"If so, I've heard no charges or accusations, and King Elroth is scrupulous about observing protocol."

"Then what happened?"

"I don't know," he said. "I've been here since I was taken, though I am not certain where we are. The vehicle that brought me here had no windows, and no way to see which roads we took."

She bit her lip, pulling back. "We are beneath a way station Lord Farras built for the king."

Her father's look of confusion said it all. He'd been no more aware of this place than she had been when Sala had convinced her to come find Ademar.

"Douse the light," Rafe whispered, urgency in his tone.

Lila didn't ask questions. She let the light go, a little relieved to spare even that small drain on her energy. They stood in the dark, still and silent. It was then she heard what had alerted Rafe —footsteps roaming near the door where the wolves had escaped. Ademar would have deactivated any magic keeping that exit secure when he'd helped Teegar escape. That wouldn't go unnoticed.

Sure enough, a moment later, she caught the charcoal stink of a fresh spell being cast. Judging by the intensity of the smell, it was strong and nasty magic. Defensive magic, no doubt. A trap or a tripwire.

"It's not safe to leave that way any longer," she whispered, glad her father and Rafe were close enough to feel their presence. The dark was absolute. "They'll be watching to see who blunders through that."

Lila had been lucky so far. No doubt Farras had sent minions to find her, but they wouldn't think to look in the hidden part of the dungeon. She wasn't supposed to know about it, and that assumption had given her time to free the prisoners.

Unfortunately, her good luck had run out. Lila took a shaky breath, feeling the confined space close in around her. The soft tread of the fae guards grew fainter as they moved down a different corridor, their voices low and urgent. They would be back, and they'd bring reinforcements for a thorough search. She couldn't hope to hide in the cells any longer.

She willed the merest spark of light to rise from her palm. "We'll have to leave the way station from the main floor and hide in the woods until help arrives."

Rafe gave her father a careful look. "It will be risky with so many guests around, but we can do it."

But her father frowned. "Guests?"

"Lord Farras is here." Lila kept her tone neutral. "Mother is hostess of a banquet in his honor."

"Galeeta is here?" Her father straightened. "Under this roof?"

"Yes, and Ademar, too," she replied. "They've been staying here."

He pressed his hand to his forehead, as if a sudden headache had struck. "So close. Why don't we just go to them?"

Lila grabbed his wrist, feeling prominent bones. "No, you shouldn't. Lord Farras has everyone under his sway, including Mother."

"Stop." He put a finger on her lips, as he'd done when she was a child. "I know Galeeta too well to believe that. She is a slave to the whims of court, but she finds her way to goodness in the end."

"Sir," Rafe said before Lila could argue. "At the very least, Lord Farras is no friend to us. And he brought approximately two hundred retainers with him, many of them soldiers. I would advise leaving now and contacting your family later."

Gareth wavered, then seemed to make up his mind. "I agree that Farras can't be trusted. Lead on."

The moment Rafe pushed the door open, they all breathed deeply, as if their lungs had starved for free air. Wasting no time, Lila took the lead, using her magic to sense any traps the guards might have set. Her father came next, leaning on Rafe's arm and shielding his light-sensitive eyes.

They made slow progress, stopping often to let her father rest. There was one near miss with a patrol, but Rafe heard him in time to duck down a side corridor. The main challenge was maintaining a reasonable pace. When they finally made it to the stairs that led up to the entry hall, her father was spent. He leaned against the wall at the foot of the stairs, face ashen. Lila reached out, ready to help, but he pushed her hand away.

"Don't you dare," he said. "You've already given me too much of your strength."

Lila frowned at the stairs. There were spells galore to keep anyone from leaving, but she had dealt with them all before. She folded the magic aside and led the way up. Rafe helped Gareth follow. Lila waited for them at the top, then cracked the door open to peer out. Her plan was to go directly to the secret passages and wait until the coast was clear.

When she saw no one, she beckoned the others into the black and white tiled hall and led them around the base of the stairway, reversing the path she had taken with Rafe earlier that night. He'd appeared ragged in the dim dungeon, but under the shimmering chandeliers, he looked like a hermit fresh from his wasteland hovel. When she noticed a man's cloak tossed over the banister, she flung it around Gareth's shoulders to hide his clothes. As an added bonus, the hood shaded his eyes from the light.

They'd almost made it to the secret door when she heard Farras giving orders in a whip-crack tone. He was somewhere close by and coming nearer, and now she heard the word *escape*. Her stomach dropped.

There was no time to fumble with the door and usher everyone through. Instead, they hurried around the corner, where the entry connected with the main part of the house. She glimpsed Farras walking past with two of his guards. The lord's hair was streaked with blood from where she'd hit him. He was gazing down at something a guard held. It looked like an amulet on a chain. Thankfully, it was interesting enough that he didn't look up until he was well past where Lila cowered. She released a gust of pent-up breath.

The place was buzzing with voices, and the mood no longer felt like a celebration. Something was happening. While it was possible her absence had been noted, she doubted the anxious murmurs had to do with her. Farras wasn't the type to admit he'd been bashed over the head by his supposed date. So, what was going on?

Groups of servers were coming through with trays of glasses, no doubt heading toward the kitchen. Not sure where to go next, she pulled Rafe and her father as far out of sight as she could behind a decorative pillar. Hopefully, they'd look to any passer-by like a cloaked noble with a pair of servants in tow.

Gareth pointed toward the banquet hall, just visible from where they stood. "Did you decorate that?"

"Yes," she replied softly, not wanting to be overheard. "Mother insisted."

Prison had done nothing to dim her father's wits. She saw the implications sink in—that after so many years, the issue of her marriage to Farras had been revived. He nodded slowly, as if putting additional pieces into place. "Did he ask for your hand?"

"Asked isn't the right word."

"How did you respond?"

"I knocked him unconscious with a wine bottle."

Rafe choked down a laugh.

"Good girl," her father said. "Lord or not, he is not for you. The longer I knew Farras, the more I saw there is a streak of evil in his soul."

"I know." She turned to Rafe. "It was Farras who took the wolves and put them under a sleeping spell. He confessed as much to me."

"And the dead? The graves we saw?" Rafe demanded.

"The spell is fatal unless someone breaks it."

Rafe's eyes flashed yellow with fury. He looked about to speak, but then his jaws clamped shut, the muscles working as if he ground Farras between his teeth.

Her father took a wary step back from the wolf. "The list of his crimes covers more than you know. Trust me on that. It's rare that he admits to one."

"He was in a chatty mood," Lila said, remembering what else the fae lord had said. "I'll tell you later. Now is not the time."

"But maybe it is," her father said. "Maybe the only way to stop him is to tell the truth in front of two hundred high-born witnesses. Violence does not concern him, but shame will."

Lila's stomach flipped over with anxiety. Her father was an idealist. If they tried to denounce Lord Farras, it was more likely that none of them would get a chance to speak before the lord cut them down. "How about—"

She never got a chance to finish the sentence. Commotion erupted outside the window, punctuated by a mighty howling of wolves. Rafe spun, eyes wide. "The pack. They're here."

For an instant, Lila was confused. The wolves she'd freed were fit enough to hide, but not to fight. But these—by the spine-shaking sound, these beasts were fresh.

The crowd of fae startled as if the wolves were already inside. A few ran, although Lila wasn't sure where they thought they could go. Others began shouting for weapons. Still others crowded the windows for a better look.

Lila and Gareth joined the crush at the window, pushing through the silk-and-velvet throng. No one was going to look closely at them now—not with chaos erupting outside. Lila cupped her hands against the glass to see out into the dark.

It looked like a painter's vision of Hell. Wolves, half-wolves, Undead, and fae were locked in bloody battle. Help had arrived, but it had come with fang and claw. When she glimpsed Rafe's vampire friend—the one he'd fought so hard to free—Lila knew who the messenger had been. Izetta had survived.

When she turned to tell Rafe, he was gone.

CHAPTER 30

*I*zetta leaped from one tree to the next, alighting on the branch of a twisted oak. It was well past midnight now, when a human place would be sunk into the peace of sleep. The forest around the way station was anything but that. Tension crept like a mist veiling the air.

Justice would be served that night. The fae were deadly, but in her experience they lacked the imagination—and humility—to properly watch their back. Yes, Izetta would enjoy herself tonight.

The invaders were a tightening noose around the way station. Vampires floated from tree to tree in a ring of silent shadows. The wolves—and one cougar—padded through the soft grass in groups of four and five. One wolf in each hunting party, including the Alpha, remained in human form to communicate with the others. Coordination would be essential to beat an army of fae twice their number.

Izetta sprang again, landing beside Malatest. He looked too tall to balance easily on a branch, but he moved lightly aside to give her room. He was in a three-piece suit and fedora, shoes shining and hair meticulously styled. He looked as if he'd stepped straight from a nightclub a hundred years past.

They'd reached the edge of the trees. Nothing but open ground stretched between them and the way station, where the party-goers wandered in and out through the open doors. A hum of conversation filled the night air, punctuated by snatches of music.

"Is that the banquet area or just the public space of the house?" Izetta asked, pointing to the door where the guests spilled out.

Malatest nudged her finger a few degrees to the left. "There. The banquet room is behind that verandah, if Teegar can be believed."

The captain claimed he hadn't spent much time in the way station—outside of the dungeon, of course—so his information wasn't as useful as they'd hoped. While Teegar knew there were magical wards and secret passages, he couldn't give their exact location. Izetta believed him, almost. Maybe. It was a shame fae blood wasn't drinkable.

They'd left Teegar in the care of the wolves, who had brought him along at fangpoint. He might prove useful yet.

Malatest and Izetta watched in silence as the wolves came to a halt beneath the trees. Yellow eyes flashed at even intervals around the property. The noose was complete, with all the players in position.

"Are we ready to start this party?" Izetta asked.

Malatest rose to his full height, waving to catch the Alpha wolf's attention. At the last moment, Devries's hand shot up, signaling a halt. There was a rustle in the bushes, as if another group of wolves were moving in a hurry.

"What is it?" Izetta whispered.

"I'll go see." Malatest floated to the ground and disappeared into the trees.

Izetta waited, schooling her impatience as she studied the way station. The fae drifting to and fro looked like exotic fish in their bright, fluttering silks. Beautiful, and probably poisonous. Izetta's side was relying heavily on the element of surprise.

She searched the ground for Malatest. He was talking to Rafe's father and nodding. *Hurry up*, she thought. There were only so many hours of darkness left, and Devries liked to talk. She prayed to whatever dark gods still heard her that it wasn't bad news about Rafe. All night she'd been wishing the wolf was at her back, but that was why she was here, wasn't it? The fae would pay for taking him, and much, much more.

Malatest leaped from the ground and landed beside her, one hand on a branch and the other on his hip in a pose of supreme satisfaction.

"What's up?" Izetta asked.

"There is definitely dissention in the fae ranks," he said with a grin that showed his fangs. "Some of the missing pack turned up. One of the fae women, a healer, released them from the dungeon with Rafe's help. They asked that we do not kill that one."

"I think her name is Lila. She is the daughter of the family who were in the house when Rafe and I were captured. She might be working with Rafe, but do not trust the mother or the son." Izetta paused. "The mother is mine to bleed."

Malatest shook his head. "Maximum damage, minimum death. Enjoy your prey, but no prisoners die until I get the identity of the Magician."

"What if they resist capture?" Izetta asked, all innocence. Fae were hard to kill, but she knew how.

"Use your imagination. You'll enjoy the exercise."

Malatest gave the signal to attack.

The wolves broke into a ground-eating trot, then a lope. They converged on the building from all sides like a silent, rushing tide of fur. The fae on the verandah had wandered onto the lawn, and it took a second for someone to notice the noiseless threat. When the cry went up, it was too late. Goblets dropped from fae hands as they turned and ran, overcome by shock. Only a handful in military dress stood their ground, swords drawn. One launched a bright ball of crackling energy straight at Malatest, but the cougar—Errata—brought the fae down in a flurry of claws and lashing tail. The first blood was spilled.

Howls ripped the air and Undead rained from the sky. The party guests scrambled for the safety of the way station, clogging the doors. Anyone trying to organize a defense was trapped inside. This had been Malatest's plan, and it was working.

The vampire king himself mowed a path to the way station, picking up his opponents and tossing them aside with the brute strength of the Undead. Wolves harried the running fae, bringing them down with brutal efficiency. The anger in every strike wasn't just battle lust. This was vengeance for their young.

Izetta jumped from the lawn to the verandah. From their perch in the trees, Malatest had pointed to the left, indicating where the banquet hall should be. Izetta strode in that direction, letting her boot heels ring on the wooden deck. She had to dodge a few skirmishes, but she found what she was looking for. There were no windows, but high up in the wall there was a row of long, stained-glass panels with a twisting floral design. They would have looked charming from the inside with the sun filtering through.

Izetta sprang up to the narrow ledge outside the panels and put her boot heel through the glass. The fae could defend the doors to their little castle, but they'd have trouble defending a missing wall. Izetta grabbed the sill where the window had been and tore at the fabric of the building. Fae-made structures were often summoned into existence, meant to fade back into nature once they were no longer required. This was no exception. It was made of wood and far easier to crush than stone or steel.

Malatest joined her, quickly understanding her plan. In moments, the rest of the Undead followed, tearing chunks from the side of the building. Fae threw offensive magic, but that only wrecked the building faster. A few of the vampires were clearing away the debris, cautious of accidental staking from the flying wood, but they had trouble keeping up. Izetta had a person-sized hole in the wall in under a minute. They'd have the whole thing down in less than ten.

She grabbed a ragged chunk of wall and gave it a twist as she heaved. With a shower of splinters, the wood gave way with a loud crack. She slung the chunk aside and was reaching for another when she saw her quarry.

Galeeta was as lovely and perfect as the fae queen from a picture book. Her sheet of golden hair was wound into a crown of jewel-studded braids. As Izetta stared, the fae woman turned the pale oval of her face toward the invading Undead.

A jolt of fear lanced Izetta as memories of the dungeon cell revived. Pain. Hunger. The desperate flight through the woods. Anger followed, more rabid than any wolf. She stepped through the hole in the wall. She hadn't survived for millennia by leaving her enemies alive.

A blinding flash froze Izetta mid-stride.

RAFE WAS inside the way station with Lila and Gareth when the first howls sounded. Pulse pounding, he surged toward the window, then checked himself. He had sworn to protect Lila, but he knew the voices calling his kin to battle. This was pack.

The sounds of war quickly multiplied, ruffling the hair along his neck. Cautiously, he moved away from the press of panicking fae. He wanted to see what was going on, too, but he was a lone wolf in the midst of the enemy. He would not attract attention by pushing his way through the crowd. He couldn't help anyone if he was back in chains.

He kept moving until he found himself in the kitchen where he'd first broken into the way station with Izetta. Smashed glass and blood smeared the floor, evidence of Lila's fight with Farras. It was all too sharp a reminder of what was at stake. If Farras won this night, the wolves wouldn't be the only victims.

Wasting no time, he pushed the window open and climbed outside, grateful for the cold air against his heated face. From there, he jumped on top of a concrete planter for a better view. At first glance, it seemed there was little action at this end of the property, but within seconds the melee came within sight. With a rush of joy, he saw Izetta, whole and well, leaping from a treetop to the ground. She had survived to bring rescuers.

Including his father. The Alpha was in pursuit of a fae who was running, not toward the way station, but across the lawn and toward the woods. Toward Rafe. He leaped from the planter and into the fae's path, spreading his arms to block the way. Wolves were fast but fae moved like lightning. If he didn't catch him now, there would be no chance.

The fae ducked, swerving to the left. Rafe sprang, grabbing him and using the momentum to toss him to the ground. The fae was cuffed, but still managed to roll to his feet. He didn't get far before Rafe grabbed him by the hair and pushed him to his knees. It was Teegar.

"What are you doing here?" Rafe demanded, shouting over the din of fighting.

"I went for help, just as you asked," Teegar replied. Dirt caked his face and the remains of his uniform. "They won't believe I'm on your side, especially that she-serpent of a vampire. She put me in these cuffs. I was running for my life."

His father skidded to a halt beside them, his eyes widening in surprise when he saw Rafe. Emotions slammed through Rafe at the sight of his father—a tangle too complex to unravel in the middle of a fight.

"You turned up at the right moment, boy." Then the Alpha turned toward the forest and whistled a series of piercing notes.

Giving commands, Rafe knew, although this was a signal he didn't recognize.

"Why is this one prisoner?" Rafe asked, keeping his tone brisk.

"Your friend, Izetta," he replied, echoing Teegar's words. "She said to keep him prisoner, or there would be blood spilled."

That was good enough for Rafe. More wolves were joining them now—the six Lila had freed from the dungeon. They surrounded Teegar, thrusting their muzzles close and baring fangs. No doubt this was who his father had summoned with his whistled command.

"Take him away," the Alpha ordered. "Don't let him budge until I say so."

One of the wolves nipped Teegar, making him scramble to his feet. With a shove, they forced him toward the edge of the battle. These wolves weren't fit for a fight, but six of them could supervise one fae cuffed in iron. They walked proudly now, stiff and sore but with their tails high.

"You found them," said his father, gesturing toward the retreating wolves. "You saved them."

"Not all. I was too late. We were too late. And I didn't save them alone." Rafe was stammering, so he made himself shut up.

"It doesn't matter." His father put a big hand on his shoulder. "I asked you for help, and you gave it. As for those we lost, they will be mourned as heroes."

"I still haven't found the Magician."

"When you open the fridge door and smell decay, it's only a matter of time before the rotten cabbage comes to light." The Alpha nodded toward the way station. "There's our fridge, and your friend is tearing it a new door."

Rafe frowned at the vampires ripping open the wall. "Fenrir's balls."

His father's laugh was evil. He slapped Rafe's shoulder again. "I always complained about your Undead friends, but I'm beginning to see the appeal."

A moment of awkwardness rose between them as the ghost of old arguments drifted past. But Rafe had seen too much in the last few days to give that ghost much weight. He put an arm around his father's shoulders and gave him an awkward, one-armed hug.

"Thank you for coming," he said.

"You're my son. I'll always come to get you."

There was pride in his father's voice. It wasn't magic, and it didn't heal everything, but it was a very good start.

"I hear there's at least one fae worth saving," his father said as they stepped apart.

"Yes." Rafe pulled his shirt off over his head. He'd been human long enough. "No one touches her."

"Then you know what to do," the Alpha said. "It's time to avenge our cubs."

Rafe snarled, fully wolf now, and bolted toward the battle.

A flash of light bleached the night sky.

CHAPTER 31

*L*ila backed away from the window, pulling her father with her. She looked around for Rafe, but he was nowhere in sight. Worry stabbed her—if wolves were attacking, he was an automatic target for the fae. So did a profound sense of loss. She'd grown used to having him near.

But there was no way to search for him. Fae were crowding in every direction, making it hard to move. She wished she was still wearing the fancy gown and jewels she'd had earlier that night. Right or wrong, the finery earned her a degree of respect. While she was dressed in ill-fitting castoffs, no one thought twice about trampling right over her and her father.

A female in a crimson skirt knocked Lila in the ribs, making her lose her grip on Gareth's arm. For a heart-stopping instant, he vanished into the crowd, carried off like a twig in a river. Desperate to find him again, she burrowed through the crush of bodies, nearly getting bowled over by running soldiers.

The military captains who had come with Farras were mustering their troops in the banquet room. That made sense. It was large enough to hold most of the fae, and it had few entrances to control. On the surface, it was the logical place for her to go. Then again, the way station was hardly a beacon of hospitality. Which would be worse—to be stuck in the room with Farras's crew or take her chances outside? Neither guaranteed safety, but her choice couldn't be for herself alone.

She glimpsed Gareth's cloak near the banquet room door. By sheer determination—and use of elbows—Lila forced her way to his side.

"There you are," she said, slipping her arm securely through his. "I thought I'd lost you."

Clearly too weary to speak, he put his hand over hers, squeezing her fingers. She looked around for Rafe, but there was still no sign of him. She hoped he'd made it outside, where he'd be with his pack.

The crowd carried Lila and her father through the banquet room door. The high-ceilinged hall looked nothing like it had just an hour ago. The lights had been turned up, dispelling the illusion of an indoor night. Most of the tables had been removed to make room for the crowd, although one or two had been pushed against the wall to hold platters of leftover food. Lila entered, immediately sensing the spell she'd cast to decorate the hall was shattered. The vines had withered and falling petals smeared the floor where a hundred heels had crushed them.

Momentum carried them to the far end of the room, where the high table had once stood. Lila steered Gareth to the right once she was finally able to get out of the crush and find a spot against the wall. Her father sank to the floor, almost boneless with fatigue. He needed more healing, but Lila felt weak-kneed herself.

She looked around. No one was fighting in here, just milling like cattle in a pen. The table with the food was only a few yards away. Lila edged toward it, not letting her father out of her sight. Even through the chaos, the scent of food was tantalizing, reminding her she'd spent too much energy and eaten too little at dinner.

Barely looking at what she took, Lila stuffed bread, nuts, and slices of hard cheese into the pockets of Ademar's fleece jacket. Then she popped a piece of nut-crusted brie in her mouth. The flavor exploded on her tongue, and she could feel the nourishment hit her bloodstream almost the moment she swallowed. She took another bite and grabbed an almost-full wine bottle that stood on the table. She hurried back toward the place her father sat, head bowed and hood pulled down to hide his face.

"Here." She pulled grapes and cheese from her pocket and offered them to Gareth, realizing she was parched. She paused to take a drink from the bottle.

And nearly spit out the wine. The two gargoyles who served Galeeta were approaching her father with a menacing tread. Lila scrambled forward, putting herself in their path. Galeeta was just steps behind the two monsters. Lila fell back out of pure dismay, nearly stepping on her father.

The gargoyles closed in protectively, flanking her mother. The chaos in the room had notched up a degree, with more people shoving to find a spot.

Galeeta put a firm hand on Lila's shoulder. Her gaze flicked from the wine bottle to Lila's clothes to the crumpled figure on the floor. Her mouth flattened in anger. "Where did you go? What have you done?"

Howls sounded from outside. Galeeta gave her a hard look.

"I didn't invite them," Lila pointed out. "But there are some things you should know."

Her mother pushed Lila aside, not bothering to reply. Lila was forced to skitter sideways to avoid the nearest gargoyle. She'd barely found her balance when Galeeta bent to examine the cloaked figure beside the wall, her emerald ballgown pooling around her feet.

"Who are you?" she said to Gareth, who was eerily still.

"Mother..." Lila began, but Galeeta held up her hand, cutting off any more words.

Her mother's gaze drifted down to Gareth's feet, which were encased in a filthy but familiar pair of slippers. Her father's captors hadn't even allowed him to find shoes before he was dragged away.

Galeeta visibly swallowed. *By the Abyss*, Lila thought. *Some part of her knows.*

"I wrote the invitations to this banquet," her mother began. "I know every guest here, and you were not invited."

Slowly, her father lifted his hand and pushed back his hood. His pallor was evident in the brightly lit hall. His gaze swept over her elegant dress and jewels before searching her face. "Hello, wife."

The gargoyles were the first to react, springing away with a soft squawk of surprise. The sound vanished beneath Galeeta's cry of horror. Her mother collapsed to her knees beside him.

"Gareth!" her mother's voice rose with surprise. She touched his face, shivering a little as her fingers found the unexpected roughness of his beard. "Oh, Gareth."

Galeeta fell on him, holding him hard. Tears turned her eyes to glimmering stars as she turned to Lila. "Where was he?"

"What is going on here, Lady Galeeta?" Farras emerged from a knot of fae nobles who huddled a dozen yards away. They were dispersing now with purposeful strides, presumably to carry out Lord Farras's orders.

Lila shrank back as Farras came forward, using his spear like a walking stick. She'd heard it was his weapon of choice, wielding it on foot or on horseback with equal ease. Light flared on its silvery tip, as if it held more than a hint of power.

Then her gaze fixed on the diamond-shaped metal amulet on a thong around his neck. Was it the object he'd taken from his henchman earlier that night? She reached to sense its power, expecting something dangerous. It was nothing of the kind, but a cheap shield against fae compulsion—the kind anyone could buy if they knew the right witch.

As he neared, his attention remained on her parents. Lila edged closer and noticed the gargoyles did, too. They were ready to protect Galeeta, even against this lord of the fae.

Her mother held Gareth close, though her features settled into a bland mask. "Lord Farras, you've already brought my husband back to me. How did you get him free of the king so soon?"

Farras looked as if he'd swallowed a porcupine. He glanced around, his eyes narrowing when he caught sight of Lila. "How did you do this?"

Before she could answer, Ademar emerged from the crowd, hurrying forward as fast as he could with his cane. "There you are, Mother. What … Father!"

"Hello, my son," Gareth replied.

Ademar spun to face Lila. "Where was he?"

She stared Farras in the eye. "In the cells beneath this way station, near the pack of wolves that Lord Farras spelled into a fatal sleep."

Galeeta's mouth dropped open, speechless. In contrast, Ademar rounded on the lord, his face flushed with rage. Lila's whole body clenched with fear.

"Ademar," she said softly. "Have a care."

"Yes," Farras repeated, loud enough for all to hear. He tilted the spear head in Ademar's direction. "Have a care what you say. You've only got one leg to stand on as it is."

Gareth managed a caustic smile at Farras. "I see you've lost none of your diplomatic touch since you threw me in a cell." Then he gave in to a wracking cough.

Lila passed the wine bottle to her mother, who held it to Gareth's lips.

Farras's lip curled in derision. "It was Teegar who arrested you."

Her father took a second swallow of wine. "Does it matter?

He never put on his drawers without your explicit order, at least until you tired of him trotting at your heels."

Farras lifted his weapon, but stopped when one of the gargoyles twitched. He backed away, eyes Arctic with displeasure. "You'll regret those words."

Ademar's sword flew from his cane, but he froze as the stained glass on the opposite wall exploded with a crash.

Someone screamed as sharp-nailed hands grabbed the window frame and ripped it away. A gaping hole revealed the pale faces of a dozen Undead, their eyes glowing as they reflected the indoor light. More hands grabbed the edges of the wound in the wall and tore. Sections of wall peeled away like the rind of a fruit.

"Impossible," Galeeta murmured, her voice shaking with terror.

Lila's knees trembled as she moved to stand beside Ademar. She'd hoped for an army to stop Farras and his troops. She'd even planned to go find one. But this—this wasn't what she'd imagined.

"Do you have a weapon?" Ademar asked without taking his eyes off the far wall—or lack of it.

"Only my magic," she replied. All she had in her pockets were leftovers from the banquet.

"Then that will have to do, but hold your fire for now."

He was right. One of the nobles lobbed a defensive spell at the vampires, but only succeeded in scorching a section of the wall.

"Stop, you fools!" Farras pounded the butt of his spear on the floor. The noise was like thunder. "Conjure a barricade!"

No one listened. Fae warriors were without peer, but this was not a field of war. It was pandemonium. Panic had seized the room, and those with the discipline to fight were swamped by terrified civilians. More spells blasted the wall to splinters before the fae realized they were doing the enemy's job.

"Where is my barricade?" the lord snarled as he stalked to the center of the room, brandishing his spear in the air.

No one replied, because it was too late. The Undead spilled into the room, Izetta in the lead. The dark-haired vampire paused long enough to scan the room before she marched straight for Galeeta, a grim smile playing around her lips. She pulled a long blade from her boot. Not a gun—some of the vampires had them, because Lila heard the rat-tat-tat of automatic fire—but a weapon guaranteed to inflict pain. The vampire tested it on her thumb as she approached, then licked the wound.

Ademar took a step forward, but Lila caught his arm as the gargoyles surged forward, blocking Izetta's path.

"I've come for you, Lady Galeeta," she said with sinister courtesy. "Call off your monsters and fight."

"I will not leave my husband's side," Galeeta responded. "He was freed from prison tonight."

At some unseen order, the two creatures parted just enough to show Lila's parents huddled on the floor. Lila's breath hitched. Her father slumped against Galeeta's shoulder, eyes closed, as if he'd used up the last of his strength. Tears tracked down her mother's face.

"Fireballs and damnation." Izetta's face twisted. "Where's the sport in this?"

She did not have a chance to say more. Brilliant light flooded the room, searing everyone's eyes. Lila flung up her arm, but it was no good. The radiance had a weight of its own, pressing into her skin and on down to her bones. It flared to a teeth-jarring pitch and then receded, the air tangibly cooling as it did.

When Lila's vision finally cleared, she saw an arch of flame where the hole in the wall had been. The Undead had fled that spot, giving the ferocious light a wide berth. Even so, not all the fighting had stopped. Wolves and fae and vampires still battled, both inside and out.

"Freeze!" boomed a disembodied voice.

The words rolled over the scene, as deep and resonant as thunder in the mountains. Lila's knees bent under the weight of compulsion. She could not move. No one could. An eerie quiet fell over the scene.

And then Lila heard the silvery tinkling of bells.

The air beneath the arch rippled, then broke like the surface of a lake. The head of a gray-dappled horse emerged, the golden bridle richly decorated with silver bells and tassels. A moment later, the rest of it was visible, including the rider. He was tall and dressed in robes rich with the shifting hues of autumn. His face was broader than most fae, with a cleft chin and square jaw. A golden crown shaped like twisting branches circled his brow. This was Elroth, the Forest King.

A dozen lesser light fae swarmed around him. No bigger than hummingbirds, they shed a sparkling radiance from their transparent wings that broke into rainbows where it glanced off the king's armor. It was like looking into a miniature sun.

King Elroth rode into the middle of the banquet hall, filling it and yet, with subtle magic, making the space stretch to accommodate him and the procession of riders that followed him through the portal.

He came, Lila thought with wonder. *He came, and now everything will be fine.* Except one person was not frozen in place. She'd forgotten the amulet.

Lord Farras's spear twisted through the air toward the king.

CHAPTER 32

*L*ight flared from the spear's tip, fracturing into an iridescent shower bright enough to sear Lila's eyes. She strained to leap forward and somehow intercept it, but King Elroth's command gripped her tight. She might as well have been trapped in amber.

She recognized the spear's radiance for what it was—a spell to guarantee Farras's weapon would strike and kill the king. With no other option, she screamed a wordless warning that was echoed by a dozen other voices.

Two of the king's retainers surged forward—one a female clad in silver mail, the other a male in armor so dark that it seemed to drink the light. The latter spurred his black steed closest to the king, ready to shield him at all costs, but he could not close the distance in time.

Farras had chosen his position well, launching his attack from the left and behind, outside King Elroth's line of sight. At the warning cry, the monarch twisted in his saddle, but not fast enough to do more than glimpse his own execution.

A huge shape eclipsed the spear's blinding sparks. Lila blinked, clearing her sight of the blazing afterimage to see an enormous gray wolf spring into the air, catching the spear in his jaws. Lila's breath stopped. *Rafe!* He had bolted in from outside the broken wall and from beyond the sphere of the king's command to freeze.

The spear, loaded with intricate spellwork, shattered in Rafe's bite before his paws hit the floor. The power banked within the weapon discharged in a single, wild eruption. A searing flash ended in a clap of rushing air. Lila flinched, unable to duck, and squeezed her eyes shut. A wave of pins and needles coursed over her body followed by a strange nothingness.

Her ears recovered first as the remains of the spear clattered to the floor. Lila rubbed tears from her light-blinded eyes, relieved to be able to move again. When her vision cleared, she saw the king still seated on his horse, his face white with shock.

Amid the shards of the spear, Rafe sprawled at the feet of the king's charger. The rush of unfocused magic had changed him back to human form, naked and unconscious.

Lila dove toward Rafe, frantic with worry. She fell to her knees and skidded the last few feet across the polished floor, heedless of the guards and the nervous stamping of the horses. One of the lesser fae dove past her head, wings buzzing in alarm, but she waved it away.

Rafe was facedown, one arm flung forward. Lila placed her hand against the lean muscle of his back, a soft cry of relief escaping her lips when she felt the rise and fall of his breath. But his skin was unnaturally cool, as if his vital spark had been seared away.

Someone was shouting at Lila, but the words were meaningless to her. She summoned the last of her strength, sending it through her touch and into Rafe's still form. His heart skipped and fluttered until it caught the rhythm of hers. For an instant, their pulses beat together, fae and wolf. Without thinking of where she was or who might be watching, she used her free hand to smooth the dark tangle of hair from his face.

Only then did she notice the prick of a blade against her spine. Lila looked up, and the warrior in silver glared down. The fierce-eyed female had dismounted and held a sword inches from Lila's flesh.

"What do you think you're doing?" The warrior demanded, casting a meaningful glance toward Elroth. "We're in a mood to strike anyone who gets too close to the king."

"I have to heal him," Lila replied, a headache pounding behind her eyes. She'd stretched her energy too far, but she couldn't stop now.

The warrior opened her mouth, but her reply was drowned out.

"Seize Lord Farras," roared the king. "Bring him forward to answer for this crime."

Lila glanced up to see Farras sprinting for the broken wall. In a swirl of capes and swords, the fae fell upon the lord, forcing him facedown and wrenching his hands behind his back. Power flared, and a fae in silk finery flew backward. But there were too many for Farras to fight all at once, especially when the king's mounted retainers joined the fray. The warrior in black produced iron cuffs, locking them around the prisoner's bare wrists.

Lila's attention returned to Rafe. His life force was steadier now, his temperature warming. Or maybe that was an illusion, because she was starting to shiver.

The warrior in silver mail grasped her shoulder. "You need to stop and step away now. You're hurting yourself."

"Not yet," Lila said stubbornly.

"He's only a wolf." The fae frowned at Rafe, who was just beginning to stir.

Lila opened her mouth to protest the *only*, but gave a sob of relief as Rafe slowly sat up. He shook his head as if trying to clear it.

"Rafe? Are you all right?" Lila asked.

He nodded, then seemed to regret the motion. Reaching blindly, he grasped her hand and squeezed it in silent thanks.

With a chime of harness bells, King Elroth dismounted next to where Lila sat with Rafe. With a sweeping gesture, he unhooked his russet cloak, draping it around the wolf's shoulders. A murmur rose from the crowd. The gesture was an enormous mark of royal favor.

With fluid grace, he knelt beside them, frank curiosity on his face. "Lila of House Fernblade, is that you?"

Her mouth went dry. "It is, sire."

"You summoned me."

"I did, sire."

"Clearly, we have much to discuss." His gaze swept over her. "For now, you've done enough. Let me finish your task."

The king spread his fingertips over Rafe's chest, releasing a pale golden glow of healing magic. Even though she was not its target, Lila felt the brush of royal power like a pressure against her skin. The touch did not last more than a second or two, but Rafe's eyes flared wolf-gold. He scrambled to his feet, as if too filled with energy to be still.

"This wolf saved my life," the king said, rising to face the room. "I owe him and his pack a boon."

"He is my son," another wolf called out.

Lila got to her feet more slowly, eager to get a look at the Alpha she'd heard so much about. He was older and not as tall as his son, but she could see a resemblance, especially in his fierce regard. Every line of his body said he would fight for his pack, and especially his child.

"King Elroth," Rafe said with a courteous bow, showing excellent manners to a monarch who was not his own. "The wolves have come for justice. There was nothing to be gained by more death."

"You risked your life," said Elroth. "I will not forget that. What is your name?"

"Rafe of Pack Devries."

"Rafe, I thank you." The king gave a deep nod. "And while I would prefer to keep on praising your bravery, young wolf, duty commands me. There is much to do before sunrise. Go to your pack knowing you have my gratitude."

With a last bow, Rafe retreated from the king's presence. He paused as he passed close to Lila, bending to whisper in her ear. "Thank you."

Then he disappeared into the throng of wolves.

A murmur rippled through the crowd, growing louder until Elroth held up a hand for silence. "I will hear your grievances, but first you will cease your battle. Fae will gather near the high table. The rest of you go to the other end of the hall."

He pointed to emphasize his orders. Lila began to move, but the king stopped her.

"You remain here, Lila of House Fernblade," he said in softer tones. "You summoned me, and you have yet to tell me why."

A vampire in a smart suit, who seemed to be the leader of the Undead, stood his ground. "You give orders easily for one who doesn't rule the Undead or the wolves."

Elroth's shoulders stiffened. "And you are?"

A beat passed before the Undead answered. "Malatest. I rule the vampires in these parts."

"You are here, Mr. Malatest, in a fae territory, where I rule everyone."

"We didn't come here for something fun to do." The vampire tilted his fedora back a degree. "We have a score to settle."

"As I said, if you have complaints, they shall be heard. Whether they are heard before the sun rises is up to you."

Malatest matched him silence for silence, then gave a short nod. "Then I'll play nice to save time, but understand we were winning the fight."

Elroth raised his brow. "Your position is noted."

Malatest retreated. By some unspoken agreement, the Undead

gathered on the left side of the hall and the shifters on the right. When Lila looked back, Rafe had between swept into the crowd of wolves. As natural as that might be, a pang of disappointment ran through her. She missed his presence at her side.

Once the noise settled, the king strode to the middle of the banquet hall, while his retinue ranged behind him and beneath the portal's glowing arch. The retainers were all warriors, armed to the teeth. Their grim faces made it plain what would happen if anyone—fae, wolf, or vampire—put a foot wrong.

Lila found a place next to the retainers and scanned the room for her parents. She saw the gargoyles first, looming like large and ugly statues. Ademar had commandeered a bench, where her parents sat together. Though Galeeta sat as upright and poised as ever, Gareth slumped, holding her hand in his. Ademar leaned against the wall on Galeeta's other side, brow creased in a frown.

Lila's chest tightened with a mix of emotions—love, exasperation, and anxiety. Mother, father, brother—they were all a piece of her. And so vulnerable. She felt adrift, caught between the desire to be with them and the need to tell King Elroth everything she knew.

She forced herself to look away. The rest of the fae stood in a crescent at one end of the banquet hall, shuffling nervously. There seemed fewer than before. Had some fled when Farras was arrested? If they'd followed him out of fear, maybe they saw their chance and ran?

Lila searched the wolves until she found Rafe among them. It was not hard since his dark head rose above the rest. He was talking to his father, and the king's cloak was gone. He wore pants and a sleeveless jacket, but no shirt, leaving his bare arms and chest on display. Lila longed to reach out and put her hand against his warm skin, but he was too far away. For a heartsick instant, she wondered when she would touch him again—or if she ever would.

Lila's heart skipped with apprehension as King Elroth raised his hands for silence. After a moment, all that they could hear was the wind in the forest, clearly audible through the gap in the wall the vampires had made.

"I was on my way to Gilden Wood," Elroth said. "Imagine my surprise when I was suddenly summoned by an urgent message to come here. It has been a long time since I received a communication by crystal of such strength and clarity."

On hearing his device had actually worked, Ademar jerked upright, grinning, then quickly smothered his expression. Lila couldn't hide an answering smile. Elroth looked her way, and she felt her cheeks grow hot.

"I responded immediately," he said. "A king comes when one of his people calls out in distress. I would ask the sender why she sent that message."

The warrior in silver mail nudged her forward. Once Lila was in motion, all her years of training for court took over. She approached Elroth, stopping at a respectful distance, and sunk into a curtsy. The gesture felt wrong in her grubby, ill-fitting clothes. "Your Majesty."

She rose, feeling the weight of so many watching. Farras stood where she could see him from the corner of her eye. His captors had hauled him to the front of the crowd and gagged him with a banquet napkin.

"It is evident that much has happened here," Elroth said with an edge of sarcasm. "Tell me your message now, in full."

"This is a long tale with several threads, sire, and I do not know every part," Lila began. "But what I do know is that there is an individual some call the Magician selling bacchante in the city."

"I have heard of the drug," Elroth replied. "That is one reason I believe the fae will benefit by retreating from the human world."

Lila tensed. "I am sorry to say, Your Majesty, that the Magician is a fae, and he sells the drug to other supernaturals as well as to our people."

The king's eyebrows lifted. "A fae is selling bacchante? A light fae?"

"Yes, Your Majesty." Lila pushed on, wanting to say as much as she could before she lost her chance to speak. "The effect on other species is most often fatal, so they are eager to find the Magician's identity."

"Understandable," Elroth said.

"Wolves tracked the Magician to this way station, but they vanished without a trace. Rafe was the last to arrive with his Undead companion." Lila gestured to where Izetta stood. "I was here when they were thrown into the dungeon beneath this building."

"Way stations do not have cells," Elroth interrupted in an affronted tone. "Or should not."

"This one does," Lila replied, leaving as little room as possible for interruption. "Lord Farras confessed to me that he spelled the wolves to sleep and put them in the prison cells. I freed those who were left alive, along with Captain Teegar and my father. They were all being held in the dungeon."

"Captain Teegar?"

"And my father. Lord Farras said that you were responsible for his capture."

"He did, did he?" Elroth's frown deepened. "That is far from the truth."

"One more thing."

The king's eyebrows rose again. "Just one?"

"So there is no doubt ever again, I would like to be formally and publicly released from any expectation that I marry Lord Farras."

Elroth made a less than kingly snort. "That I grant without reservation. Allow me a moment to consider what you've told me. Remain here in case I have questions."

Lila curtsied again and retreated to her place beside the retainers.

The silver-clad warrior gave her an approving nod. "Quick and concise," she said under her breath. "That's how he likes it."

And it didn't take long for Elroth to digest what she'd told him. Barely a moment later, he addressed the room.

"I have heard a great many disturbing things in these last minutes. First among them is that a fae is responsible for deaths in other communities."

Malatest stepped forward. "Like I said, we have a score to settle."

"As do we." That was Rafe's father, matching the vampire move for move.

Elroth looked from one to the other. "Then I ask you, does anyone know the identity of the Magician?"

CHAPTER 33

Izetta hadn't taken her eyes off Galeeta of House Fernblade. Since the moment Izetta had escaped the way station, she'd daydreamed of exacting revenge. It wasn't just pain Izetta objected to—a professional killer couldn't complain too hard about flesh wounds.

It was the damage the fae had done to others—to Rafe, to Sadie, to the youngsters who didn't know any better because the young should be able to live and learn from their mistakes. She loathed whoever put a prison under a place meant for hospitality. Who thought like that?

Galeeta was guilty—maybe not for everything, but for enough. But now she was propping up her mate with a look of bottomless, helpless grief Izetta would not soon forget. Grief, with a side order of guilt. There was nothing Izetta's blade could do to top that kind of suffering.

Vengeance was all about timing. Izetta would get her justice, but it would have to wait. The realization left her more than a little disgruntled.

Until the fae king who looked like a storybook Prince Charming began asking about the Magician. That perked her up.

"Please, sire." Izetta strolled toward the king, making a perfunctory bow. "I have evidence of the Magician's identity."

"And you didn't tell me?" Malatest protested from the sidelines. Then he and the Alpha began shouting at once, making a confused, angry babble.

"Silence!" Elroth barked and waved for Izetta to continue.

"I just figured it out," she said, addressing Malatest as well as Elroth. "And it's not as simple as you think."

She pulled out her phone and fussed with it for a moment, then held it up so that Elroth could see. He took the phone from her with a respectful nod, seeming not to notice her battle-stained clothes and wild hair.

"This is security camera footage of the Magician," she said. "I've personally verified it with half a dozen witnesses who were present in the same venue that night. It's the only image we have of him."

As he watched, she took the opportunity to study the king's profile. His features were a little more rugged than most fae, his hair a shade darker and tinted with auburn lights. Definitely handsome.

Elroth remained silent until the video ended. "Unfortunately, we do not see his face."

Izetta scrolled the video back, tapped the image on her phone and expanded it. "Look at his hair ornament."

Elroth peered at the phone again, a frown of concentration pleating his brow. "I know that design. I know the silversmith who created it."

Izetta pulled Teegar's hair clip from her pocket and held it up. The clip was about four inches wide, shaped in a twisting infinity loop. What made it unique was that the loop was an elongated, striped cat, with fangs and claws extended. "I would say this is a match."

The king took the clip from Izetta's hand. An angry flush rose

along his cheekbones, and his fingers closed around the ornament so tightly his knuckles grew white.

"Teegar was trusted by my father first, and then by me," the
king said roughly. "He was a good leader of his men. A simple,
honest soldier—or so I thought."

A surprised murmur rippled through the fae, but it quickly
grew angry once the wolves and vampires joined in. The tension
made Izetta twitchy enough to scan the room for possible
threats. Her eye caught the prisoner who had thrown the spear.
The gagged fae met her gaze with an insolence that made her itch
to break his neck.

Fireballs. He wore Errata's amulet. That's what had left him
free from the spell that froze everyone else—and able to throw
his weapon. She took two steps forward and, vampire-quick, she
ripped it from his neck. It must have hurt, because Farras let out
a grunt.

"He stole that from my friend," she said to anyone listening,
but no one stirred.

"Teegar? Where is he?" the king bellowed. "Where is Captain
Teegar?"

A gasp rose from the fae. Izetta felt as much as heard the panic
in it, like the vibrations from a badly-tuned instrument. She cast
a sideways glance at Elroth. He was obviously a master at hiding
his thoughts, but the downward twitch of his sculpted mouth
gave him away. He'd heard it, too.

Some of the fae knew Teegar's secret. That made sense, if
what she'd heard about fae using the drug was true. They had to
know who sold it to them, and now their playtime was over.
Names would be named, and judging by the royal frown, it
would not go well for those on Elroth's naughty list.

The six wolves who had been imprisoned under the waysta-
tion escorted Teegar into the hall. The fae standing near the
entrance parted to make way for the strange procession, holding

back their cloaks and skirts as if afraid the wolves might brush against them.

Teegar's hands were still bound and his clothes ragged and caked in mud. Leaves stuck in his snarled hair. But when he caught sight of Farras, his bruised and dirty face blazed with defiance.

His escort positioned him directly before the king. When the wolves drew back, Izetta shoved Teegar to his knees. He hit the floor with a thump.

Elroth regarded his captain for a long moment. "I trusted you."

"But you never thought to make me more than what I was," Teegar replied so quietly that Izetta barely made out the words. There was an ache in his voice that spoke of enduring disappointment.

"I can only grant my subjects what they earn."

"I deserved more. You are the king. You could have changed everything."

Elroth heaved a weary sigh, as if he'd heard this argument countless times before. "Not even I can make you something you are not prepared to make yourself."

Teegar looked confused.

"You see, the problem, sire," Izetta said. "This is the Magician's body, all right, but I can't believe this blank canvas represents the Magician's brain. That's why I wasn't about to let my friends play chew toy with him just yet. He's not your final answer."

The wolves whined. The king looked from them, to Izetta, and finally at Teegar. "Then who is your partner?"

The color drained from Teegar's face. There was no way out of the hole he'd dug for himself, whether or not he answered the king.

Izetta enjoyed the moment until one of the fae—Galeeta's husband—struggled to his feet. Her gut twisted in sympathy. It took a lot to weaken a fae, but time in the cells had done it. His strength was clearly spent.

She couldn't help glancing at the female fae—Lila—who stood to the side with King Elroth's retinue. The young fae was disheveled and dirty, but what Izetta noticed was the way she looked at her father. That much shock and grief left a mark.

"May I speak, Your Majesty?" Lila's father asked in a cracked voice. "I believe I may shed some light on this matter."

"Lord Gareth, is that you?" Elroth said with obvious shock.

"Indeed, sire. I have been reflecting on my choices in the privacy of a cell."

The king beckoned him forward. "Please come and share what you know."

At Elroth's signal, Lila hurried to her father's side to help him approach. A fae warrior in silver armor followed. Together, they bore Lord Gareth's weight as he slowly made his way toward the king. He stumbled once, nearly taking Lila with him, but as soon as they drew close, Gareth waved her off and approached the king, bowing low.

"As always, I am at your disposal, Your Majesty."

"As always, old friend," the king said gently. "Please rest assured that you were not apprehended on my authority. It grieves me to see you in distress."

"Your concern does me honor, sire." Gareth pulled himself upright and cast a hard look at Teegar. "As does your interest in what I have to say."

"Please share what you know."

"I was arrested by Captain Teegar for the possession of a trunk containing, so I am told, wealth gained by illegal means."

As he spoke, his voice shook with fatigue. Izetta took a step closer, reluctant to miss a single word.

"What illegal means?" Elroth asked. "Stolen goods? The sale of bacchante?"

Gareth shrugged. "I do not know the particulars of my criminal career. In fact, I do not remember it at all."

A ripple passed through the crowd, more horror than amusement at the jest.

"However," Gareth continued, "it was Lord Farras who stored the trunk—along with other household goods—at my residence while his own house was being redecorated. I postulate that he is the captain's partner in crime. It would take someone that unprincipled to bring bacchante to our streets."

If the fae had been shocked when Teegar was accused, this time the crowd responded with a din. A handful of bystanders chose that moment to slip out the door and into the night.

"That would make sense, sire," Izetta said, looking at the fae king, "if your would-be assassin was the brains of the operation and the one who supplied the product. But then why was Teegar in the cells? And why was this man arrested?"

Gareth shook his head, his smile crooked. "Madam, I was unwittingly in possession of all the lovely gold. That made me theoretically guilty, and that gave Lord Farras leverage over my family. As for Captain Teegar, I would suggest our two culprits had a partnership that soured, and he wasn't clever enough to make himself scarce."

"Partnership?" Teegar exploded, loud enough that several people jumped. "Farras is a *spider.* Once his fangs are in, he sucks you dry. When I finally came here to settle things, I woke up in a cell."

"Were you aware that there was a prison here?" Elroth asked pointedly. "In a way station where any fae who asks should be guaranteed safety?"

Teegar scowled. "Even the dungeons have dungeons here, my king. The cells are where I picked up my supply, nice and hidden. Lord Farras never built this nightmare to be a safe place."

Izetta glanced at Farras, who stood bolt upright, eyes blazing with fury. Teegar had doomed them both.

"That is all the confession I need for now." Elroth nodded to his warriors. "Teegar is henceforth stripped of rank and title and shall be held for trial. See to it that representatives of the wolves and Undead have equal rank with the fae when it comes to judgment. The crimes of the Magician are not against us alone."

The wolves and Undead made approving noises. Malatest and the Alpha stepped forward to nod their heads in thanks.

King Elroth returned the gesture. Then his attention went to Izetta. "Many thanks for your assistance, my lady."

"You are welcome, sire, though I'm not a lady. I am Izetta."

"Izetta. Your name is known even in the Gilden Wood. I am glad we met in pursuit of a common goal."

She smiled, showing her fangs. "One word of advice, sire, if you don't mind."

"Of course not," he replied, his brows rising.

"The Magician had customers among your people. Don't forget they'll need you now."

He put a hand to his heart. "I'm taking my people to a place of healing. I promise you they will have whatever they require."

Izetta had heard plenty of promises from men with crowns, but Elroth seemed to mean it. She retreated to where the vampires stood while Lila and the silver-clad warrior returned Lord Gareth to his family.

Teegar was taken away. He cried and cursed as he vanished through the portal between two of the king's warriors, while the wolves and vampires cheered.

"And now," the king said, his eyes growing sharp. "What shall we do with Lord Farras?"

"Elroth is angry," Malatest murmured as Izetta reached his side. "If I were Farras, I would grovel very hard."

Errata appeared on her other side. Silently, Izetta handed her back her amulet.

The werecougar stuffed it in her pocket. "Good work up there. Can I get a copy of that video?"

Izetta didn't reply. The warrior in black was dragging Farras before the king. The fae lord had lost none of his insolence, but his hands were shaking now. Whether it was fear or rage, she could not tell.

"Why?" Elroth asked Farras. "You are my cousin, wealthy and talented, and you have always had my ear. What could you want so dearly that I must die?"

The room grew so silent, Izetta thought she could hear the shadows slide along the floor.

"The sovereign power of the throne," Farras said simply.

Color rose again in Elroth's face. "Treason."

"Call it creative self-interest."

"Let me guess," Elroth said dryly. "Killing me would only get you so far without the support of your peers, so you invented your drug to addict, bankrupt, or blackmail your way to an army of obedient hangers-on."

"Oh, I did not invent bacchante, merely discovered a source." Farras smiled, showing bloody teeth where a blow had cut the inside of his mouth. "And I rarely got involved in the details. There were so many other transactions that required my personal touch."

A rustle of indrawn breath circled the hall. How many here had got that personal touch? By the sullen mood among the fae, Izetta guessed quite a few.

"Why involve other supernaturals?" Elroth demanded.

"For the gold," Farras replied, catching and holding the king's gaze. "If you got out more, you'd know money is as good as magic in the real world. You talk about a decline in fae power, but instead of navigating the future, you run back to the forest like a startled deer. Change happens, cousin, whether you embrace it or not."

Elroth's head jerked back as if a snake had reared before him. "Oh, cleverly spoken, Farras. You do enjoy the sharp edge of your honest wit."

Farras shrugged one shoulder, his bound hands robbing the gesture of his usual grace. "So cut my head off."

"You expect to die, do you?" Elroth's smile was pitying, and for the first time, Farras's defiance faltered.

"What—"

"I did not give you leave to speak, fool." The king grabbed the top of Farras's head, spreading his fingers wide to grip his skull. "If you long to be close to the throne, I can ensure you will always have a place beside it."

Eyes wide with sudden understanding, Farras screamed. "*No!*"

Magic slammed into Farras with the force of a war hammer, making him shudder wildly. Light flickered around Elroth and his prisoner, but not the usual light fae glow. This was an absence of color—jagged scraps of nothing ripping the air around them. The backwash alone made Izetta stagger, but Farras curled forward until his forehead touched the floor. This was the power of the sovereign he had wanted so badly, but now it was turned against him.

Farras slowly shriveled—Izetta could think of no other word as his flesh seemed to evaporate from twisting bones. When Elroth finally released him, he stayed curled up on the floor, slowly rocking back and forth.

"Get up, fool." Elroth nudged him with his foot. "You have new duties."

Farras pushed himself to his knees. When he looked up, the bones of his face had altered, so that chin and nose were too sharp, like a child's nutcracker doll. His hair had crisped and frizzed to a ragged sun around his head.

"My liege," he wheezed.

A collective shudder passed through the fae huddled against the walls. One of the wolves threw up. Izetta wished she could. Every vampire understood transformation, but she'd never seen anything like this.

"Be it known that you, Farras of the Forest Fae, are stripped of wealth, of title, and of all your magic," Elroth said, his voice carrying the full weight of authority. "You will never be king of the fae, but I sentence you to be the Lord of Misrule."

Farras let out a shriek of rage that sounded like tearing metal.

"It has been many years since I had a court jester," the king said. "But you are fully qualified for the position."

Farras scrambled to his feet but could not pull himself upright. His bones were no longer straight. He stumbled, caught himself, and howled in defiant anger. When he finally got control of his limbs, he weaved and bobbed with a strange, hopping gait.

"I will kill you in your sleep," he rasped, brandishing claw-like fingers. "I will tear out your eyes and devour them. I will drip poison in your wine."

"Then I shall pen you with the hounds until you mend your ways," the king said blandly. "You will have to earn your comforts, cousin."

"This is not who I am!" Farras shrieked.

"It is exactly who you are," Elroth retorted. "Every monarch who sits the Throne endures the test of this particular magic. The purpose is to reveal a fae's true spirit, to manifest their nature in the flesh, and so it has done with you."

Arms raised, Farras hurled himself at the king with another ear-splitting scream. The warrior in black grabbed the jester by the back of his torn silk tunic, holding him in place while his feet still tried to pedal forward.

Elroth looked on, his face pale. "Let this be an education for anyone tempted to treason. The Throne is not a prize to be taken, but a trust to be defended. Until Farras understands his own folly, he will remain a fool."

Wolf, fae, or Undead—they all stared in profound shock. The shifters shuffled closer together, needing the comfort of touch. When Errata's shoulder brushed hers, Izetta slipped her arm through the cat's.

"Vlad's fangs," Malatest said under his breath. "And I came here looking for revenge."

Izetta made a soft noise that might have been a stillborn laugh. "We're rank amateurs, my friend. There's a reason we're scared of the fae."

The king addressed his retinue. "Take my jester away and find him motley. Perhaps Bronkin left something he can wear."

The moment Farras approached the portal, the way station he had built began to tremble.

CHAPTER 34

The vibration beneath Lila's feet deepened to a shudder, and then stopped. Everyone in the hall shuffled nervously, glancing around as if looking for the cue to run. The king's retainers closed in around Elroth, one of them gesturing toward the portal.

Lila immediately understood what was happening—she'd seen the problem herself on various job sites. Farras's magic was broken, and enough minutes had ticked by that the spell that built the way station was adjusting to the fact. If the building's magic had been set properly—the spell anchored across a large group of casters for safety—the transition should have been seamless. This was sloppy work.

Unless … A thought occurred to Lila, but she pushed it away. Not even Farras was so arrogant. The idea came again, except this time there was a smell in the air that made her queasy. No, not a smell exactly, but a feeling like something scratching on the inside of her skull.

A lot of power went into building an ordinary way station, let alone one this extravagant. Such magic didn't run down quietly, like a battery gone dead. Half the time it rebounded like a rubber band.

The vibration beneath Lila's feet deepened to a shudder. Around the hall, the crowd was growing restless while Elroth seemed to be in deep conversation with one of his counselors. The warriors were fanning out, weapons drawn, intent on keeping order. No doubt they believed the tremor was the way station's magic adjusting to the loss of its designer. It took experience to know the quality of this disruption signaled something far worse.

Gooseflesh coursed down her arms. Every instinct screamed that the place was about to get very dangerous.

She looked around for her mother's servants, but the gargoyles were gone. They'd been present when she'd brought her father back to the bench, but had vanished the first time she actually wanted their help.

Fine. No time for irritation, much less a search party. Her family would have to manage on their own.

Lila grabbed Ademar's arm and gestured to their parents. "Get them to the door. Fast."

She turned to go, but he caught her sleeve, holding her in place. "Why?"

"I know building spells. Something doesn't feel right. I'm going to warn the king."

To his credit, Ademar believed her at once. "I'll do my part. Good luck."

She began a sprint across the hall, waving to catch the eye of the warrior in silver mail. But the magic was failing too fast. Halfway there, she stumbled as the polished wood planks of the floor began to lift. Lila fell to her hands and knees, skidding only a few inches before another bit of oak jammed her knees. The floor shook violently. The remaining plates of food slid from the tables and smashed as the furniture rocked.

"Outside!" King Elroth roared, far too late.

A giant crunching, grinding noise sounded from beneath the floor. Lila picked herself up just as tendrils split the boards at her feet. They wormed past the cracks and edges, pale green fingers that thickened and stiffened into twigs, then saplings unfurling a crown of leaves. The forest was reclaiming the way station.

She bounded forward, fully focused on getting out alive. No place was safe to stand on—the whole floor had burst open with untamed growth. The room heaved, rocking the pillars. The remains of her decorations slithered down their fluted surface, crumbling to dust.

She'd almost made it across the hall to the exit when the room exploded. A great tree, almost as wide as the room itself, pounded upward from below. The force flung Lila like chaff.

She landed on her back with enough force to spin her like the hands on a clock.

When she stopped moving, it took a moment for her lungs to work again. She dragged in air in a whooping rush and struggled to sit up. Her first sight was of Farras, his twisted form crouched like a spider about to pounce.

"This is all your fault," he rasped.

He crawled forward, oblivious to the rolling destruction around them. Lila scuttled backward, frantically searching for the king's warriors.

Farras gave a nasty grin. "Oh, I gave His Majesty's brutes the slip. They were far more concerned about his precious head getting a bump once the shaking started. They believe I'm quite harmless now."

"But you're not," Lila said, stalling while she groped for a plan of escape. "You broke every rule about magical constructs. You never anchored this way station. You held onto its magic by yourself, with no help, and now it's a death trap."

"A group anchor required that I share my secrets." He laughed. "Give away my plans for this place. Why would I trust anyone?"

For the barest instant, Lila felt sorry for him. "But now it's falling apart."

A chunk of the ceiling crashed just yards away, sending up a plume of dust and debris.

Farras ignored it. "I never create something I'm not prepared to sacrifice, and I never leave my enemies alive. That's why I always win."

Snatches of memory stuttered through her brain—the castle in Gilden Wood, the stables, Farras beating his horse. She'd been terrified of Bronkin, the old jester who had chased her through the castle halls. He'd been deranged, but nothing like this. Farras's eyes held a sheen of fury she'd never seen anywhere before.

Old fear welled up in her, as if her girlhood nightmares had reared from their grave. But she wasn't a child any longer. Lila summoned her power, remembering the battle spell she'd used on Rafe the night he'd arrived with Izetta.

"No, your reign of terror is over. You're off the board." With a cry of satisfaction, she made her shot. An orb of energy flew from her hand, straight into Farras's chest.

He batted it away as if it were a gnat. Lila's stomach dropped like a stone.

"You've drained your magic already today," he said with a sneering laugh. "Poor Lila, I bet you tried to save everyone and have nothing left for yourself."

He picked up a long shard of wood, like the one he'd used on his horse that day in the stables, and stood. Lila seized the opportunity to roll away from him and scramble to her feet. She staggered as the floor pitched again as if a giant creature tunneled under it, pushing up the boards with its spine. She grabbed what she thought was a table leg, but it was stuck in a crack. Fresh roots plunged downward, into the dirt, as the forest called it back home.

Dirt? Lila's thoughts skittered. If there was earth beneath this floor, the lower levels of the way station had vanished. Time wasn't running out—it was already gone.

"Poor Lila, not a weapon or wine bottle in sight," Farras crooned. Then his tone turned angry. "Did you think you'd get away with setting this rebellion in motion? With turning your back on *me*?"

She sent a plea to the forest, using the last scrap of her power. She wasn't relying on magic—she'd used that up—but her affinity with the wood mattered. The table leg came free in her grip.

"Contrary to your own opinion," she said, "you're not the center of the universe."

He swung the shard of wood, and she blocked his strike. The blow made her stumble backward, pain lancing up her arm. He struck again, and this time, his stick shattered. He tossed the remains aside, but not before Lila smashed her table leg against his skull. He dropped to his knees, grabbing her legs as he fell forward. Lila went over backward, landing hard on the pitching ground.

Farras crawled up her body, his hideous, bloodied face rising into view. His hands locked around her throat. Lila struggled for breath, chest heaving in vain. Pain sang through her whole body as she clawed at his grip. Her vision went black, random splotches of light dancing in the void.

The floor tilted again. Lila rolled with the momentum, flipping her attacker to his back. The motion loosened his hold just long enough to suck in a breath. She blinked Farras into focus and gazed into his rage-filled eyes.

Her hand found the table leg, and she jabbed one end into his breast bone. The angle was awkward, because he was still doing his best to strangle her, but aim wasn't important. Neither was force.

You can have this back now, she said to the forest. *Thank you for the loan.*

The table leg sprouted roots again, shooting them down through Farras's body and into the earth below. His scream seared through her as he gave a last painful spasm before finally letting go of her throat.

Lila's head bowed with exhaustion. Regret died beneath a wave of relief. She'd survived. Thinking would come later.

The wood spearing him exploded into a tree, flinging her off and absorbing whatever was left of the king's jester. She fell, rolling several times before crashing into a wall.

White-hot pain lanced through her from jaw to tailbone. It took her a moment to realize that she'd been tossed into the passage just outside the banquet hall. The huge glass windows cracked, then shattered, glass raining from the frames. Lila curled into a ball, arms over her head. Seconds passed as tiny slivers of glass stung her skin.

"Lila!" Rafe bent over her. His eyes had flared wolf-yellow, startling beneath the fall of his curling dark hair. "Get up."

She tried. Cracks spidered up the wall, mirroring the agony scampering along her nerves. Lila hissed air through her teeth, digging her fingers into Rafe's arms.

In one swift move, he picked her up as if she were no more than a toddler. The motion hurt, and she couldn't stifle a cry.

"Hush." Rafe glanced over his shoulder, turning pale as he caught sight of the massive tree trunk blocking their way back to the banquet hall. More tendrils were creeping through the floor.

Lila's courage wobbled. "Leave me and go. You might still have a chance."

"I swore to your brother I'd protect you."

"I release you from that promise."

"Busy now," he growled. "Talk less."

He ran toward the entry hall, reaching the space just as something crashed behind them. Destruction ruled here, too. The stairway that led to the floor above crumbled at the base, bits of elaborate trim dropping off as the banister sprouted leaves. Then the floor gave a heave, throwing them against the wall. Lila's head bumped something solid, but the knock barely registered. She already hurt in too many places.

Rafe stumbled, catching his footing at the last second.

"Put me down!" She wiggled out of his grasp.

"Can you run?"

"I can try."

"Okay." He grabbed her hand, dragging her out of the way as a piece of the ceiling sheared away, spraying plaster and wood shards into the air. The overhead light crashed to the floor at the base of the stairs. Rafe leaped over it, swinging her past the explosion of crystal and sparks.

"This way!" Rafe shouted.

They lunged for the massive front door. Somewhere deep in the house, a support beam whined as it torqued and splintered. The roof buckled to the chorus of more breaking windows.

Something slammed into her shoulder, sending her staggering forward. Her palms hit the floor, but she pushed up and kept running. Rafe was heaving at the door, fighting against a frame that was losing its proper shape. In another minute, that too would fall to rubble—with them under it.

Rafe had the door open a few inches. He wrapped his fingers around the front edge of the heavy oak planks and planted his feet. Plaster coated his hair and clothes, sweat streaking his dusty face like war paint. He strained against the door, bare arms bunching and feet pushing against the floor. The door moved, but only inches.

Lila joined him, bracing her back against the frame and pushing while he pulled. It probably cost her more effort than it helped Rafe, but the door moved another foot before it wedged against the buckling floor. With a massive crunch, the high ceiling of the foyer collapsed in earnest. Chunks of wood fell like gigantic hail.

Wasting no time, she wriggled through the opening. Rafe barely squeezed through behind her. The air outside was cold and fresh, the stars like ice chips above.

CHAPTER 35

He caught her hand, pulling her across the grassy clearing until they were well away from the way station—and just in time. The remains of the building finally crashed to the earth. A faint glow clung to the rubble, the last of King Elroth's fiery portal. Perhaps the way station's collapse had rendered it unstable. The release of that much magic was as good as a detonation.

Bit by bit, the rubble of the way station dissolved to nothing. Soon, the hilltop would be as pristine and wild as the rest of the woods. Lord Farras's hidden prison in the woods was truly gone.

"Thank you," she said, still holding Rafe's hand.

"For pulling you out of a building that wanted to be a forest?"

She gave him a sidelong look. "And other things."

He frowned. "What happened back there? Why didn't you leave with the other fae? When I couldn't find you, I went looking."

"Farras. He triggered the building to collapse and came back for a last hurrah. A tree ate him."

Rafe's brows rose.

Lila sighed. "He blamed me for everything that happened to him."

Weariness swamped her, and she leaned against Rafe's side.

He squeezed her hand. "You set us free by refusing to fall in line with his plans. Remember that part."

"Lila!" Ademar stood a few yards away, at the crest of a rise in the grass. He beckoned frantically. "Come here."

As she tried to move, all her bruises made themselves felt. Another time, she would have eased them with magic, but she was spent.

"Hurry!" Ademar called.

She started to walk. "I'm coming as fast as I can."

Her brother quickly moved in to take her arm, putting himself between Lila and Rafe as he urged her along. The wolf's eyes flashed yellow, but Lila shook her head, silently asking for patience.

"Come along if you must," Ademar said to Rafe. "There's no time to waste."

"What's the matter?" Rafe asked.

"You'll see. Maybe you can help."

"Fine."

Rafe took Lila's other arm and fell into step beside them. When they reached the top of the rise, Lila saw what was left of the crowd. Fae lights hung over the scene, supplementing the starlight. From what she could see, most had fled or dispersed to the woods and were now gathered in small knots, some talking but more sitting in silence as if to digest everything they'd just learned.

She glanced to the left. The walkways and pool had vanished. The tents and vehicles of Farras's followers were swallowed by dense brush. Only the horses had escaped unscathed and were now happily grazing on the new growth.

Then she looked toward where the lawn had been and understood Ademar's urgency. King Elroth was there with two of his warriors and the leaders of the Undead and the wolves. The king had his hand on her father's arm, holding him back from—she tried to make sense of what she saw.

"Come on!" Ademar shouted, trying to hurry down the slope with the aid of his cane. "You're the one they trust. You try talking to her."

Lila wasn't sure what he meant, but she leaned on him and Rafe as they hurried toward the scene. At first, all she could make out was the vampire leader—Malatest—in his pinstripe suit, with Izetta beside him. They were looming over her mother, who was on the ground with her tattered green gown pooling over the grass. Izetta held a long blade.

"Wait!" Lila cried, all injuries forgotten. "Don't touch her."

"Lila," her father cried, still struggling to reach his wife. "Lila, help her."

"Halt." The king held up a hand. "All of you, halt or I will make you."

Malatest stepped back, raising his palms in a gesture of surrender. Izetta remained where she was. The vampire's dark eyes never wavered from Galeeta's face.

"We're asking for justice," Izetta said in a cool, even tone. "Not vengeance, but equitable payback for our imprisonment."

"She put shackles on my son," the Alpha said. "Wolves died."

Malatest spoke up. "While we recognize that the two leaders of this treasonous scheme were dealt with tonight, one remains."

"Lady Galeeta protected that piece of troll-dung," Izetta said. "She knew full well what she was doing. And she tried very hard to hurt me."

"Please. *Please*," Lila begged. "You don't know the full story."

Izetta ignored her. "I demand justice, Your Majesty. That is my right."

Malatest folded his arms. "What do you say, sire?"

Lila's heart thundered. The accords between the supernatural species were simple. All players more or less observed basic principles of justice in order to avoid costly war.

"Galeeta of House Fernblade," the king said. "Our allies have brought charges against you. How do you respond?"

"I did what I did to protect my family," Galeeta said from her position on the ground. "And for the record, I truly believed my husband was in your custody, my king."

"But—" Lila interjected, but the king held up his hand to silence her.

Rafe put his arm around her shoulder. Ademar went to their father, all but holding him upright. The others remained stock-still.

"Izetta of the Undead, though your charges are indeed grave, might we conduct this with all players on their feet?" Elroth asked with a drop of sarcasm.

"No," Izetta replied, still as death as she loomed over Galeeta. "I've caught her. I keep her."

Elroth exchanged a look with Malatest. "The rules of this proceeding state that all parties are equal, free to speak, and none shall stand on ceremony. However, this is beyond the bounds of civilized behavior."

Malatest shrugged. "Izetta, give it up. You'll get your chance if the verdict is a thumbs-down."

Slowly, very slowly, the vampire stepped aside, sheathing her blade. Lila darted forward to help her mother to her feet. Galeeta barely glanced at the vampires as she smoothed back the hair that had escaped her elaborate braids. Her face was a pale, haughty mask that failed to hide her fear. Lila's chest tightened with grief. There was no way her family would walk away from this unscathed.

The group—fae, Undead, and wolf—regarded Lila, clearly expecting her to retreat now that Galeeta was on her feet. She looked around for Rafe. His expression held the same fear and confusion she felt.

She stubbornly stuck by her mother's side.

"Very well," Elroth said. "Galeeta, what did you know of Farras's plan to commit treason?"

"Nothing, Your Majesty." Galeeta swallowed, as if still feeling the shadow of Izetta's knife. "It was supposed to be a celebration. No one knew we would be attacked. No one knew you would come, Your Majesty. Whatever plans Lord Farras had, tonight he simply seized the opportunity. That is my guess, at least."

The king looked unimpressed. "And what do you know for certain?"

Lila wanted to hear the answer and yet didn't. She held her breath and lifted her gaze, meeting Izetta's eyes. The vampire was close enough to touch. The look she gave Lila held a shred of pity, but she looked back to Galeeta with the intensity of a hawk.

"I knew he meant to deliver Lord Teegar into your custody," Galeeta replied. "Lord Farras desired to win your trust."

"And then once that happened, he would slit my throat?"

Galeeta swallowed again. "He did not say that to me. I would not doubt it."

Silence hung over the group long enough for a wolf to howl in the distance. Another answered. Once again, she sought Rafe among the wolves, their gazes meeting. She took a shred of courage from the warmth and concern she saw there.

"Tell them what he used against you," Lila said unsteadily.

"My children," Galeeta said softly. "Sala and her children were the latest."

"What do you mean *latest*?" Elroth asked.

"I bore five children. Four were daughters—Sala, Rosemund, Arabelle, and Lila. Rosemund and Arabelle were serving at the court of the May Queen when I received a letter to say they had vanished without a trace."

"I remember," Elroth said with a nod. "There was a search."

"I found out later what became of them." Tears stood in Galeeta's eyes.

"You did?" Lila cried. She heard Ademar and her father's voices rise in shock, too. "Why did you say nothing?"

"Did Farras kill them?" Ademar asked, furious now.

"Worse." Galeeta fell back a step, putting space between her and Lila. She hugged her arms, as if suddenly cold. "The gargoyles. He twisted my daughters' bodies and minds into monsters."

"What?" Lila cried, but the word was drowned in the general chorus of surprise.

Gareth sagged in Ademar's arms, and Lila helped him lower their father to the ground. Images flashed through her mind—the creatures disappearing around corners, avoiding the light, and fading away when they might have captured their father. Her head swam as if she might faint.

"Farras swore me to silence on pain of their deaths," Galeeta added, sobbing openly now. "And he promised to restore them if I did everything he said."

"That's tragic," Izetta said, still fingering the hilt of her blade. "But a sad story doesn't make up for what she did."

"I'm sorry," Galeeta cried. "I apologize for what I did to you. I was certain you had come to harm my family."

"Izetta," Rafe said. He stood with his father now, back with his own pack. "I know what she did to us and agree there must be a price, but Lila helped us. She freed the wolves. She freed me."

"Lila is not on trial." The vampire shot him a quelling look.

But she was. Her family was. What happened to Galeeta would impact them all. If her father had been the heart of the family, her mother had been their muscle, bone, and mind. And now, with a long recovery ahead, Gareth would need her more than ever.

"Your Majesty, is no one here to defend my mother?" Lila asked the king. "Will no one argue her case?"

His expression softened, but not much. "This is not that kind of trial, and she has spoken for herself."

Her mother struggled to silence her weeping. "There will be a vote, Lila."

"Guilty," Malatest said, wasting no time.

Lila sucked in a breath. Galeeta was utterly still.

"Guilty," Rafe's father said. "Though I am heartily sorry for everything that she suffered. No one's children should be threatened. But that includes mine."

King Elroth shook his head. "I couldn't change the verdict even if I desired it. But I don't. Lady Galeeta of House Fernblade, you are guilty of treason and of harming our friends."

~

GUILTY.

Rafe bowed his head as the word settled over the clearing. The verdict made sense in a tragic way. Whatever her reasons, Galeeta had collaborated with the fae who had tried to murder the king—among a long list of other heinous acts. That was a death sentence.

"Good," said Izetta.

Galeeta stiffened, drawing herself up as if leaning into a strong wind. Gareth deflated where he sat in the grass, collapsing into his son's arms.

"No, no please." Lila fell to her knees, her expression stricken with grief. "I beg for mercy, sire. She is my mother."

"Lila." Lady Galeeta stared straight ahead, but her mouth worked as if unable to decide what to say.

Rafe expected her to silence her child, to say that fae didn't beg.

Instead, she surprised him. "Thank you for being my daughter."

"This is very touching," Malatest said. "However, there is a verdict and a debt to pay, and we're wasting darkness."

The words were like battle lines, keeping the species in their separate corners. No one truly trusted the fae and recent events had done nothing to bridge that gulf.

"I know that look, son," his father said softly. "Don't you dare start a fight."

There was a shadow of their old fights in his tone. He was still an Alpha, and Rafe was still his rebellious son. This was no time for that fight.

"I won't." Rafe understood Izetta's anger—he had been in the dungeon, too, and although his imprisonment had been longer, it had been far gentler than hers.

But there had to be another way forward.

Rafe went to Lila and lifted her from where she knelt on the grass. She raised her face to his as she stood, her eyes wide and frightened. The sight stopped his breath, and the ground seemed to move all over again.

"You and I built a bridge," he said. "It shouldn't have worked, but it did because I told you the truth and you listened. You showed me fae were capable of a kind of honor I understood."

"We both wanted the truth," she said softly. "But how does that help now?"

"My question exactly," Izetta put in, her voice like ice.

Rafe squeezed Lila's hands, then released them as he turned to face Izetta. "While we agree on guilt, we have yet to decide on a sentence."

So much was in the balance. He'd just started to feel like pack again, but that wouldn't last. His father was angry. So was Izetta. His life would be so much easier if he kept his mouth shut and stayed within the boundaries of expected discipline.

But duty looked different tonight. He turned to the king. "The fae have stood apart from the supernatural community for too long. Tonight proved we're stronger together. Let's learn to work together before another Farras or Teegar comes along."

The king raised his brows. "And you believe sparing Galeeta's life will further that goal?"

"Life leaves room for options." Rafe folded his arms. "Death does not. And you granted me a boon, sire. I want a better solution."

"I vote with my son," the Alpha said. "If he's calling in a royal favor, I should listen."

Rafe closed his eyes for a moment, drinking in his father's words. They had finally achieved at least some understanding now.

"I will listen," Izetta said, exchanging a glance with Malatest. "I'm not in the business of mercy, Rafe Devries, but that's what you're asking from me. Make this good."

Rafe was acutely aware of Lila beside him. A hollow place was opening up inside him. Soon the king and his Forest Fae would fade into the woods, leaving nothing but a jumble of memories behind. He should have known better than to let himself imagine a future with them—with Lila—in it. Years ago, Rafe had learned the hard way to keep all four paws on the ground, but that resolve was fading like the stars before the approaching dawn.

"I'm not looking to give the fae a pass," Rafe said quietly. "I'm looking for a world where our communities can learn from each other instead of ending up at war."

"I've rarely granted a wish that pleased me more," Elroth said with a regal nod.

CHAPTER 36

*L*ila stood beside her mother, holding Galeeta's hand as if afraid she would disappear. In that moment, it was hard to say if Lila was the protector or the one in need of care. Perhaps they played both roles, and that was how it was meant to be with mothers and daughters. They'd never given each other the chance to find out.

Now, thanks to Rafe, maybe she'd learn.

The wolf had returned to his place next to his father. He'd saved her more than once since they'd met, but convincing the others to spare Galeeta's life was his greatest gift. None of the court nobles would have squandered a king's boon that way.

There were no words vast enough to contain her gratitude to him. But even as she tried to imagine telling him that in some bright future, she couldn't. There was only terrifying anticipation, one moment after the next, until her mother's sentence was pronounced.

"Galeeta of House Fernblade," King Elroth began, "you have transgressed our laws. Your guilt has been proven by your own account and the testimony of others."

Lila's gaze strayed to Rafe, as if she could draw strength from the sight of him. His expression was grave, a line of concentration between his dark brows. With a sudden rush of loneliness, Lila wanted him back at her side.

"In penance," the king continued, "you shall be severed from our court. You will not pass into the Gilden Wood with our people, but stay in the cities among the other species, both human and supernatural, until you are released by my word."

Shock ran through Lila. Her mother in the human city? He might as well drop an exotic koi into a cactus garden.

"I have taken the young wolf's desire for cooperation between our peoples to heart. Of necessity, you will learn the ways of those around you. If you are wise, you will forget your name and pedigree and present yourself on the strength of your true skills and character."

Galeeta flinched but said nothing. Lila had gone to the city, but she had wanted the adventure. This ran against every one of her mother's instincts.

The king went on. "You are a healer, and you will give your services to all in need, free of charge or obligation. You are to conduct yourself as an ambassador of goodwill from my court, so that all may know we are as good as we are powerful. This is your act of contrition and path to redemption."

Finally, her mother spoke in a low but steady voice. "Am I to go alone, Your Majesty?"

"If your family wishes to be with you, they may join you in your exile. I would suggest that you ask your daughter for advice on how to live there. You will be given enough wealth to survive, but no more."

Lila pressed her hand over her mouth, not sure if she would laugh or cry. The humans had a concept of Hell. This was it for Galeeta. There would be many dark days ahead.

Galeeta raised her head to regard the king. "You are taking your people away from the human cities to preserve their magic against the taint of human cities. What if I lose mine?"

"Remember your crimes." There was no sympathy in Elroth's face. "If you lose your power, then that shall be part of your punishment, Lady Galeeta. At least you will still have your life, thanks to a wolf you no doubt despise."

Her mother's mouth dropped open. "No, I—"

Elroth pushed on, riding over her words. "I don't believe a change of heart comes from one night alone, even if that night is fraught with terror and mercy in equal measure."

Galeeta was silent, no doubt because what Elroth said was true.

"If you hear nothing else, my lady, hear this. I nearly lost my life and my throne to a monster tonight. That wolf is correct. If we were one with our neighbors, even in some small part, we would have brought him to justice long ago and avoided much pain and death for the fae and for our neighbors. Our young have shown us wisdom. It is up to us to embrace that lesson."

The Alpha put an approving hand on his son's shoulder.

Lila caught Rafe's gaze one last time, making sure he saw her before mouthing a silent *thank-you*. He'd given her a gift beyond price. Rafe ducked his head, uncharacteristically flustered.

Izetta and Malatest nodded, but cautiously watched the lightening horizon. Dawn was not far away.

Elroth paused long enough to look around the clearing before turning to Izetta. "My lady, may I borrow your blade?"

Izetta silently handed it over, hilt first. The king sliced open his palm and used his thumb to mark Galeeta's forehead with his blood. "Your penance has been spoken and shall not be broken until recompense is made."

The spell was simple, ancient, and powerful. Galeeta bowed until her face was hidden against her knees. Elroth's sentence struck at the heart of Galeeta's pride. After holding herself together through so much, now she wept like a broken child.

The family crowded around her, giving as much comfort as they could. Lila barely paid attention when the king opened another portal for the fae, taking them back to the forest they considered their true home.

Lila didn't notice the vampires leave at all, and only looked up from her distraught mother when distant wolf howls signaled that the pack had left, too. Rafe had gone with them, at long last welcomed at his father's side. The long and terrible night was ending and taking him with it.

The future Lila had struggled to imagine was upon her. She had her family, closer than ever before. She was free from any obligation to marry someone she didn't choose, free to build her life as she chose. And yet, tomorrow was an unexpectedly lonely place.

ONE MONTH LATER, Lila juggled her shoulder bag, coffee, and croissant to her usual table at the bistro. It was late on a Saturday afternoon, so she had the luxury of scrolling through the online news while drinking her latte. It was the first time she'd relaxed in the weeks since she'd returned from the way station.

The first sip of coffee was heaven as she let her fae senses explore the bold taste. There was a snatch of song and sun-warmed earth coupled with the crisp air of the high mountains. She'd never tasted coffee or a croissant before coming to the city, but now that she had, there was no way she could give up such colorful flavors.

While she'd been at the way station, she'd missed the pleasure of the bistro, with its glass-topped tables, blue-checked curtains, and busy chatter. That had been the least of her problems, but now she appreciated the place even more. It sat next door to her apartment building in East Bay and was lively but never overly crowded. People spread their visits out according to their schedule and, given the mixed clientele in the area, the bistro served breakfast all day and all night, too.

Lila began scrolling on her tablet, skimming without really reading. There was a going-out-of-business sale as the light fae owners left for Gilden Wood and a new story from Errata about bacchante—sadly, the drug hadn't vanished along with the Magician. The reporter had tried to write about Farras and the destruction of the way station, but Elroth had put a stop to that. Some fae business would always remain hidden, and no one who'd seen the king's justice in action was likely to defy his wishes.

Lila's family had been lucky, thanks to Rafe. Still, nothing had been simple. She'd held herself in a fist of worry while she'd found a place for her parents and organized the thousand necessary things to set up their lives—bank accounts, utilities, bus schedules, and even library cards. She missed Rafe's steady presence every minute. She'd done everything with no help from other fae, who all seemed to feel she was the one with the time and expertise to handle the assignment.

The result of her efforts was a mixed success. Her father adored the library. In contrast, it had taken a monumental effort to convince her mother that their budget would not extend to a housemaid, and an automatic dishwasher would have to do. One might have thought civilization had crashed around Galeeta's ears.

No, it had not been an easy beginning. Even so, it was progress. They had their space now, and Lila could reclaim hers. She could sit and have her coffee in peace. When someone pulled up a chair to her table, she was ready to blast the intruder at least three tables away. She set down her cup and looked up, barely wiping away a scowl.

It was Rafe. Her mouth went dry, as if she'd been drinking sand. She hadn't seen or heard from him since the trial. "Hello."

"Hello." He smiled, and it was the first true, carefree smile she'd seen from him. There were dimples involved. "I hope I'm not disturbing you."

She stuffed the tablet back in her bag. "No, not at all. How are you?"

"Fine. How are you?" He took a sip of his drink.

"Fine." Hearing the bland politeness of their words, she stopped.

They had united, wolf and fae, in a desperate search for truth. They'd risked death for it. She owed it to him now.

"Actually, it's been dreadful. I've had to introduce my mother and father to the modern world."

"Parents," he said, saluting her with his mug. A paper tag identifying his drink as English Breakfast hung over the edge of the mug.

"Siblings," she countered. "Sala and her family have joined King Elroth in the woods. So did Ademar. I doubt I will see any of them for a while."

"And you? Are you staying here?"

He asked the question lightly, but she heard more beneath it. This conversation—and everything that came after—depended on her answer.

She looked away, desperately uncertain. "I think so."

"You aren't certain?"

"Maybe. I don't know. The fight with Farras shook me."

That was a mild way of describing the nightmares she'd had since planting a tree through his body. She'd jolted awake too many times, covered in perspiration and utterly alone.

"I'm not surprised," Rafe said. "No one with an ounce of sanity could easily shake that off. We're still mourning our fallen kin."

"I've wondered over and over again what made Farras like that. He was the last survivor of his own House when he arrived at court. Something bad happened to him, but I've never known what that was."

"Did you find your other sisters?"

"We did, but not until the next day. They were wandering in the woods beyond the way station."

Lila turned to the window, but she wasn't seeing the street outside. Her older sisters had been shocked, bewildered, and terrified, but no longer gargoyles. Rosemund had a mane of curling hair that surrounded her like a cloak. Arabelle wore hers straight, but when they'd been found, they both looked as if they'd been rolling in a pile of leaves.

"The spell that bound them was broken," she continued. "It failed when Farras was stripped of his power. Even so, they will not recover all at once. They are physically themselves, but they have not regained their power of speech. They may not remember much of what happened."

Rafe set down his mug hard enough that it clicked against the glass tabletop. "Where are they now?"

She turned back from the window. "King Elroth took them. He has the finest physicians among the fae."

He reached across, putting his hand over hers. "I'm glad they were found."

She pulled her hand away. "You left without saying goodbye."

She hadn't meant to say it, but there it was. Regret flickered over Rafe's face, but he quickly hid it.

"Your family wouldn't have welcomed the intrusion. Not right then," he replied sitting back in his chair. "And I knew I could always find you if you were in town."

Of course, he could. He was a tracker. "So you did."

And he was here now. That was something. She broke her croissant in two and pushed the plate across to him, keeping half for herself. He gratefully accepted the pastry and bit into it.

"So I did," he said after swallowing the bite. "I wanted to see how you were doing. Whether my boon was doing any good."

"It's early days," Lila said with a shrug. "One of the braver neighbors took Mother up on her offer of healing, although it was for a sick labradoodle. Father is amusing himself trading chess lessons for wine. I fear the reputation of the light fae will be classified less as a benevolent powerhouse and more as a collection of hapless eccentrics."

Rafe chuckled. "It will take time. Shifters, Undead, witches—we have to get used to each other when we all share the same laundromat and drugstore."

"I moved here to learn what that was like," Lila mused, dusting the pastry crumbs from her fingers. "It was easy when I was on my own, with no responsibilities to anyone but myself. I could leave my past and immerse myself in a new environment. It's different with my parents here, and I have to explain why taxes are a thing."

"It's harder?"

"It makes me question myself more. I believe in love and truth between all the human and supernatural communities, but when I see their blind spots, I wonder where mine are."

He made a face. "Family has a way of making us overthink everything. My father is mellower than he was when I left home, but not enough to make things completely comfortable."

"I hear a story there." Lila drank the last of her coffee. "Shall we take a walk?"

If she'd wanted to end the conversation, send him out of her life, she missed her chance right there. Once they were out on the street in the summer sun, peace flooded into her. He was at her side again, his gray T-shirt and blue jeans showing long, lean muscles.

"My father wants to step down as Alpha," Rafe said as they turned toward the park at the end of the street. "He wants me to step up. That's changed the dynamic between us. Made it easier in a way."

"What do you want?" she asked. "Do you want that more than your job as a tracker?"

They reached the park. It was a few acres of trees with a playground and community garden at the other end. It felt good to get off the pavement and stand on the chip trail that ran around the park's perimeter. She could think better with dirt and bark under her feet.

"I used to want nothing more than to escape this place," he said. "Now I'm fine with sticking around here. Enough time has passed, and the pack needs fresh blood."

It was his future. She could hear it in his voice—he would accept the challenge because that was who he was. "But?"

"It's not all I want."

Lila's heart made an unexpected skip. So, the fork in the road hadn't been when they left the bistro—it was now, under the chestnuts that lined the park. *Wolves and fae don't mix.* But here they were, standing too close to pretend that they were polite acquaintances.

It was time to make a choice—not out of drama and defiance or under the cover of secrecy, but in the Saturday afternoon sunlight. Wolves and fae mixed because they said so.

"Is that why you followed your nose to my favorite coffee shop?" she asked.

"After what happened, you needed time," he said, his voice soft and low. "Now I need to know if I'm welcome."

She cupped his face between her palms, pulling him down for a kiss. It had only been four weeks, but all at once it felt like an eternity since she'd last breathed in his warmth. "You are welcome."

And they kissed, deep and long. A skateboarder whizzed by on the sidewalk, letting out a whistle as he passed. Lila wrapped her arms around Rafe's neck, drawing him closer. He grasped the small of her back, holding her steady as they repeated the kiss. Then a car horn honked. There was no such thing as privacy on the neighborhood streets. She didn't care.

By unspoken consent, they headed deeper into the trees. He took her hand, engulfing it in his warm fingers. There were many questions, many bumps in the road ahead, but none of them were impossible now. Magic was the meeting of will and power, and they had both.

Dappled shade danced on the lawn. Most of the trees were young, new plantings from when the park was built a dozen years ago. Lila had discreetly shaped them—a nudge here and there—to make a canopy over the path. After the ancient forests of the fae, it had seemed odd at first to be in a place where it was still possible to so boldly leave one's mark. Whether humans knew it or not, their cities were still new, raw creations with infinite futures.

"What shall we do today?" she said, savoring the *we*. "Where should we go?"

"Home," Rafe said, stopping with his back to a tree. "Right here."

He circled her waist, drawing her in until she stood between his legs. His eyes danced with happiness. Lila leaned into him, her cheek against the hollow of his collarbone. With curious fingertips, she traced the landscape of his hard chest. He laid a hand over hers, stilling her movements.

"What are you thinking?" he asked, his low voice a husky whisper.

"That this moment is an end. We're both free. The nightmare is over."

"And a beginning?"

"Of everything that comes next," Lila said, lacing her fingers through his. "I can't wait to see what that will be."

THE END

AFTERWORD

Thank you so much for reading *Hidden* and stepping into my story world for a time. While you're immersed in the book, you're helping to create the place and people with your imagination. I hope this journey together was fun!

If you enjoyed the story, please tell a friend or leave a review. Reviews help other readers find good stories and are incredibly important to authors. Your opinion matters!

Also, if you'd like to keep up on what's happening with my books, please sign up for my newsletter at www.SharonAshwood.com.

I promise that I won't share your email or information, and I won't send you spam. Around once a month I'll send you an email with contests, new releases, and previews of what's coming.

If you'd like to see more of the Dark Forgotten world, turn the page to learn about the series. It begins with a young witch named Holly and her vampire business partner, when a ghost-busting job goes horribly wrong…

RAVENOUS

THE DARK FORGOTTEN, BOOK 1

One kiss is all it takes to lose your soul…

Holly Carver is a small-time witch who busts ghosts for tuition money, but ends up wrangling a demon when a haunted house job goes bad.

Her Undead business associate, Alessandro Caravelli, suspects the demon is somebody's not-so-secret weapon. The supernatural community is at war, and Holly's unpredictable magic holds the key to hell's doorway. Soon Holly is on everyone's "must have" list, and not in a good way.

Alessandro wants her for more than magic. A lover with six centuries of experience, the vampire is walking seduction, but he's also a predator. Every moment he spends guarding Holly, every second he spends falling under her witch's spell, he becomes more and more of a threat himself. As Holly's sharp-tongued grandma warns her: vampires are like a box of rich chocolate—they seem so tempting, but over-indulgence is a killer…

Start reading Ravenous now!

SCORCHED

THE DARK FORGOTTEN, BOOK 2

Cracking the case will cost Mac the last of his humanity. Walking away means Constance loses her son.

Detective Macmillan has a taste for bad girls, but his last lover took the cake—and his soul. Now half-demon, Mac's lost his friends, his job, and his freedom.

Constance is a vampire trapped inside the Castle prison. Her adopted child has been kidnapped, and she turns to Mac for help. The trail leads them deep into the dungeon, where the stakes are beyond even Mac's worst fears—beyond even death itself.

Fiery, vulnerable Constance will do anything for those she loves, including Mac. And he'll be damned if he turns his back on her . . . and a demon forever if he doesn't.

Welcome to the Castle. The price of admission is your soul.

This Romantic Times Book Reviews Top Pick blends the best of urban fantasy with sizzling hot paranormal romance.

Start reading Scorched now!

UNCHAINED

THE DARK FORGOTTEN, BOOK 3

Been there. Slain that.

Ashe Carver is one kick-ass monster killer—and she has the scars to prove it. But faced with a custody battle for her ten-year-old daughter, Eden, she's hung up her stakes and taken a job at the public library, determined to prove she's as good a mother as she is a hunter.

Easier said than done. Lovelorn vampires haunt the library, a slime demon is hanging out at the mall, and, after centuries guarding a supernatural prison, dashing Captain Reynard strides into her world like a hero from a classic novel. He has only weeks to live unless Ashe finds the thief who took his soul—and he's just too drop-dead gorgeous to die...

Bitten by Books writes: "Unchained by Sharon Ashwood is everything I'd expect from a kickass paranormal romance and more . . . Ashe is such an amazing heroine, I couldn't help but love her."

Get your copy of this multi-award winning paranormal romance today!

Start reading Unchained now!

FROSTBOUND

THE DARK FORGOTTEN, BOOK 4

Every dog might have his day, but the hellhound guards the night …

As a snowstorm locks down the city, more than the roads are getting iced. Someone's beheaded the wrong girl, and vampire-on-the-lam Talia Rostova thinks it was meant to be her. Now she's the prime suspect in her own botched murder—and the prisoner of her smoking-hot neighbor.

Lore is a hellhound, bred to serve and protect, so he's not freeing Talia until he's sure that she's the prey and not the hunter. You'd think a beautiful woman in his bedroom would be a good thing, but trouble-prone Talia has run afoul of someone more sinister than your average lunatic killer. An ancient Undead is wreaking vengeance on the city—and on her—and Lore will have to go far beyond a stake to put him back in his grave …

Start reading Frostbound now!

GIFTED

THE DARK FORGOTTEN, BOOK 5

Who says the holiday season is just for humans?

For all the holly-jolly times, family gatherings are complex no matter who—or what—you are. When you're hunting for the latest "it" toy to stuff a stocking, it doesn't matter if you're alive or Undead, fanged or furry—you're just as desperate to be the cool dad. And then there are the family grumps who never send cards, the ones who eat all the good candy, and those who drool and dig up the neighbor's yard.

No, the Yuletide Season isn't for the faint of heart—and sometimes it's downright demonic—but holiday miracles make it all worthwhile. Chance encounters and unexpected forgiveness remind us that joy doesn't come in a gift-wrapped box.

This novella from the Dark Forgotten world catches up with favorite characters for a fresh take on the holidays. Those visiting the world for the first time will understand why *Chicago Tribune* called it "simply superb."

Grab this book and return to the world of the Dark Forgotten. Santa Claws is waiting!

Start reading Gifted now!

ABOUT THE AUTHOR

USA Today Bestselling author Sharon Ashwood is a novelist, desk jockey and enthusiast for the weird and spooky. She has an English literature degree but works as a finance geek. Interests include growing her to-be-read pile and playing with the toy graveyard on her desk. As a vegetarian, she freely admits the whole vampire/werewolf lifestyle would never work out, so she writes her adventures instead.

Sharon is a winner of the RITA® Award for Paranormal Romance. She lives in the Pacific Northwest and is owned by two naughty black cats.

www.SharonAshwood.com
Sharon@SharonAshwood.com

ALSO BY SHARON ASHWOOD

Crown of Fae Series

Flicker

Shimmer

Shatter

Smolder

Quake

Dark Forgotten Series

Ravenous

Scorched

Unchained

Frostbound

Gifted

Fragile Magic (short story)

Hidden

Dragon Lords novellas

Lord Dragon's Conquest

Valkyrie's Conquest

Camelot Reborn series

Enchanted Warrior

Enchanted Guardian

Royal Enchantment

Enchanter Redeemed

Horsemen series

Possessed by a Warrior

Possessed by an Immortal

Possessed by a Wolf

Possessed by the Fallen

Audiobook

Enchanted Warrior

Corsair's Cove miniseries

Kiss in the Dark

Secret Seed

Long Road Home

www.ingramcontent.com/pod-product-compliance
Lightning Source LLC
Chambersburg PA
CBHW051322190726
48290CB00001B/275